## *On Your Mark, Get Set ...*

I turned and tested out the new leather seat of my bike.

"Just do me one favor, Frank," Dad said when I reached for the ignition. "Don't take this new mission too lightly. They must have named it 'Extreme Danger' for a reason."

"That's what I told Joe."

"Well, be careful," said Dad.

Joe and I slipped our helmets over our heads and revved up our engines. Then, waving good-bye to Dad, we roared out of the parking lot and headed down the highway.

**UNDERCOVER BROTHERS™**

#1 *Extreme Danger*

## Available from Simon & Schuster

# THE HARDY BOYS

*UNDERCOVER BROTHERS*

**#1** **Extreme Danger**

**FRANKLIN W. DIXON**

**Aladdin Paperbacks**
**New York   London   Toronto   Sydney**

❧ ALADDIN PAPERBACKS
An imprint of Simon & Schuster
Children's Publishing Division
1230 Avenue of the Americas
New York, NY 10020

Designed by Lisa Vega
The text of this book was set in Aldine 401BT.
Manufactured in the United States of America
First Aladdin Paperbacks edition June 2005
10 9 8 7 6 5 4 3 2
Library of Congress Control Number: 2004113061
ISBN-13: 978-1-4169-0002-3
ISBN-10: 1-4169-0002-0

# TABLE OF CONTENTS

# Extreme Danger

# 1.

## Terror at 12,000 Feet

*I'm going to die.*

That's what I thought when I pulled the cord of my parachute—and nothing happened.

*Definitely not cool.*

As I plummeted downward through the sky, it felt like I was floating. The earth below, on the other hand, was rushing up to greet me at a speed of 120 miles per hour.

To make matters worse, it was my first solo jump.

And probably my last.

I tried not to panic. I looked over at "Wings" Maletta, the jumpmaster of Freedombird Skydiving School. The big bearded man was Freedom-falling about ten yards away from me. I waved to him like a maniac, pointing at my broken parachute cord.

1

And guess what he did?

He *laughed*.

Seriously. Like some sort of cartoon villain on Saturday morning TV, he threw his oversized head back and *laughed*.

Then it hit me.

*He knows who I am.*

In case you haven't figured it out, I'm no ordinary thrill-seeker who jumps out of planes. I'm Joe Hardy—undercover agent for ATAC (American Teens Against Crime)—and I was on a mission. A pretty dangerous mission, as it turned out. The police had reason to believe that the Freedombird Skydiving School was just a front for a fly-by-night smuggling ring. Wings Maletta wasn't a real diving instructor—he was a DVD pirate. So the ATAC team asked my brother Frank and me to go undercover to crack the case.

Hey, why not? Who would suspect a couple of teenage boys taking skydiving lessons?

Wings Maletta, that's who.

I stared at the broken pull cord in my hand and the big-toothed grin on Wings's round furry face. He looked right at me—then pointed up at the plane.

My brother Frank stood in the open doorway, getting ready to jump.

"Frank! Wait! Don't jump!" I shouted through the walkie-talkie in my helmet.

Too late.

Frank leaped out of the plane.

"They're onto us, Frank!" I yelled. "Maletta cut the pull cords!"

I waited for a response.

Nothing.

"Frank! Can you read me?"

Static.

I didn't know what to think. Did Frank hear me? Did someone sabotage his parachute too?

One thing I *did* know. If I didn't grab onto Wings Maletta in the next few seconds, I was going to be digging *really* deep for clams in the sandy beach below.

And I *hated* clams.

So I angled my body headfirst toward the dude who wanted to kill me—and tried to "swim" after him.

Hey, it works in the movies.

But this wasn't a movie. This was real life, and I didn't have a stunt double.

I didn't even get five feet before a wicked blast of air sent me spinning off course. I quickly straightened my arms into a diving position and managed to catch a "wave" of wind. Before I knew it, I was sailing right toward my target.

It was almost like body surfing, except I was swallowing mouthfuls of air instead of water.

And, oh yeah, my life depended on it.

Like a human rocket, I zeroed in on Wings Maletta and—*pow*—the guy didn't even know what hit him. I plowed into his bulging beer belly with a soft thud. Then, throwing my arms around his barrel chest, I held on tight.

Wings was totally stunned. You should have seen his face. With his eyes bulging in his goggles and his furry beard poking out of his helmet, he looked like a very large—and very confused—teddy bear.

Except teddy bears don't usually throw punches when kids hug them.

*Whack!*

Wings's huge hairy fist slammed into my jaw and sent me flying backward.

*Man! That hurt!*

It was still daylight, but I was seeing stars. And clouds. And the earth, too—spinning around me.

Time to get a grip.

I spread out my arms and legs to steady myself, then tilted downward. Wings reached for his parachute cord.

*Oh, great.*

If I didn't grab onto him in the next second or

4

two, I was going to plunge to my death. Not an option.

So I bucked against the wind like a wild bronco and thrust myself headfirst at Wings. With all my strength I lunged at him with my right arm.

Somehow I managed to grab his wrist—before he could pull the cord.

*All right!*

But Wings wasn't having it. He tried to brush me off like a bug, smacking my hand and swatting me away. I reeled back from his blows.

Then my hand started to slip off his wrist. One inch. And another.

*Get a grip,* I told myself again. But this time I meant it. Literally.

Suddenly the walkie-talkie in my helmet crackled with sound.

"Joe! Hold tight!"

It was Frank!

I glanced up. There he was! Swooping down like a bomber plane!

I grabbed onto Wings Maletta with both hands—and braced myself.

*Wham!*

Bull's-eye.

Frank crashed into us with shocking force. The collision sent the three of us tumbling through the air like a clumsy circus act. Frank clung on piggyback-style while I swung from my arms. And Wings? He kicked and screamed with every twist and turn.

"Get off me, you brats!" he howled. "The chute won't hold us all!"

I pulled myself up until we stopped spinning. But Wings wouldn't stop yelling.

"You idiots!" he bellowed. "When I pull the cord, you'll be flung off! You don't stand a chance!"

"Oh, no?" Frank shouted back. He held up a pair of tandem cords and clipped both of us to Wings's backpack.

I had to hand it to Frank. That kid is always prepared.

Wings let out a sigh. "We're still too heavy," he shouted.

"Just pull the cord," I said.

Wings shrugged—and pulled.

*Whoomp!*

With a massive jolt, Frank and I were ripped away from our bear-sized enemy. We plummeted downward, then shot back up again, held by the tandem cords. The parachute opened above our heads, but it sagged with our weight. In seconds we were drifting toward the drop zone below.

Problem was, we were drifting too fast.

"I told you," Wings grunted. "At this speed, we'll all die!"

Frank and I ignored him as we scrambled up the cords and grabbed onto Wings's legs.

"Let go!" the phony instructor yelled, trying to kick us off. "One of you has to let go—if you want to save your brother!" he added.

I looked Frank in the eye. I knew what he was thinking: *No way. We're a team.*

"I have another idea, Wings," I said, shimmying my way up the guy's body. "Maybe you can break our fall."

Wings cursed. I ignored him and straddled his thick neck. Then I reached down to help my brother until we were both standing on Wing's shoulders, holding the parachute lines for support.

"But wait! The fall could kill me!" Wings protested as we floated swiftly to the field below. "I'll break my legs, for sure!"

I glanced at my brother and shrugged. "That's a risk we're willing to take," Frank said with a smile.

The earth was only a couple hundred feet below us. Wings was freaking out. "No! My legs! I'll be crushed!"

"I have a suggestion, Wings," I said.

7

"What's that?"

"Tuck and roll."


As it turned out, Wings *did* break his legs in the fall. Which made it impossible for him to run away when the police arrived. They'd been watching the whole thing from the ground—and had an ambulance waiting to pick up the pieces.

I was just happy that none of the pieces had "Hardy" written on them.

"Good job, boys," said Lieutenant Jones, smiling and shaking our hands. "Sorry we got here a little late. By the time we realized your cover was blown, you were already in the air with Maletta."

"I can't believe that guy actually tried to kill us," Frank said, shaking his head.

"Well, he *is* a pirate," I pointed out.

"A *DVD* pirate," Frank added. "It's like he made us walk the plank for a bootleg copy of *Spider-man 6.*"

I laughed. "Hey, we survived," I said, punching his arm.

Frank returned the favor by pushing me off-balance.

"You boys need a lift back to the skydiving school?" Lieutenant Jones asked, opening the door of his squad car.

8

"No, thanks. We're undercover," Frank explained. "Some kids from our school showed up for diving lessons today."

The police officer nodded and said good-bye.

Five minutes later Frank and I reached the Freedombird Skydiving School. We were totally beat, not to mention a little bruised. But it felt good to complete another successful mission. Wings and his smuggling ring were safely behind bars. And the Hardy brothers were ready to relax and chill out with some friends.

Unfortunately, Brian Conrad was the last "friend" we wanted to see—and the first person to spot us approaching the Freedombird School.

"Why did Brian have to show up for lessons today?" I moaned to my brother. "Talk about a bad coincidence."

"More like Murphy's Law," Frank chipped in.

"Hey, Hardys!" our least favorite classmate yelled from the parking lot. "I saw you jump. What's up with the double tandem diving? You girls get scared, or what?"

I glanced at Frank and rolled my eyes.

Let me tell you about Brian Conrad. The guy is like that public access TV—nothing but bad news, twenty-four seven. If the yearbook committee was voting for Boy Most Likely to Need a Good Lawyer, he'd win, hands down.

Of course, he hated Frank and me. In case you hadn't noticed.

"Too scared to go solo, huh?" Brian taunted as we approached the school building.

I growled under my breath.

"Ignore him, Joe," my brother whispered. Then Frank looked Brian in the eye and said, "Our parachutes malfunctioned, Conrad. We almost died."

"Yeah? I almost believe you," Brian shot back. He leaned against his SUV and shouted to his sister in the backseat. "You hear that, Belinda? Your boyfriends are too scared to jump solo! What a pair of wimps!"

Belinda glared at her brother. She opened her mouth to say something—but she was interrupted by a high-pitched voice inside the school building.

"Wimps! Wimps! Wimps!"

Brian Conrad burst out laughing.

Frank and I turned toward the small brick building and exchanged puzzled glances. We didn't know who it could be. The police had rounded up all of Wings's men. So we headed for the door and carefully peeked inside.

"Wimps!"

The sound came from a large gold cage in the corner.

It was Wings's pet parrot—the official mascot of the Freedombird Skydiving School.

"Figures," I muttered. "The pirate had a parrot."

Frank entered the small reception room and walked to the cage. "Poor thing," he cooed to the red and green bird. "Your daddy's behind bars now. Just like you."

The parrot tilted its head as if it understood.

"Maybe we should set you free." Frank opened the cage door and the bird flew out.

I ducked as it fluttered past my head. "Easy there, flyboy," I said.

The parrot circled the room a few times—and landed on Frank's head.

"Looks like you have a new friend, Frank," I said.

Frank rolled his eyes upward. The bird squawked.

And then Brian Conrad walked in.

"What do we have here?" the jerk sneered. "One parrot and a pair of chickens!" He pointed and laughed.

*Okay, stay cool,* I told myself.

If my brother and I could survive a parachute

jump without pull cords, we could put up with Conrad's obnoxious jokes.

But come on. Did the bird have to join in, too?

"Chickens! Chickens! Chickens!"

# 2.

# Duck!

"I can't believe you really want to keep that bird," my brother Joe complained as we headed for the parking lot. "It keeps making fun of us."

I held the bird with one arm and opened the car door. "It's a parrot, Joe," I said. "That's what parrots do. They repeat things. And the poor thing is an orphan now. It needs a home." I gently placed the bird on the backseat of our Aunt Trudy's old Volkswagen Beetle.

Joe slid into the passenger seat and sighed. "But why couldn't it say 'Heroes! Heroes!' instead of 'Wimps! Wimps!'?" he asked.

The parrot flapped its wings. "Wimps! Wimps! Wimps!" it squawked.

I laughed while Joe closed his eyes and

13

groaned. "It's just so annoying," he said.

"It's only a bird, Joe," I reminded him again.

"I'm not talking about the parrot," Joe explained. "I mean, dude, we jump out of a plane with busted parachutes, take on a killer at twelve thousand feet, smash an international smuggling ring . . . and then get teased by a windbag like Brian Conrad."

"Hey, that's the price we pay for going undercover, Joe," I said. "And don't worry about Conrad. We won't have to see his face again till school starts in the fall."

Aunt Trudy's car engine died as soon as I tried to start it. And guess who we had to get a ride home from?

Brian Conrad.

I guess I spoke too soon.

I had to wave the guy down before he pulled out of the parking lot. Needless to say, my brother was not thrilled.

"Okay, I'll accept a ride home from that kid," Joe muttered under his breath. "But you owe me. Big time."

Brian's SUV screeched to a stop next to Aunt Trudy's dusty VW. "You boys need to be rescued twice in one day, huh?" he teased us yet again.

14

"Why are you driving that toy car, anyway?"

"Our motorcycles are getting a tune-up, Conrad," Joe said defensively.

I told my brother to chill out while we loaded our stuff into Brian's SUV.

"At least you get to sit in the backseat with your girlfriend," Joe whispered to me.

"Don't even start," I warned, my face turning red.

I guess I should explain. Brian's sister, Belinda, is smart, funny, blond, beautiful—the whole package. And she smiles and touches my arm every chance she gets.

Problem is, I get a little flustered around girls.

"Jump in, Frank," Belinda said, opening the rear door of the SUV. She flashed a smile that made me feel weak in the knees.

Okay, maybe I get more than just a little flustered.

Joe hopped into the front seat next to Brian. I knew the little creep grabbed shotgun just so he could watch me squirm next to Belinda.

I tried to play it cool as I slid into the backseat—with a parrot on my shoulder.

*Real cool.*

We fastened our seatbelts and Brian peeled out of the parking lot like it was the Indy 500. "Um, we're not really in such a hurry, Brian," I pointed out.

"Sorry, I forgot the Hardys are allergic to danger," he said, slowing down only slightly.

"Put a lid on it, Brian," Belinda scolded her brother. "They were almost killed today. I hope you're all right, Frank." She placed a hand on my forearm.

"Well, yeah . . . um . . . it was . . . you know . . . a little scary," I stuttered.

*What a dork.*

"Don't worry. I'm fine," I said, clearing my throat.

Brian started clucking like a chicken, which caught the attention of the parrot on my shoulder. It raised its feathered head and squawked.

"I like your bird," Belinda commented with a smile.

I blushed. "Oh, yeah. Wings had to go to the hospital, so we're taking care of his pet."

"What's his name?" she asked.

I shrugged. "I'm not sure."

"Didn't Wings call him Birdbrain?" Brian said with a nasty laugh.

The parrot ruffled his feathers and made a loud raspberry sound.

"I wouldn't like that name either," I said to my

16

new feathered friend. The bird responded by poking my head with its beak.

Belinda giggled. "How about calling him Pokey?" she suggested.

The parrot puffed up its chest.

"Puffy?" Joe chimed in.

"Polly?" Brian added.

The bird squawked back. "Pokey! Puffy! Polly!"

"Man, he's like a tape recorder with wings, isn't he?" I said. "I guess I can throw away my digital mixing board. With this bird on my shoulder, who needs playback?"

The parrot flapped its wings with excitement. "Playback! Playback! Playback!" it chirped.

"That's it!" said Belinda, slapping my knee. "You can call him Playback!"

"Totally," Joe agreed.

"Okay. Playback it is," I said, petting the parrot's belly. I turned to Belinda and made a lame attempt at flirting. "I think he likes the name. I mean, who wouldn't . . . you know . . . like your . . . um . . . bird name."

*Real smooth.*

"It's perfect," I added, trying not to blush. I gave Belinda a cool sideways glance and nodded shrewdly.

Saved!

Well, until the parrot decided to poop on my shoulder.

"Gross," I muttered.

Everyone burst out laughing.

But really, did they *have* to make jokes about it the entire ride home?

"It's a parrot, Frank. That's what parrots do," my brother said, mocking my own words.

Belinda offered her sympathy—and a pack of tissues from her purse—but, boy, was I relieved when Brian pulled up in front of our house.

"Thanks, Brian," said Joe, hopping out and dashing to the porch of our old house. It was clear to everyone that Joe really hated thanking Brian for *anything*. He just wanted to make a quick escape.

Which left me alone with Belinda in the backseat.

"You take care of yourself, Frank," she said. "You had a rough day, poor guy."

Then she gave me a peck on the cheek.

I'm sure my face turned redder than Playback's tail feathers. "Um . . . well . . . thanks, Belinda," I stammered. "And, ah, thanks for the ride, Brian."

Before I could embarrass myself any further, I ran up the porch stairs as fast as I could. I followed Joe into the house—and almost crashed right into him.

The entire family was sitting in the dining room, staring at us. Mom, Dad, Aunt Trudy—and they all had strange, surprised looks on their faces.

"Is that a parrot?" Mom asked.

"Parrot! Parrot! Parrot!" Playback responded.

Mom chuckled. "I guess that answers my question," she said. "I suppose you boys want to keep him?"

"Can we, Mom?" I replied. "He needs a home."

Aunt Trudy was horrified. "Is he housebroken?"

"Of course he is," I lied.

I might have gotten away with it if Playback hadn't chosen that exact moment to drop a little gift on my shoulder.

"I knew it!" Aunt Trudy exclaimed. "He's going to poop all over our nice clean house! When I was a little girl on the farm, we had some ducks and that's all they ever did. Poop, poop, poop all over the place."

"He's not a duck, Aunt Trudy," I argued. "And I promise to clean up after him."

Aunt Trudy stood up and started clearing plates off the table. "I think we all know who does the cleaning up around here," she said. "Not to mention cooking for a pair of boys who are always late for dinner."

"Sorry, Aunt Trudy," Joe and I said in unison.

Mom stood up, came over to me, and petted the parrot. "Isn't he a pretty thing?" she said. "I guess you can keep him, but he's your responsibility. I'll download some parrot info from the Web tonight for you."

"Thanks, Mom," I said, kissing her cheek.

I glanced at Dad. I could tell he was concerned about the skydiving mission. But we'd have to talk about it later, when Mom and Aunt Trudy weren't around.

"Did you pick up some Band-Aids for me?" Aunt Trudy questioned us.

Oops.

That was the reason Aunt Trudy had lent us her VW. "Um, there's something I have to tell you about your car, Aunt Trudy," I said, wincing. "The engine died on us."

"Yup," Joe confirmed.

"Well!" she said, shaking her head. "You know, something's fishy here. I send you boys out with my Beetle to buy some Band-Aids, and you come back with bruises and a bird. What *really* happened?"

Joe and I glanced down at the bruises on our legs.

"We'll tell you all about it . . . after you warm up some leftovers for us, Aunt Trudy," said my brother, thinking fast. "Thanks! We need to wash up first."

We both gave our aunt a kiss and bounded up the stairs before she could ask any more questions. Playback clung to my shoulder and squawked.

When we reached the second floor, Joe turned to me and said, "Well, Frank, I bailed you out of that one. You owe me again."

I swatted the back of his head and followed him into my bedroom. "Where are we going to put this bird until we get a cage?" I asked.

Joe walked to the window and turned around. "Let's see. We could push a couple of chairs together, and—"

I stopped listening, because something outside the window caught my eye.

A big red brick sailed through the air. Right toward our window.

"Joe!" I yelled. "DUCK!"

21

# 3.

## Extreme Danger

*Duck?*

I ducked.

A split second later, something sailed past my head and crashed on the bedroom floor. I looked up to see what it was.

A brick?

I slowly raised myself to the window and peeked outside. The yard below was empty. Whoever threw the brick was gone.

"It's clear," I told Frank.

"Hey, want to give me a little credit here?" asked Frank. "It's a good thing I told you to duck—or you'd have another rock in your head."

"Very funny. But if you're so smart, why didn't you pick another word besides *duck*? I mean, dude,

22

after all the jokes today about ducks and chickens and parrots, I didn't know what you were talking about."

"What should I have said?" Frank asked. "Stoop? Bend? Lower yourself into a safe position? Hey, you figured it out. Now you owe me one."

"Let's just say we're even," I said. "Now stoop or bend down and check out that brick."

Frank leaned over and picked it up. The brick was your basic red brick—nothing unusual. But it was tied to a small padded envelope.

"What's that?" I asked. "A death threat from Brian Conrad? 'Stay away from my sister or the bird gets it. . . .'?"

Frank stood up. "No, it's our next mission."

He opened the envelope and pulled out a wad of cash, a hotel reservation, a small laser pointer, and a CD.

"Very clever," said Frank, turning the CD around in his hand.

"What's it say on the label?" I asked.

Frank looked me in the eye. "'Extreme Danger,'" he said.

"Cool," I replied, nodding. "But not as cool as this." I snatched the laser pointer out of Frank's hands and snapped off the lights.

Then, aiming toward the wall, I pressed the end

of the pointer with my thumb. A tiny pinpoint of light danced across the room.

Playback squawked.

With a flutter of wings, the large bird flew off Frank's shoulder and chased the pinpoint from one side of the room to the other. It was pretty hilarious watching Playback go. By swirling the laser, I could even make him fly in a perfect circle above our heads!

"Okay, knock it off," said Frank.

"But he likes it," I insisted.

"Joe."

"Okay." *Fun* wasn't in my brother's vocabulary. I aimed the laser above the TV set until Playback came to rest on top of it.

The parrot touched the tip of his beak to the pinpoint of light and screeched so loud it made me jump.

"Look!" said Frank. "The laser is burning a hole in the wall! Quick, turn it off!"

I released my thumb. The pinpoint of light disappeared instantly, but it left a small burn mark on the wall.

"Give me that," said Frank, snatching the pointer away from me and snapping on the lights. "Make yourself useful, Joe. Turn on the game player."

"Hey, I'm useful," I said, reaching for the game

controls. "I figured out we can use the laser pointer to burn holes, didn't I?"

"Yeah, and you almost burned a hole in my bird."

I had to bite my lip to keep from laughing.

"All set," I said, taking the CD from Frank and loading the game player. We plopped down on the beanbag chairs in front of the monitor and prepared ourselves for our next mission.

*Bring it on.*

I pressed PLAY.

The picture turned black. A low electronic hum grew louder and louder until it sounded like a chorus of spinning wheels. Suddenly the wheel sounds screeched to a halt, and two red slash marks crisscrossed the screen to form a giant X. Then there was a sizzling noise—like the sound of a burning fuse—and a huge explosion. The giant X burst into a fireball of tiny cartoon flames.

"Killer graphics," I said.

"Shhh," Frank responded.

The flames burned a bunch of holes in the screen, revealing a dozen little scenes—videostream clips of people skateboarding, bungee jumping, rock climbing, motocross racing, you name it.

"Extreme sports," a deep voice boomed over the soundtrack. "Pushing the limits of human skill and endurance, extreme sports have taken America by storm. Daredevil skateboard stunts, motocross mega-races, Big Air ramp-jumps, death-defying bungee dives—these are just a few of the pumped-up thrills that have captured an entire nation of brave young risk-takers. The highs are higher, the lows are lower, and the dangers . . . are extreme."

"Man, look at that ramp!" I said, slapping Frank's knee. "That must be fifty feet high! How can anyone—" On the screen a leather-jacketed motocrosser flipped backward on his bike and crashed headfirst on the ground.

"Oh, man! Wipeout!"

"Ouch," said Frank.

"Extreme events are more popular than ever," the deep-voiced narrator continued. "Once an underground phenomenon, extreme sports now receive international television coverage. Extreme Olympic-style games and events are popping up all over the world."

"Cool. Let's go," I said.

"Careful what you wish for," Frank warned. "You might end up flying over that fifty-foot ramp."

"Piece of cake."

I turned my attention back to the screen. The

videostreamed sports footage was suddenly replaced with tourist shots of Philadelphia.

"Philadelphia, Pennsylvania. Birthplace of the American Constitution," the voice went on. "City of Brotherly Love, home of the Liberty Bell. And proud host of the Big Air Games, the newest and biggest extreme sports competition in the country. If you are interested in this exciting midsummer event, tickets are still available. Hotel rooms are conveniently located, with all-day shuttle service to and from the stadium. Just call our 800 number located at the bottom of the screen. Be sure to ask about our special group rates."

I looked at Frank. "What is this? A commercial?"

"Sure sounds like it," he agreed. "All it needs is a catchy jingle."

Then another voice came from the speakers. It sounded like it was making fun of the narrator. "If you would like to attend the Big Air Games as an undercover agent, however, please press CON-TINUE and you will be briefed on your mission."

"*That's* more like it," I said, grabbing the controls and pressing the button.

"Somebody at the home office must have a sense of humor," said Frank.

The tourist shots disappeared. A detailed map of Philadelphia filled the screen.

"Hello, boys," said the second voice. "Sorry about that introduction. I just thought I'd show you the tourist board's ad for the Big Air Games. We got you both tickets for all the events and reserved a room at the Four Seasons Hotel in Philadelphia."

A yellow square flashed on the map, indicating the hotel's location.

"Some of the top extreme athletes in the country are coming to the games—and staying at your hotel. Because of the size of the event, we're taking extra precautions. In dangerous times like these, it's important to always be prepared for the possibility of trouble. As teenagers, you'll be able to access more information than police officers could. Blend in, mingle with the fans and the athletes. But always, keep your eyes and ears open."

This was going to be great!

Frank didn't seem as excited. "It doesn't sound like much of a mission," he muttered. "Just hang out and watch other people take risks?"

"One more thing, boys," the voice spoke up. "We have reason to believe that several threats have been made to participants. Some skateboarders claim they saw a few strange postings on one of the extreme sports Web sites. There are thousands of those sites. The feds are checking the threats out, but it could take months to find something. Ask around. Gather all the information you can. I suggest you pack and leave as soon as possible."

I glanced at Frank. He sighed.

"This mission, like every mission, is top secret," the voice went on. "In five seconds this CD will be reformatted into an ordinary music CD. Five, four, three, two, one."

The Beastie Boys blared from the speakers.

The music was so loud it scared Playback off the TV. He flapped his wings and flew into the air, then landed on Frank's shoulder. He looked a little shaken. But after a moment or two he was grooving to the beat—and squawking the lyrics.

"Party! Party! Party!"

Frank walked over to the computer, turned it on, and logged in.

"What are you doing?" I asked. "We're supposed to leave as soon as possible."

"I'm going online to search some of those Web sites," he replied. "I'll only be a few minutes."

"Are you kidding?" I said. "The feds are looking for those threats day and night, and you think you can find them in a few minutes?"

"Hey, I'm the Search Master, remember?" he said, tapping his head with a finger. "My Web search talents are unmatched . . . except maybe by

Mom. But she's a librarian. It's part of her job."

"Sometimes I wish we could ask her to help," I said.

"Don't even think it. We're undercover, remember? We're on our own," he said, hunkering over the computer.

While Frank launched his Web search, I went to ask Dad to drive us to the garage to pick up our motorcycles. He was sitting by himself at the dining room table.

"Another mission? Already?" he whispered, looking up from his newspaper. "You haven't even told me about the last one."

"We'll fill you in later, on the way to the garage. Don't worry, Dad," I said, noticing the concerned look on his face. Then I turned around and headed back upstairs.

Frank hadn't moved since I'd left him.

"Find anything, O Mighty Search Master?" I asked.

Frank squinted at the screen. "I don't know. Maybe. Look at this."

I leaned over his shoulder—the shoulder *without* the parrot—and studied the screen. In a tall, narrow window, there was a long scroll of postings. I started reading.

"So?" I said. "It just looks like a bunch of dudes talking about the Big Air Games."

"Look at this one posted by 4567TME," he said, reading out loud. "'I hope you Xtreme sports nuts know how to dial 911.'"

I shrugged. "4567TME has a point. Extreme sports *are* dangerous. Most of those athletes wind up in the hospital sooner or later."

"Maybe," Frank admitted. "But it *could* be a threat. Maybe 4567TME plans to *put* those athletes in the hospital. And *sooner,* not later."

I rolled my eyes. "Man, you're making something out of nothing. I think you're just bummed out because we don't have a detailed mission—or even suspects. No smugglers to bust. No bank robbers to catch. I think you're afraid to just kick back and have fun . . . for once."

Frank sighed. "Maybe you're right," he said, logging off the computer.

"I know I'm right. This'll be like a vacation, man! So pack your bags and get ready to tear up the mega-ramps with your brother. Okay?"

Frank smiled. "Okay."

I turned around and started filling my backpack with clothes and socks and underwear. Frank got up from the desk and walked to the video game player. He pressed EJECT and pulled out the disk.

I stopped packing. "What is it, Frank?" I asked. "Why are you staring at that disk?"

Frank paused. "I don't know," he answered. "You're probably right about everything. But I wonder. If this mission is nothing but fun and games, why is it called 'Extreme Danger'?"

I didn't know what to say.

But Playback did.

"Danger! Danger! Danger!"

# 4.
## Warning Signs

Call me paranoid. But I couldn't shake the feeling that there was more to this mission than met the eye.

*Extreme danger.*

The phrase reminded me of a road sign warning—sort of like FALLING ROCKS or SLIPPERY WHEN WET.

I really wanted to do a little more snooping around online—check out some other extreme sports Web sites—so I packed my laptop along with my clothes.

"Ready to roll?" I asked Joe. He strolled into my room with his backpack and motorcycle helmet.

"Dad said he'd drive us to the garage," he said.

"Did you fill him in on our mission?"

33

"No, not yet," Joe answered. "Prepare to be interrogated by the master."

My brother wasn't kidding. Our dad, Fenton Hardy, used to be one of the New York City Police Department's top investigators. He could wrangle a confession out of anyone—mobsters, counterfeiters, jewel thieves, and yes, even his own sons. But even though he'd had more than his share of danger, he still got nervous when he heard what we were up to.

"We probably shouldn't tell Dad about our little skydiving incident," I said to Joe.

"No way. He'd totally freak."

"Okay, so here's our story. We found the pirated DVDs and handed the evidence over to the police, who arrested Wings after the dive. No snags. No surprises. Got it?"

"Got it."

"Good."

I zipped up my backpack, grabbed my helmet, and followed Joe downstairs. Mom and Dad were sitting in the living room watching the six o'clock news on TV.

"Okay, we're ready to go, Dad," Joe announced.

Mom looked up and frowned. "Go where?" she asked.

Dad shifted nervously in his chair. "Honey, I,

34

um, told the boys they could take a little trip to Philadelphia for a few days," he told her.

"Oh, you did, did you?" she said. "And what, may I ask, is the purpose of this little trip?"

I thought fast. "We're studying the birth of American democracy in history class next fall," I lied. "Joe and I figured we could get a head start with an educational tour of Philadelphia."

"Oh, really?" Mom said, narrowing her eyes.

"Yeah," Joe jumped in. "You know, I've always wanted to see the Liberty Bell."

"Uh-huh," Mom responded with more than a hint of suspicion. "And I suppose your little trip has nothing to do with the Big Air Games, which happen to be in Philadelphia this week?"

She pointed to the TV set. A reporter was interviewing a group of extreme sports athletes while skateboarders zipped up and down a ramp in the background.

Clearly Mom had learned a few tricks from Dad.

"Well, you know—if we have time," I said, "we *might* check out a *few* of the Big Air events."

Mom nodded and sighed. "Okay, you can go," she said. "But promise me you won't get any crazy ideas about all this extreme sports stuff. I don't want you taking risks like that. I don't even want you to ride your motorcycles at night. It's too dangerous."

"Don't worry, Mom. It won't be dark for a couple more hours," Joe assured her.

"We'll be extra careful," I added.

Dad stood up and fetched his car keys from the entry hall. "If you want to make it to Philly by nightfall, we'd better get going, boys," he said.

Joe and I grabbed our stuff and headed for the front door. But we froze in our tracks when we heard a familiar voice behind us.

"Those boys aren't going anywhere."

We turned around to see Aunt Trudy standing in the dining room with two plates of food.

"That's right," she said. "Those boys aren't going anywhere until they finish their dinner. They're growing boys, and they need to eat."

"Wow, that's awfully sweet of you, Aunt Trudy," I said, trying to butter her up. "But we have to hurry off to Philadelphia now. You wouldn't want us to ride our motorcycles in the dark, would you?"

Aunt Trudy adjusted her glasses. "No, I guess not. But let me pack you a doggy bag. It'll just take a minute."

"We don't have a minute, Aunt Trudy," I explained. "We really have to go. Now."

She sighed. "All right, then," she said. "But what's the big rush? What's waiting for you in Philadelphia?"

"The Liberty Bell, Trudy," Mom chimed in. "The boys are going to learn that the bell cracked in 1753, the very first time it was rung. And the note it plays is E-flat."

Mom winked at Joe and me.

Pretty cool for a librarian.

But Aunt Trudy wasn't satisfied. "What about my VW?" she asked.

"I'll tell the guys at the garage to check it out," Dad volunteered.

*Phew.*

"Okay, but what about that bird?" said Aunt Trudy. "It doesn't even have a cage. It's going to poop all over the house."

I gave her my sweetest look. "Do you think you could take care of him while we're gone?" I asked with a smile. "It'll only be for a couple of days." I worked harder at my sweet smile.

Aunt Trudy melted. "Oh, all right," she gave in. "I'll feed him. But I won't clean up his messes!"

"Love you, Aunt Trudy," I said, giving her a peck on the cheek.

Joe and I hugged Mom and headed out the door. "Bye!"

"If you can remember, pick me up some Band-Aids!" Aunt Trudy shouted after us.

Once we were loaded into Dad's car, I let out a big sigh of relief. "Glad to get that over with," I whispered to Joe.

I'd spoken too soon.

"Okay, boys," said Dad, pulling out of the driveway. "Tell me all about your last mission."

Once again Joe and I were forced to tell some little white lies—and Dad was harder to fool than Mom and Aunt Trudy. Taking a deep breath, I gave Dad the watered-down version of our skydiving mission. He listened quietly, waiting until I was done.

Then he said, "That's an interesting story, Frank. But you left out the part about your pull cords being cut."

My jaw dropped open. "How did you—?"

"Lieutenant Jones is an old friend of mine," he explained. "We were on the police force together in New York. And he told me everything that happened. Unlike you."

I felt my face get warm. "Dad, we hate lying to you, but . . ."

"We didn't want you to freak out," said Joe.

Dad glanced at us through the rearview mirror. "Look, guys. When I left the force and started up

American Teens Against Crime, I knew it would involve risks. But I also knew that you boys can take care of yourselves . . . and each other."

Joe nudged me in the ribs. I nudged him back.

"I was always impressed with the amateur detective work you did a couple of years ago," Dad continued. "The cops at the station used to call you the Sherlock Brothers of Bayport. You solved some major crimes. Cases even the police couldn't crack. And you mixed with some major criminals. Sure, I was worried. But I couldn't be prouder."

I smiled. "Thanks, Dad."

"Yeah, thanks," said Joe.

Dad's expression changed. "But now . . . I don't know," he said, lowering his voice. "It's a tough world out there. Maybe it's too much to ask teenagers to go undercover. It's just too dangerous. And now that I'm semiretired, I can't keep a close eye on you boys."

"But Dad, we have the entire ATAC team looking out for us," I told him.

"Yeah, man, we're covered," said Joe.

Dad took a deep breath and let it out slowly. "I guess you're right," he said. "But you can't blame a guy for worrying about his kids. Especially when they're jumping out of planes and busting smugglers."

"That's what we live for!" said Joe.

Dad chuckled. "So tell me all about this new mission. What's up with the Big Air Games? Are the athletes using steroids, or bribing judges, or what?"

"I wish it was that specific," I said. Then Joe and I filled him in on the details.

"Basically they want us to keep an eye on the other teenagers," Joe explained.

"We're just undercover baby-sitters," I added with a sigh.

"Don't be so sure," said Dad. "The ATAC team wouldn't be sending you unless they detected something suspicious. Just stay on your guard. And have some fun . . . within limits. Remember my motto."

"Suspect *everyone*," Joe and I said at the same time.

"Good boys." Dad steered the car off the highway and pulled into the front lot of the Bayport Auto Garage. "Go get 'em," he said.

My brother and I hopped out and dashed into the garage. We were dying to see our bikes. Butch, the head mechanic, had promised to upgrade our motorcycles with some new parts.

"Yo, bros," Butch greeted us. "You prepared to be blown away?"

"Go ahead," said Joe. "Make my day."

The mustached mechanic waved us into the garage. "Feast your eyes on these babies," he said.

One word: *Wow*.

These were no ordinary motorcycles. These were total high-tech speed machines decked out with all the latest features! Polished chrome controls, high-grade leather seats, stainless steel exhaust pipes—the works—and they were customized with flaming red double Hs.

"This is *too much*!" Joe yelped. "This *kicks butt*!"

I couldn't believe my eyes. "What . . . ? How . . . ? Why did you do all this, Butch?" I said, stammering. "I mean, we just brought our bikes in for a tune-up."

Butch laughed and walked over to the motorcycles. "Check this out," he said, demonstrating the new features. "Hydraulic clutch. Optimized suspension. Fog lamps with flint protectors. Hazard warning flashers. Digital clock, CD player, and CB radio. Electric power socket for accessories."

"Dude! Stop! You're killing me!" Joe whooped out loud, faking a heart attack.

"But wait. That's not all," Butch went on. He flicked a switch, and a series of digital panels lit up on the dashboard. "Check it out, guys. Here you have your security tracking device and computerized navigation system."

41

"Unreal!" Joe hooted.

I stared in shock.

This was unbelievable.

Finally I managed to speak. "You weren't kidding when you said you'd upgrade our bikes, Butch. But the problem is, I don't know how we're going to pay for all this."

"Forget about it," said the mechanic. "It's taken care of." He nodded toward a man standing in the doorway.

"Dad!" Joe shouted. "You totally rock!"

"You boys deserve it," Dad said with a big grin. "Now saddle up and make your father proud."

Joe hooted and hopped on his bike. I looked my father in the eye. "You didn't have to do this," I said.

He shrugged. "I just thought you boys should have all the new safety features when you're chasing down bad guys."

I smiled. "Okay, cool. Thanks." Then I turned and tested out the new leather seat of my bike.

"Just do me one favor, Frank," Dad said when I reached for the ignition. "Don't take this new mission too lightly. They must have named it 'Extreme Danger' for a reason."

"That's what I told Joe."

"Well, be careful," said Dad.

Joe and I slipped our helmets over our heads and revved up our engines. Then, waving good-bye to Dad, we roared out of the parking lot and headed down the highway.

Joe was so happy he looked like he was going to self-destruct.

I glanced over my shoulder for one last look at Dad. He was standing in the middle of the lot, watching us ride off. Even from a block away, I could see the concern on his face.

A warning sign.

Unfortunately, I should have been paying attention to *other* signs—like the road signs in front of me.

Because I'd missed the turn for the interstate.

And Joe was nowhere in sight!

# 5.
# Killer Wheels

*Philadelphia, here we come!*

Man, I was having a blast. With the new killer wheels beneath me and the open road in front of me, I was ready to take on the world—or, at least, tackle our latest mission.

There was just one problem: Where was Frank?

Turns out he'd fallen behind. But thanks to our new navigation systems, he was able to catch up with me on the next interstate ramp. Zooming up next to me, he grinned and gave me a thumbs-up.

*All systems go.*

We made good time. Weaving our way through the rush-hour traffic, we reached the outskirts of Philadelphia by eight o'clock. My motorcycle handled like a dream.

Heck, I could have kept riding all night long.

Minutes later we found the hotel and pulled our cycles into the parking garage. "Do I have to leave my bike here?" I asked Frank, turning off the engine. "Do you think they'll let me park it in my room? I could say it's my luggage."

"You could also say you're Elvis, but I don't think they'll go for it," said Frank. "Come on. Let's check in."

We gathered up our stuff and grabbed an elevator to the lobby. When the doors opened, we thought we'd come to the wrong place.

The joint was rocking!

It was a total zoo. Every inch of the hotel lobby was crawling with punked-out dudes and dudettes sporting Mohawks and Day-Glo dye jobs. Across the room, a gang of bikers in red leather knocked their helmets together and cheered. A pack of T-shirted skateboarders did railslides down the entry steps. A ponytailed trio of identical triplets zipped past us on Rollerblades.

"Hey, Frank," I said, nudging my brother. "If they can skate around in here, maybe I can ride my bike, too."

"Give it a rest, Joe."

Frank pointed me toward the reception desk. Zigzagging our way through the crowd, we walked up to the check-in sign—and found ourselves face-to-face with a bald-headed desk clerk who didn't look at all amused by the hotel's current clientele.

"May I help you, gentlemen?" he said with a tired sigh.

"I'll take care of this," Frank told me.

"Sure, knock yourself out."

My brother loved handling this sort of official business. Fine with me. It gave me a chance to scan the room and check out the action.

I turned around—and nearly knocked a girl over.

"Whoa! Sorry," I said, grabbing her wrist before she fell. "Are you okay?"

The girl looked up. "No problem. I'm okay."

She was more than okay. She was a total knockout—a brown-eyed beauty with jet black hair, ruby red lips, and a hot-pink skateboard tucked under her arm.

This mission was looking better all the time.

"I'm Joe. Joe Hardy." I extended my hand.

The girl slapped it and smiled. "I'm Jenna Cho. And I'm *so* embarrassed."

"Embarrassed? Why?" I asked.

She held up her skateboard and shrugged. "Well, it's like this. Twenty minutes ago I did a 540 air spin on the half-pipe and had no problem landing

46

on my board. Then this dude bumps into me in a hotel lobby and I totally wipe out."

I laughed. "This dude sounds like a jerk," I said.

"No, not really," Jenna said with a wink. "In fact, he's kind of cute."

*Nice.*

"Are you competing in the games?" Jenna asked me.

"No, I'm just a fan," I said. "But I skateboard a little myself. I wish I'd brought mine with me."

"Well, if you want to borrow mine, I'll be practicing in FDR Park tomorrow," said Jenna. "All the Big Air boarders hang out there."

"Sure, I'll drop by," I said, even though I wasn't thrilled about riding a hot-pink skateboard.

"Jenna! Come on!" someone yelled across the lobby. I looked over to see a group of skateboarders in front of the elevators.

"Chill out! I'm coming!" Jenna yelled back at them. She threw her board on the floor and hopped on. "I'm in room 514," she whispered. "Call me if you want to hang." Then she skated away.

*Excellent.*

"Who was that?" asked Frank, coming up behind me.

"A beautiful girl who just gave me her room number," I bragged.

"Why was she whispering?"

"Probably because she didn't want *you* to hear it."

"Or maybe she has something to hide."

"Oh, come off it, Frank. Stop playing detective for two minutes and enjoy yourself."

My brother looked annoyed. "We're here on a mission, Joe," he said, lowering his voice. "We're supposed to be gathering information."

"Yes, and the best way to do that is by blending in and hanging out with the athletes," I replied. "And besides, I *did* get some information. Jenna told me that all the skateboarders practice in FDR Park."

Frank raised an eyebrow. "Okay, well, that's useful," he admitted. "Anyway, I have our room keys. Let's go."

We took the elevator up to our hotel room, unpacked our stuff—and suddenly realized we were starving.

"We should have taken Aunt Trudy's doggy bags when we had the chance," said Frank.

"Let's go out and grab a slice of pizza," I suggested. "We have the whole city of Philadelphia at our feet."

Frank agreed.

We left our room and went downstairs, passing through the circus in the lobby and heading for an exit. When we got outside, we were surprised to see that the sidewalks were just as crowded as the hotel.

"Man, the whole city is buzzing," said Frank, staring at all the extreme athletes and fans passing by.

I could tell he was trying to eavesdrop on their conversations—listening for anything suspicious. That was my brother. Always on the case.

We walked a few blocks, just enjoying the sights, until we stumbled on a small skateboard store. The place was a little run-down but seemed to carry all the latest boards and equipment. A sign above the door said OLLIE'S SKATE SHOP.

"Let's go in," said Frank. "We can ask the owner if he's heard any rumors about an attack."

I was starving, but I didn't feel like arguing with my brother. He was a man on a mission.

A little bell jingled when we opened the door and stepped inside. The place was packed with merchandise, but not many customers. There were just a few teenaged boys trying on helmets, and two girls looking at T-shirts.

"Hey! You boys!" a deep gravelly voice shouted from behind the counter.

Frank and I turned to see who was shouting. It was a middle-aged man with a bad sunburn, a walking cane, tattooed arms, and long blond hair tied in a ponytail. He looked kind of like an angry surfer.

Lucky for us, he was pointing at the other boys in the store. "Don't put those helmets on your greasy little heads unless you're serious about buying them," he barked.

"Oh, get over yourself, dude," one of the boys shot back. "I don't care if you *were* the national champion. That was years ago. Right now, you're a knobby-kneed has-been!"

The ponytailed man fixed his cold blue eyes on the boys—then slowly reached under the counter. "Get out of my store," he snarled. "Now."

Nobody moved for a moment or two. Then the boys put down the helmets and walked out of the store. "Loser," one of them mumbled as the door closed with a jingle.

Frank tapped my arm, then nodded at a handwritten sign next to the register. It said, AS AN AMERICAN CITIZEN, I FULLY EXERCISE MY RIGHT TO BEAR ARMS. SHOPLIFTERS: BEWARE.

I glanced back at Frank. He raised his eyebrows and tilted his head toward a bulletin board.

I turned and looked. The board was covered with photos of Ollie looking young and fit—and soaring through the air on a skateboard. There were newspaper clippings, too, with headlines like OLLIE PETERSON: NATIONAL SKATEBOARD CHAMP 1986 and OLLIE WINS AGAIN! I had to squint to read the small clipping on the bottom: SKATEBOARD LEGEND TAKES A FALL.

"What are you boys looking for?" Ollie grunted, slamming his cane down on the counter.

I tried to think fast. "I need a new skateboard," I answered. "Something top-of-the-line."

Ollie growled and lowered his cane, then limped toward a large skateboard display. "Over here, kid," he said. "I got all the latest models."

Why not buy one? That way I wouldn't have to share Jenna's tomorrow.

It took only about three minutes for Ollie to convince me to buy a brand-new THX-720 with red flame detailing. And it matched my motorcycle!

Frank, in the meantime, was studying the articles on the bulletin board—gathering information, as usual.

As Ollie rang up my purchase, one of the girls walked up to the counter and said, "Excuse me? Mister? Do you have any T-shirts for the Big Air Games?"

Wrong question.

Ollie almost threw a fit. "Big Air *Heads* is more

51

## SUSPECT PROFILE

<u>Name:</u> Owen Peterson, aka "Ollie"

<u>Hometown:</u> San Diego, CA

<u>Physical description:</u> 40 years old, 5'11", 170 pounds, shoulder-length blond hair, blue eyes, walks with limp, carries cane, dragon tattoos on forearms

<u>Occupation:</u> Owner/operator of Ollie's Skate Shop in downtown Philadelphia

<u>Background:</u> Former professional skateboarder (career ended after accidental injury in 1990)

<u>Suspicious behavior:</u> Threatened customers, reached for (alleged) gun under store counter, talked about replacing skateboard bearings with nitroglycerin

<u>Suspected of:</u> Attempted sabotage

<u>Possible motives:</u> Revenge against Big Air Games (business dispute), personal resentment

like it!" he snapped. "Those big-business money-grubbers won't allow me to set up a stand outside the stadium. So, fat chance I'll fill their greedy pockets by selling their ugly shirts."

The girl blinked her eyes. "So that's a no?" she asked.

"YES, IT'S A NO!" he boomed.

The girl shrugged and left the store with her friend.

A few seconds later Ollie calmed down enough to take my money and complete my purchase.

Frank strolled over to the counter. "I guess those Big Air Games are a big deal, huh?" he said to Ollie.

Ollie rolled his eyes. "A big pain," he sneered. "The whole city is tied in knots, with all the traffic and the cops everywhere."

"Well, an event that big must attract a lot of weirdos," said Frank. "Maybe even terrorists. Someone told me they heard a rumor that someone was going to sabotage the games."

Ollie laughed. "That would be fine with me," he growled. "I even know how they could do it."

"Oh, really?" said Frank, leaning over the counter. "How?"

Ollie grabbed a skateboard off the display and flipped it over. "See the axis of the wheel here?" he said, giving it a spin. "That's where the ball bearings usually go. But some of these new models use liquid bearings. No balls, just liquid. Understand?"

Frank and I nodded.

"Well, imagine this," Ollie continued. "What if

53

someone replaced the liquid with an explosive like nitroglycerin? Think about it. The faster the skater goes, the hotter the nitro gets. Faster and hotter, faster and hotter, until . . . *KA-BOOM!* I think you get the picture."

Yes, we got the picture.

And it wasn't very pretty.

*Talk about killer wheels.*

I grabbed my new skateboard and nudged my brother. "Come on, Frank. We better get going. It's late."

My brother agreed. "Bye, Ollie," he said as we left the store. "It was nice talking to you."

*Yeah,* I thought. *It's always nice to talk to a crazy washed-up skateboarder who wants to blow people up.*

# 6.

## Attacked!

Joe and I didn't get to eat until ten o'clock at night. *(My fault, because it was my idea to go inside Ollie's Skate Shop.)*

And we didn't get to sleep until one o'clock in the morning. *(Joe's fault, because it was his idea to call up Jenna Cho when we returned to the hotel.)*

Anyway, Jenna convinced my brother that we should skip the pregame events in the morning. The official opening ceremonies would be held the following day. She suggested we sleep in, grab a late breakfast, then meet her in the park with the other skaters.

Sounded good to me. I was exhausted.

After a full day of skydiving, motorcycle-riding,

55

skateboard-shopping, a whole pizza at ten o'clock—and listening to Joe yammer on with his new girlfriend—who could blame me for being tired?

*Ah, sleep.*

"Wake up!" said Joe, hitting me with a pillow. "Are you going to sleep all day? Move your lazy butt!"

I rubbed my eyes and looked at the clock radio.

*Nine forty-five?*

I think it was the first time in history that Joe woke up before I did. "Breakfast," I mumbled sleepily.

"No time for that," said Joe, tossing me a pair of shorts and a shirt. "We promised to meet Jenna. Move it."

I crawled out of bed, hopped in the shower, and got dressed as quickly as I could. Joe insisted that we ride our cycles to the park.

"We don't want to be late," he said, adding, "and girls dig the bikes."

About twenty minutes later, we arrived at FDR Park. Jenna Cho was waiting with her pink skateboard at the entrance.

"Yo, dudes!" She greeted us with a big smile and a thumbs-up. "Awesome set of wheels! I'm impressed."

"Told you so," Joe whispered to me. Then he

flashed a smile at his new friend. "How's it going, Jenna?"

Jenna swung her skateboard like a baseball bat. "It's going, it's going, it's gone!" she said, laughing. "Come on, park your bikes so we can grab some cheese steaks."

"Philly cheese steaks?" I asked. "For breakfast?"

Joe swatted my arm. "This is my brother," he explained to Jenna. "Frank is the logical Hardy."

"Yeah, and Joe is *hardly* logical," I added.

After the introduction we found a spot to park our bikes and ordered three cheese steaks at a nearby stand.

"Wow," I said, taking a bite. "This is incredible."

Jenna nodded. "Now you know why they're world famous."

We strolled through the park, chomping on our cheese steaks, while Jenna showed us the sights. "I'm taking you guys to a skatepark underneath the overpass," she said. "It was built by the city. All the cool Philly kids skate there."

"Can't wait," Joe said, waving the new skateboard he'd bought at Ollie's.

"Where's your board, Frank?" asked Jenna.

I shrugged. "With pros like you around, I didn't want to risk looking like a dork."

"Too late for that," my brother teased.

I decided to change the subject. Now was my chance to ask about the rumors of a possible attack. "Speaking of risks," I started off, "someone told me they saw some threats posted on one of the extreme Web sites. Some people even think someone plans to sabotage the games. You heard anything, Jenna?"

Jenna thought about it, then said, "I don't know, just the usual rivalries. Competition can get pretty fierce. There's a lot of money at stake."

"There is?" I asked.

"Well, the top prizes are ten thousand dollars," she said. "And if you win the nationals, you could land a million-dollar endorsement deal from the sports gear companies."

*Definitely a motive for sabotaging your opponent,* I thought.

We were almost in the middle of the park. A few kids on skateboards and motocross bikes whizzed past us. "The skatepark is over there," Jenna said, pointing past some trees.

Suddenly a loud siren blasted right behind us.

"Look out!" Joe yelled.

We jumped out of the way as a white EMT ambulance barreled past us with its lights flashing.

"It's heading for the skatepark!" Jenna shouted. "Maybe there's been an accident!"

"Let's go," I said, slapping my brother's shoulder.

The three of us dashed after the ambulance, pushing past dozens of gawking skaters and bikers. The siren stopped blaring. The vehicle pulled to a halt in front of a graffiti-covered ramp under the highway overpass. We rushed over to the center of the action.

A muscular dark-haired boy lay on the concrete next to his skateboard. "It hurts! It hurts!" he howled in pain.

"I know that boy," Jenna whispered to Frank and me. "That's Gongado Lopez. He's from New York City, and everyone says he's a sure thing for a gold medal this year."

*Not anymore.*

A tall skinny paramedic applied bandages to the boy's knees and shouted over his shoulder, "Jack! I need some help here!"

A short stocky technician jumped out of the ambulance with a small case of supplies. I watched the two men do their job and I checked out the ID badges on their chests.

The short guy was named Jack Horowitz, and the tall skinny guy was Carter Bean. Carter seemed to be the more experienced of the two. He filled a hypodermic needle and gave Gongado a shot of painkiller in about fifteen seconds flat.

"Gongado!" a high-pitched voice cried out. "Gongado! What did that dirtbag do to you?"

A short frizzy-haired young woman pushed past us and rushed toward the stricken boy. Carter blocked her with his arm. "Stay back, miss," he said firmly. "Let us do our jobs."

The girl backed off but kept talking. "Gongado! Sweetie! What happened? Tell me!"

Gongado blinked his eyes. Obviously the painkillers were kicking in, but he was able to talk. "Baby, I was attacked! Somebody jumped me and knocked me over and whacked me in the knees with my own skateboard."

The girl burst into tears. "Was it him?" she asked. "Was it Eddie?"

Gongado shook his head. "I don't know. I didn't see his face." Then he closed his eyes and passed out.

A man with a camera stepped forward. "Did anyone see anything?" he shouted into the crowd.

Nobody said anything.

"Are you a police officer?" Carter asked the man.

"No, I'm a reporter for the *Philadelphia Freedom Press,*" he told the paramedic. "I was just walking through the park when I heard your siren. Do you mind posing for a picture? Just crouch over the victim and try to look concerned."

"I *am* concerned," Carter said calmly. He turned to help his coworker lift the boy onto a stretcher and into the ambulance.

The reporter snapped away with his camera. Even after the ambulance drove off, he kept pursuing the story. But instead of taking pictures, he interviewed half the kids in the crowd.

After a while, the reporter went away—and the scene returned to normal. The skateboarders practiced their kickies and heelies while the bikers hurtled over ramps. Jenna, Joe, and I found a spot under a nearby tree.

"Do you know that girl? Gongado's girlfriend?" I asked Jenna.

"I don't know her personally," she said, "but I know *about* her. Her name's Annette, and she only dates the hottest skateboarders in town. She used to go out with Eddie Mundy . . . until Gongado beat him in the last regional contest. Now she goes out with Gongado."

"Eddie Mundy," I said. "Annette mentioned Eddie's name. So she thinks Eddie attacked Gongado?"

"Of course she does," said Jenna. "Gongado stole Eddie's title. Then he stole Eddie's girl. You do the math."

"What's this Eddie guy like?" I asked.

Jenna pointed across the park. "That's him over there. In the red bandanna." She poked my brother's arm. "Come on, Joe. Want to try out the vert ramp?"

Joe and Jenna ran off with their skateboards.

And me? I decided to have a little talk with Eddie Mundy.

"Hey, man," I said, approaching him during a break. "I hear you're the best skateboarder in town."

Eddie sat down on his board and looked up at me suspiciously. "Who told you that?" he asked. He was lean, lanky—and a little scary-looking, I had to admit.

"Some of the other athletes said you were the best," I said, nodding at the other skateboarders.

Eddie shrugged. "I *used* to be the best," he grunted. "Until Gongado Lopez snatched my title away."

"Well, they just took Lopez away in an ambulance," I said. "His knees are all busted up. So I guess he's out of the contest now."

"Yeah," said Eddie, squinting his eyes. "So I guess that makes *me* the best." He let out a little laugh.

"Did you and Gongado get along?" I asked.

Eddie didn't answer. He just stared at me. "Why do you ask so many questions, man?"

"I'm writing an article on the Big Air Games for my school paper," I lied.

"Well, watch your back," said Eddie. "It's dangerous to ask too many questions. *Extremely* dangerous."

He gave me a hard look. I figured I was pushing my luck, so I simply said thanks and good-bye.

## SUSPECT PROFILE

**Name:** Edward Mundy, aka "Eddie"

**Physical description:** 18 years old, 6'1", 180 pounds, brown hair, green eyes, wears red bandanna

**Hometown:** Philadelphia, PA

**Occupation:** Hardware store clerk, amateur skateboarder

**Background:** Former titleholder in regional skateboard contests, currently competing in Big Air Games

**Suspicious behavior:** Laughed about Gongado Lopez's attack and leg injuries, referred to Frank's questioning as "extremely dangerous"

**Suspected of:** Assault and battery

**Possible motives:** Professional revenge (Lopez stole his title), romantic triangle (Lopez stole his girl)

I walked around the skateboard park looking for Joe. I wanted to get him up to speed.

We had another suspect.

A few minutes later I managed to drag Joe away from the concrete ramps—and away from Jenna. She said she needed to practice for her upcoming event, so my brother and I headed off on our own.

I waited until we were about a hundred yards away from the skatepark—safely out of everyone's earshot—before I told Joe about my talk with Eddie Mundy.

"Man!" Joe said, after hearing my story. "That dude is *so* guilty."

"We don't know that for a fact," I pointed out. "Sure, Eddie has the motives—and the attitude— to commit a crime like that. But there's no real evidence."

"But come on," Joe argued. "How else do you explain his comment about your 'dangerous' questions?"

I scratched my head. "I don't know," I said. "It's definitely suspicious. And we definitely should keep an eye on Eddie Mundy."

"So that's it?" Joe said, throwing his hands up. "We just keep an eye on the guy? We don't turn him in to the cops?"

"No. Not yet."

Joe stopped walking. "But Frank," he persisted. "What if Eddie Mundy hurts someone else?"

I thought long and hard about my brother's question. But I never got the chance to answer him.

Because somebody started screaming.

# 7.

## Blood on the Half-Pipe

*Man! What a scream!*

Frank and I stood still and listened.

There it was again!

I don't know what freaked me out more: the fact that the scream came from the skateboard park, or that it sounded like Jenna doing the screaming. I took off like a bolt of lightning, sprinting as fast as I could toward the concrete overpass. Frank's footsteps echoed behind me. Other skaters and bikers were dashing toward the half-pipes—but I outran them all.

A group of people were crowded around one of the pipes. I spotted a dark-haired girl hunched down in the middle of the circle.

"Jenna!" I yelled, pushing past the onlookers.

Jenna sat on the curve of the ramp, leaning over the lifeless body of a curly-haired boy.

I dropped to my knees beside her. "What happened? Is he okay?"

Jenna looked up at me, her eyes filled with tears. "I don't know," she said. "We were practicing our air jumps, and Jeb just collapsed in front of me. Then my skateboard slammed into his head. I tried to stop, but . . ."

I carefully examined the boy's scalp, parting the locks of his curly hair. "I don't see any head wounds," I said. "And he's still breathing. Somebody call 911!"

"I already did," said Frank, shoving his cell phone back in his pocket and stooping down next to us. He looked at Jenna. "Who is he? Do you know him?"

Jenna nodded. "Jeb Green. He's an old friend of mine from California. An amazing skateboarder. He knows how to take a fall. But this time . . . it was weird . . . he fell with a bang."

"A bang?" I said, glancing at Frank.

"It's all my fault," Jenna sobbed quietly. "I tried to stop before I ran into him, but my skateboard shot out from under me. I might have given him a concussion."

"I don't think your skateboard did this," I said,

pointing to the upper curve of the ramp. "There's blood on the half-pipe."

"And here, too," Frank added. "In the middle of the guy's chest."

We quickly unbuttoned the boy's shirt—and exposed a small bullet hole in his skin.

"Jeb was shot!" Jenna gasped.

The crowd started buzzing like flies. Some of them took off running, while others moved in for a closer look. One man kept saying, "Excuse me, pardon me, coming through," until he pushed his way in.

It was the reporter from the *Philadelphia Freedom Press*.

"So what happened here?" he asked. "Any eyewitnesses?"

Jenna started to speak, but I stopped her.

There was something about this guy I didn't like. Maybe it was the way he hoisted up his camera and started snapping away whenever people got hurt.

"Hey, buddy," I said. "This boy might be dying here. Give the camera a rest."

The reporter scoffed. "Are you kidding? This is front page material."

I felt like punching the guy. But Frank had a better idea. He simply stood up—and blocked the reporter's view.

In the distance a siren began to wail.

"Okay, everybody move out of the way!" Frank yelled to the crowd. "Make room for the ambulance! Come on, guys! Move it!"

Slowly the kids backed away, leaving space for the approaching EMT van.

Soon the ambulance came to a halt in front of the ramp. The doors flew open and out stepped Carter and Jack—the same paramedics who'd treated Gongado Lopez about an hour before.

"Busy day," I said, stepping out of their way.

"Not really," replied Carter. "Accidents happen every day."

"This wasn't an accident," Frank told him.

"Oh, I see," said the thin paramedic, examining Jeb's chest wound.

"Is he . . . is he going to live?" Jenna asked.

"Well, the hole is too small for a regular bullet," Carter said. "This looks like it was made by a pellet gun." He inspected the wound further. "Yes, here it is, lodged in his sternum."

Jenna sucked in her breath. "But is he . . . ?"

"Yes, he's going to live," the paramedic added.

The crowd of onlookers cheered. Even the reporter from the *Freedom Press* looked happy—although he didn't stop taking pictures for a single second.

The EMT guys ignored all the attention. They were completely committed to their work. I was amazed at how fast and efficient they were. In only minutes Carter and Jack had the boy safely strapped onto a stretcher and hooked up to an IV drip.

I put my arm around Jenna's shoulder. "Jeb's going to be okay," I told her. "These guys know what they're doing."

Jack, the shorter paramedic, climbed into the driver's seat and revved the engine. Carter stayed in the back with the patient. Just before the ambulance pulled away, Carter peered out the rear window and gave the skateboarders a thumbs-up.

Everybody cheered.

"Beautiful! Just beautiful!" the reporter exclaimed, capturing the whole scene with his camera. Then he pulled a handheld tape recorder from his pocket and started asking people questions.

I looked down at Jenna. She looked pretty shell-shocked. "Maybe you should sit down for a minute," I suggested.

"There's a bench over there," Frank said, pointing.

The three of us walked over and sat down. Hidden away beneath a big shady tree, the bench offered a perfect view of the skateboard park. Nobody was skating or riding. Everyone was milling about and talking.

We didn't talk for a while—just watched the others from a distance.

Finally Jenna spoke. "Why would anyone want to shoot Jeb? It doesn't make any sense." She kicked an empty soda can back and forth between her feet.

I glanced at Frank.

I knew he was *dying* to ask Jenna some questions, but he didn't say a word.

"I just don't get it," she said softly. "Everybody loves Jeb. He's one of those sunny California guys. Always happy, always smiling. No enemies, no rivals. He's just a cool, laid-back kind of guy. I wish you two could meet him."

"Maybe Frank and I can visit him at the hospital," I said.

"Would you?" she said, her eyes lighting up. "That would mean a lot to me. Maybe I should skip practice and go with you."

"I bet Jeb would want you to practice and kick butt on the ramps tomorrow. Don't you think?" I asked.

She nodded. "Yeah, you're right. But tell him that I'm pulling for him, and I'll try to visit him tonight."

I gave her a big hug. "Go practice," I said.

Jenna smiled and stretched. Then she threw

down her board and skated off toward the ramps.

I couldn't take my eyes off of her, for two reasons.

One, I was falling for her.

Two, I was worried about her.

"The shooter is still out there, Frank," I said. "He could be watching right now . . . and waiting to pull the trigger again."

"Maybe not," said Frank. "Here comes Eddie Mundy."

Warning bells went off in my head.

Eddie skated toward us with a red bandanna on his head, a backpack on his shoulder, and a hot dog in his mouth. He screeched to a stop in front of our bench.

"Hey! Mr. School Newspaper Reporter!" he barked at Frank. "What did I miss? What was up with the ambulance in the skatepark again?"

*As if you don't know,* I thought.

"There was another accident," Frank told the skater. "Jeb Green ran into a bullet."

Eddie stopped chewing his hot dog. "You're kidding me," he said.

"Why would I kid? I'm Mr. School Newspaper Reporter, remember?"

"Dude, that's pretty heavy-duty news," said Eddie, shaking his head. "Is Jeb dead?"

"No, he's in the hospital," Frank answered. "Seems he was shot with a pellet gun. You know, the small kind you could probably fit in a backpack."

Eddie glanced at the pack on his shoulder then smiled. "Hey, man. I wasn't even here, so don't even think it." He took another bite of his hot dog.

I couldn't take this guy another minute.

"So where were you, Eddie?" I asked.

He smirked at me. "I was grabbing a dog. See?" He opened his mouth and showed us the chewed-up food.

"Where did you buy it?" Frank asked.

Eddie shrugged. "A vendor."

"Which vendor?"

"Dude, how do I know? There are like a hundred vendors in this park!" He laughed—until he saw the look on our faces. "You guys are serious, aren't you? You really think I'm picking off the other skateboarders. Why? You think it's the only way I can win a medal? Give me a break, man!"

Eddie hopped on his board and skated away.

I looked at Frank. "I think I'm going to hang around the skatepark for a little bit. I don't like the idea of Jenna practicing while that creep is around."

Frank nodded. "Here's an idea. I'll go question

some of the hot dog vendors in the area, see if Eddie was really there during the shooting. Meet me at the park entrance in about a half hour. Cool?"

"Cool."

We parted ways. I headed into the skatepark and found a spot under the overpass where I could keep an eye on both Jenna and Eddie. After a while my fears started to fade. Everything seemed back to normal.

*But it had seemed normal right before the attacks.*

"Hey, you. Kid," someone said to me.

I turned my head and groaned. It was the reporter from the *Philadelphia Freedom Press*. He had his tape recorder in one hand and his camera in the other.

"What do you want?" I asked him.

"You were here for both of the accidents," he said.

"Yeah, so? So were you."

"So what's your story, kid?" he asked. "You a skateboard freak? Would you kill to win the Big Air Games?"

I shot him a dirty look. "How do I know you're really a reporter?"

He pulled out a wallet and showed me his press

ID. I glanced at his grainy face shot and credentials: Maxwell Monroe, journalist/photographer, *Philadelphia Freedom Press.*

"Nice picture, Max," I said. "So why do you like taking pictures of violent crimes? What do you get out of it?"

"A Pulitzer Prize for journalism if I'm lucky," he answered, chuckling. "Maybe I'll stumble onto another attack today. It's crazy. Two teen assaults at the same place on the same day? And I happen to be right here to catch it all on camera? I mean, what are the chances of that?"

*Yes,* I thought. *What* are *the chances of that?*

"I tell you, most reporters would kill for this kind of story," Max went on. "I can see the headlines now. 'Big Crimes at Big Air Games! An exclusive report by Maxwell Monroe.' I'll be famous."

"Sure you will, Max," I said, slowly backing away. The guy was creeping me out.

"Well, kid, I have to get back to the office if I want to make my deadline." He slipped his little tape recorder into the inside pocket of his jacket.

That's when I noticed something: He was wearing a gun holster.

"Good luck with the games, son! Break a leg!"

Monroe turned and walked away, laughing to himself.

I turned my attention back to the ramps. Eddie Mundy was leaving the park with a group of friends. Seemed safe to leave Jenna.

I watched her do an amazing jump, said good-bye, and headed off to meet Frank at the park

## SUSPECT PROFILE

**Name**: Maxwell Monroe

**Hometown**: Philadelphia, PA

**Physical description**: 48 years old, 6'2", 200 pounds, balding, brown eyes, glasses

**Occupation**: Journalist/photographer, Philadelphia Freedom Press

**Background**: Graduate of Farmdale Community College, former fact-checker for Weekly World News

**Suspicious behavior**: Just happened to "stumble" onto two crime scenes, harassed victims with camera, joked about possibility of more attacks

**Suspected of**: Assault, battery, attempted homicide with firearm, journalistic fraud

**Possible motives**: Pulitzer Prize, fame, fortune

entrance. I couldn't wait to give him the latest news.

If my suspicions were correct, tomorrow's headline just might read: LOCAL REPORTER WILLING TO KILL FOR GOOD STORY.

FRANK

# 8.

## Dead on Arrival

The emergency room at Pennsylvania Hospital was crowded, noisy, and hectic. The patients with the most severe injuries were wheeled past us on gurneys. Others had to wait in the seating area until a nurse at the desk shouted their names.

I shifted back and forth on the hard vinyl chair and tried to sort through the clues and suspects in my head. But it was hard to concentrate with all the moaning and groaning in the room. The patients were losing their patience. And so was I.

My brother wouldn't shut up about Maxwell Monroe.

"I'm telling you, Frank. That newspaper guy is a

total freak," Joe yammered on. "He'd do anything to get a good story."

"I don't know, Joe," I said. "It seems pretty far-fetched."

"But he was *there,* dude, for *both* attacks."

"So were we," I pointed out. "So were a lot of people."

"But what about his gun?"

"You didn't see a gun. You saw a shoulder holster. Maybe it was just the guy's camera strap."

"Maybe," Joe said, standing up and stretching his legs. "But maybe not."

It was hard to take Joe seriously. He was holding a bouquet of fresh daisies.

"Okay," I said. "I'll add his name to our suspect list. Let's see now. We have Maxwell Monroe, Ollie Peterson, Eddie Mundy . . . and every skateboarder competing in the games. That really narrows it down."

Joe sighed and rubbed his eyes.

"Hardy! HARDY!"

The desk nurse shouted out our names like an army drill sergeant. Joe and I rushed over to the desk.

"You can see Jebediah Green now," the nurse informed us. "They just moved him to room 418."

We left the emergency waiting room and headed

for the elevators. On the fourth floor, another nurse pointed us toward Jeb's room. I knocked lightly before we entered.

"Come in," said a gravelly voice.

My brother and I entered the room. Jeb was laid out in the hospital bed with a big gauze patch taped to his chest and an IV drip stuck in his arm.

Joe held out the bouquet of daisies. "These are from Jenna," he said. "We're friends of hers."

Jeb smiled weakly. "Thanks, dude."

"She wanted to come, but we told her you'd probably want her to stay and practice."

"Definitely." He looked a little woozy—but surprisingly strong, especially considering he'd just been shot in the chest with a pellet gun.

"I'm Frank Hardy," I said, shaking his hand. "This is my brother Joe. How are you feeling?"

"Beats me," he said with a goofy grin. "I got so many painkillers in me, I don't feel a thing. But they tell me I'm going to live."

Joe set the flowers on a table and pulled up a chair. "My brother and I are trying to figure this thing out, Jeb."

"You and half the cops in Philly," said Jeb. "Those guys asked me like, a zillion questions down in the emergency room."

"Mind if we ask a few more?" I said.

"Sure. Why not? Who's counting? But first let me tell you what I already told the cops. No, I don't have any enemies—none that I can think of, at least. No, I can't think of any reason why someone would go after both Lopez and myself. And no, I'm not one of the top competitors this year—so it's pointless to take me out of the games."

I nodded and sighed. "Thanks, Jeb. You just answered most of my questions."

"The cops were pretty thorough," he said.

I was stumped. And, judging by the look on my brother's face, so was Joe.

Then I thought of something.

"I have another question for you, Jeb."

"Shoot," he said, smiling.

I laughed at his word choice, then asked my question. "What can you tell me about Ollie Peterson? The owner of Ollie's Skate Shop?"

Just then the door swung open—and in walked the tall skinny paramedic who had treated Jeb in the park.

"Hello, Jeb," the man said, smiling. "I was told you can see visitors now." He glanced at Joe and me.

"No problem, dude," said Jeb. "Join the party."

The paramedic introduced himself. "I'm Carter Bean. You probably don't remember me, but I'm one of the emergency medical guys who picked you up at the park."

"Thanks, man. You saved my life," said Jeb, shaking his hand. "These are friends of mine, Frank and Joe Hardy. They're in town for the Big Air Games."

"We're also fans of your work," Joe told Carter. "We saw you handle both of those emergencies today in the park. You're a real pro."

Carter nodded. "Thanks. It's always nice to be appreciated." He looked at Jeb. "So how are you doing? Did they patch you up good?"

"Check it out," Jeb answered.

Carter pulled away the bandage and examined the wound. "Nice job," he said. "That'll heal up before you know it. Good thing the gunman must have been standing far away. If he had fired at a closer range, you'd have been DOA."

"What's that mean?" asked Jeb.

"Dead on arrival," Carter explained.

"How far away would you say the shooter was?" I asked.

Carter scratched his head. "Well, you'd have to ask a forensic expert, but I would guess a couple hundred feet, at least."

I made a mental note of it. Maybe it was a clue. Maybe not.

After a few minutes of chitchat, the paramedic announced that his lunch break was over. As soon as he left the room, I asked Jeb again about Ollie Peterson.

"What can I say, man? Ollie is Ollie," Jeb explained. "Everybody knows him and everybody hates him. But he's got the best skateboard shop in town. He really knows his stuff. Ollie was a former champ, you know. He was the hottest thing on wheels back in the eighties. He had a huge career ahead of him."

"So what happened?" I asked.

"Two things," said Jeb. "First, he claims he invented the 'ollie'—the move you make by smacking your foot down on the back of the board. Everybody knew that Rodney Mullen came up with it, though. He's a legend among skateboarders. Ollie was just a big joke, especially after he insisted that everyone call him Ollie. His real name is Owen."

"Okay. What's the second thing?"

"The accident," said Jeb. "It happened in 1990, at the peak of his career, in the FDR skatepark. Ollie was really pushing himself. He flew about ten feet in the air and slammed down knee-first on the edge of the half-pipe. He's lucky he can walk at all."

We thanked Jeb for the information. He asked

us to give Jenna a message—"Go for the gold, baby"—and gave us the peace sign. Then Joe and I exited the hospital, hopped on our motorcycles, and returned to the hotel.

"Man, I need a shower!" Joe said when we got back to our room. "I'm drenched in sweat." He peeled off his shirt and headed for the bathroom.

I decided to plug in my laptop and check out a few Web sites. Maybe people were chatting about the attacks this morning. I logged in, did a quick search, and found the official chat rooms of the Big Air Games.

*Bingo.*

The chat rooms were packed. Everybody was typing in their theories on the skateboard assaults. Some blamed terrorists. Others thought it was the work of motocross bikers. But nobody suggested anything that made any sense.

I was about to give up when something caught my eye.

It was one little message, posted among all the oddball conspiracy theories.

It said, "I told you this was going to happen. I warned you."

It was posted by 4567TME—the same person who had posted the strange warning to "Xtreme sports nuts."

I knew it! That message I read yesterday was a threat!

I scanned the rest of the chat list, scrolling down to see if 4567TME had posted anything else.

Nothing—just that one message.

*But what a message.*

Joe stepped out of the bathroom drying his hair with a towel.

"Joe. Come look at this," I said.

Joe leaned over the laptop and read the message. "We have to tell the police," he said. "Maybe they can trace the source of the message through the Web site."

"Not if the message was bounced there," I said. "It could take days, even weeks, to track it down."

"We don't have that much time. The games start tomorrow."

"I know," I said, reaching for my cell phone and dialing 411. I asked for the number of Ollie's Skate Shop.

"What are you doing?" said Joe.

I shushed him, then dialed the number. It rang.

"Yeah? What do you want?" Ollie's gruff voice snarled over the line.

"What are your store hours?" I asked.

"Noon to ten."

"Noon?" I said. "That seems pretty late to open a store."

"Who asked *you*?" he snapped back. "It's *my* store and I'll do whatever I want." He hung up.

I looked at Joe. "Ollie doesn't open his store until noon," I explained. "Which means he wasn't working this morning. He could have been at the park."

Joe brought up another piece of evidence. "The paramedic said the pellet gun was fired from several hundred feet away. So it wasn't one of the skateboarders who did it. They were all hanging around the ramps."

"But Eddie Mundy was buying a hot dog," I pointed out. "The vendors are several hundred feet away."

Joe shook his head. "I don't know, man. Eddie looked pretty bummed out when you told him about Jeb. I really think Ollie is the prime suspect here."

I had to agree. "He's bitter about his career. He hates the Big Air Games. He dreams up ways to sabotage skateboards."

"And he has a gun under his counter," Joe added.

"Ding, ding, ding!" I said. "It looks like we have a winner, folks."

"Definitely," Joe agreed. "Ollie's our man. So

what do we do now? Are we ready to turn him in?"

I shook my head. "We still don't have enough evidence to convict the guy."

Joe groaned. "You and your evidence." He flopped down on his bed. "So what do you suggest, Mr. Law and Order?"

"I think we should pay Ollie another visit," I said. "Let's see how he's taking the news about the skateboard attacks."

Five minutes later we left the hotel and walked the three blocks to Ollie's street.

Joe was getting more excited with every step.

"We have to nail that guy," he said under his breath. "He's so guilty I can smell it."

I think Joe was looking forward to some sort of big showdown—the kind you see in the movies. Ollie certainly had what it takes to be a big-screen villain. Even with his cane and his limp, he'd probably put up a good fight.

*Be prepared for anything,* I told myself.

Even so, I was totally shocked when Joe and I turned the corner.

Ollie's shop was surrounded by police cars and fenced off with yellow tape. The place was crawling with cops. Behind them an ambulance flashed its lights and blared its siren, then drove off down the street.

Joe and I pushed our way up to the police line. "What's going on? What happened?" Joe asked the officers.

Nobody would talk.

"I'll tell you what happened," said someone behind us.

Joe and I spun around.

It was Maxwell Monroe, the reporter from the *Philadelphia Freedom Press*.

"Ollie's been murdered," he said.

# 9.

## Who Is Mr. X?

*Ollie? Murdered?*

I couldn't believe what I was hearing. Our prime suspect had just become the latest victim.

"How did it happen?" Frank asked the reporter.

"He was poisoned," Max told us. "I overheard the cops talking. They think someone slipped something into Ollie's coffee. They're sending a sample off to the lab to be tested."

*Ollie? Murdered?* I kept thinking. *Who would want to murder Ollie?*

Then I remembered the way he snapped at those customers in his shop last night. Ollie may have owned the best skateboard shop in Philly, but he certainly seemed to have a lot of enemies. According to Jeb, everybody hated the guy.

But did they hate him enough to kill him?

Max raised his camera and snapped more shots of the crime scene. "Mr. X strikes again," he said.

"Who's Mr. X?" I asked.

"Haven't you seen the evening edition of the *Freedom Press*?"

"No. It's only two o'clock now."

"We went to press early today. Had to beat the other papers with our scoop," Max explained. "Anyway, the cover story is by yours truly. Photos, exclusive interviews . . . all mine! Even Mr. X was my idea."

"Phantom of the Big Air Games," Frank muttered.

Max looked at Frank. "Yeah, I came up with that, but . . . I thought you hadn't seen the evening edition yet."

Frank pointed to the crime scene. Lying in the doorway of Ollie's shop was a crumpled copy of the *Freedom Press*. The headline read, WHO IS MR. X? PHANTOM OF THE BIG AIR GAMES ATTACKS XTREME ATHLETES IN PARK.

"Mr. X. Xtreme sports. Get it?" said Max.

"We get it," I said.

"Better yet, buy it," the reporter added. "My editor-in-chief is hoping to double, even triple, our circulation with this story."

"We'll grab a copy on our way back to the hotel," Frank promised.

"Aw, heck. Officer! Excuse me!" Max yelled and waved to a police officer in front of Ollie's shop. "Toss me that newspaper! There, on the ground!"

The officer glanced down at the rumpled paper in the doorway. "Sorry, sir!" he shouted back. "It's evidence!"

"Evidence," Max muttered to us. "It's the biggest story of my career, and that joker calls it evidence. Can you believe it? He's probably just too cheap to buy his own copy! Evidence, my foot."

I shot a glance at Frank and twirled a finger at my temple.

What a fruit loop.

"Mr. Monroe. You said Ollie was poisoned," my brother said, trying to change the subject. "Did you see his body before they put him in the ambulance?"

"You bet I did," answered the reporter, patting his camera. "Got it all on film. He was already dead when they loaded him in. I wanted to get a shot of his face, but he was covered up by the time I got here. I did get a good shot of his cane lying next to him on the stretcher, though."

"How did you hear about it?" Frank asked.

"I didn't. I was on my way here to talk to Ollie. He called and left a message at my office. Said he wanted to talk to me about Mr. X. I show up here just as they're dragging him off to the morgue."

"When did Ollie leave you a message?" Frank asked.

"About a half hour ago," Max told him. Then he narrowed his eyes. "Hey, kid, you should be a reporter. You ask a lot of questions."

Frank smiled nervously. "Well, sir, I'm thinking of studying journalism when I go to college."

"You are?" I asked.

Frank kicked my leg and kept smiling.

"You look like a good kid," said Max. "But here's a little advice. Don't put all your eggs in one basket. Study a whole bunch of subjects. I mean, look at this Ollie guy here. He used to be a big skateboard star. It was his whole life. Then he busted up his leg real bad. Turned into a bitter old man, from what I hear."

"Who do you think killed him?" Frank asked. "And why?"

The reporter rubbed his jaw and shrugged. "My professional opinion? I think Mr. X is just some nutcase looking for attention. When you look at the different victims, the possible motives . . . it just doesn't make sense."

*You can say that again,* I thought.

"Come on, Joe," said my brother. "Let's grab some lunch."

"Sounds good, man. I'm starved."

Frank reached over and shook hands with the reporter. "It was good to talk to you, Mr. Monroe. Thanks for the advice."

"No problem, kid," said Max, turning back to the crime scene.

Frank and I walked around the corner and found a little Chinese restaurant. We went inside and were quickly seated at a small table under a giant menu on the wall.

After the waitress took our order, I leaned forward and whispered to Frank, "What did I tell you about Max Monroe? The guy is a nutcase. But he's right about Mr. X. Mr. X is a nutcase, too. Because Max *is* Mr. X. There's even an X in his name!"

"Slow down, Joe," Frank said. "I really don't think Max Monroe is crazy. An interesting character, yes. But crazy, no. I think he's telling the truth about getting a message from Ollie and showing up here after the guy was dead. If he had killed Ollie himself, you can be sure he would have taken some pictures of Ollie's face."

*Good point,* I thought.

"Ollie wanted to talk to a reporter," Frank continued. "He knew something."

"About the Big Air Games?" I asked.

Frank shook his head. "Don't you get it? Ollie knew the identity of Mr. X. And I bet it was something in Max's article that made him figure it out. That's why he called the newspaper."

I had to admit, it made sense.

"We have to get a copy of that paper," I said.

The waitress brought us our order. Frank and I wolfed down our chicken lo mein and moo shu shrimp as fast as we could. We were dying to get a look at the newspaper, but the waitress took forever bringing us our check.

Finally we paid and headed back toward the hotel. We stopped at a newsstand along the way and bought the evening edition of the *Philadelphia Freedom Press*.

I studied the pictures on the front page.

There was a shot of Gongado Lopez being carried on a stretcher; a picture of Jenna, Frank, and me leaning over Jeb Green on the half-pipe; and another one of that paramedic, Carter Bean, giving a thumbs-up through the rear window of the ambulance.

"Dude! We made the front page!" I said.

"Come on," said Frank, pushing me along. "We can read it back at the hotel."

A few minutes later we were crossing the lobby

of the Four Seasons Hotel, weaving our way through the swarming crowd of skateboarders and bikers and other athletes. We walked up to the bald-headed receptionist and asked him if we'd gotten any messages.

He sighed and turned around to check. If possible, he looked even more tired than he had yesterday. "Yes, indeed you do," he said, handing Frank a small pile of envelopes.

Frank thanked the man but didn't examine the envelopes until we were alone in the elevator. "Let's see. What do we have here? Ah. The first one's for you. Very pretty."

He handed me an envelope. My name was handwritten in large swirling letters in hot-pink ink. I opened it and read it out loud.

"Hey, Joe. Thanks for visiting Jeb in the hospital and giving him the flowers. He really appreciated it. He left me a message saying he really liked you guys and was sending you something you might want to see. I don't know what. Anyway, I have an athletes' dinner to go to tonight. Then I plan to crash early. Tomorrow's the big day! See you at the games. Jenna."

"What?" said Frank. "She signed it just 'Jenna'? Not 'Love, Jenna' or 'Yours forever, Jenna'?"

"None of your business," I said, smiling to myself.

We got out of the elevator, went to our hotel room, and flopped ourselves down on one of the beds. I started to read the Mr. X article while Frank opened the second envelope.

"Check this out," said Frank, holding up two plastic-coated badges. "The ATAC team sent us press passes to the games. According to our ID badges, we work for a teen magazine called *Shredder*."

"Cool."

Frank opened the third envelope. It was bigger than the others and stuffed with newspaper clippings.

"What are those?" I asked.

"I'm not sure. Oh wait, here's a note. It's from Jeb." He read it out loud. "'Hi, Frank. Yo, Joe. Thanks for the visit. My mom dropped by right after you left. Get this: She brought all my old scrapbooks for me to look through while I'm getting better. As a kid, I started saving any article I could find about skateboarding. So here I am, flipping through the scrapbooks, and I stumble on some articles about—guess who? Our friend Ollie Peterson. I figured you might want to check them out, so I'm having Mom drop this off at your hotel. Hope you find what you're looking for, dudes. Peace. Jeb.'"

Frank pulled out some of the news clippings and spread them across the bed.

"It was really cool of Jeb to send these," I said. "Too bad we don't need them anymore."

"You never know," said Frank, sifting through the pile. "There might be a valuable clue buried in here."

"He's dead, Frank. You can scratch him off the suspect list."

"Well, Dad once told me that the best way to catch a killer is to investigate the victim. There's usually some sort of link between the two. Murder is hardly ever random."

"Okay, then. Keep looking," I said, turning back to my paper. "And I'll keep reading about Mr. X."

Frank looked up. "See anything interesting?"

I shrugged. "Nothing we didn't already know," I said. "But the photo captions are pretty funny. Listen to this one. Under the picture of us leaning over Jeb, it says, 'Xtreme shock: Freaked-out teens comfort skateboard star and pellet victim Jebediah Green.'"

"'Freaked-out teens'?"

"Yeah. And listen to this. Under that thumbs-up picture of the ambulance guy, it says, 'The Real Hero of the Games: EMT paramedic Carter Bean saves lives and wins hearts of today's troubled youth.'"

"'Troubled youth'? Give me a break," said Frank.

"Maybe you're right about that reporter. He *is* a nut case."

I started to read some more but suddenly remembered something. "Didn't we get a fourth envelope?"

"Oh, yeah," said Frank. "Where did it go?" He looked underneath the news clippings about Ollie. "Here it is. Nice stationery."

He opened it up and read it.

"What is it?"

Frank didn't say anything. He just stared at the note with a stunned look on his face.

"Frank?"

I reached out and took the paper from him. Then I read it.

The message was three simple lines, neatly typed in capital letters.

**STOP ASKING QUESTIONS**

**AND STAY AWAY FROM THE GAMES**

**IF YOU WANT TO LIVE.**

Pretty uncreative for a threatening note. But effective.

# 10.

## Let the Games Begin

As soon as I woke up the next morning, I started getting nervous.

The Big Air Games were about to begin. A crazed killer was on the loose—assaulting, shooting, and poisoning people in the extreme sports world. And we'd received a threat. The mission known as "Extreme Danger" had turned out to be just that.

"Joe! Wake up!" I said, shaking my brother in his bed. "We have a criminal to catch. Come on!"

Joe and I were running out of time—and out of suspects. The newspapers were asking, "Who is Mr. X?" And we didn't have a clue.

"I'm up, I'm up," said Joe, still half asleep. "Where's the bad guy? Let me at him."

"I'm guessing he'll be at the Big Air Games," I said. "And so will we. Get moving."

We showered, dressed, and headed down to the lobby. The hotel had arranged a big continental breakfast for the Big Air guests. All the athletes and fans were there, reading the morning paper and talking about Mr. X.

I glanced down at a copy of the *Freedom Press* on one of the tables. The headline read, MR. X STRIKES AGAIN: EX-SKATEBOARD STAR POISONED!

There were old pictures of Ollie in the prime of his youth—and a new photo of his dead body covered in a sheet right outside his shop.

Joe went to grab us some bagels and juice. I sat down and started to read. A public statement from the police confirmed the presence of poison in the victim's coffee. But Max Monroe's article didn't say anything about Ollie trying to contact the newspaper before he was killed.

"More bad news, huh?" Jenna Cho stood by the table, holding a large glass of juice and a fresh fruit plate. "Mind if I join you?" she asked.

"Have a seat," I said. "Joe is getting us bagels. So I guess you heard about Ollie."

Jenna nodded grimly. "It's so twisted. I mean, the guy was totally obnoxious, but he didn't deserve to be killed."

Joe returned with a big tray in his hands—and a big smile on his face. "Jenna! What's up? Ready for the games?"

"You kidding? I'm ready to win," said Jenna. "The women's freestyle event is this afternoon."

Joe sat down and looked her in the eye. "You know, there's some serious stuff happening right now. I'm a little worried about you."

"Well, I can't quit now," she said. "I've trained too long and too hard. And besides, I like taking risks. The day before yesterday I gave my room number to some strange boy in the lobby."

Joe looked shocked. "What strange boy? Who is he?"

"She's talking about *you*, Einstein," I said without looking up from my newspaper.

We finished our breakfasts and wished Jenna luck before she rushed off to join the other athletes in the shuttle van. Joe and I headed down to the parking garage to get our motorcycles. The Big Air Games were being held in one of the four stadiums in South Philadelphia. The traffic got worse the closer we got, but we made it. We even arrived ahead of schedule.

The stadium complex was a total zoo.

A giant banner greeted us at the entrance: THE CITY OF PHILADELPHIA IS PROUD TO WELCOME THE

BIG AIR GAMES. Hundreds of extreme sports fans were lined up at the gates. Parents with binoculars and kids with skateboards wandered through an obstacle course of food stands and souvenir tables. Some of the sports gear companies were even giving away free hats and T-shirts.

"Outrageous," Joe muttered. "Totally."

I slapped his shoulder and pointed toward a couple of TV news vans. Some men were unloading equipment in front of a large tent. A sign said: PRESS REGISTRATION.

"Come on," I said. "We can use our press passes and skip all these lines."

We steered our motorcycles toward the press tent and parked them next to one of the vans.

"Okay, we're reporters for *Shredder* magazine," I whispered to Joe before we entered the tent.

"Frank! Joe! What are you doing here?"

We should have known Maxwell Monroe would be here too. He waved us over toward the registration desk. We held up our badges to a tall woman who wrote down our ID numbers and said hello to Max.

"You're reporters, too?" he said. "I should have known. You ask too many questions." He chuckled. "So are you ready for big trouble at the Big Air Games?" Max paused for a second. "Hey! I should use that for my next headline! If we're lucky, Mr. X will make a special guest appearance today. Right, boys?"

*Jerk.*

"Let's go, Joe," I said, grabbing my brother by the arm. "Let's try to get some pregame interviews."

"Catch you later!" Max yelled after us.

The opening ceremonies were about to start. Joe and I quickly found a place near the locker rooms that had a clear view of the field.

A heavyset sportscaster from Channel 7 walked onto the center stage and made some opening remarks. His voice echoed through the loudspeakers. "And without further ado," he said, winding up, "I am honored to introduce you to . . . the extreme sports athletes of the Big Air Games!"

The fans went crazy.

The field exploded with activity. A heavy-metal rock band erupted with sound. Fireworks burst from a cannon. And hundreds of athletes swarmed across the field.

It was hard to know where to look. Inline skaters circled the track. Skateboarders zoomed up and down the long rows of half-pipes. Bungee jumpers were hoisted into the air by gigantic cranes. Then a small army of motocross bikers hurled full-speed into the killer curve of the Monster Loop—up, around, and down—in rapid-fire succession.

"Man! That's insane!" I gasped.

"Look! There's Jenna!" Joe said, pointing toward the half-pipes. She was easy to spot because of her hot-pink skateboard.

"And there's Eddie Mundy," I said. "In the red bandanna."

Joe looked over at the skateboarder. "We should keep an eye on him."

Suddenly all the activity in the field screeched to a halt. The athletes lined up, standing straight and tall, as the band launched into an electric-guitar version of the national anthem.

"Let the games begin!" a voice announced at the end of the song. Some of the athletes started to leave the field.

"Come on, Joe," I said. "Now's our chance. We can talk to the players in the dugouts."

We hurried down the stairs and got as close as we could. A security guard stopped us. "Athletes only beyond this point," he grunted at us. We showed him our press passes. "Maybe they'll let you in the locker rooms."

We walked around to the locker room entrance. Another guard let us through when we flashed our passes.

The men's locker room wasn't very crowded. A few guys were doing stretches. Others were fussing with their gear. One boy with a Mohawk sneered at us. "What are you preppies doing in here?"

"We're reporters," I told him. "Do you mind answering a few questions?"

"Get lost! Go back to your fancy prep school!"

"Yeah!" someone else yelled. "Get in the game or get out!"

Frank tugged my shirtsleeve. "Let's go, Frank," he said. "I have an idea."

When we got outside, Joe hustled me past the guard, then showed me something tucked in his pocket: a pair of official Big Air athletes' passes.

"Where did you get those?"

Joe smiled. "I spotted them under a bench in the locker room. So I snatched them while you were talking to those guys."

I was skeptical. "The security guards saw us, Joe. They think we're reporters, not athletes."

A big smile crept over my brother's face.

"How do you feel about getting an extreme makeover, Frank?"

Before I knew it, we were riding our motorcycles up and down the streets of South Philadelphia, looking for a clothing store. But we weren't having much luck.

Finally Joe pulled over. "Look," he said, pointing across the street. "I bet we can find something in there."

I turned and looked. "You got to be kidding, Joe."

The place was called HOLLYWEIRD.

It looked like a vintage clothing store. There were two mannequins in the window—one in a wedding dress with a hunting vest, the other in a skin-diving suit and a purple wig.

"Come on," Joe said. He wouldn't take no for an answer. We circled around and parked in front of the store.

A little bell tinkled when we walked through the door. Two girls looked up and stared at us. They were sitting in old beauty parlor chairs, reading magazines—and they looked as bizarre as the mannequins in the window.

"Can I help you guys?" asked the tall one. Her hair was bright blue and spiky, and her jeans were held together with safety pins. "I'm Holly."

"And I'm Weird," said the other one. Her face was powdered white, but everything else—hair, lips, clothes—was completely black.

Joe did the talking. "We need to change our look. It could be biker, skateboarder, punk, whatever—as long as it's wild. We want to look . . . you know . . . *extreme*. Can you help us?"

The two girls looked at each other—and grinned from ear to ear.

Grabbing Joe by the shoulders, Holly pushed him toward the changing room and started pulling clothes from a rack. "Here, try these on," she said, handing him a big pile of pants, shirts, and accessories.

The girl named Weird looked at me and motioned with her finger. "Your turn," she said.

"I don't know if I . . ."

It was useless to resist. The girls were thrilled to make us over. We were like a pair of life-sized dolls for them to play with. They made us try on nylon tracksuits, snakeskin pants, flowered surfer shorts— you name it.

Finally, Joe ended up in a black punk-rock concert shirt, oversized army shorts, and a cool racing jacket.

And me? They dressed me in blue camouflage pants, black boots, a tie-dyed tank top, and a leather jacket.

"We approve," said Holly, standing back to admire her work. "You guys look fierce."

I stood next to Joe and looked in the mirror.

Pretty cool, I had to admit.

"You know what would really top it all off?" said Weird, holding up an electric hair trimmer. "Mohawks!"

"Oh, yeah! Totally!" Holly agreed.

I laughed and shook my head. "There's no way I'm going to get a Mohawk."

"I'll do it," said Joe.

I turned to argue, but my brother had already hopped into one of the beauty parlor chairs. Weird spun him around, wrapped a towel around his neck, and plugged in the clippers.

"You, too. Grab a seat," said Holly, pushing me into the other chair.

"Wait! No!" I protested. "I don't want a haircut!"

"Then I'll just spray in some blue dye," she said, picking up an aerosol can. "It washes out . . . and it'll match your pants."

"Go on, Frank," said my brother. "Just do it."

I closed my eyes. "Okay," I said. "Do it."

Holly started spraying—and Weird started shaving.

*Bzzzzzzzzzz.*

# 11.
## Crash and Burn!

*Man! The wind feels cool against my scalp!*

I roared along on my motorcycle, right behind Frank, through the streets of Philadelphia. We had gotten a little lost on our trip to Hollyweird, so Frank was using his bike's navigational system to find our way back to the stadium. I followed.

I had to laugh a little at the sight of Frank with blue hair.

Then I reminded myself that I had a Mohawk.

Aunt Trudy and Mom would have my head on a platter.

Well, it was too late to worry about it now. My head was shaved and smooth and shiny, with a spiky stripe of hair down the middle.

Besides, I looked *crazy* cool. And I have to confess: Even *Frank* looked cool.

Finally we spotted the banner for the Big Air Games. Riding past the press tent, Frank and I circled the stadium until we found the athletes' entrance. A security guard held up his arm to stop us. We flashed our passes—the ones I'd swiped from the locker room—and the guard waved us through.

We rode our motorcycles up a large cement ramp and down a long hall. It led us right through the stadium and out onto the south side of the field.

Frank and I must have been quite a sight, because the audience cheered when they saw us.

"Maybe we should pop a few wheelies or something," I said to Frank.

I waved to the crowd. They cheered again.

"Man, I could learn to like this."

"Knock it off, Joe," said Frank, getting off his bike. "Let's go talk to some of the athletes."

"But what about my fans? They want me! Frank! Wait!"

I hopped off my bike and ran after my brother. We walked past a group of inline skaters—and almost collided with Maxwell Monroe.

"Sorry, excuse me," said the reporter. He did a double take. "Hey, wait! It's you guys! Let me check you out! Wow. Great disguises. Now that's one way to infiltrate the inner circle of the extreme sports world. Very clever. I'd try it myself, but I'm too old to pull off a Mohawk or blue hair."

"Lower your volume, Max," I whispered. "You're going to blow our cover."

Max smiled. "Sure, kid. I understand," he said. "We're all journalists here. But let me give you boys a little advice."

*Again?* He leaned toward us and spoke in a hushed voice. "When Mr. X makes his move today—*and he will*—you don't want to be standing in the line of fire. I'd be careful about getting too close to the athletes if I were you."

Then he said something that sounded strangely familiar.

"And stay off the field . . . if you want to be safe."

I glanced at Frank. He didn't react to Max's words.

"Well, I hope to see you later, boys," the reporter said. "I'm going to the press box. They have sand-wiches up there."

We said good-bye and watched Max disappear into the crowd.

"Did you hear that?" I asked Frank. "He used almost the same words as that warning we got: '*And stay away from the games if you want to live.*'"

Frank ran a hand through his blue hair. "Maybe it's just a coincidence," he said.

"Or not," I added. "He seems so sure that Mr. X is going to attack today."

"He's a reporter. Joe. He's *hoping* Mr. X attacks."

We walked around the perimeter of the field as we talked. Soon we came upon the skateboard dugout. I spotted Jenna, so I waved.

She looked at me like I was a total stranger.

*Oh, yeah. The Mohawk,* I reminded myself.

"Jenna! It's me, Joe!"

She squinted, then smiled and came running out of the dugout. "Look at you guys!" she said. "Extreme Hardys! I like it!" She ran her fingers through my Mohawk.

"Where's your skateboard?" I asked her.

"Over there in the dugout."

"Look," I said. "Keep your skateboard with you at all times. And check the wheels, the axle, everything. Make sure nobody's tampered with the board. And tell the others to do the same. Promise?"

"Promise," she said. Then she told us that her

event would start in about an hour in the stadium next door.

"I'll be there," I told her.

Frank and I said good-bye and started to walk toward the north end of the field. We still hadn't talked to any of the motocross bikers.

Suddenly my brother stopped. "You know what, Joe? What you told Jenna was really smart. No one should leave their equipment unattended."

"Thanks, man," I said. "You never tell me I'm smart. What's the catch?"

"The catch is, we shouldn't leave our motorcycles back there. They could be sabotaged."

"Oh, yeah," I said. "I guess I'm not *that* smart."

Frank laughed. "Come on. Let's get our bikes and ride them up the field."

We turned around and started walking the other way.

"Well, well, well. Check out the posers."

It was Eddie Mundy.

The cocky skateboarder walked right toward us with a big sneer on his face.

Did he ever wash that thing?

Eddie stepped in front of us, blocking our path and giving us the once-over.

"I'm diggin' the new duds. But you still look like

**113**

a pair of preppy boys," he teased. "Give it up, dudes. The blue hair and Mohawk aren't fooling anyone."

"Ignore him," Frank whispered. "Just keep moving."

But Eddie wouldn't let it drop.

When we tried to walk around him, he threw his arms over our shoulders and walked along with us.

"Look, guys," he said, lowering his voice. "I know who you are. Really."

I shrugged his hand off. "What are you talking about?" I said. "What did you hear?"

"There you go with the questions again," Eddie said, sighing. "Those questions are getting you both in a lot of trouble. I think you know what I mean."

Frank stopped and stared at him. "What are you saying?" he asked.

Eddie grabbed us both by the arms and squeezed. "I'm saying drop it. Leave. Now."

Then he let go and walked away.

Frank and I didn't say a word for a moment or two. I guess we were a little stunned. Finally I turned to Frank and looked him in the eye.

"Okay," I said. "Things are getting freaky around here. What do you think is going on?"

"I don't know," said Frank. "But I intend to find out."

Clenching his jaw, he stalked off toward our motorcycles at the end of the field. I just stood there and watched him go.

*Easy, Frank.*

But hey, I wasn't about to let my brother take on Mr. X all by himself. We were a team.

"Frank, wait!" I yelled, running after him.

After stopping to watch one of the bungee jumps, Frank and I reached the south end of the field without incident.

I mean, nobody threatened to kill us if we didn't leave.

Our motorcycles appeared to be okay. But Frank insisted that we inspect them carefully before starting the engines.

"Someone could have cut the brake lines or punctured the gas tanks," he said. "Or a dozen other things."

"Everything checks out," I reported after a quick inspection.

"Check again."

"Frank."

"Check again," he repeated. "This is serious, Joe. People know we've been asking questions. Both

Max and Eddie warned us to back off. Maybe they're concerned. Maybe they're killers. Who knows? We can't take any chances."

Once Frank was satisfied with the inspections, we jumped on our cycles and revved them up. Then we took off, riding slowly along the perimeter of the stadium.

We had to warn the motocross bikers: Don't leave your bikes unattended, not even for a minute.

As we approached the motocross zone, I couldn't stop staring at the huge Monster Loop rising up in the distance.

The thing was humongous!

The highest point of the curve must have been fifty feet high. But as I got closer on my cycle, I swear it seemed more like a hundred. How could anyone get up enough momentum to ride the entire loop without falling?

I was about to find out.

There were six motocross bikers lining up, getting ready to tackle the Monster Loop.

Frank and I pulled up on the sidelines and parked our motorcycles. We jumped off and ran toward the motocross bikers.

"Wait!" Frank yelled. "We need to talk to you!"

We were stopped in our tracks by one of the event directors.

"Hold it right there, boys," he said. "Everyone has to stay back here until the stunts are completed."

Frank tried to explain. He told the event director about the possibility of sabotage and asked if the bikers kept a close watch on their bikes.

"Don't worry, we're taking care of everything," the man assured him. "With Mr. X on the loose, everybody is taking extra precautions. We've got more security, more safety inspectors, more emergency medical teams . . . you name it."

I looked around and saw all the security guards walking along the sidelines—and an ambulance waiting near the Monster Loop. It didn't make me feel any better.

I had seen more than enough medical emergencies in the past two days.

Frank finally gave up trying to get past the event director. He came over and stood next to me, gazing up at the Monster Loop and shaking his head. "That thing is scary."

"Totally."

The motocross bikers were all revved up and ready to roll. Then a man waved a flag and they were off.

The bikers tore up the dirt as they headed for the first series of ramps. Up and over, up and over, the roaring machines sailed through air, then plunged back to earth, wheels spinning faster with every jump.

"Dude!" I shouted out.

The six bikers skidded and swerved past us. Hurtling toward an even bigger ramp, they picked up speed, hit the curve, and shot into the air again, even higher than before.

"All right!" Frank cheered.

Finally the bikers were making their final round—their last chance to build up momentum for the big finish. . . .

*The Monster Loop.*

Faster and faster, they flew around the track with their engines roaring.

And that's when I noticed something.

One of the bikers' wheels was wobbling.

"Frank!" I yelled. "Look at number four's front wheel!"

We watched helplessly as the biker headed straight for the Monster Loop.

"Stop! No!" my brother and I screamed.

One, two, three of the motocross bikers hit the loop, rising up—thirty, forty, fifty feet in the air— one after the other. Up, up, and over.

Biker number four was right on their heels. The guy must have noticed that his front wheel was wobbling, but it was too late to stop. He hit the curve and rose straight up, his whole bike shaking. Higher and higher he went, until he was nearly upside down at the top of the curve.

"He's not going to make it," Frank gasped. "He's going to fall!"

But no, he didn't fall. The bike completed the upper part of the arch, then plunged its way downward.

That's when the front wheel snapped off.

The front of the bike started grinding into the metal edge of the loop, sparks flying everywhere. The biker tried to lean back—but then the whole bike went tumbling forward, somersaulting down, falling and falling.

Finally biker number four slid to a stop at the bottom of the Monster Loop. The last two bikers managed to swerve out of his way.

But that wasn't the end of it.

Number four's bike burst into flames.

# 12.

## The Biker in Black

I couldn't believe my eyes.

*Mr. X had struck again.*

And we were too late to stop him.

As the motocross support crew rushed to the burning bike, dousing the flames with fire extinguishers, I lowered my head and replayed the tragedy in my mind.

*If only we'd gotten there sooner. We could have warned them. We could have told them to double-check their bikes for sabotage.*

I watched in stunned silence as the ambulance pulled up to the scene. Paramedic Carter Bean and his partner, Jack, jumped out and rushed to the biker's side. On the sidelines Monroe held up his camera and clicked away.

120

I felt like I was reliving the same nightmare, over and over.

Suddenly biker number four sat up, coughed, and threw his hands in the air.

"He's all right! Look!" Joe shouted.

The crowded whooped and cheered.

The biker tried to pick himself up, but Carter and Jack insisted on helping him onto a stretcher. I guess they wanted to make sure he didn't have any broken bones or other injuries. They loaded the guy into the ambulance and turned on the flashing light on the roof. Then they began to drive away.

But not before Maxwell Monroe could snap a few more pictures of Carter and his patient through the rear window.

Everybody—athletes and fans alike—broke into applause as the ambulance left the stadium. I stared down at the ground for a few moments, then looked up at Joe. I didn't know what to say.

"We tried, Frank," he said. "We did everything we could."

"Let's go talk to some of the other bikers," I told him. "Maybe they saw someone suspicious hanging around."

We walked over to a group of guys in motocross jackets standing with the crew. They were all talking about the "accident."

"Do you think it was Mr. X?" one of them said.

"It had to be," said another.

"I can't believe Mike's okay. Did you see how he fell? Head over heels, man!"

"Mike's lucky he's alive."

I interrupted the conversation and asked them if they'd seen anything strange before the race. "Did you notice anyone near the bikes?" I asked. "Someone you didn't know?"

A biker with long hair shook his head. "No, dude," he told us. "There're too many security guys around. Everyone's worried about Mr. X."

Another biker agreed. "The only people I saw had official clearance. You know . . . guards, crew, medics, safety inspectors."

I nodded. The guys went back to talking about Mike McIntyre—biker number four—and his amazing Monster Loop crash. Apparently Mike was not only a star athlete, but also a great guy. Everybody seemed to like him.

"Who's that over there?" I asked, pointing to the sidelines.

In the middle of the crowd was a motocross biker dressed head to toe in black. He sat on a black bike and wore a black helmet, too. The shield was lowered, so I couldn't see his face.

"Huh, I don't know," said the long-haired biker. "Never saw him before."

I turned to ask the other guys if they knew him. They all shook their heads. When I turned back for a second look, the mystery man was gone.

"Frank, we have to go," Joe said, looking at his watch. "It's almost time for Jenna's event."

I wanted to stick around and track down the biker in black—but my brother had promised Jenna we'd be there to cheer her on. Jumping on our motorcycles, we headed for the nearest exit.

We almost didn't make it in time. It took forever to weave our way through the outdoor food stands and vendors to get to the next stadium. But with our athletes' passes, we were able to zip right through and ride our cycles out to the field.

The women's skateboard competition was starting.

"Jenna! Hey!" Joe yelled, spotting her on a bench.

Jenna picked up her skateboard and ran over to meet us. "Hey, guys! You made it!"

"Just barely," I said.

"Man! I am so pumped!" she said with a huge smile. "I'm ready to go for the gold, baby. Look out!" Then her expression changed. "So what's up with you guys? Any sign of Mr. X yet?"

I glanced at Joe.

He shot me a quick look, then smiled at Jenna. "No. Everything's cool," he said. "Go out there and show the world what you can do."

Jenna gave us both a big hug, then dashed back to the bench.

I looked at Joe and raised an eyebrow.

"What?" he said. "I didn't want to give her bad news right now. It could break her concentration."

I smiled. "Joe and Jenna, sittin' in a tree . . ."

"Whatever, Frank."

We watched the first skateboarder, a young girl from Florida. She was incredible, riding the half-pipe like a pro. Then it was Jenna's turn.

I could tell Joe was nervous by the way he clenched and unclenched his hands.

*Please, no more accidents,* I thought to myself.

Jenna took her place on the edge of the half-pipe. Taking a deep breath, she hopped on her board and went hurtling down the hard concrete curve. She swiveled and swerved, then rode the arch upward, leaping and spinning in the air like a ballerina, smooth and graceful. I'd never seen anyone do skateboard stunts like this before.

"Go, Jenna, go!" Joe shouted beside me.

She ended her routine with a wild 540-degree spin—and the crowd went crazy.

"That's my girl!" Joe hooted.

I turned to tease my brother about his choice of words when I noticed someone on the side-lines.

It was the biker in black.

He sat there on his motocross bike with his arms folded across his chest. He was still wearing his helmet—and shielding his identity. I don't know what it was about him, but he made me itch.

"Joe, look," I said, pointing to the man in black.

Joe spun around.

The mystery man spotted us.

Then he jumped up, kick-started his motocross bike, and took off across the field.

"Come on!" I yelled to Joe. "After him!"

We ran and leaped onto our motorcycles, revving them up as fast as we could. A second later we were racing across the stadium in hot pursuit of the mysterious motocross biker.

The audience cheered and clapped wildly. They must have thought we were part of the games.

But this was no game.

The faster Joe and I went after the guy, the more recklessly he rode—zooming to the left, skidding to the right, then heading straight for the concrete half-pipes.

My brother and I nearly flew off our cycles when we hit the concrete, swerving back and forth between the arching curves like a swinging pair of pendulums.

Finally the biker in black jumped off the final ramp and hit the ground hard, wheels spinning in the turf. Joe and I were right behind him—and he knew it. So he headed for the inline skating track.

My brother and I soared off the last ramp. We both landed hard but managed to steady our bikes and take off after him.

Once we hit the track, the mystery rider didn't stand a chance. His motocross bike didn't have the power or the speed that our motorcycles had.

But he was one step ahead of us. Rounding the bend, he slammed on his brakes and made a hard turn off the track.

Joe and I zoomed right past him—and plunged straight into an inline skating race!

Oops.

Lucky for us, the skaters saw us coming. They veered out of our way, skating to one side or the other so fast that they looked like blurs. Finally we were in the clear.

But where did he go?

Joe and I screeched to a halt and looked around the stadium.

"There he is!" Joe shouted out, pointing across the field.

The biker in black shot out from behind a half-pipe. He headed right for the south exit—and disappeared.

I wasn't about to give up. I nodded at Joe, and we raced to the exit. Rocketing up the ramp, we hurtled headlong into a dark hallway. People screamed and jumped out of our way. Seconds later we were out of the stadium—and lost in a maze of food stands and vendors.

Where was he?

I skidded to a stop, my rear wheel swerving beneath me and bashing into a ring toss booth. Dozens of stuffed animals showered down on me.

"Sorry, ma'am," I said to the startled booth lady. "I'll pay for this. I promise."

I hopped back on my bike and rode slowly through the crowd until I found my brother.

Eating a hot dog.

"Joe!"

"Hey, I was hungry!" he said, taking a bite.

I was about to respond when I spotted the biker in black. "There he is! He's going into the main stadium!"

127

Joe shoved the rest of the hot dog into his saddlebag. "For later," he explained.

We revved up again and headed for the athletes' entrance. Minutes later we were inside the stadium, searching for the mystery rider.

"Frank! I see him!"

My brother pointed me toward the motocross track. Our mystery man was trying to blend in with the other bikers. But since he was the only guy wearing all black, his plan didn't work.

Joe and I raced up the field after him. As soon as he saw us coming, he revved up his engine and hit the racetrack at full speed.

We kicked into high gear and followed him. In seconds we were gaining on him—until we hit the first series of ramps. The speed of our motorcycles sent us flying too high and too far into the air. We landed with a bone-crunching thud on the top of each ramp, our bikes bucking with each jolt.

*Ow.*

Back on level ground, we were able to pick up speed again, closing in fast on our target. But the mystery rider was going straight for the last and largest ramp—and he was totally gunning it.

Up, up, and into the air he soared, with Joe and me right behind him.

*Whoa! Watch out!*

For a second I thought we were going to land right on top of him. Flying and falling, I looked below me. The biker bounced out of the way in the nick of time—and kept right on going. But Joe and I were hot on his heels.

From this point on, it was full speed ahead.

Straight into the Monster Loop.

*No,* I thought. *Not that.*

There was no turning back. We were just too close—and going too fast.

The three of us hurtled into the giant upward curve of the Monster Loop—the biker first, then Joe, then me. The roar of our engines echoed inside the loop. I watched Joe and the biker go up, up, up, higher and higher, until they were no longer in front of me—they were *above* me.

My stomach turned.

And so did we.

The whole world, it seemed, was rolling beneath my wheels. I glanced down and saw nothing but blue sky below me. At first I didn't understand. Then it hit me.

I was upside down!

But not for long. Soon we were plunging downward on the other side of the loop. Joe and the motocross biker were right below me.

We were coming down to earth now—and *fast*.

The mystery rider plunged downward and outward. Swerving and wobbling, he hit the level ground, rode straight out of the loop—and totally wiped out.

Joe and I had to hit our brakes as hard as we could to avoid hitting the guy.

Finally we came to a stop. Jumping off our cycles, we dashed over to the fallen biker in black.

He lay on the ground next to his bike and moaned. But he didn't seem to be injured, because when he saw us, he jumped to his feet and tried to run away.

Joe and I grabbed him and held on tight.

"Okay, mystery rider," I said. "Let's see who you are."

Joe reached up and pulled off the biker's helmet.

I couldn't believe it.

# 13.
## "Meet Me at Midnight"

Frank and I had risked our lives, raced with death—*even rode the Monster Loop*—and for what?

To unmask a mystery man who turned out to be . . .

*Chet Morton?*

Chet was one of our best friends from home and, until now, we'd never seen any hint of his wild side. He was definitely the last person I expected to see underneath that black helmet.

"You're not Mr. X," said Frank.

"More like Mr. Y," I said. "As in *W-H-Y* are you here, Chet?"

Chet looked embarrassed. "I dropped by your house yesterday, and your mom said you were at the Big Air Games. At first I was a little insulted.

Why didn't you ask me to come along? Then I figured you must be working on a case. So I decided to help you out and go undercover. Just like you."

He pointed at my Mohawk and Frank's blue hair.

"When you spotted me, I guess I freaked out," he went on. "I was afraid you'd think I was a suspect."

"Well, yeah," I said. "We did."

Just then the biker crew and medical team swarmed around Chet to see if he was okay. Joe and I backed away from the crowd.

"What are we going to do with him?" I asked Frank. "Chet could ruin the whole mission."

Frank shrugged. "Maybe he could help us out," he said. "It wouldn't be the first time."

"Yeah, but he helped us out when we were amateur detectives. We're on the ATAC team now, Frank. These are serious missions . . . with major risks involved."

Frank looked at me. "Did you see how he jumped those giant ramps and tore into that Monster Loop? You have to admit, Joe. The guy is fearless."

Maybe Frank had a point.

A few minutes later—after Chet convinced the paramedics that he didn't need to go to the emergency room—we invited our friend to stay with us in our hotel room, if he needed a place to crash.

"Can I? Cool!" he answered.

We decided to hang out for a while and watch a few more events—but then I remembered something.

*Jenna.*

I told Frank and Chet that I wanted to go back to the other stadium. They weren't thrilled about riding through that maze of food stands and vendors again, but once I told them why I wanted to go, they agreed. Believe it or not, Chet's bike was still in working order.

As we slowly rode our way out of the stadium, Maxwell Monroe started shouting to us from the press box.

"Joe! Frank! I want to talk to you guys!" he yelled at the top of his lungs.

Frank rolled his eyes. "He probably wants to interview us about our little bike chase," he said.

Neither of us was in the mood to answer the reporter's questions. So I waved back at Max, pointed to my watch, and shook my head. Then we rode our bikes through the exit and headed for the other stadium.

Jenna was thrilled to see us.

"I was so worried about you guys," she said. "What was up with that crazy bike chase? Who were you chasing?"

We introduced her to Chet.

"So? Did you win?" I asked her.

Jenna held up a medal. "Second place!"

I gave her a big hug. "Congratulations," I said. "Second place, huh? That's great."

"Yeah. But it's not first place."

"Hey, there's always next year."

"Will you come to watch me?" she asked.

"Of course," I replied.

"Promise?"

"Promise."

I also promised to join Jenna and some of her skateboard buddies later that night to celebrate her victory. Frank and Chet were invited too, of course.

The four of us found some seats and watched a few more events. My favorite was the skysurfing contest. The competitors were actually dropped from planes overhead. These dudes "surfed" through the air, doing all kinds of crazy spins and twirls, before landing with their parachutes right in the middle of the stadium. It was totally awesome.

I would have enjoyed it even more if my own parachute cord hadn't been cut the other day.

The rest of the games were pretty uneventful, which was cool with me. By the time we got back to the hotel, Frank, Chet, and I were pretty hungry and tired. We flopped down on the beds and considered ordering in some food.

That's when Frank noticed the blinking light on the hotel phone.

"We got a message," he said, picking it up and pushing a few keys on the touchtone pad.

Frank listened for a minute. Then his face turned white.

"Frank? What is it?" I asked.

Slowly he handed me the receiver and pushed a couple of keys to replay the message. I put the phone to my ear and listened.

"Hello, Frank, Joe."

The voice was scratchy and muffled. It creeped me out.

"I know the identity of Mr. X."

I sucked in my breath and waited to hear more.

"Mr. X, you see, is misunderstood. You should be thanking him, really. Would you like to know more about him?"

There was a long pause. The voice got deeper.

"Meet me at midnight. Tonight. In Love Park. And don't call the police. This will be our little secret."

*Click.*

That was it. End of message.

I handed the phone back to Frank.

"Who was that?" asked Chet.

"Nobody," I told him.

"Well," said Chet, "it seems like *nobody* just scared the living daylights out of you two. What's up?"

"Should I tell him, Frank?" I asked my brother.

Frank sat down on his bed, staring at the scattered press clippings about Ollie's tragic career. He seemed to be lost in thought. "Okay," he finally said. "Let's tell him."

We ordered up three Philly cheese steaks from the hotel's room service and spent the next hour filling Chet in on all the details of the Mr. X case. Of course, we didn't tell him we were on an undercover mission for American Teens Against Crime. ATAC was a top-secret organization, and he wouldn't have heard about it, anyway.

"Let me get this straight," said Chet. "Mr. X has attacked four people, one of whom is dead. He sent you a warning to stop asking questions if you want to stay alive. And now you plan on meeting this wacko in a park tonight at midnight?"

Frank sighed and nodded. "Yup. That pretty much sums it up."

"Cool," said Chet. "Can I come with you?"

"No," I said. "It's too risky."

Frank looked at me. "We *could* use a lookout, Joe," he said. "He could stand back and watch from a distance. That way, if there's any trouble . . ."

"I jump in and start kicking butt!" said Chet, striking his goofiest kung fu pose.

"No, you call the police," said Frank. "Deal?"

"Deal."

"Okay. Everybody synchronize your watches."

Exactly four hours and thirty-seven minutes later, we were standing in a dance club near John F. Kennedy Plaza and celebrating Jenna's second-place victory. Her skateboard friends were really cool and lots of fun. They loved going wild on the dance floor. The music was kicking, the lights were flashing—and Chet, to everyone's surprise, turned out to be a moving, grooving, one-man dancing machine.

"Come on, Frank!" he shouted to my brother sitting near the bar. "Get up and boogie!"

I could tell Frank was nervous.

So was I. But I tried to hide it so I could show Jenna a good time.

"Jenna, do you know a place called Love Park?" I shouted over the music while we danced. "Is it close to JFK Plaza?"

137

"It *is* JFK Plaza," she answered. "Everyone calls it Love Park. The place is part of skateboard history, one of the coolest spots on the planet for doing street stunts. It's legendary. But nowadays the police arrest people for skateboarding there. Still, that doesn't stop some kids. They'll risk anything so they can tell everyone they skated at Love Park. It's like a badge of honor."

I narrowed my eyes. "Have *you* ever skated at Love Park?" I asked her.

Jenna smiled mysteriously. "A woman never reveals her deepest secrets," she said.

Frank came up behind me and tapped my shoulder. He pointed at his watch.

Almost time.

I told Jenna that we had to leave now. It was getting late.

"Don't go," she pleaded. "It's not even midnight yet."

I apologized and promised to talk to her tomorrow. Then Frank, Chet, and I headed out of the club and into the darkened streets of Philadelphia.

"I thought we should get there early to find a hiding place for Chet," Frank explained as we walked down the sidewalk toward the park.

It was a hot, muggy night. The air was damp, and the atmosphere was thick. Heavy gray storm clouds settled over the city, raising the temperature. Even the streetlamps, with their dull hazy glow, seemed to feel the heat.

"There it is, over there," said Frank. "Love Park."

I started to sweat. We were about to meet Mr. X—or at least someone who claimed to *know* Mr. X. I thought about that strange raspy voice on the phone message, and I shuddered.

We walked toward the huge round fountain in the center of the plaza. I watched a tall geyser of water shoot up into the air. Then I turned and scanned the rest of the park. It was easy to see why the place would be a skateboarder's dream. There were marble benches and steps and ledges everywhere—perfect for street skating.

Frank stopped in front of a tall modern sculpture. "I guess this is why it's called Love Park," he said.

I looked up at the cube-shaped structure. It was made of four giant letters cast in steel—a large L and a tilted O stacked on top of a V and an E. It looked like a design from the 1960s.

"Maybe you can hide right here, Chet, in the shadow of the sculpture," said Frank. "Joe and I will circle the fountain until Mr. X shows up."

Chet nodded and crouched down at the base.

"How's this?" he asked. "Can you see me?"

"Not if you stay in the shadows," Frank told him. "Just stay low and keep an eye out for us. Do you have your cell phone with you?"

"Cell phone. Check," said Chet.

"Okay. It's almost midnight. Let's go, Joe."

We headed quickly and quietly toward the fountain. The city lights bounced off the rippling water and cast tiny flickers of orange and blue across the park. We stopped at the low curving edge of the stone landmark.

I gazed across the street to see if there was anyone on the sidewalk.

*Where are you, Mr. X? We're ready for you. Come out and play.*

I couldn't see a soul. And I couldn't hear a thing either—just the gurgling jet sprays of the fountain.

"I don't like the looks of this," I whispered. "I think we're being set up."

"Just hang in there, Joe," said my brother. "It's almost midnight."

Slowly and steadily we circled the fountain until we reached the far side of the plaza. A low rumble of thunder rolled overhead.

Suddenly Frank stopped.

"Turn around," he said. "Let's go back."

"Why?" I asked.

"The fountain is blocking the view. Chet can't see us here."

We couldn't see Chet either.

But we could hear him.

"Frank! Joe!"

It sounded like he was struggling. A loud scream echoed across the plaza.

# 14.

## A Real Shocker

*It's Mr. X. He's here.*

Joe and I dashed to the other side of the fountain as fast as we could. A sudden flash of lightning lit up the park.

"Chet!" Joe shouted. "Hold on! We're coming!"

I heard footsteps running off as we circled the plaza and sprinted toward the Love statue.

*Where's Chet?*

I could only make out a dark shape lying in the shadows. A bolt of lightning flashed again—and revealed the still body of our friend underneath the sculpture.

"Chet!"

Joe reached him first. Dropping to his knees, he pressed his ear against Chet's chest. "He's still

142

alive," he shouted, his voice echoing through the park. "Call 911!"

I pulled out my cell phone. "Hello, we have an emergency here!" I barked. "A boy's been hurt in JFK Plaza! Under the Love statue! Send an ambulance!"

I crouched down next to Joe and leaned over to examine Chet. "I don't see any serious injuries," I said. "He's breathing okay."

Joe stood up and scanned the park. Another boom of thunder rumbled overhead, but louder than before.

"The storm's about to break," Joe said. "And Mr. X is still out there. He's probably watching us right now."

I felt a drop of rain on my hand.

A siren wailed in the distance. It sounded like it was only a block or two away—and getting closer. Thirty seconds later, I spotted the ambulance. It barreled down the street, lights flashing, and pulled up to the curb. The door flew open. Carter Bean hopped out from the driver's seat and raced toward us.

Chet let out a little groan. Slowly turning his head and blinking his eyes, he gazed up at Carter. His eyes widened.

I jumped up and stood in between Chet and the paramedic.

"Hello, Carter," I said. "Or should I call you Mr. X?"

Thunder and lightning filled the sky. The storm was ready to hit—and it was going to be a big one.

---

### SUSPECT PROFILE

_Name_: Carter Bean

_Hometown_: Philadelphia, PA.

_Physical description_: 35 years old, 6'3", 165 pounds, thin wiry build, short brown hair, hazel eyes

_Occupation_: EMT paramedic, Pennsylvania Hospital

_Background_: Grew up in poor neighborhood in Philadelphia, worked his way through medical school, became local hero for saving skateboard legend Ollie Peterson's leg after 1990 accident

_Suspicious behavior_: Treated every victim in the Big Air Games attacks (unlikely in a city this size)

_Suspected of_: Assault, battery, sabotage, and murder

_Possible motives_: To draw attention away from extreme sports heroes, relive past glory, gain fame and recognition for lifesaving work

---

The rain came down hard and heavy, but in spite of the sudden downpour, nobody moved.

Carter Bean glared at me, his eyes narrowing. "What are you talking about?" he said. "I'm here to help. You called 911, didn't you?"

I looked Carter straight in the eye. "No, I didn't," I said. "I just pretended to call. I knew you would show up anyway."

The paramedic smirked. "How did you know? What proof do you have?"

"I saw your picture in the old news clippings of Ollie's accident in 1990," I explained. "You got a lot of press coverage, didn't you? How did the newspaper put it? Oh, yeah. 'A Legend Falls. A Hero Is Born.'"

"So?" said Carter, blinking the rain out of his eyes. "Everyone in the medical profession is a hero. I was just getting the recognition I deserved."

"Maybe," I said. "But real heroes don't do it for the recognition. Real heroes do the right thing because it's the right thing to do. They don't plan 'accidents' . . . like you did at the Big Air Games."

"Like I said before. What proof do you have?"

"Oh, come on. Every time someone got hurt, you were right there, ready to jump out of your ambulance and save the day."

Carter scoffed and shoved his hands in his pockets. "That doesn't prove that I attacked anybody. It's just a coincidence."

I pointed to his medical ID badge. "Is that a coincidence, too? Your ID number is EMT7654. But backward, it's 4567TME. That's the name you used to post threats on the Internet."

Carter sneered. "You think you're pretty smart, don't you?" he said. "I must admit—I'm stunned by your cleverness. Absolutely stunned. And I think I should return the favor."

He pulled a small stun gun from his pocket and thrust it straight at my throat.

"Frank! Look out!" Joe yelled.

I ducked fast. The stun gun swooped over my head with an electric crackle and a little zap of light.

Carter cursed me and lunged again. I tried to sidestep his attack but my knee slammed against the base of the Love sculpture. The impact sent me spinning and stumbling to the ground.

Carter stood over me. "Be a good patient now and take your medicine," he said.

He lowered the stun gun to my shoulder.

Joe tackled him to the ground.

*Get him, Joe!*

The two of them hit the wet concrete and rolled

146

across a puddle. Carter held the stun gun between them, aiming it at Joe's face.

I crawled to my feet and limped toward them. My knee throbbed with pain.

The stun gun buzzed in Carter's hand, a tiny bolt of electricity sizzling at the tip. Joe gripped the guy's wrist, struggling to push it away.

"Don't be afraid, kid," Carter growled. "It's just a little electroshock therapy."

The stun gun moved closer to Joe's face.

I staggered forward—but I knew I wouldn't make it in time to save Joe.

"Hey, Carter! Think fast!" I yelled.

I threw my cell phone like a baseball. It hit the paramedic in the ear, knocking his head back.

*And he's out!*

But no, Carter Bean was still in the game. Even though he lost his grip on Joe, he held on tight to the stun gun. In seconds the paramedic was up on his feet and waving the defense weapon like a sword.

Joe jumped back with every swoop of Carter's arm. The rain pounded, even harder than before. My brother almost slipped and fell as Carter forced him backward toward the fountain.

"Careful, kid," he said. "Accidents happen every day."

I had to do something—and fast. My knee throbbed, but I had to help my brother.

The lightning illuminated the way as I staggered after them. "Carter! I called the cops! They're on the way!"

"Liar!" Carter shouted, taking another lunge at Joe. "You threw your phone at me! Remember?"

He zapped the stun gun near my brother's head, forcing Joe back to the edge of the fountain. I limped forward as fast as I could, until I was right behind them.

I threw my arm around Carter's neck.

He spun around and kicked me in the knee.

I went down.

But Joe managed to get away. Slipping to the side, he took a few steps back, then charged full-force at our opponent.

Carter was too fast for him. He swung his right hand—stun gun blazing—at my brother's neck. When Joe tried to block it, Carter brought up his left fist and punched my brother in the jaw.

Joe reeled back—and collapsed to the ground.

"Joe!" I shouted.

He didn't move. It looked like he was unconscious.

Carter turned to me and smiled. "Looks like this is it, Frank. If you think you can get away from me now, you're in for a real shocker." He came after me with the stun gun.

I didn't stand a chance. My knee was hurting even more now. When I tried to scramble away, Carter stepped down on my leg and pinned me to the ground.

I stared up helplessly, the rain stinging my eyes.

Carter pointed the stun gun at my head.

"It's a shame, really," he said. "No matter how hard a paramedic tries to save lives, some patients just don't pull through."

He brought the stun gun closer to my face. Blazing sparks of electricity danced on the tip. He aimed it at my neck and . . .

*Wham!*

Carter was knocked off his feet.

A bright streak of red zoomed past me. A set of wheels skidded on the wet concrete.

It was Eddie Mundy!

The skateboarder in the red bandanna had plowed right into the paramedic. Carter was flat on his back, groaning.

"Eddie? What are you doing here?" I asked.

"I'm not who you think I am," he said, skating around the fallen paramedic. As Eddie started to explain, I saw Carter's arm move.

He still had the stun gun!

"Eddie! Look out!" I shouted.

Carter jabbed the weapon at Eddie's leg. The skateboarder kicked down hard on the back of his board. The front end flew up, slamming into Carter's arm and knocking him down.

The stun gun went flying into the fountain.

"Nice job," I said.

Eddie helped me to my feet. I had to lean against him for support because of my knee—not to mention the fact that my clothes were totally drenched and felt like they weighed a ton. I looked over at my brother. Joe was sitting up in a puddle, rubbing his jaw and smiling.

"Did we get him?" he asked.

"Yeah," I said. "Eddie skated right over the guy like he was a half-pipe."

"Eddie?"

The skateboarder offered Joe a hand and helped him up. "Actually, I'm an ATAC agent, just like you guys," Eddie said.

"Dude!" Joe exclaimed. "We thought you were bad news, man. You threatened us at the games today."

"I was warning you," Eddie explained. "Back at ATAC headquarters, they were afraid you two were going to be Mr. X's next targets."

"Turns out they were right," said Joe. "Hey, where is that psycho nurse anyway?"

Eddie and I spun around.

Carter was gone.

"Later, boys!" a voice rung out from the other side of the fountain. "I have to go now. It's an emergency!"

Carter laughed as he dashed around the fountain, heading for his ambulance. Eddie started running after him, with Joe and me staggering behind.

*There's no way we can catch him.*

Then I heard something strange. The rumbling sound of wheels seemed to be circling the plaza. Suddenly, out of the darkness came a whole gang of skateboarders, bounding down steps, grinding across benches, and jumping off curbs. They headed straight for Carter Bean and surrounded him, a human fence of skateboarders, zooming so fast that their prisoner couldn't escape.

"Look! There's Jenna!" Joe pointed out. "And her friends! They must have followed us out of the club."

Just then a small brigade of police cars came speeding down the street. One of them blared its siren, and they all pulled up to the curb and stopped. There must have been a dozen officers. Most of them charged at the skateboarders, breaking up the circle and apprehending the suspect. Two of them ran to the Love statue to help Chet, and the others came over to Eddie, Joe, and me. "Are you boys all right?" a tall officer asked. "Sorry it took us so long to track down that missing ambulance."

"Missing ambulance?" I asked.

"We wanted to question Carter Bean," the officer explained. "When the hospital tried to find him, they discovered he was gone—and one of their ambulances was missing."

Chet came over to join us. He looked a little stunned—no pun intended. "How did the police get here so fast?" he asked.

"You didn't call them?" asked Joe.

"No, I never got the chance. I got jumped by some guy with a stun gun. He must have stolen my cell phone."

"So who called the police?" I asked.

"I did," said a voice behind us.

It was Maxwell Monroe.

The reporter strolled up and smiled. "I had reasons to suspect Bean," he told us. "After Ollie was killed, I dug up all the old articles about him in our records. Then I saw that Carter Bean was the ambulance hero who saved Ollie's leg, and I got suspicious. But I didn't have enough to go on for a cover story. So I told the cops they should question the guy. You can read all about it in tomorrow's paper."

My mind was reeling with questions. But I never had a chance to ask them. Carter Bean started yelling as two of the police officers tried to handcuff him.

"Careful! You're hurting me!" he cried. "You're hurting me!"

"Well, Carter," I said. "Maybe you should call 911."

# 15.
## Heroes

Okay. So we caught the bad guy. Mr. X was safely behind bars. The Big Air Games were a huge success. Our mission was accomplished.

Still, I was totally confused. Why was Ollie poisoned? Why didn't Carter save Ollie's life, like he did for the others?

"Maybe Eddie Mundy can tell us," Frank said.

We got up early the next morning and sneaked out of the hotel room while Chet was still sleeping. We had agreed to meet Eddie at an out-of-the-way diner to discuss the details of the case. He was already waiting for us when we arrived.

"Eddie! My man!" I said. "Looking good, dude."

Without the red bandanna, Eddie was like a

154

totally different person. His hair was neatly combed, and instead of skateboard gear, he wore a button-down shirt and khaki pants.

Frank and I, of course, still had the blue hair and the Mohawk.

"Hey, Frank, Joe," he said as we slid into the booth. "I think I owe you guys an apology. I thought you knew I was an ATAC agent after I dropped that hint."

"What hint?" I asked.

"In FDR Park, I said it was 'extremely dangerous' to ask questions," he explained. "From the looks on your faces, I thought you understood. I was referring to the name of our mission."

"Actually," I said, "that only made me suspicious. You?" I looked at Frank. "Definitely," he agreed. "But now I get it."

Then we asked Eddie about the murder of Ollie Peterson. We wondered why it seemed different from the other attacks. Why would Carter want Ollie dead?

"Here's our theory," Eddie began. "Ollie may have resented Carter for becoming a hero after the accident in 1990. Some of the papers barely mentioned Ollie's awards and reputation in the skateboarding community. They focused on this young resourceful paramedic, fresh out of school. He was a poor kid from Philly who worked a bunch of night jobs to pay for medical school . . . an everyday hero who saved a man's leg and looked good in photographs."

Frank and I nodded.

"Okay, so years later, Ollie has his own skateboard shop," Eddie continued. "He probably forgot all about the kid who got famous from his tragedy. Then one day Ollie buys the evening edition of the *Freedom Press,* and there's that same paramedic—and he's a big hero again. So what does Ollie do? Well, we traced his phone records and found out that he called information and got Carter's number. He called Carter and talked for two minutes, then dialed up the *Freedom Press.*"

"Maxwell Monroe told us that Ollie left a message at his office," said Frank. "He wanted to talk to the reporter about Mr. X."

"Ollie obviously suspected Carter Bean," said Eddie. "We believe that he called Carter on the phone to question him or accuse him—or maybe just harass him. Either way, Carter felt threatened. Ollie had to be silenced. So Carter stole some medication from the hospital and slipped a fatal dose into Ollie's coffee."

I let it all sink in. "Okay," I said. "That explains Ollie. How did you know we were meeting Mr. X at midnight in Love Park?"

"I was following you," Eddie answered. "I was even there in the dance club last night. Man, your friend Chet is one crazy dancer."

"He's also the mystery biker in black," I added.

"That was some mean riding," said Eddie, laughing. "I freaked when I saw you guys head for the Monster Loop."

"*You* freaked?" said Frank.

I asked Eddie another question. "What about Jenna and her friends? They all scattered when the cops showed up. But why were they there in the first place?"

Eddie gave me a sly smile. "You'll have to ask Jenna yourself."

"I plan to."

We talked a little more about ATAC and some of our missions. When it was finally time to go, Eddie reached under the table and pulled out a box.

"I have a little souvenir for you guys."

He slid it across the table. I laughed when I saw the wrapping paper. It was the front page of the *Philadelphia Freedom Press*. The headline read, MR. X

X-POSED! MANIAC MEDIC BUSTED BY DAREDEVIL DUO. There was a picture of Carter in handcuffs next to one of Frank and me chasing Chet through the Monster Loop.

"Open it," said Eddie.

We tore away the paper and laughed again. It was a first aid kit full of bandages.

"I found it on the curb last night next to Carter's ambulance," Eddie explained.

We thanked Eddie for the memento and rushed back to the hotel. Then we dashed up to our room to pack our stuff and check out.

We'd almost forgotten about Chet. He was still sleeping—and snoring and mumbling. I had to laugh. And I had to mess with him a little too. So I took a long gauze bandage from the first aid kit and tied a big bow in his hair.

"Shouldn't we wake him?" Frank asked. "We can't just leave him here like this."

"But he looks so peaceful," I said.

"And so pretty," Frank added.

We sneaked out of the room, trying not to laugh too hard. Then we headed to the elevator with our backpacks and helmets. Jenna had left a message that she'd meet us in the lobby at ten o'clock—and she had a surprise for us. When we got downstairs, we found her sitting on the steps with Jebediah Green.

"Jeb! Dude!" I said. "How are you feeling?"

"Not bad. Just a little sore," Jeb said with a smile. "How's the Daredevil Duo?"

Frank rubbed his knee and winced. "Just a little sore. Thanks for sending us those clippings, man. They helped us figure out who Mr. X was."

"Ah, yes. The Maniac Medic," said Jeb, holding up a copy of the *Freedom Press*. "That's one twisted dude."

While Frank and Jeb laughed over the headlines, I took Jenna aside to say good-bye. We swapped e-mail addresses and home phone numbers and agreed to stay in touch. I promised to visit her in Atlantic City before the end of the summer. Then Frank interrupted, saying we had to hit the road now.

I looked into Jenna's eyes, hating to say good-bye. "Tell me something," I said. "Why did you follow me to Love Park last night with your skateboard buddies?"

"Because I knew you were looking for trouble," she answered. "And because I wanted to help out. And because I care about you."

I smiled. "Good answer."

*She cares about me!*

Frank cleared his throat. "Time to go," he said.

Jenna kissed me on the cheek and gave Frank a hug. Then we waved good-bye to Jeb and headed down to the parking garage. On the way I noticed that Frank was quieter than usual. I asked him what was up.

"I don't know," he said, shrugging. "Maybe I'm just a little jealous. I mean, the mission's over, and you have this new friend who just happens to be a gorgeous girl and an extreme skateboard champ. And what do I have?"

I tried to cheer him up. "You have a parrot waiting at home for you, Frank."

He reached over and messed up my Mohawk.

The ride home was a nice way to unwind after the extreme dangers of our mission. The sky was clear and blue, and our motorcycles—I swear— seemed to enjoy cutting loose on the wide-open highway. In just a couple of hours we roared into our hometown and turned down the road to our house.

Aunt Trudy's Volkswagen was sitting in the driveway looking good as new. Dad must have driven it through a car wash after he had it fixed. I was glad the repairs hadn't taken long. As a joke, my brother and I parked our motorcycles right behind the VW, blocking it in. Just to drive Aunt Trudy a little crazy.

"Home sweet home," said Frank, pulling off his helmet and fluffing his hair.

"It's our *crib*, Frank. Get with the times." I took off my helmet and followed him to the porch.

The old house looked exactly the same.

Frank and I, however, did not.

Mom screamed when she saw us. "Oh, my gosh! What did you boys do to your hair? Frank! You're blue!"

Frank walked across the living room and gave her a kiss. "You dye your hair too, Mom."

"I do not."

"I've seen you touch up the gray."

"Not me. I don't have any gray hair. And if I did, I wouldn't dye it blue. Green, maybe, but never blue. And *you*!" she said, pointing at my head. "What made you think it's the 1980s? You're not in a punk band. People don't wear Mohawks anymore."

"Sure they do, Mom," I said, giving her a kiss. "Your son wears one."

Dad sat in his chair, laughing. He was always happy when we got home safe and sound after a mission—and always a little concerned. "Welcome back," he said. "I can't wait until your Aunt Trudy sees you boys."

"Where is she?" I asked.

My dad rolled his eyes. "Actually, you might want to hop back on your bikes and travel across the country for a while."

"Why? What's up with Aunt Trudy?" asked Frank.

Mom started to laugh. "Ask your parrot."

Just then, we heard a bloodcurdling shriek upstairs—and the flapping of wings.

"Get off of me!" Aunt Trudy screamed. "Get your stinking claws off me, you darn dirty bird! Off! Off!"

Playback came swooping down from the staircase and flew around the room. The parrot circled three times, squawked, then landed on top of Frank's new blue hairdo.

"Playback! Don't mess with the hair! I just styled it!" Frank lifted the parrot off his head and set him down on the mantel above the fireplace.

I heard footsteps coming down the stairs. Frank and I turned around to greet Aunt Trudy.

"I've had just about enough," she was saying. "Those boys better bring back a cage for that winged demon or I'm going to . . . AAAAAUUUGH!!! Stay

162

back, you, or I'll chop you in half, I swear! I know judo!"

Aunt Trudy waved her arms wildly in the air.

"Aunt Trudy, it's us," said Frank, laughing.

Our aunt stopped waving and squinted at us. "Of course I knew it was you. I was just . . . just playing along." She straightened her shirt and hugged us. "Did you remember to get me the Band-Aids?"

I reached into my backpack and handed her the first aid kit that Eddie had given us.

"Oh, my, these look so professional. Like the kind you see in hospitals. Thank you very much."

"Oh, it was nothing," I said.

Frank glanced at me and laughed. We turned to go upstairs and unpack.

"Wait, I'm not done with you two yet," said Aunt Trudy. She disappeared into the kitchen and returned with a bucket of warm soapy water.

"What's this?" I asked.

"This is for cleaning up after that parrot of yours," she explained, handing us each a sponge. "I told you that bird was going to poop all over the house. Look! Right here on the table! And look! On the carpet! And oh my goodness, look! He's pooping right now on the mantel!"

Frank and I started laughing.

"Well, if you think it's so funny, then you should have a load of laughs cleaning it up," said Aunt Trudy. "And you might think about using the sponge on your hair while you're at it!"

Frank and I took the bucket and sponges and started scrubbing the mantel. What could we do?

Dad turned on the television. "Boys! Look! It's the Big Air Games!" Frank and I turned to see the videotaped footage of our Monster Loop jump, ending with the helmeted Chet's wipeout.

Mom shook her head. "Anyone who would do something like that is just crazy," she said.

"But Mom, that's the Daredevil Duo and their sidekick, Hatchet," I said, winking at Frank.

"I don't care *who* they are. If you want to talk about *real* courage, I saw something on the news yesterday about this paramedic who saved two of those extreme sports kids at the park. Now that's what the world needs today. Real heroes."

Playback squawked.

"Heroes! Heroes! Heroes!"

Frank and I looked at each other.

"Get back to work, boys!" said Aunt Trudy. "That poop isn't going to clean itself up."

Cleaning up crime? I'm into it. Cleaning up parrot poop? Not so much. But hey, a job's a job. Glancing at Frank's hair, I smiled and went back to sponging.

# Exciting fiction from three-time Newbery Honor author Gary Paulsen

Newbery Honor Book

Newbery Honor Book

Aladdin Paperbacks and Simon Pulse
Simon & Schuster Children's Publishing
www.SimonSays.com

# PENDRAGON

Bobby Pendragon is a seemingly normal fourteen-year-old boy. He has a family, a home, and a possible new girlfriend. But something happens to Bobby that changes his life forever.

## HE IS CHOSEN TO DETERMINE THE COURSE OF HUMAN EXISTENCE.

Pulled away from the comfort of his family and suburban home, Bobby is launched into the middle of an immense, interdimensional conflict involving racial tensions, threatened ecosystems, and more. It's a journey of danger and discovery for Bobby, and his success or failure will do nothing less than determine the fate of the world. . . .

### PENDRAGON

by D. J. MacHale

Book One: The Merchant of Death
Book Two: The Lost City of Faar
Book Three: The Never War
Book Four: The Reality Bug
Book Five: Black Water

Coming Soon: Book Six: The Rivers of Zadaa

**From Aladdin Paperbacks • Published by Simon & Schuster**

## Lost—and Found

I rooted around in my backpack and pulled out a pair of binoculars. I used them to take a better look at the vehicle.

"It's a Seussmobile," I told Frank.

"What does that mean?"

"You know, it looks like something out of a Dr. Seuss book." What else was it supposed to mean?

Frank took the binoculars and checked out the van for himself. "See?" I asked. "It has all those weird metal things poking out all over it."

"I think they're solar panels," he said. "Which explains why we aren't hearing any motor."

It hadn't even registered with me how quiet the van was—but my brother was right. It was as silent as a submarine under water.

"There's a good chance we've found Arthur Stench," Frank told me. "Or he's about to find us."

# THE HARDY BOYS
### UNDERCOVER BROTHERS™

#1 *Extreme Danger*
#2 *Running on Fumes*

**Available from Simon & Schuster**

# THE HARDY BOYS

## BOYS

*UNDERCOVER BROTHERS*

**#2    Running on Fumes**

**FRANKLIN W. DIXON**

**Aladdin Paperbacks**
New York   London   Toronto   Sydney

✿ ALADDIN PAPERBACKS
An imprint of Simon & Schuster
Children's Publishing Division  ·
1230 Avenue of the Americas
New York, NY 10020

Copyright © 2005 by Simon & Schuster, Inc.

All rights reserved, including the right of
reproduction in whole or in part in any form.

THE HARDY BOYS MYSTERY STORIES and HARDY BOYS
UNDERCOVER BROTHERS are trademarks of Simon & Schuster, Inc.
ALADDIN PAPERBACKS and colophon are trademarks of
Simon & Schuster, Inc.
Designed by Lisa Vega
The text of this book was set in Aldine 401BT.
Manufactured in the United States of America
First Aladdin Paperbacks edition June 2005
10  9  8  7  6  5  4  3  2
Library of Congress Control Number: 2004113932
ISBN-13: 978-1-4169-0003-0
ISBN-10: 1-4169-0003-9

# TABLE OF CONTENTS

# Running on Fumes

# 1.

# Crash or Burn

I grabbed the closest chair and hurled it at the huge
window behind the desk.

Nothing. Not even a crack.

"Safety glass," I told my brother, Frank.

"Standard in an office building. Especially on
the twenty-second floor," Frank answered. He
didn't look up from the computer. His fingers
scurried over the keyboard.

I grabbed the chair and slammed it against the
glass again. *Bam! Bam! Bam!* I could feel the impact
all the way up my arm bones to my shoulders.

The smell of smoke was getting stronger. We had
to get out of here. The floor was shut down. The
elevators were off—not that you should use elevators
in a fire. The doors to the stairs were locked tight.

1

Somebody wanted us dead.

"Break, you piece of rat poop! Break!" I swung the chair like it was a bat and I was trying to knock the ball out of the stadium.

*Yeah!* Finally, a hairline fracture appeared in the glass. I beat on the place where the glass had weakened. The crunch of the glass under the chair was the best sound I'd ever heard.

"Frank—we've got an escape hatch."

I stuck my head through the shattered window and my stomach shriveled into the size of a BB. It was probably a tenth of a mile to the ground. And take it from me—when it's a tenth of a mile straight down, it's a long, long way.

"You've got the chutes, right?" I asked Frank.

He grunted. He doesn't appreciate my sense of humor. Maybe 'cause he has none himself!

"Okay, so . . . rope. We need rope," I muttered.

We were going to need rope if we were going to rappel down the side of the building.

Problem is, your average high-powered—and totally corrupt—lawyer's office doesn't come with rope. I scanned the room looking for a substitute. Cords off the two standing lamps, maybe? I snatched the letter opener off the massive wooden desk and started hacking away at the closest cord. Smoke was starting to creep into the room from

2

under the door. Not much time left. Why couldn't the office have steel doors like the stairwells did?

"How's it going, Frank?" I asked as I started to work on the second electrical cord.

"This firewall is like nothing I've ever seen before. Elegant," my brother answered, eyes still glued to the monitor.

"I'm more worried about the firewall on the other side of the door!" I shot back.

"I gotta get through it." The keys clacked under Frank's fingers. "If I don't—"

He didn't finish the sentence. But I knew what would happen if he didn't get through that firewall to the list of witnesses.

*You worry about getting you and Frank out of here alive,* I ordered myself. *Let him worry about the witnesses.*

With a figure-eight knot I tied the two pieces of cord together. The combined length would get us down about a story and a half. That left nineteen and a half stories to go.

Wait. Twenty and a half. I'd forgotten about the lobby.

I yanked the cord out of the phone. The phone was dead anyway. Another piece of the kill-Frank-and-Joe-Hardy plan. I guess it wouldn't have done much good to trap us in a burning building if we could just call the fire department.

I strode around the room, jerking the cord free from the little metal staples that held it to the wall. *That'll get me another few stories,* I thought as I added the phone cord to my rope.

The computer had some decent cordage I could use. But I couldn't have it until Frank was done. And even with that, we still needed more.

What else? What else?

The carpet that covered a big section of the polished wood floor. Perfect! But it would take me hours to cut it into strips with a letter opener. . . .

Wait—I'd just busted through a window. There were shards of glass everywhere! I snagged a piece and set to work on the carpet. Good thing it was thin.

You'd think hitting the ground would save me from the smoke—but there was no escape. In seconds my eyes were watering. Each breath was like swallowing sandpaper.

I ripped off my shirt and hoisted myself onto my feet. I'd spotted a mini-fridge in here the first time I'd visited Frank on his intern job. That was his cover—high school intern at the law firm. Mine was annoying brother of high school intern.

I dashed to the fridge and helped myself to two bottles of water.

"Frank! Heads up!" I tossed him one of the bottles and poured one on my shirt. I used the

4

shirtsleeves to tie the damp cloth over my face and then got back to work.

I tied the strips of carpet together as fast as I could. Added them to the rope.

Still not enough.

I added strips of the heavy drapes. The smoke was as thick as fog now. Orange-tinted fog. The flames were eating the door to the office. Any second they'd start on the ceiling.

"I'm through!" Frank called, voice muffled by the wet shirt tied over his mouth and nose. "Just got to copy the names." He hit a few keys, and the file started to download onto a CD.

I tied one end of my rope to one leg of the desk. "Nothing to use as a hook in here, right?" It's not like I could make some strong metal rings out of paper clips. "We'll have to Dulfersitz."

"File's done," the computer announced.

A second later Frank had the CD in his hand. I added all the computer cables to my rope. I still wasn't sure it was long enough to get us to the ground.

"Go, go, go!" Frank ordered.

I didn't have to be told twice. I wrapped the rope around my body and under my butt; the *sitz* part of the Dulfersitz rappelling technique means you sit on the rope.

Then I took a deep breath, turned around, and climbed out the window.

The breeze was strong up there, swinging me out to the left. I managed to get my feet positioned against the building and started to slide down the rope. Moving from phone cord to carpet to curtain to computer cord to . . .

To nothing.

No more rope. And my feet hadn't hit the pavement yet. I twisted my head around, trying to see the ground.

"Joe! Jump!" Frank shouted.

I looked up and saw that the cloth part of the rope had started to burn above my brother's hands. Frank needed me out of his way. Stat.

I closed my eyes and let go.

# 2.

## Fatal Blow

"Good morning, morning glory. Time to get up."

I rolled over and checked my alarm clock. "I have three more minutes," I called to Aunt Trudy. And I wanted every second of them.

Aunt Trudy pushed open the door. "I am not letting you be late when you have finals, Frank. And that's that."

I knew the progression. If I didn't get up now, Aunt Trudy would pull off the covers. If I still didn't get up, she'd dump a glass of water over my head.

"Okay, I'm up. I'm up." I sprang to my feet. Other than extreme lack of sleep and a smoke-fried throat, I felt pretty good.

7

Aunt Trudy nodded her approval. "No backsie-insies," she warned as she left my room. Sometimes Aunt Trudy thinks I'm still five years old. Although I have to admit, it was sort of tempting to crawl back into the sheets.

Instead I pulled on my jeans and a clean shirt, then trotted down the hall. I couldn't stop myself from cracking up when I spotted Joe halfway down the stairs. His blond hair was plastered to his head with water. Aunt Trudy got him good.

Plus, he was limping.

"Hey, are you all right?" I asked as I caught up to him. "As all right as possible after crash-landing onto a cement sidewalk and then having you crash-land on top of me," Joe answered.

He was careful to keep his voice low. Aunt Trudy and our mom don't know anything about the missions Joe and I take on for ATAC. They've never even heard of the American Teens Against Crime organization. Even though Dad is the one who founded it.

ATAC is top secret. The whole reason the squad exists is because teenagers can get into certain places adults can't, no questions asked. If everybody knew there were teen crime fighters around, that wouldn't be true anymore.

We grabbed our backpacks on the way out the

front door and almost tripped over Mom. She had the whole veranda covered with junk.

Well, I call it junk. Mom thinks of it as treasure.

"Careful," Mom said. "I just got the aluminum and the tin divided." She pointed to two of the piles of trash.

"You don't have to separate those, do you?" Joe asked. "Metal is metal to the recycling plant."

"Yes, but the kids are going to make luminarias out of the tin cans at the library's after-school program," Mom explained.

"Recycling isn't just throwing things into the blue garbage can," she continued. I'm saving up corks from wine bottles to make a bulletin board." Mom nodded toward another one of her piles. "And I'm thinking of making picture frames out of those CD cases."

"Merry Christmas!" Playback, our parrot, called from his perch in the sun. "Ho, ho, ho!"

"It's June," I told the bird. He ignored me.

"And don't give her any ideas," Joe added, smiling at Playback.

"Ho, ho, ho!" Playback said again. He sounded freakishly like Aunt Trudy. She'd spent the holidays ho-ho-ho-ing. The parrot can imitate anything. You should hear his impression of the doorbell.

"Okay, no CD-case picture frames for Joe next Christmas," Mom said. "How do you feel about a wastepaper basket made of egg cartons?"

Joe groaned. Mom laughed.

"Come on," I told my brother. We carefully began weaving our way around the piles and headed toward the front steps.

A squawk cut through the air—and it didn't come from Playback.

Aunt Trudy rushed across the porch, knocking the tin cans into the tower of used foil.

"I can't believe I let you two sleep so late that you don't have time for breakfast. And on the day of your finals!" Aunt Trudy shoved sports bottles into our hands. "At least drink some water. You can't think clearly when you're dehydrated. I told your father that this morning. But would he listen? No!"

"Where is Dad, anyway?" Joe asked.

I took a swig of water so Aunt Trudy would calm down.

"One of his breakfasts with the other retired cops," Mom said. She started to get her piles back in order.

"Breakfast." Aunt Trudy snorted. "Donuts and black coffee in some diner with sticky tables. As if that counts as a decent breakfast!"

I doubted he was there, though. Dad usually said he was meeting up with friends from the force when he had ATAC business himself. I knew he'd be disappointed that he didn't get to hear the details of Joe's and my mission first thing.

"Drink! Drink!" Aunt Trudy urged.

I took another long swallow, tasting smoke along the way. I wondered how long that would last.

"Your Aunt Trudy is right," Mom agreed. "The body needs water for transporting hormones, chemical messengers, and nutrients. Did you know the brain is eighty-five percent water?"

Can you tell our mom is a research librarian?

"With prolonged dehydration, the brain cells actually start to shrink," she told us.

I drained the rest of the bottle, and I heard Joe slurping down his.

"Thanks, Aunt T," Joe said. It came out sounding like Auntie. "Now my brain cells are nice and fat and ready to kick it on those finals!"

Aunt Trudy beamed.

"See you later," I called over my shoulder.

"Wimps! Wimps! Wimps!" Playback called in farewell. Must have been something he picked up from his previous owner. Nothing to do with me and Joe.

I mean, do you know any wimps who ride

11

motorcycles? Motorcycles with hydraulic clutch. Optimized suspension. Fog lamps with flint protectors. Hazard warning. Digital CD player and CB radio.

Didn't think so!

Joe and I climbed on our bikes and roared off to school. Well, roared off at the speed limit. Teenage guys riding motorcycles are traffic cop bait. Just FYI.

"I'm not liking how that looks," Joe said when we parked our bikes in the school lot.

I followed his gaze. I didn't like the scene either. Brian Conrad was talking to our friend Chet Morton.

The thing is, guys like Brian never talk to guys like Chet. Guys like Brian insult guys like Chet. They bully guys like Chet. They punch guys like Chet.

But talk? No.

I hurried over to them. Joe was right behind me.

"I think I saw you looking at my sister," we arrived in time to hear Brian say. He was right in Chet's face. Chet's pale face.

Chet's a great guy and everything. But he hasn't ever figured out that the way to deal with the Brians in the world is to show no fear.

"Belinda isn't Chet's type," Joe jumped in.

Brian whipped his head toward Joe. "You're saying my sister isn't good enough for this dillweed?"

Chet took the opportunity to move away from Brian—and closer to Joe and me.

"Everyone knows Belinda is gaga over my brother here."

I felt heat flood up my neck. *Don't let me be blushing.* That's all I could think. *Do not let me be blushing.*

I have this thing. This minor problem. I kind of turn into a moron around girls. Especially hot girls like Belinda. Even hearing Joe talk about her and me . . . Well, you can't get more moronic than blushing.

"I don't get it myself. Everyone knows I'm the better-looking one," Joe added.

The bell rang.

"I don't want any of the three of you sniffing around Belinda." Brian nailed each of us with a look that was supposed to be chilling. He kept his eyes on me the longest.

Like I'd even attempt to talk to Belinda. Not because I was scared of Brian, but because I was scared of making a total fool out of myself.

I held Brian's stare until he turned and walked away.

"So *were* you checking out Belinda?" Joe asked Chet as we headed inside.

"Hey, she was checking *me* out. I was just standing there." Chet flexed—as if he had muscles to flex.

*Yeah, right,* I thought. Chet's a good friend, but he's kind of a dork sometimes.

I mean, he was all attitude now that he was alone with me and Joe. But I noticed he couldn't stop himself from looking over his shoulder. To make sure Brian hadn't heard.

"See you guys at lunch," I said when we reached the door to my first-period class.

Chemistry. Final number one.

It wasn't that hard. At least not with my super-hydrated brain. Which was lucky, because Joe and I hadn't gotten much studying done last night.

Make that no studying. None. Although the story for Mom and Aunt Trudy was that we'd come home so late because we'd pulled a late-night study fest at Chet's.

English was a little more difficult. But only because I sit behind Belinda in English. And that's sort of distracting.

Next up, PE. A break from the brainwork. Nice. I was looking forward to it. That is, until I found out we were fencing. And who did Mr. Zwick assign to be my fencing partner?

Yep. Brian Conrad.

I slid my mesh-front mask into place. Brian and I faced off.

"Don't forget what I said this morning, Hardy." Brian thrust his foil at me. Going on the attack.

I parried. Now it was my turn to attack.

"Have you ever noticed how people who talk all the time never actually do anything?" I asked.

I jabbed my foil and hit Brian on the arm. That didn't count. To get a point in fencing, you have to touch the tip of your foil to the torso of your opponent. Head and arms don't get you any points.

"If my sister could see you now, she'd get over her little crush. She goes for jocks."

I didn't bother to reply.

Brian came at me again. I blocked. Thrust. He blocked.

We circled each other, foils clashing. A line of sweat trickled down my back as the clanging of metal on metal filled my ears. Brian's eyes stayed on mine. I could see them through the double layers of mesh—mine and his.

Then he glanced left. I jerked my foil in that direction, sure he was going to strike that way.

Instead he brought the foil to my heart. "If this was a real fight, you'd be dead," Brian announced. "This steel would slice right through your heart." He turned and walked away.

I was still thinking about his words at lunch when I met up with Joe at my locker. *If this was a real fight, you'd be dead.*

Brian was right. If there hadn't been protective tips on our foils . . . if I hadn't been wearing padding . . . if we hadn't been just two guys in gym class . . .

I would be dead right now. I'd blown it.

I twirled in the combination and opened my locker. Brian's voice continued in my head. *This steel would slice right through your heart.*

My heart.

I blinked twice. It was still there.

There was a heart inside my locker.

# 3.

# THE NEXT ASSIGNMENT

"Oooh! Frank's got a secret admirer."

I reached for the big, red, heart-shaped box of candy jammed in the bottom of my brother's locker. "I call the ones with nuts."

Frank slapped my hand away.

"Is there a note?" I asked. "A mushy note? 'Oh, how I love you, Frankie, baby, honey, dollface.' Whoever sent it is calendar-challenged. Valentine's Day isn't this week."

Frank blushed. My brother actually blushes.

And girls still like him. I seriously don't get it.

He opened the heart-shaped box. And suddenly I wasn't thinking about girl psychology anymore.

There was no candy in the box. Only a nice wad of cash, a folded map, and a video game disc. The label on the front read: RUNNING ON FUMES.

We were about to get our next ATAC assignment. This is how they always came. Disguised as video games.

"We need some privacy." Frank led the way out onto the quad and over to the oak tree at the far corner.

I pulled my portable game player out of my backpack and plopped down on the grass. Frank sat next to me and handed over the "game." I slid it into the slot.

I love the sound of that click when the disc is in place. My heart actually starts to beat faster. Every single time. I never get tired of the moment when we're about to find out the next assignment.

I hit PLAY. The Earth appeared on the small screen. A small blue and white ball. Spinning.

That didn't tell me much. Our assignment was somewhere in the world. Duh.

"Humans share the earth with as many as one hundred million other species." As the narrator spoke, trees and fungus and animals and insects and single-cell organisms took over the screen, new ones appearing every second. Filling every inch.

"But two hundred and seventy thousand of these species become extinct every year." Red Xs

18

slashed across the monitor, crossing out creatures I hadn't even known existed in the first place.

"This extreme extinction rate has occurred only five times before in the history of the earth, caused by meteors, volcanic eruptions, or rapid climate change."

"Meteors. That's one of the theories about what killed off the dinosaurs," Frank commented.

"Thanks, Mom." Sometimes my brother sounds like a research librarian himself. "What I want to know is what this has to do with us."

"But nature has nothing to do with the massive extinction going on today," the narrator continued. I couldn't get my eyes off all those red Xs. How could that many species disappear every year?

Entire *species*. It made my head hurt to think about it.

"The current extinction explosion is caused by"— a photo of Frank and me appeared—"humans."

"Somebody at the home office has a warped sense of humor," Frank said.

"I'm still not seeing the connection to us," I complained. "What's the mission?"

Pictures of tons more people appeared on the screen. "Humans consume nearly half of all the Earth's resources. This man wants to change all that. His name is Arthur Stench."

One man replaced all the people filling the screen. He looked like he was in his fifties. He was losing his hair, but he had a long beard—with enough hair for his whole body. It looked like he worked out.

"Arthur Stench has a compound in the California desert. It's a place where people gather to live in harmony with the land. Where they can give back to the earth."

I felt like giving the game player a shake. Was I watching a PBS special or what? Where was the assignment?

Stench's photo faded and a picture of a desert came up. All scrubby brush and cactus and rocks, with some mountains in the background.

"We have no visual of the actual compound. Visitors are not welcome. That's where you two come in. Many of Stench's followers are teenagers. Your assignment is to infiltrate the compound."

"I don't get it," I said. "Stench sounds like one of the good guys."

It was like the narrator had heard me. "Stench may be a harmless man. Even a hero. But we have received information about his using extreme measures to force people into following his beliefs. Threats. Arson. Bombing. Even murder. We need to put an end to it. But first, we need to determine whether or not he really is a threat."

"So it's not all about recycling," I muttered. I stared at Stench's picture, like if I stared at it long enough, I'd be able to see into his brain.

"There are no roads leading to the compound. You won't find any hotels or fast-food places. It's

---

## SUSPECT PROFILE

Name: Arthur Stench

Hometown: Santa Cruz, California

Physical description: Caucasian, age 55, 5'9", 175 lbs., balding, beard, left-handed, muscular.

Occupation: Leader of the Heaven compound.

Background: Both parents died while he was attending the University of Southern California; founded several companies that went bankrupt; divorced; estranged from children; antitechnology.

Suspicious behavior: House has no windows; needs a bodyguard so must have enemies; overheard making threats against oil companies.

Suspected of: Ecoterrorism.

Possible motives: Willing to use violence to enforce his beliefs if that is what it takes.

unlikely you'll see any people until you arrive. We recommend using your motorcycles."

Our juiced-up bikes appeared on the screen, flying across the desert. No roads—no speed limits! Cool.

"This mission, like every mission, is top secret. In five seconds this disc will be reformatted into a regular music CD."

Exactly five seconds later, some Cher song started playing at top volume.

I heard a few laughs from some of the other kids on the quad before I could rip the disc out of the player.

"You know what this means?" Frank's dark brown eyes were gleaming.

"Yes, I do, my friend. It means—"

"Road trip!" we said together.

No boring stay-at-home summer for us. We were taking the bikes all the way across the country. How excellent was that?

# 4.

## Good or Evil?

Joe flopped down on my bed the next morning. Without bothering to take his shoes off. Did I mention my brother is a slob?

"Got the GPS on both bikes programmed," he announced. He blew a big purple bubblegum bubble. The hypercharged fake grape smell almost made me sneeze.

He sucked the gum back into his mouth and started chomping. "The route is 2,741.3 miles. Almost a two-day drive."

"If you drive nonstop. Without eating. Or sleeping," I corrected him. I slid a set of lock-picking tools into my backpack. They'd been useful on other missions, and I liked having them along.

"I was thinking about that. I know we need to

23

get out to the compound and check things out. But we probably have a little time to—"

"—see some stuff," I finished for him. I was totally with Joe on this one. "I was thinking a little detour to Mount Rushmore might be nice."

"Wait." Joe used the corner of my bedspread to clean out one of his ears. "Say that again."

"You're washing that." Joe kept on cleaning, but I didn't bother repeating myself. I knew he'd heard me just fine.

"We have the whole country to see. And a bunch of stone heads are at the top of your list? Unbelievable."

I added some underwear to my pack. Joe was probably planning on wearing the same pair of boxers for the whole ten days. He thought if you turned them inside out it made them clean again.

"What's at the top of your list?" I asked him.

Joe sat up. "Okay, tell me if this is not cool. I read about this place where they train animals for fairs and stuff. All the tic-tac-toe-playing chickens come from there."

"You'd rather see farm animals playing the dumbest game imaginable than go to one of the most famous places in the country?"

Before he could answer, Mom came into the room. "I printed out some info on petroglyphs for you guys. Some of them could have been carved eight thousand years ago."

I felt my face getting hot. It's not just being around girls that makes me blush. Lying to Mom does it too.

Joe and I had told her we wanted to use part of our summer break to check out the petroglyphs in the Mojave Desert. The designs Native Americans had chipped into rocks sounded pretty cool.

But that's not why we had chosen this cover story. We picked it for two reasons. One: Mom was likely to approve something so educational. And two: There were petroglyphs in the same general area as the compound.

If you're gonna lie, it's better to put some truth in there.

Joe took the printouts from Mom and started scanning them. "Is any of this talk about the connection between the petroglyphs and aliens true? I heard that some of the glyphs are actually of UFOs the Indians had seen."

Can you tell my brother is a fan of Art Bell? That guy's talk show is all about UFOS and conspiracies and how there are real vampires roaming around. Joe eats that stuff up with a big spoon.

"Actually, I did come across one site that talked about 'glyphs and aliens," Mom told Joe. "I didn't print anything, but there's some great stuff about how some archeologists think the petroglyphs were drawn by medicine men while they were in a trance state."

"You mean they were wasted?"

"Well, there may have been some mind-altering plants used in some of the ceremonies," Mom admitted.

I zipped my backpack and slung it over one shoulder. "Ready?" I asked Joe.

"Yep." He grabbed his own backpack off the floor and stuffed Mom's printouts in the front pocket.

"I guess I don't have to give you any mother speeches. Like, always wear your helmets. And try to eat something that's not fried once in a while."

"Don't worry. Aunt Trudy's made her mark on us," I told her.

"You know when you two are gone it's *me* she lectures," Mom complained.

"She means well," Joe teased. That's what Mom always tells us when we complain about Aunt Trudy. We love our aunt and everything, but she can be a pain sometimes.

I was surprised Aunt Trudy wasn't upstairs right at that moment, supervising the packing. Her absence was explained when we headed outside.

She was already out there, polishing the handlebars of Joe's motorcycle.

It took us fifteen minutes to get through all the good-byes and Aunt Trudy lectures and Mom suggestions. It would have taken longer if Dad hadn't been at another one of his "breakfasts." He always has a lot of advice before a mission.

We were outta there.

Once I'm on my bike, I never want to get off. It's nothing like riding in a car. It's like the motorcycle is an extension of your own body. Like you're running down the highway. Wind blasting past you. We'd been riding for a day and a half now—with a short stop for sleep—and I still wasn't tired of the bike. I could ride forever.

Our first major stop was Mount Rushmore. Joe and I had made a deal—we got to alternate destinations on the way across the country.

And, yeah, he was right. Mount Rushmore was just a bunch of big stone heads.

But big stone heads of men who helped make America what it is. Washington. Lincoln. Jefferson. Theodore Roosevelt. It was like being in the presence of a hundred and fifty years of history.

"Okay, my turn now," Joe said when we got on our bikes in the monument's parking lot.

"The brainiac chickens, right?"

27

"Nope. Even better. The Thing in the Desert."

"I need more information."

"It's this *thing*. Someone found it in the desert. It's supposed to be amazing."

"But what is it?"

"That's what's so cool." Joe pulled on his helmet. "It's indescribable. You have to see it for yourself. People come from all over."

"Where did you even hear about it?"

Joe tapped his helmet. He couldn't hear me.

Whatever. It was his pick.

When we hit Arizona, we started seeing signs for the Thing. YOU ARE A HUNDRED MILES AWAY FROM THE THING IN THE DESERT. WHAT IS THE MYSTERY OF THE DESERT? That kind of stuff. None of the billboards gave any indication of what this famous thing actually was.

About twenty-two billboards later, we finally arrived at a big gas-station–souvenir-shop combo. Joe was practically dancing as we headed inside. We each paid two bucks and started following the big green footprints that we were told would take us to the Thing.

"How cool is this?" Joe asked, making sure to place his feet right inside the monster tracks.

"Right now all I'm seeing is pieces of wood that are supposed to look like animals." I squinted at the closest log. I guess it looked sort of like a squirrel. A mutant squirrel.

"You're the one who wanted to see rocks that looked like heads." Joe picked up his pace. The monster tracks led us out of the shed we were in and into another one. We passed some bedroom furniture from France. And a car that Hitler supposedly rode in once. Maybe.

Finally, in shed number three, we reached the Thing. I'm sure you all want to know what exactly it is, right?

Sorry. I can't tell you. I couldn't figure it out.

It's kind of a mummy. Maybe. With possibly a mummy baby. The sign above it says, YOU DECIDE.

Great.

I looked over at Joe, figuring he'd be ready to demand his money back. Or at least admit that Mount Rushmore was a much better destination.

"That thing is unholy *awesome!*" he declared.

Okay, so I was wrong. But at least the next destination pick was mine. Had to wait for the trip back, though. We needed to get our butts in gear and get to Arthur Stench's compound.

We decided to continue on to Phoenix, then crash. The next day we'd have about a four-and-a-half-hour ride to Palm Springs. Stench's group was set up in the desert, about another hour from the city.

"So, want to place a bet?" Joe asked when we stepped into our motel room.

"On what?" I pulled off my boots and stretched out on the closest bed. It felt like the mattress was vibrating. It always takes a while for the sensation of being on my bike to fade.

"On what we're going to find tomorrow." Joe did his usual shoes-on bed flop.

Didn't bother me this time. Wasn't my bedspread.

"Do you think Stench will be just some tree-loving guy? All peaceful? Or do you think he'll have a tent full of bombs and stuff?"

"I don't think ATAC would have sent us out here if there wasn't some chance the guy is dirty," I answered. "Not that I'm complaining. It's been a great trip."

"I knew you were grooving on the Thing!"

"The gift shop was better. Too bad we didn't have enough cash for that stuffed rattler."

"Yeah," Joe agreed. "Although Aunt Trudy probably would have made us keep it in the garage."

I closed my eyes. The image of Arthur Stench filled the blackness behind my eyelids. Good guy? Bad guy?

Trying to protect the earth was definitely good. But not if you used violence to do it.

The image of Arthur Stench seemed to smile at me. Daring me to figure him out.

Tomorrow Joe and I would get the chance. We'd be face-to-face with Stench.

# 5.

# BLOWOUT

I didn't have to look at the GPS to know we were getting close. Hundreds of white windmills stretched out over the desert.

This had to be the San Gorgonio Pass. Frank had been telling me about it last night. I was having trouble falling asleep. Adrenaline was pumping through me just thinking about what we might find at the compound.

When I'm feeling that way, one thing that can calm me down is hearing Frank yammer. He comes up with some interesting stuff sometimes. And last night he filled me in on the windmills.

I told you he's part reference librarian, right? The good thing is, he's part cop, too. A solid combo.

But anyway, before all the facts conked me out,

I got the scoop on the wind turbines. It's pretty amazing. See, hot air rises over the Coachella Valley and forces cooler air through a pass between the San Bernardino and San Jacinto mountains.

The wind gets up to twenty miles an hour. And that gets the windmills really spinning. The people who own the land sell the electricity the wind turbines generate. They farm wind.

I think next time my guidance counselor asks what career I have in mind, I'm going to say that. Wind farmer. But really, I'm pretty sure I'll end up a detective or a PI or something. I need the excitement.

Frank pulled up alongside me. He tapped his GPS. I looked down at mine.

Blank screen.

Uh oh.

I took the next exit off the highway and pulled into the first gas station I spotted. The first and only gas station. The exit hadn't even led to a town—just the station, and a diner that looked like it had been closed for fifty years. The newspaper over the windows was torn and yellow.

I checked the GPS again. Still dark. I was hoping the malfunction was a windmill thing. But no.

Frank rolled up behind me and took off his helmet. So did I. "Guess we're out of GPS signal range. We're going to have to do it the old-fashioned way," he said. He took the map that had been delivered with our assignment out of his backpack.

I leaned close so I could study it too. "Seems like we should get on this access road instead of the freeway."

"Yeah. Then we should see a road cutting into the desert a couple miles down." Frank returned the map to his backpack.

I started to put my helmet back on, then I hesitated. It seemed like we were dead center in the middle of nowhere. The dinky gas station was probably the last place to get supplies.

"I'm going to stock up on water," I told Frank.

"I'll fill up the bikes."

I headed into the little store—not much more than a couple of food racks and a fridge next to the cashier. The place smelled like unwashed feet.

I grabbed a few bottles of water and some sodas for each of us, along with an assortment of chips, some beef jerky, and some of those neon pink marshmallow cakes.

The old guy behind the counter rang up everything without comment. I paid for the grub and gas and returned to Frank. We stowed everything in our backpacks and headed for the access road.

It ran alongside the highway for a while. But unlike the highway, we had this road all to ourselves.

It was kind of cool—and kind of freaky. I mean, what kind of road has zero traffic?

Our bikes ate up the road, mile after mile.

Wait. Shouldn't we have made a turn by now? According to the map, we were supposed to go only a couple of miles before we hung a left.

Except there hadn't been any place to turn.

I slowed down a little. Frank brought his bike up even with mine. "Did you see a turn?" I shouted. He shook his head.

Maybe we'd underestimated the mileage. A paper map is no GPS. I checked the odometer. Watched as another mile clicked off. Then another.

Frank waved for me to pull over. "Whaddya think?" I asked when I came to a stop next to him.

"I think maybe one of those dirt tracks back there might actually have been a road."

"One of those things that looked like bunny trails?"

Frank had the map out again. "Has to be. At least if we believe the map."

I stared in frustration at the blank screen of the GPS. What good was the thing if it didn't work in isolated areas? Isolated areas were where you needed it most.

"So which bunny trail do we pick?" I asked Frank. "We went by about four of them."

He frowned. "I guess we do it by mileage. The road we're supposed to take is . . ." He laid his pinkie finger on the map, calculating. "I'd say it's three and a quarter miles back in the other direction."

We turned around. I watched the odometer click one, two, three miles. I scanned the left side of the access road. A fifth of a mile later I spotted a dirt path heading out into the desert.

It had to be what we were looking for. Clearly Frank thought so too. He swung his bike onto the trail.

I followed him, slowing down. The bumpy path wasn't made for speed. Good thing we were on our motorcycles. A car wouldn't have cut it.

I didn't really miss the speed, though—even though I usually want to go everywhere as fast as possible. I thought there wouldn't really be anything to look at in the desert, but I was wrong. There were those cacti that look like guys with their hands up. And these stunted spiky trees. Tumbleweeds. Actual tumbleweeds. Huge piles of boulders.

I was so busy looking around, it took me a minute to realize that Frank had come to a stop. I pulled my bike up next to his. Right away I saw what the problem was.

The road forked. On the map it didn't do that.

"You think we chose the wrong route?" I asked.

"This should be the right road. We calculated the mileage correctly."

I pulled out my cell phone. No juice.

"Well, the fork to the right heads more in the direction I think we're supposed to be going." I cracked open one of my sodas. The carbonation stung my dry throat.

"Yeah," Frank agreed. "We might as well try it. We can always turn around." He opened a bottle of water and drank. "Caffeine dehydrates you, you know. You should drink some water with that soda."

"Next stop." I drained the can, then took the lead down the trail we'd chosen. It got narrower. And narrower.

Then it disappeared.

Frank and I stopped for another strategy session. I took his advice and had some water and marsh-mallow cake.

We decided to go down the other path for a while before we returned to the access road. It was a good choice. The path headed in the wrong direction for about a mile and a half, but then it looped back.

I was pretty sure we were going the right way, but it would have been nice to see a road sign. There was nothing to indicate that any human had even been out here before.

The sun beat down on my helmet. I shrugged out of my leather jacket and used one hand to stow it in the container under my seat.

A long shadow appeared across the sand in front of me. At first I couldn't figure out what was casting it. Then I looked up.

A huge bird flew overhead. Black with an orange head and a wingspan that was wider than my whole body. Two of the bird's buddies joined it. *Vultures,* I realized.

I hoped they weren't after me and Frank.

A moment later I spotted exactly what the vultures were after. A sheep lay on the ground ahead of us. One of the vultures perched on its back. In an instant I could see a strip of the sheep's flesh in the bird's sharp beak.

I stopped for a closer look. How many times do you get to see vultures in action?

"That bighorn has to weigh more than two hundred pounds. Wonder what took it down," Frank said.

I eyed the sheep. Something other than vultures had already been eating it. "Isn't there a bear on the California state flag?" I asked.

"There are supposed to be some black bears out in the desert."

I looked over my shoulder. I felt like Chet, trying

to make sure Brian Conrad wasn't around.

The other two vultures swooped down on the sheep. There was a little squabbling with the first one about who got to eat what, then they settled down.

Probably whatever had killed the sheep wasn't around, or the vultures wouldn't be there. Right?

Maybe not. I heard a long, high, quavery howl. Followed up by a *yip, yip, yip*.

"Coyote," Frank said.

The vultures didn't seem too bothered by the sound.

"Four o'clock." My brother's voice was low and calm.

I turned my head to the right. A coyote was crouched beside some prickly-looking shrubs, its eyes on the sheep.

It gave another howl. The hair on my arms stood up, even though the coyote was only about the size of a collie. Same basic head and body shape too.

Now, don't go thinking I'm a wimp. But even though this coyote probably weighed in at about twenty pounds and looked kinda like a pet, I knew he had to be tough. Nobody was pouring him Alpo every night. He had to go out and hunt.

And he had the teeth to do it.

"It doesn't look interested in us. But we should probably—," Frank began.

"Yeah," I agreed. The coyote's yellow eyes shifted to me as I moved to start up the bike. He started toward me, belly low to the ground. In total stalking mode.

The hair on the back of my neck went up this time—and the hair on my arms hadn't even fallen back into place yet.

Stare back? Don't stare back? Yell? Don't yell?

Frank had chosen to be still and quiet, so I did too.

Looking directly into a dog's eyes is a dominance thing. I figured it was probably the same with a coyote, so I deliberately lowered my eyes.

Of course, I couldn't see if my strategy worked. The coyote could be about to leap on me. I shot a quick glance in the direction of the animal. I had to.

The coyote was moving toward the sheep. I let out a breath I didn't even know I was holding, then took the opportunity to rev up the bike. Frank and I left the birds and the coyote to duke it out over the sheep.

A few miles later we stopped again. I did a bear and coyote scan, then moved my eyes lower to check for rattlers and scorpions. All clear.

"Maybe we should go back and try another road," Frank said. "We should be heading southeast by now."

The sun was pretty much directly ahead of us. And since the sun still sets in the west, we had a problem.

I pulled out a couple of pieces of jerky and handed one to Frank. "What if we went off-road?" I asked. "Just headed in the right direction?"

Frank considered it. "I do have my compass. And we could make some markers with pieces of one of our shirts so we could find our way back."

"We're not using one of my shirts. You brought enough clean underwear to last you till the next millennium. We can use a few pairs of those."

I drank some water to wash down the Slim Jim. When I put the bottle back in my pack, I realized I'd just drunk half of the last one I had. I'd thought I had one more.

"What?" Frank asked.

"Just have to pace myself on the water," I answered.

"I have a bottle left."

"I have half of one and another soda. Plus three little bags of chips."

This would have been no biggie in normal circumstances. In normal circumstances there's at least a mini-mart within blocks. A mini-mart and a fast-food place.

But in the desert . . . there was nothing but desert.

I did another cell phone check. No juice. I knew that's what I'd see, but I had to look.

Frank pulled a pair of boxers out of his backpack. He used his Swiss Army knife to cut a strip of cloth. Then he tied the cloth to the closest cactus.

"We have enough hours of daylight to try your plan," he said. He climbed back on his bike.

We veered off the path and zoomed along. I felt like we could ride forever without hitting civilization.

Then I saw something that made me feel like cheering: a NO TRESPASSING sign nailed to a big cactus.

I let out a whoop and put on the brakes so hard that the bike skidded in a semicircle.

"You're happy that we have to turn around?" Frank asked.

"Don't you get it?" I asked. "That sign means that there's something to trespass onto! That means people. We can ask for directions. Get more water."

"You're right. Let's get trespassing!" Frank led the way past the sign.

A few miles later we saw another one: TURN BACK. PRIVATE PROPERTY. This sign was posted next to a road! It wasn't paved or anything, but it was a road.

I shot Frank a thumbs up. We were getting closer to . . . something.

I jammed on the gas. I could get a little speed going now. Yeah! I was flying down the flat, straight road.

Then—

*Bang!*

My back tire blew out.

I spun out of control.

# 6.

## NO TRESPASSING

Suddenly I hit the dirt. The weight of my bike pinned me to the ground.

I killed the motor and looked over at Joe. He'd been tossed too.

"You okay?" I asked. I shoved the bike off and scrambled to my feet.

"Yeah." Joe sat on the ground next to his motorcycle. "What the heck just happened?"

I leaned over and examined my front tire. A small, sharp spike was imbedded in it. I jerked the spike free and held it up. "*This* just happened."

Joe found a similar spike in his back tire. "I guess when they said 'no trespassing,' they really meant it."

"No kidding." I walked back a few feet. Now

44

that I was looking for them, I saw a bunch of the spikes scattered in the dirt.

"So, do we walk deeper in, or back out?" Joe asked.

I thought about the one and a half bottles of water we had between us and the small amount of food. If you could call chips and candy food.

"In, I think. I'm hoping the guy who left these spikes is closer than the access road."

Joe nodded. "Yeah. It's not like the access road would even do us that much good. We didn't see anybody on it."

"We'd probably end up having to go back to that gas station."

And that was a lot of hiking. In the desert. With almost no water.

*Stop thinking about the water,* I ordered myself. It wasn't helping anything, but it kept slamming back into my brain.

No water basically equals death—no matter where you are. But in the desert, death comes faster.

We were on a mission, though. We couldn't turn back.

Joe picked up his bike, moved it to the side of the road, and hid it behind some brush. I moved mine, too. Don't get me wrong, it wasn't easy leaving them behind. We love our bikes. But we had business. And besides—who was around to steal them?

We started to walk.

And walk.

And walk.

Sweat dripped down my face and down my back. At least I was still sweating. You know your body is really going into crisis when you don't.

"What do you think? Drink the soda or not?" Joe asked.

"It'll just make you thirstier."

"I guess the chips are a bad idea."

"They'll definitely make you thirstier. But I guess we might need the carbs for energy."

"I'll save 'em," Joe decided.

Neither of us had mentioned the heat. What was the point in talking about it? But it was like a solid presence on top of my head. Pushing down. Making every step harder.

I got an idea. I pulled a T-shirt out of my backpack and wrapped it around my head. "You should do this too," I told Joe. "Use anything white. It will reflect the sun—keep you a little cooler."

He followed my lead, also using a T-shirt, and we kept walking.

And walking.

And walking.

I didn't like the way Joe was looking. He wasn't picking up his feet as he walked. Each step was stirring up the sand—which we both ended up breathing. His eyes seemed sort of sunken in, and his lips were cracked.

I probably looked about the same. I flashed on what Mom had said about water. How you need water to transport nutrients, and how your brain cells shrink without it.

How long did it take for that to happen? Joe and I needed to be sharp out here.

"Do you think ATAC would be able to find us out here?" Joe asked. "I mean, do you think we're ending up anywhere close to where we're supposed to be?"

"If the signs were put up by Stench and his group, we are," I answered. I didn't point out that ATAC—and Dad—weren't expecting us back for almost a week.

We kept on walking. That's all we could do.

Walking, walking, walking.

"Do you think ATAC would be able to find us?" Joe asked.

I shot a glance at him. Did he remember he'd already asked that question? Was he getting delirious?

I pulled my water bottle out of my backpack and

took a small swallow. Then I handed it to Joe. "You should drink a little."

"I still have some of mine."

"Go ahead. We'll share yours later."

Joe took a swig, then immediately coughed it back up. "Sorry," he muttered. "Wasted it."

"Try it again," I urged.

He managed to keep the next swallow down. When he handed back the bottle, I noticed that his skin felt clammy.

Not good.

I checked the compass. We were going southeast. But that didn't mean anything, because we didn't really know where we had started from. The map I kept looking at was useless.

I jabbed a piece of cloth onto one of the spines of the nearest cactus. If we had to turn around and retrace our steps—and our motorcycle ride—back to the access road and then back to the gas station, would Joe make it?

Would I?

"How about if we stop for a while?" Joe asked. "I'm getting really sleepy. Maybe we could nap until dark. We have flashlights and everything."

My watch read 3:14. "The sun's going to be out for hours, and there's no place to take cover," I answered. "We'll bake out here. We've got to keep going until we find at least some kind of shelter."

"Shelter, right." Joe stopped. He used one hand to shade his eyes as he turned in a slow circle. "There's nothing—"

His mouth dropped open. "Do you see that? Or is it a freaky desert mirage?"

I followed his gaze. We both stared at the metallic dot moving toward us. Was it—?

I yanked a small pair of binoculars out of my pack.

"It's a van," I told Joe.

# 7.

# NOW ENTERING HEAVEN

A van. Yes! Our butts were saved.

Unless Frank and I were both having heat hallucinations. I asked Frank for his binoculars and used them to take a better look at the vehicle.

"It's a Seussmobile," I told Frank.

"What does that mean?"

"You know, it looks like something out of a Dr. Seuss book." What else was it supposed to mean?

Frank took the binoculars back and checked out the van for himself.

"See?" I asked. "It has all those weird metal things poking out all over it."

"I think they're solar panels," he said. "Which explains why we aren't hearing any motor."

It hadn't even registered with me how quiet the

van was, but my brother was right. It was as silent as a submarine under water.

"There's a good chance we've found Arthur Stench," Frank told me. "Or he's about to find us. What else would an extreme environmentalist drive?"

I took the binoculars again. The van was close enough for me to see the driver now. "It's not Stench," I announced. "Not unless he's had an extreme makeover."

A girl was operating the solar-powered van. A complete killer of a girl. With all this curly light red hair. Dark freckles on her shoulders. Shades covered her eyes—but I was thinking they were green.

Maybe this was a mirage after all.

Frank held out his hand for the binoculars. I handed them over. Then I pulled the T-shirt off my head and used my fingers to comb through my sweat-soaked hair. I'd been thinking this vacation would be girl-free. How happy was I that I was wrong?

"I'm still thinking the thing is a Stenchmobile," Frank said. "The girl could be one of his followers. There are supposed to be a bunch of people our age at the compound."

I knew that. But somehow I'd pictured Stench's followers differently. I mean, you don't usually think of normal teenager types living out in the middle of the desert. No movies. No malls. No skateboard parks. No candy. No fun.

I thought all the people at the compound would be, well, geeks. But the girl in the van was no geek. Geeks aren't hot.

Frank stared at me like I was crazy as I licked my fingers and used them to wipe the dirt off my face. "That's gross. You're smearing spit all over yourself."

Who cared? First impressions count. And the red-haired girl was about to get her first impression of me. She pulled the van to a stop next to us and leaned out the window.

"Welcome to Heaven!" she called.

"Does that mean we're dead?" Frank asked.

The girl pulled off her shades. I was wrong about her eyes. They were brown, not green. Light brown. Almost gold.

Okay, I sound like a potatohead. Sorry. Just lost it for a minute.

"You don't look like a ghost to me," the girl answered Frank. She smiled as she stared at him. Stared—as in, checked him out. After I washed my face with spit for her!

"Heaven's what we call this place," the girl added. She squinted, trying to see through the sun.

"I guess I should tell you what I'm called too. My name's Petal Northstar."

Huh? That girl's parents did *not* name her Petal. I kept my mouth shut, though. There was still a chance Petal might realize I was the Hardy who was worthy of her. I didn't want to blow it.

"I'm Alex Jefferson," Frank said. "And this is my brother, John."

Do you think he could have come up with a more boring alias for me? John. Come on. "You can call me J. J.," I quickly told Petal. "For John Jefferson."

I knew it was safer to use a fake name. But that didn't mean the name couldn't be somewhat cool.

"How'd you guys end up all the way out here?" Petal asked. Her voice was soft.

Like a petal.

Man! I just went potatohead again.

"We were just doing some off-road motorcycle riding. Then we ran over a couple of spikes, and they blew our tires out," Frank answered. "But we kept on walking."

"Maybe you should have obeyed the No Trespassing signs," Petal said. It didn't sound like she had any problem with using spikes to keep out unwanted guests.

"Yeah. It's just that you have to get almost this

deep into the desert to get the full impact of the terrain. All the way out here, the world is untouched. No soda cans. No graffiti."

Got to hand it to Frank. If Petal was from Stench's compound, he'd said the perfect words. He'd made himself look like someone who would want to live with a bunch of save-the-Earthers. I also gave him points for spitting the words out. He tended to be super-shy around girls.

Petal climbed out of the van. She walked around to the back door, opened it, and pulled out some canteens for me and Frank.

"I actually saw a cactus with graffiti carved into it once. Cut right into the cactus flesh," she said as we both took long drinks.

Nothing tastes as good as water in the desert. Nothing.

"That's so wrong," I told her. She really looked at me for the first time—then turned her attention back to Frank. I don't know how he does it. Because he doesn't even *do* anything! It's like how mosquitoes go for some people more than others. Girls swarm to Frank. And what does he do about it? Nothing. What a waste!

"Mr. Stench is expecting me back. I guess I should bring you guys with me. We can make plans to get you home later." She smiled at Frank. "Or maybe you'll want to stay awhile. Really experience the desert."

Bingo. She was definitely from Arthur Stench's compound.

"Great," Frank said. "Thanks." He climbed into the back of the van, and I was right behind him. I was hoping I could get the shotgun seat next to Petal, but it was loaded with boxes.

I wondered what was in them. Guns? Bombs? Vegetable seeds?

"Did that water taste weird to you?" Frank asked as Petal walked back around the van to the driver's side door.

"It tasted awesome," I answered.

"Don't drink too much, okay?" he said. He dropped his voice to a whisper as Petal got behind the wheel. "I think it might be poisoned. It tasted off to me."

Poisoned? But why? Did Stench somehow get advance notice that Frank and I were coming? Did he know about the mission?

The thoughts made me feel dizzy. Or maybe it was all those hours in the sun. I drank some more water. It really did taste good. Maybe a little metallic from being in the canteen, but good.

Frank shot me a disapproving look. But it's not like it was any better to die of dehydration than poison. You were dead either way.

Petal powered up the solar van, and we bounced away. It felt great to be moving *and* sitting.

"You two must be hungry." Petal said "you two" but she was using the rearview mirror to look straight at Frank. Even though Frank was still wearing a freakin' T-shirt turban and had grit all over him. He looked like one of those sand people in *Star Wars*.

"Yeah. All that walking," Frank answered.

"There are some energy bars in that bag behind your seat. Help yourself."

I didn't need to be asked twice. I grabbed bars for me and Frank, and had half of one down my gullet in about a second.

"Chewy," Frank said, the word coming out garbled because he was having trouble swallowing his bite of energy bar.

Mine wasn't going down too smooth either. The more I chewed, the bigger the lump in my mouth seemed to become. Although it couldn't really be growing.

Could it?

"Tofu and cactus fiber," Petal told us. "We make them ourselves at the compound."

Frank looked like I felt. He looked like he was about to hurl. Somehow he managed to swallow his wad of cactus tofu. I figured if he could do it, I could do it—so in one huge gulp, I forced the gunk down my throat.

"Is that what you mostly do at the compound? Cook?" I asked.

"We don't have assigned jobs like that," Petal explained. "We each do what Mr. Stench asks us to."

She answered Frank, even though I was the one who had done the asking. "She likes you," I signed to Frank, keeping my hands low so Petal couldn't see. He and I had learned American Sign Language on another mission. It came in handy when whispering was too loud.

Frank blushed. Even the tips of his ears turned fiery red. "She's pretending," he signed back. "She wants to put us off guard."

I checked to make sure that Petal's eyes were on the road and not my brother. They were. So I signed my answer. "Who cares if she is? She's smokin'."

Frank's fingers moved fast as he shot back his reply. "I don't trust her."

"You don't trust anybody," I signed back to Frank. It's true. My big brother has a suspicious nature. Which I guess is good for an ATAC member. But still.

Me? I usually trust people until I have a reason not to.

"Hey, we didn't even say thanks for saving our lives. We'd be vulture chow if you hadn't shown up," I told Petal.

I meant it. But I was trying to remind Frank that this girl had done us a huge favor.

"My pleasure," Petal said. "My complete pleasure," she added, again with the long look at Frank.

Frank's blush had started to fade—but those words from Petal got it going again.

"Hey, here we are!" Petal exclaimed. "I can't wait for you to meet Mr. Stench and everybody."

I couldn't wait to meet Stench either. The mystery man. What would he be like? Slowly, we drove past a sign that read: NOW ENTERING HEAVEN.

<u>SUSPECT PROFILE</u>

<u>Name:</u> Petal Northstar, aka Paula Northum

<u>Hometown:</u> La Quinta, California

<u>Physical description:</u> Age 17, 5'6", 128 lbs., red hair, brown eyes, hummingbird tattoo on left shoulder blade.

<u>Occupation:</u> Member of the Heaven compound.

<u>Background:</u> Only child; dentist father, schoolteacher mother; 3.8 GPA; created a Web page called Toxic Avengirl.

<u>Suspicious behavior:</u> Heard to say she would do absolutely anything for Arthur Stench, extremely skilled with a bow and arrow.

<u>Suspected of:</u> Aiding Arthur Stench in acts of violence.

<u>Possible motives:</u> Desire to stop the use of technology and oil.

# 8.

# THE FAMOUS MR. STENCH

*Now Entering Heaven.* I wondered if that was true. Or if we were really entering some kind of hell.

Actually, the place didn't look like either. The compound didn't look like much of anything. Just a cluster of tents of different sizes, a short row of Porta-Pottis, and in the distance, one wooden building with no windows that I could see.

Petal pulled the van up next to the biggest tent. Two guys about my age trotted up to meet us. They started unloading the boxes from the front seat without a word.

"I've got some stuff to take care of," Petal said. "But I know Mr. Stench will want to see you guys and help you get wherever you need to go."

She smiled at me. Was Joe right? Did she like

me? I'm not the best girl smile evaluator.

It didn't matter. I had to stay objective. About Petal. About Stench. About the whole compound. Joe and I were on a fact-finding mission. And I needed to focus on facts. Only facts.

"That is, if he doesn't convince you to stay," Petal added. "A lot of people do. It's the kind of place you find when you're the kind of person who belongs here. I—"

"Hey, Petal. My blowin' in the wind girl," someone called, interrupting.

I turned toward the voice and saw a guy wearing a metal suit with what looked like a metal top hat on his head. Additional sheets of metal poked out from his back like mutant angel wings.

"Oh, Dorothy!" Joe said out of the side of his mouth.

I tried not to crack up. But now that Joe had pointed it out, I realized the guy did have a Tin Woodsman look going. He literally clanked as he headed over to us.

"Solar Man." Petal gave the guy a half hug. Half was all she could manage with those metal wings the guy was sporting.

"Whatcha got there?" the man asked, nodding at me and Joe.

"I found these boys wandering in the desert,"

Petal answered. "Alex and J. J., meet Solar Man. He's been with the compound from the beginning."

I made a mental note: He'd be a good source of information.

"Can you take care of them for me? I know Mr. Stench will want to talk to them."

"Of course, my little bit of flower," Solar Man told Petal.

"See you guys later," Petal told me and Joe. She headed into the large tent.

"Yeah, like she's ever actually *seen* me," Joe muttered. He's always complaining about how girls like me more. I don't get it.

"The chief is in a confab right now," Solar Man said. "Cannot be interrupted. But you two can hang with me until he's done. Come on, I'll take you to my abode."

It wasn't hard to figure out which tent belonged to Solar Man. It was the only one covered with solar panels. There was a lawn chair made entirely of foil sitting out front.

Solar Man adjusted the chair so that it was facing directly toward the sun. Then he sank down onto it with a sigh. I blinked as his solar-suit shot reflections of the sun into my eyes.

"All made of recycled materials. Found 'em myself," Solar Man told us, patting his foil chair.

"Aren't you hot?" Joe asked.

I'd wanted to ask Solar Man that myself, but I thought he might get offended.

"I'm storing up energy, little brother." Solar Man tapped a power pack strapped to his side. "Don't you think it's worth a little pain to save our planet?"

His voice was mellow, but his dark eyes were sharp.

Did he think it was worth pain to *other* people to save the planet?

"It's definitely worth some pain," Joe agreed. "I was just wondering how you can survive it. We were out in the sun for only a few hours, with no panels, and we almost didn't make it."

"I've been doing this a long time. I've built up an endurance," Solar Man explained.

I wondered what he meant by a long time. A year? Five? Twenty-five? Forty? The guy was in his sixties at least.

"Did you start when you met Mr. Stench? Or were you doing it before then?" Joe asked.

Solar Man shifted in his seat. I bet it was hard to get comfortable with those metal wings. Even if they sort of sunk down into the foil of the chair.

"I was a sun god long before I met Arthur. That's how we met, actually. He saw me gathering energy and knew I should live at the compound.

## SUSPECT PROFILE

_Name:_ Solar Man, aka Danny Sunshine, aka Daniel Templeton

_Hometown:_ Woodstock, New York

_Physical description:_ Age 63, 6'1'', about 160 lbs., African American, bald, brown eyes, missing one toe on right foot.

_Occupation:_ Member of the Heaven compound.

_Background:_ Followed the Grateful Dead selling T-shirts for twelve years; no family; no driver's license; first member of Arthur Stench's compound.

_Suspicious behavior:_ Wrote a paper about how people who don't agree to use solar power should be locked in a dark cellar until they see the light.

_Suspected of:_ Assisting Arthur Stench in acts of ecoterrorism.

_Possible motives:_ Stench makes him feel important; Stench helps him get his message out to the world.

Even though the compound was just a dream in my man's head back then."

"How long ago was that?" I sat down in the small

patch of shade thrown by the tent. Joe flopped down next to me.

"More than a year now. First Arthur and I traveled around a little. Finding the other people who we knew belonged."

"How did you find them?"

"I feel it right here." Solar Man tapped the solar panel covering his chest. I figured he meant he felt it in his heart. Not the panel. But with a guy like Solar Man, who knew?

"I can feel their soul touching my soul. Some are like me—folks who have found their own way to make a difference." He ran his hand lightly over his metal top hat.

"A lot are like little Petal. Young ones who realize the earth is dying and have dedicated their lives to saving it."

Joe and I exchanged a look. I knew my brother was trying to make the same call I was. Harmless wacko—or should-be-behind-bars wacko?

"Arthur created a place for all of us," Solar Man went on, talking faster and faster, his voice rising with each word. "Other people—businesspeople, reporters, scientists, the president—may think we're crazy. But Arthur understands that all geniuses look a little crazy. He knows the ideas we develop here will change everything."

"I can't wait to meet him," I said.

"Be patient, tumbleweed. The man has lots of things to attend to. But he'll make time for you," Solar Man answered.

"What's that one wooden building?" Joe asked. "The one with no windows."

Excellent question. The building was definitely the winner in the one-of-these-things-is-not-like-the-other game.

"That's Arthur's thinkatorium. That's where he thinks all his big thoughts," Solar Man answered.

"And the no windows are because . . . ?" I asked, waiting for him to fill in the blank.

Solar Man sat up suddenly, solar panels clattering. "You two ask a lot of questions."

My gut muscles tightened. Had we blown our cover?

"We're curious," Joe said quickly. "Seekers."

"I like it," Solar Man told him. He turned to me. "Windows equal distractions, little brother. That's why you don't find them on Arthur's place. People equal distractions too. That's why he has a lock on the door. He needs his thinking time."

Interesting reason for having no windows and a lock on the door. It didn't seem like the most logical reason, though.

I was getting more and more curious about

Stench. No. Make that more and more *suspicious*.

"Looks like the meeting of the minds is over." Solar Man nodded to a mid-size tent. Two men walked out, followed by Petal.

"I'll take you over." Solar Man stood. "I gotta frisk you first. The chief is big on security. You have to be when you're trying to change the world. Look at what happened to JFK. And Martin Luther King."

"We're not going to assassinate anyone," Joe promised as Solar Man frisked him.

"Standard op. No exceptions," Solar Man said as he moved over to me. "Nothing personal."

When Solar Man was done checking us out, he led us over to the tent where the little meeting had just broken up. This was it.

"I've gotta go catch some more rays. Go on in," Solar Man told us. It made me feel like a little kid, but for one second I wished he was coming with us.

I pushed my way through the tent flap. My eyes went directly to a refrigerator of a man. A massive guy. Tall. Wide. With arms like slabs of meat.

"That's Mondo. He's my bodyguard. He never leaves my side."

I jerked my gaze away from Mondo and saw Arthur Stench looking at me. He was smaller than Mondo. Everyone was smaller than Mondo.

But it was absolutely clear who was in charge:

this man dressed in a long white robe, with a sword strapped to his waist. He looked like a cross between those pictures you see of Obi-Wan and samurai soldiers.

His beard was grayer than we'd seen in the photo. And although he was balding on top, he'd grown a long ponytail.

"Freak-y," Joe whispered, so quietly that only I could hear him.

Stench *was* freaky looking. Almost goofy. It was like he was wearing a costume—except that sword of his wasn't plastic. And there was something about him that made me feel like he wouldn't be afraid to use it.

"Alex and J. J. Jefferson. Can I offer you anything?" Stench asked.

Before either of us could answer, he whirled toward the wooden table to his left, whipped his sword out of the scabbard, and—*whoosh, thud*—cut one of the pineapples sitting there exactly in half.

Yeah, I was right. He'd use that sword in an instant.

Stench sheathed the sword again and gestured to Mondo. The bodyguard did the grunt work of carving the pineapple into smaller pieces. He served them to me and Joe on wooden plates.

"As you see, Mondo has many uses," Stench said.

## SUSPECT PROFILE

**Name:** Michael "Mondo" Callihan

**Hometown:** Wakulla, Florida

**Physical description:** Age 42, 6'3", 340 lbs., blond, blue eyes.

**Occupation:** Arthur Stench's bodyguard.

**Background:** Former linebacker for the Florida Gators; two ex-wives, no kids; served a jail term for manslaughter.

**Suspicious behavior:** Bottle of steroids fell out of his pocket, observed flying into rages.

**Suspected of:** Doing Arthur Stench's dirty work.

**Possible motives:** Seems like hired muscle.

"Petal seemed to think you two might want to join our family. Is that true?" Stench asked.

"Uh, before we answer that, can I ask why you're wearing that sword?" Joe stuck a piece of pineapple in his mouth and sucked on it.

Count on my brother to ask the question everyone else wants to ask, but doesn't have the guts to.

Stench pulled the sword free again and turned it back and forth in the light pouring through the tent flaps. "It's beautiful. Elegant. Exactly what it needs to be, and no more. Unlike most creations of the modern age."

He looked at the sword like he was in love with it. "I don't allow any modern technology at the compound. That's something you need to know. I forbid it."

I would have felt better if he put the sword away. But he kept holding it out, admiring it. "We live off the land here. We live in peace with each other and the planet."

Stench sliced the sword through the air. It gave a faint whistling sound. He smiled so widely I could see the gold fillings in two of his molars.

"Still, sometimes people make their way to the compound who don't believe in peace. I need to be prepared for them. I need to be able to protect myself."

Finally Stench slid the sword back into its scabbard again. I noticed the scabbard wasn't leather. It was some kind of heavy plastic. Recycled, I assumed.

"With Mondo to protect you, who needs a sword?" Joe joked.

"Good observation," Stench said to Joe. "But

you have neglected to consider the possibility that Mondo might be my attacker."

Paranoid much? If he didn't trust his own body-guard, who did he trust?

Stench laughed long and hard. After a few seconds Mondo joined in—but the bodyguard's laugh sounded completely fake.

"Now, is it true that you're interested in joining us here in Heaven?" Stench asked.

"We were led here, man," Joe answered. "It's like the place was calling to us. Our GPS conked out, and our cell phones went dead. Technology totally failed us. But we kept on coming. It was like we were on some kind of vision quest."

What a load of garbage. I thought maybe Joe had laid it on a little thick—but Stench was nodding in approval. I jumped in, trying to sound like as much of a fruitcake as Joe had.

"It's like that Buddhist expression. When the student is ready, the master appears." I'd heard that in some kung fu movie. It seemed appropriate. "You're supposed to be our master, man."

I could tell Stench liked that. The guy had an ego the size of Mondo.

"I wouldn't have picked you two out as part of our spirit family. A little mainstream. A little clean-cut. A little too tied to the material world."

Maybe Joe shouldn't have mentioned our cell phones and GPS systems. At least he'd left his leather jacket back with the bikes. The head of the tofu-eaters would have hated it.

"That's what we were, man," Joe assured Stench. "It's not what we want to be."

"Looks can be deceiving," I added.

"Yes, they can," Stench agreed. "Do you know much about oil?"

I shrugged. "A little."

"It comes from the ground," Joe volunteered.

"Oil is the reason I created Heaven. The way we use oil is going to bring about the downfall of civilization," Stench told us. "Because soon the supply will be gone. And if there are no alternatives—which no one seems interested in developing—the modern world will come crashing to a halt."

Stench pulled his hair free of its ponytail and shook his head. "Everyone here at Heaven is expected to help stop this world-shattering crisis. It is our mission to create alternative fuel sources."

That explained why Solar Man was one of Stench's draft picks. He was all about alternative energy.

"Is that something I can expect from you?"

We had to come up with something to satisfy

him. He had to give us permission to stay at the compound.

"The wind turbines!" I burst out. "J— J. J. and I are fascinated by wind as a source of energy."

"I want to be a wind farmer!" Joe jumped in.

"Excellent." Stench nodded. "Excellent. Mondo, have Dave show the boys where to shower and bunk."

He turned back to me and Joe. "I think you two will fit in nicely. Stay as long as you like. Stay forever! There's nothing worthwhile to return to."

Mondo walked to the tent flap and whistled. Almost immediately, one of the teenage guys who'd helped unload the van appeared. Mondo gave him instructions in a low voice.

"Come with me," the guy—I assumed he was Dave—said. "Mondo said you'd want showers," he continued as we followed him out of the tent. "This is the best time of day for it. The water's been heating up since sunrise."

Forty minutes later we were showered, fed (more tofu, unfortunately), and in our own small tent.

"So besides him being freak-y, what did you think of Stench?" I asked Joe.

"I haven't decided." He rolled onto his back. "I mean, he *is* weird. But he's doing good stuff here.

One of the people at the compound really might come up with an alternate fuel source."

"Maybe," I agreed. "But I don't trust him."

Joe snorted. "You just don't trust anybody, Frank."

"Well—I trust him less."

# 9.

# AN UNPLANNED MISSION

"Good morning, morning glory!" Frank said into my ear.

"Good morning, Aunt Trudy," I said without opening my eyes. "Go ahead. Dump some water over my head. It would feel outstanding."

Frank laughed. "It would, wouldn't it? But I'm drinking all I have. I guess it's not poisoned after all—since here we both are. Alive."

I sat up. "Maybe we both had a little heatstroke yesterday. Made us think twisted thoughts."

"Maybe," Frank agreed. "Let's go look around. I want to check things out without an escort."

I pulled on my jeans. The feel of the heavy material was foul. It was only about ten in the morning, but the desert was already like a barbecue pit.

That robe Stench had been wearing was probably the best thing you could wear in the heat. Not that I'd walk around in a nightgown-looking thing.

Frank led the way out of our tent. "It's like Colonial Williamsburg," I said as we walked down one of the rows of tents.

Colonial Williamsburg is this place in Virginia where we went on a vacation once. They call it a living museum, because everyone in the town acts like they're living in colonial times. No modern stuff at all.

The compound was a little like that. Not colonial, and people weren't dressed funny or anything. But there was nothing high-tech.

Which made the place pretty quiet, for starters. No TVs on. No CDs playing.

We passed a man who was using a cactus spine needle to mend a rip in a shirt, and a teenage girl who was using a frond from a palm tree to sweep the area in front of her tent.

"Isn't it kind of a waste of time to sweep dirt?" I asked her. I didn't really care about the answer. I just wanted to talk to her. She had these awesome long blond braids. And green eyes. I'm a sucker for green eyes.

"There are a lot of creepy crawlies around," the girl answered. Her eyes drifted from me to Frank and stayed there. "I love them and all. And I know we share the world as equals. I just don't want them sharing my tent!"

"I'm not a creepy crawly," I began. "Does that mean I'm welcome to—"

"Hey, guys!"

The shout interrupted me. I guess it didn't matter. It's not like I was really expecting an invitation to share the girl's tent.

"How's it going?"

I turned toward the voice and spotted Dave a few tents down. He was using a hand-cranked clothes wringer to squeeze the water out of a pair of pants. The excess water fell into a bucket under the wringer.

"Hey, Dave!" Frank called. He started toward the guy.

"See you later," I told the girl with the braids. She waved at me. "Give me a call if you need help with the sweeping. We're neighbors now." I pointed to our tent.

"Both of you are staying there?" the girl asked.

Translation: I have no interest in you—but your brother is a different story.

"Yeah," I said. Then I headed after Frank. There was no point spending more time talking to Braids. She'd made her choice.

"Guess I don't have to ask how you slept," Dave said when we reached him. He dropped the pants in a basket made of woven branches. Then he pulled a T-shirt out of the tub next to him and started cranking it through his wringer.

"I think I nodded off before I even lay down," Frank answered.

"You missed breakfast, but there's probably some rutabaga muffins left." He pointed to the biggest tent. "That's the dining hall. Just go grab some if you want."

My stomach rolled over at the thought of eating a rutabaga anything. "I think I'll wait for lunch."

"Yeah," Frank agreed. "So, how long have you been living here anyway?"

Dave held up his cranking hand. "You can tell how long someone's been at the compound by the hands. I've still got blisters. That means I'm a newbie. You should see the calluses on some of the guys around here. And the girls."

He dropped the T-shirt on top of the rest of the damp clothes. "So are you two going to hang here for a while?"

"A little while, at least," Frank said.

"We're thinking we might just have found a home," I added. "Let me ask your advice. How'd you tell your parents you were moving out here?

Or did you? 'Cause I can't think of any way that our parents won't freak."

I was trying to suss out if Dave was a runaway or what.

"They told me," Dave answered. "Mr. Stench convinced my mom that this was a much better place to do her research."

"That must kind of suck for you," I said. "Being forced to leave all your friends and everything."

If Dave wasn't all that happy being here, we might get some good information from him. Unhappy people tend to blab.

"At first, yeah," Dave agreed. "But there are a lot of cool people at the compound. And I want there to be a planet to live on when I'm my parents' age, you know. And that means making some changes."

He took the bucket from under the wringer and dumped the water into the tub. "I'll take that over to the gardens later. We recycle water as much as we can."

I wondered how they got the water to begin with. I definitely hadn't seen any water sources on our way into the compound. And I'd been looking.

"So is your mom one of the people trying to develop alternate energy sources?" Frank asked.

"Yeah. You want to see?" Dave picked up the basket full of clothes.

## SUSPECT PROFILE

<u>Name</u>: Dave Simkins

<u>Hometown</u>: Toledo, Ohio

<u>Physical description</u>: Age 16, brown eyes, brown hair, 5'11", 140 lbs., wears wire-frame glasses.

<u>Occupation</u>: Member of the Heaven compound.

<u>Background</u>: On track team before he left school; one sister in college; vegan since birth.

<u>Suspicious behavior</u>: Carves knives out of wood, says that humans are the worst things that have happened to the world.

<u>Suspected of</u>: Ecoterrorism.

<u>Possible motives</u>: Wants his mother's inventions to be recognized.

"Definitely," I told him.

"Come on."

Dave led us behind his tent. He dumped the basket at the feet of a short, skinny man hanging clothes on a line. "All done, Dad," Dave said. "I'm taking these guys to see Mom's lab. They're thinking of joining us."

"Welcome," Dave's dad said.

80

Everyone around here was so friendly. Well, except Mondo. But bodyguards aren't supposed to be friendly. I could almost see myself living here. Except for the food.

"Hey, Mom, you've got guests!" Dave called as he ushered us into the larger tent on the other side of the clothes line.

I felt like rubbing my eyes. The inside of the tent looked like the AP chem lab at school, but with even more stuff. And none of it was made with twigs or cactus needles or palm fronds.

"Mom, this is Alex and J. J.," Dave said. He turned to us. "Don't be offended if she doesn't remember your names. She's the total stereotypical absent-minded professor. She doesn't remember my name half the time."

"Not true!" Dave's mom said. But I noticed her shoes didn't match.

"What are you working on?" Frank asked. He's a science geek. I bet his fingers were itching to play with all the equipment laid out on the long tables in the tent.

"Mom just set up this system to generate water," Dave explained. He sounded really proud. "Until she showed up, everyone in the compound had to trek out to this underground spring about eight miles away and haul water back."

"It's nothing too innovative," Dave's mother said. "Everyone knows that water is made of hydrogen and oxygen, and they are both incredibly common. All it takes is some energy to combine them—solar, wind, what have you—and you get $H_2O$."

"And you generate enough water for the whole compound that way?" Frank asked.

"Well, we recycle whatever we can," Dave's mom said.

"But the answer is yes," Dave jumped in.

"Janet!" A plump man with Einstein-wild hair burst into the tent. He wore a T-shirt with Einstein's picture and the words GREAT SPIRITS HAVE OFTEN ENCOUNTERED VIOLENT OPPOSITION FROM WEAK MINDS on the front.

Clearly the Einstein hair wasn't an accident. I wondered if I should tell the guy that it was the brain, not the 'do, that made Einstein a genius.

"Janet, you have to come look at the machine. I think I almost have it," Einstein Wannabe said to Dave's mother.

He turned to me and Frank. "Perpetual motion," he clarified. "The secret is magnets. Who would have thought it could be so simple?"

"Everything should be made as simple as possible, but not simpler," Frank said.

Huh?

Einstein Wannabe clapped Frank on the shoulder. "Yes! Exactly! I see there is a fellow devotee in our midst."

Oh. I got it. Frank had just hauled out an Einstein quote. My brother can actually quote Einstein. I told you he was a science geek.

---

## SUSPECT PROFILE

<u>Name</u>: Samuel Fisk, aka Wannabe Einstein

<u>Hometown</u>: San Jose, California

<u>Physical description</u>: Age 32, prematurely gray hair, blue eyes, 5'3", about 145 lbs., freckles.

<u>Occupation</u>: Member of the Heaven compound

<u>Background</u>: BS in physics, BS in biology, PhD in psychology; six-week voluntary stay in state mental facility; has daughter who lives with ex-wife.

<u>Suspicious behavior</u>: Gathers rattler venom and poisonous plants.

<u>Suspected of</u>: Ecoterrorism.

<u>Possible motives</u>: Determined to get his ideas out to the world at any cost.

---

"Come on!" Einstein Wannabe grabbed Dave's mom by the hand and towed her out of the tent.

Frank moved closer to one of the tables. "My mom doesn't like people in here when she's away," Dave said. "But you should come back later. She'll give you the full tour."

"That would be great," Frank said. We left Dave helping his dad hang the wash, and continued exploring the compound.

The smell of something baking took us in the direction of the dining hall tent. Whatever was cooking didn't smell like rutabagas. Or tofu. Actually, tofu doesn't really have a smell—or a taste.

It didn't take long to find the source of the smell. A rack of rolls was baking under a spiderweb of magnifying glasses.

"This is ingenious," Frank said. "Sun-powered cooking. No electricity."

"Why don't they just use a fire?" I asked.

"You mean burn trees—one of our greatest natural resources?" a familiar voice asked.

I turned and saw Petal standing behind me. "Well, yeah, I guess that's what I meant."

"It isn't as bad as burning fossil fuel," Frank said, attempting to bail me out. "No harm to the ozone layer."

"True," Petal said. "But trees moderate the climate. They improve air quality and conserve water. And animals depend on them for food and shelter."

She stepped closer to Frank and put her hand on his arm. "They are much too valuable to be used when there are so many other sources of energy."

"T-true," Frank stammered.

Yeah, he actually stammered. The guy can rappel down the side of a burning building, leap from a plane without a parachute. But he can hardly spit out a sentence around a pretty girl.

And Petal was looking especially pretty. She had her curly red hair in one of those Pebbles Flintstone ponytails on the top of her head. Is it just me, or is Pebbles hot? For a cartoon character, I mean.

"So what are the bow and arrow for?" Frank asked. He'd gotten his tongue back in working order. "Hunting tofu?"

I shouldn't rag on Frank. I hadn't even noticed that Petal had a quiver of arrows over one shoulder and a bow in the other hand. I'd been too focused on her hair.

"We don't hunt at the compound," Petal said. "You've probably noticed that we don't eat meat."

That would be a yes.

"Mr. Stench doesn't believe in eating anything

that has a face," Petal continued. "Neither do I."

"So why the bow and arrow?" I repeated Frank's question.

"Just for fun. See that bale of hay down there?" Petal didn't wait for an answer. She strung one of the arrows, then let it fly.

It hit the bale dead center.

Petal immediately got another arrow in place. I heard the string *twang*. Then I saw the second arrow neatly slice the first in half.

It was even better than Stench's attack on the pineapple. "Either of you want to try?"

A loud gong prevented me from uttering a big, "Totally."

"Time to go into town with Mr. Stench," Petal said.

Stench was leaving the compound. Score. That meant Frank and I could do some serious investigation. Maybe get into that locked "thinkatorium."

"He wants you guys to come with us." Petal propped the bow and the quiver of arrows against the tent. "Come on. He hates to be kept waiting."

Clearly, we had no choice. Frank, Petal, and I ran over to the Seussmobile and climbed in. Dave and a couple of guys we hadn't met were already in the back. Stench had the wheel. Mondo had shotgun.

I squeezed my way past a bunch of paint cans

and took a seat. I couldn't help noticing that Petal made sure to sit next to Frank.

"So what are we going to do in town?"

It seemed like everyone at the compound lived off the land, but there were a few things they had to buy. Stuff for the labs, clearly.

"Just a little mission," Stench answered for Petal. "Don't worry. You two will have fun. I promise."

A mission. I didn't like the way that sounded. You didn't call running errands a mission.

What exactly did Stench have planned?

# 10.

## SPLASH!

The van hit a bump. Petal knocked into me—and stayed there. Her shoulder pressed against mine.

I caught Joe rolling his eyes. It's not like I'd done anything to encourage Petal. Her name was Petal, for one thing. It was hard to imagine going out with a girl called Petal Northstar. Especially because I suspected she'd chosen the name herself.

But more important, Petal was a suspect. And you can't get emotionally involved with a suspect. That's pretty much Crime Fighting 101.

"How'd you know that stuff about how burning wood doesn't affect the ozone layer?" Petal asked me.

It wasn't a hard question. But my girl difficulty was kicking in. It's not just the blushing, which is bad enough. My tongue also seems to double in size, so I can hardly talk. And my brain goes into low gear. So even if I could talk, I wouldn't have anything human-sounding to say.

"Alex is a science geek," Joe volunteered.

*Thank you, Joe.* Even I could have come up with an answer that made me look less like a dork.

"I used to have a crush on Bill Nye, the Science Guy. You know, from TV?" Petal confessed. And she actually blushed. It looked okay on her. Just turning her cheeks a nice pink.

"Are you serious?" Dave asked from behind us.

"I know, I know. He's so goofy with that little bow tie and everything," Petal said. "But I just loved how he got all glowy when he talked about science. He had passion, you know?"

I inched over on the seat to put a little space between the two of us. But Petal used another bump to get right back up against me.

Joe let out an extra long, extra loud sigh. "We're almost there," Dave said, misinterpreting the cause of the sigh.

Almost there. Those words almost made me forget about Petal. The mission—whatever it turned out to be—was getting close.

I glanced up at Stench. He seemed calm and happy, but he still had his humongo sword.

The ride grew smoother as Stench pulled the van off the dirt road and onto a paved one. A few moments later we entered a small town.

We passed a park with a white gazebo in the center, then turned onto what was clearly the town's main street. Shops lined both sides. I spotted a little grocery store. A movie theater. A drugstore. Some clothes shops.

Stench pulled into an empty parking place. "Get ready," he told us. "I need to make a purchase. It's go time as soon as I get back."

He climbed out of the van. Mondo, too.

"Great, they're back," I heard someone outside say.

Dave squatted next to the closest paint can and used a Swiss Army knife to pry off the top. The paint inside was a deep red. He moved on to the next can. More red.

"So what is this mission, anyway?" Joe asked. "I'm ready for the fun!"

I knew him well enough to tell that his enthusiasm was fake. But I bet he had everyone else fooled. Joe is first-rate undercover.

"It's going to blow your mind, little brother," Solar Man said. "Just go with the flow. It makes the first time so much better."

"Cool," Joe said.

What else could he say?

"Go back where you came from, hippie freaks!" a man shouted as he walked past the van. He slammed his fist down on the windshield. Hard.

The van rocked. Paint sloshed out of one of the open cans and on to the floor. The smell filled my nostrils.

"The chief is back!" Solar Man announced.

A second later the van's front door swung open. Stench deposited a paper sack on his seat. "Let's move," he ordered.

Petal slid open the side door. She grabbed an open can of paint and stepped out. I glanced around for rollers or brushes but didn't see any.

I had an idea where this was headed. And I didn't like it.

Solar Man grabbed a can of paint, then joined Petal next to the van. Dave handed cans to Mondo and Stench, then took one for himself and jumped out.

"I opened cans for you guys too," he told Joe and me.

We picked up the cans and joined the others, huddling there between the van and the SUV parked next to it.

"Alex and J. J., just follow the others," Stench instructed. He turned his head and eyes on the sidewalk. I heard the voices and footfalls of people approaching.

"Now!" Stench shouted.

He rushed the sidewalk. Lifted the can of paint. And dumped the contents on the shoulder of a woman carrying a leather purse.

"Let the animals live!" he shrieked. "Industrialization is evil!"

"Killer, killer, killer!" Dave raced up to a man wearing leather loafers and doused the guy's shoes with the deep red paint.

"This is their blood!" Solar Man joined the fray. He managed to splash a woman and her little girl with one swoop of his can. Petal was right behind him, ready to pour her paint on the next innocent bystander.

I glanced at Joe. There was only one thing to do.

"Animal murderers!" I tore up to the sidewalk and splashed the paint onto the ground where there was already a puddle of red.

Joe pretended to trip. He spilled his can into the gutter.

"Back, back, back!" Stench ordered.

I joined the dash back to the van.

Two teenage boys from the town blocked our path.

The shorter one advanced. "Get those tree-loving freaks!"

# 11.
## RUN!

A third guy joined Beefy and Scrawny—and I heard more feet pounding toward us. In a second, the group from the compound could be outnumbered.

I didn't think any of the anti-tree-loving-freak group was going to want to hear how Frank and I didn't really throw paint on anyone. Or how we barely knew the actual paint throwers.

So there was only one thing to do.

"Run!" Dave yelled.

Yeah, that was the one thing.

Mondo hustled Stench down the sidewalk to the right. Dave and Solar Man went left. Frank, Petal, and I bolted down an alley between the drugstore and Ye Olde Toy Shoppe.

An alley that happened to dead end at the back of another building.

At least there was a door. I grabbed the doorknob with both hands. Twisted. It didn't budge.

Petal shoved up beside me and pounded on the door. I shot a glance over my shoulder. We didn't have time to wait for anyone to let us in.

Scrawny and two new friends—I'll call them Red Face and Buzz Cut—were bearing down on us.

"Up!" Frank yelled.

That was the only safe direction to go. I used the doorknob as a foothold. That got me high enough that I was able to grab the rain gutter.

It creaked under my weight as I hauled myself onto the roof. "Come on, come on!" I urged Petal. I dropped to my stomach and leaned down.

Frank cupped his hands and gave Petal a boost. I grabbed her wrists and hauled her up beside me. Then Frank started climbing up the gutter drain.

The gutter held for him. Barely.

I hoped it wouldn't for Scrawny and company—because they were definitely coming after us. Red Face already had his sneaker positioned on the doorknob.

"Let's move!" Petal shouted as we got to the top of the building. She pulled herself to her feet and raced across the roof—and when she got to the edge, she didn't hesitate. She leaped across to the next one.

Frank and I were half a step behind her. And the *thud, thud, thud* I heard made it clear that the townies were right behind us.

"Get those mutants," one of them shouted.

Pain exploded in the center of my back. One of those butt breaths had thrown a rock at me!

"Over here!" Frank yelled.

He veered across the roof. "Jump!" he ordered. He hurled himself off the building.

I didn't think. I just followed my brother.

I didn't go splat on the sidewalk. I went *ka-bang*—on the top of the van! A second later, Petal landed half on top of me.

What's the deal? Do I look like a big foam mattress or something?

I used one hand to grab tight to one of the solar panels. I used the other to wave good-bye to Scrawny, Buzz Cut, and Red Face.

"I'm going to miss those guys," I told Frank as the van took a corner.

Frank didn't laugh. What did I tell you? No sense of humor.

The van slowed, then came to a stop.

"That was beyond belief!" Dave cried as he slid open the side door.

Frank, Petal, and I scrambled off the top of the van and climbed inside. I shoved the door shut behind us and we were off.

"Inspiring," Stench said. He sounded impressed with what the other had done.

*Yeah,* I thought. *Real inspiring.* We'd managed to escape from some guys who were pissed off that we'd thrown paint on a bunch of innocent people.

It's not like Scrawny and Beefy and the gang didn't have a good reason to come after us. They were the good guys in a way.

And Frank and I were in the van with the bad guys. True, we didn't throw paint on anybody. But we were there. We didn't stop it from happening. No time.

Plus, it would have blown our cover.

There was no way to feel okay about what went down. But Frank and I had made what we thought was the best call.

I glanced over at my brother. Petal was all snuggled up against him again—and he looked like he couldn't wait to get away from her.

She didn't seem quite as cool to me anymore. Not after I'd seen her throwing that paint.

Half an hour later, we were back at the compound. Just in time for lunch: spinach and tofu patties with salad.

Salad never looked so good to me.

I heaped another helping onto my wooden plate and passed the bowl to Einstein Wannabe, who was sitting next to me on the palm-frond floor mat.

"I appreciate your love of the solar panels," he told Solar Man. "But they can only take us so far. Geothermal energy is my pick. There's all that heat at the core of our planet. Just waiting to be turned into steam."

Petal nodded in approval from her seat next to Frank. "Mama Earth is ready to provide. With the right turbines you can run almost anything with steam."

"Why go to the center of the earth for something we have right over our heads?" Solar Man argued. "You don't have to dig for what Papa Sun provides."

Mama Earth and Papa Sun. Gag me with a tofu patty.

"What we need is more wind turbines," Dave's dad chimed in. He smiled at his wife. "I'm no scientist like Janet, but wind seems the way to go. There are acres and acres of land that could be wind farmed."

"The problem with that is lack of infrastructure," Janet said.

"So we set up the systems we would need to get

the energy to the places it's needed," Dave's father said.

"There's always hydroelectricity," a man in a long robe like Stench's suggested. "The motion of the tides can create energy."

"Why not use them all?" Petal suggested. "Sun, water, the earth's natural heat, wind. Anything but fossil fuel!"

At the words "fossil fuel" the whole group erupted. I couldn't even figure out who was saying what. "Wasteful." "Ozone destroying." "Polluting."

Stench headed over to see what the hoo-ha was about. He jumped right in. "The use of fossil fuel will bring about the destruction of civilization," he boomed.

Every head in the dining hall turned toward him. "Fossil fuel makes us slaves," he continued. "Slaves to the countries that produce the most oil. And every drop of that oil we use brings us one step closer to annihilating the earth."

Solar Man gave a hoot of agreement. Everyone else in the place applauded. I joined in. Frank did too.

"But they won't see, will they?" Stench asked. He moved past our group and began pacing around the dining hall. "We tell them and tell them, but they won't hear."

Stench threw up his arms. "We are trying to save their lives, and they call us madmen. So what are we to do?"

It felt like everyone had stopped breathing. The big tent was silent as we waited for Stench to continue.

"We give them a taste, that's what we do," Stench finally went on. "We give them a taste of the destruction to come. The only thing that will get their attention is pain."

He began to pace more quickly. "When they feel the pain, they will change. And the world will be saved!"

More applause. No one asked what kind of pain and destruction Stench was talking about. No one suggested other ways of communication.

"I have a plan. You will all have the chance to play a part when the time comes. And it is coming soon. Be ready. Stay strong. You will be given assignments when the time is right. And we will be the ones who have saved our precious planet. We will be—"

"I've gotta hit the bathroom," Frank whispered to me.

"Me too."

Guys aren't like girls. We don't go to the bathroom together. But no one in our little circle seemed to think it was strange. They were all too busy listening to Stench. Keeping low to the ground—and out of Stench's view—we snuck out.

"I figured this was the perfect time to look around a little," Frank said once we were in the clear. "Stench didn't seem like he was going to shut up for a while. And clearly he wasn't going to give any solid information about his plans."

"All that stuff about pain and destruction. I think he was talking about more than throwing some more paint."

"Yeah," Frank agreed as we walked. "The guy has lost it. I think he's capable of anything."

"Do you think he really has a plan? Or do you think it's all talk?"

"That's what we have to—"

"Quiet." I grabbed Frank's arm and pulled him into a crouch beside me. "Mondo," I whispered.

As we watched, Stench's bodyguard laced the flap of a large tent closed. Then he headed toward the row of Porta-Pottis.

"I've never seen Mondo away from Stench," I commented.

"Which makes me think whatever is in that tent is important," Frank answered. "It's too big to be his sleeping quarters. Let's check it out."

We waited until Mondo was in one of the potties

with the door shut behind him. Then we raced toward the tent. I untied the flap, and Frank and I stepped inside.

"That thing isn't solar powered," Frank said.

I couldn't say anything for a second. And that hardly ever happens to me.

"A helicopter," I finally managed to get out. "What does Stench need a helicopter for?"

"Maybe for emergencies. To get one of his people to a hospital if they needed it?" Frank suggested.

He moved up to the cockpit and opened the door. "You've got to see this."

I was still trying to take in the fact that we'd found a copter in the antitechnology compound. They didn't even use washing machines. Or have TV. And Stench had a helicopter?

"What are you waiting for?"

I hurried up to Frank and stared into the cockpit. Low airspeed indicator. Doppler NAV. Tachometer. "Notice anything weird?"

"Like what?" Frank said.

"No stick!" I burst out.

"Right. There's no way to fly this thing!"

"Can I help you boys?"

I spun around. Mondo stood in the entrance to the tent. For a huge guy, he sure was quiet.

My brain felt like a hamster on a wheel. We needed an excuse for why we were in here—but I couldn't think of anything.

Searching for a bathroom, maybe? No. A tent and a Porta-Potti don't look anything alike!

"Dave's mom invited us to take a look at her lab," Frank told Mondo.

My brother sounded completely calm. But I knew he had to be freakin' the same way I was.

"She didn't give you very good directions. Janet's lab is only a few tents away from yours."

"We were just going by size," I jumped in. "We figured the lab had to be in a big tent—and this is one of the bigger ones. Besides the dining hall. And we knew it wasn't in the dining hall."

*Enough,* I ordered myself. When you're lying, it's better not to blab too much. You just get yourself in trouble that way.

Mondo ran his hand over his crewcut. Did he believe us?

What would he do if he didn't?

"Go back to your own tent," he told us.

Were we under house arrest?

"We all take at least an hour's rest in the middle of the day. A siesta. It's the best way to survive the desert," Mondo continued. "You can pay a visit to Janet's lab later."

"A siesta sounds good," Frank said. We hurried past the bodyguard and went straight to our tent. We'd have to do more snooping later.

"That helicopter is definitely suspicious," I told Frank. I flopped down on my sleeping bag. "He had to get it custom-made. And why? Why a copter with no controls?"

"The only answers I can come up with are bad ones. Like you want to drop a bomb without putting a pilot in danger. Or you want to spray hazardous chemicals."

"Or spray gas and start a fire," I added. "Pain and destruction."

"We've got to work this assignment fast." Frank stretched out on his bag and tucked his hands underneath his pillow. "We don't know when Stench is going to make his next move."

He frowned and sat back up.

"What?" I asked.

"Somebody left something under my pillow."

# 12.

# ON FIRE

"What is it?" Joe demanded.

I reached under my thin pillow and pulled out a folded sheet of paper. I opened it and read the message aloud: "Check Stench house."

Joe snatched the note away. "No signature." He flipped the paper over just to double-check. "But at least someone is on our side."

"Maybe," I answered.

Joe makes decisions quickly. I like to have more time to think.

"You think it could be a setup?"

"I think the only person I trust in this place is you," I told my brother.

"We do have to get a look in Stench's house. Possible setup or not." Joe refolded the note and handed it back to me. "The one building with a lock and no windows is definitely the place to keep information on a secret plan."

"Yep."

"You brought the lock picks, right?" Joe reached for my backpack.

"They're in there. But I have a feeling Mondo's going to be watching us," I answered. "We're going to have to choose our time carefully."

"If only Stench hadn't dragged us on that mission today," Joe complained. "With him and Mondo gone, it would have been the perfect time for a little breaking and entering."

"I've been thinking about that. I bet Stench brings every newbie on a mission as soon as possible," I said. "To make sure they're his kind of people."

"Or to *turn them into* his kind of people," Joe suggested. "I still feel slimy about today. We didn't really do anything—"

"—but it feels like we did," I finished for him.

We waited out the siesta time. If Mondo was keeping an eye on us, I wanted him to see we were following his instructions. But as soon as the hour was up, Joe and I headed back out into the compound. I did a Mondo scan. Didn't see him anywhere.

Petal, however, hurried right up. Had she been watching our tent? Had someone asked her to? Mondo? It seemed strange that she was on us the second we stepped out of the tent.

Joe here. I have to step in because Frank is so out of it. It's not weird at all that Petal came right up to us. Of course she was watching our tent. She wanted more Frank time.

Do you understand, Frank? The girl liiiikes you.

Go away, Joe. I'm telling the story.

Okay, maybe Joe's right. Maybe Petal was hanging around because she wanted to accidentally-on-purpose run into me. See my famous blush. Hear me stammer like Elmer Fudd. Whatever.

"I'm on my way to do a little more target practice." Petal waved her bow. "Want to come?"

"Sure," I said.

Joe looked at me in surprise. But I figured we needed to get a sense of Stench's routine. That way we'd know when we should make an attempt to search his house.

Why not use Petal to get some info?

"Have you ever tried archery?" Petal asked as she led the way over to the bales of hay she used as targets.

"Only a couple of times," Joe answered. "We're more track and field guys."

"That's cool." Petal stopped about thirty yards from the target. "A bullet will go about a hundred yards without any drop in trajectory. An arrow starts dropping a lot faster. That's something to keep in mind when you're aiming."

Joe raised his eyebrows. Why was this girl talking about bullets? How much did she know about firearms? And why? Just another hobby?

Petal handed me her bow. She moved close behind me and practically hugged me as she helped me position the arrow.

"Get a room," Joe joked.

Not funny. He thinks I have no sense of humor. What he doesn't get is that a lot of the time, he's not funny.

"I wish I could," Petal answered. She grinned. "I wouldn't mind giving up a tent for an actual room."

"Stench only believes in rooms for himself?" I asked.

Petal stepped away. "Go," she said. Not smiling anymore.

I let the arrow fly. It hit the hay at least.

"Mr. Stench has a lot of demands on his time," Petal told me, her voice cool. "He needs more privacy than the rest of us."

"Right. It's a thinkatorium," Joe said. He held out his hand for the bow. I gave it to him.

"Any tips?" he asked Petal.

"Aim and shoot," she told him. No hugging for Joe. He should be grateful.

"Mr. Stench really does get the best ideas in there," Petal said once Joe's arrow had landed. Landed closer to the center of the bale of hay than mine had.

"He's in there right now," Petal continued. "Sometimes, once he's inside, we don't see him for days. But when he comes out, he always has a million new plans."

*For pain and destruction,* I silently added.

"Days, huh?" Joe asked.

"Sometimes days. Not always," Petal said. "Your turn, Alex." She took the bow from Joe and handed it to me. Then she got her arms wrapped around me again.

"Did I mention Alex is one of my favorite names?" she asked just as I let the arrow fly. It missed the target. Entirely.

Petal laughed, but not in a mean way.

I reminded myself that she'd been hurling paint on people a few hours ago. I couldn't trust her.

I suddenly spotted Dave pushing a wheelbarrow of what looked like vegetable peelings. "Need some help?" I asked. I was ready to get away from Petal.

"Sure," Dave answered. "I'm going to add this to

the compost heap, then do some weeding in the garden."

Perfect. The garden had a clear view of Stench's house. If he came out, Joe and I would know about it.

We weeded until the sun started going down, but the door to Stench's windowless house stayed shut. Mondo left once and came back with a couple of pineapples—snack or sword practice. That's it.

When it got dark, the compound shut down. That's the way it is when you live in a place with limited electricity. (Solar Man could only do so much.)

Joe and I headed back to our tent. The sun had gotten to me again. I knew Joe was saying something, but I couldn't keep my eyes open.

I fell into a dream. I was back in the lawyer's office, where Joe and I had had our last mission. But Joe wasn't with me. Petal was.

In the dream it was easy to talk to her. And in the dream I didn't suspect her of anything.

"Do you smell smoke?" Petal asked.

I told her not to worry about it. Yeah, the building was on fire. But we could just rappel down. And it was only a dream. One of those dreams where you kind of know it's a dream.

I started to cough. Which was weird. I mean,

there was smoke in the office. But it was dream smoke. And I knew that.

*Wake up,* I told myself. *This is annoying.*

Don't you wish you could channel surf in dreams? But no. I was stuck in this one.

"The place is on fire!" Petal exclaimed. But her voice came out sounding like Joe's.

"Wake up, Frank!" Joe shouted. "The tent is on fire."

My eyes snapped open.

This was no dream.

Flames covered the ceiling of the tent!

# 13.

## PAYBACK!

Frank and I grabbed our packs. As I stumbled out of the tent, a motorcycle almost ran over my toes. Beefy was on the back. "Go back where you belong, hippie!" he howled.

He splashed gas on the tent next to ours as he zoomed past. Scrawny was right behind him. Without slowing his bike down, he touched a torch to the gas-splattered canvas.

*Whomp!*

A fireball exploded.

A bearded man raced out of the tent and started after Beefy and Scrawny. So did Frank and I.

Helpless. We didn't have our bikes. We didn't even have a garden hose to turn on the tents!

"Bucket brigade!" Frank cried.

111

I tried to remember how much water was produced in Janet's lab. Didn't matter. We had to try something.

"There are some buckets behind the dining hall," the bearded man shouted.

The three of us raced toward the dining hall. I couldn't see much. Just flashes lit by headlights or flashlights or torches.

A Jeep zigzagged through the garden, tearing up the crops.

Red Face ran past on foot. He used a knife to slash one of the tents as he went. "This is payback!" he screamed. "You thought you got away—but we followed you. You're going down, freaks!"

A stink bomb hit Frank on the back of the neck. I didn't even see where it came from.

"Get outta here!" a man shouted as he used a baseball bat to smash the magnifying glasses of the stove.

A teenage girl behind the wheel of a beat-up convertible backed over two of the compound bicycles. She blew me a kiss as I tore by her.

And then it was over. There must have been a signal, but I missed it. The shouts stopped. The motorcycles and vehicles roared off.

The sound of my own heartbeat filled my ears as we retrieved the buckets and filled them with water.

But it was too late. There was nothing left of our tent to save. Nothing left of our neighbor's.

As the sun began to come up, Frank and I wandered through the compound, joining with the others in a sad, silent parade as we took in the destruction.

"Everyone to the garden!"

Stench's voice filled the compound. He spoke through the megaphone again. "Everyone to the garden immediately."

It didn't take long for everyone in the community to gather. I stared at the tire tracks running across the neat rows of vegetables. Smashed vegetables.

How long would it take to repair the damage that had been done in less than half an hour?

We all formed a circle around Stench. He dropped the megaphone. "Now, first things first. Was anyone hurt?"

There were a bunch of "no"s and headshakes.

Stench nodded. "So they stuck to property damage." He began to pace. "Can anyone tell me why you think we were attacked tonight?"

I thought it was pretty obvious. Payback, like Red Face had yelled. We'd attacked people in the town. People in the town attacked us.

Of course, I didn't say that. I was supposed to

seem like a good little Stench follower. Nobody else said anything either. I guess everybody knew Stench liked to answer his own questions.

"Oil," Stench said.

Huh?

"The oil companies have been out to get me ever since I started Heaven," Stench continued. "They know if we succeed in our mission to create alternate energy sources, they will be out of business."

Stench pulled his sword free of its scabbard. "Now, it may have looked like it was just a few hotheads from town who did this to us. But the oil companies were behind it. Oil company dollars."

*Swish! Swish!* The sword cut through the air.

"Yes, they're out to get us." He pointed the sword at Solar Man. "Out to get you, my brother. Because they know your way works."

"Yes!" Solar Man's panels clanked as he thrust his fist into the air.

"Out to get you"—Stench pointed his sword at Einstein Wannabe—"because they are afraid of the very idea of geothermal."

Einstein Wannabe nodded, his wild hair getting even wilder.

"They tremble at the very word hydroelectricity," Stench said to the man dressed in the long white robe identical to Stench's—the one who had been praising hydroelectricity at lunch.

Man, Stench was a genius. He was stroking egos like crazy. Making everyone feel so important.

"Those oil companies think all they have to do is pay off a few townies to take care of us." Stench brought his sword to his forehead and sighed. "They think they are so smart. With all their MBAs and scientists working for them."

Stench spun in a fast circle. "But I say that there is no one working at one of those fat cat oil companies who is smarter than any one of you."

Applause burst out in the circle.

"I say the oil companies' reign of terror is about to come to an end! We aren't going to take this from them, are we?" Stench's eyes blazed.

"NO!" everyone in the circle yelled.

I mouthed the words. I couldn't bring myself to become part of the mob. I think Frank did the same.

"Are we gonna make 'em pay?" Stench bellowed.

"Yes!" the crowd shouted back. Smiles on every face.

"You're damn right we are! Tonight at midnight is payback time!" Stench exclaimed. "Be ready. Because we are going into town!"

Cheers. Screams. Applause.

My stomach churned. Maybe this would be a good thing. I pulled Frank aside. "This is it. Our shot. They go into town. We go into Stench's house."

I glanced over at the building. It had escaped the torches.

"It is the perfect time," Frank agreed. "But we have to go into town with Stench. You heard how furious he is. If he gets too out of control, we have to be there to stop it."

"Tonight's not his big plan," I argued. "He didn't know this attack was coming. He'll probably just do something like the paint again."

"We can't know that, Joe."

"But we have to risk it. We have to find out what his big plan is. If we don't, we might not be able to put an end to it."

Frank didn't look convinced. "What if he is going to put the big plan in motion tonight? What if he decided to move up the schedule because of what happened?"

He had a point. "How about this? We know that the coptor without the controls has a part in his plan. It *has* to, right? You don't have a thing like that just sitting around."

"Agreed."

"So tonight, we hide out in the tent with the coptor. We don't want to be in sight when Stench and the others leave for town, anyway," I said.

"But if Stench is putting the big plan in motion, we'll know," Frank agreed. "Because somebody will come for the helicopter."

"Right!"

We slid under the back of the helicopter tent just after sundown. We figured it was better to be hidden away early.

My biggest problem was trying not to doze off. Sitting there in the dark and everything. But that stopped being a problem when somebody grabbed me by the back of the neck.

Did I mention how quiet Mondo can be?

He looked from me to Frank. "Mr. Stench requests the honor of your presence."

# 14.

## THE FUSE

Mondo marched us over to the van and shoved us inside. Petal, the guy Joe had named Einstein Wannabe, and Solar Man were already in place.

"You're late," Stench said from the driver's seat. "I said midnight."

I waited for Mondo to tell Stench where he'd found us. He didn't.

Did that mean the copter was a secret? Stench seemed to keep a lot of secrets from his followers.

"Lateness shows a lack of attention to detail," Stench continued as we started down the road through the desert. The solar panels had clearly stored up plenty of energy during daylight hours. We were going at least seventy.

"That can be deadly in our missions." Stench's voice filled every corner of the van.

"Sorry," Joe muttered.

"One mistake, and someone could die tonight."

"Got it," I said.

It definitely didn't sound like we were going to do more paint splattering—and that thought was confirmed by the absence of paint cans.

And something else was different from the last trip to town. Something besides Dave being replaced by Einstein Wannabe.

The van was bumping and jerking like last time. Petal had managed to get herself situated tight up against me. Mondo had shotgun again. Stench was driving.

What was it? The inside of my brain started to itch. Whatever it was was important.

I looked over at Joe. He signed one word to me. "Gas."

That was it! The inside of the van reeked of gas. And the van ran on solar power.

Something was very wrong. I scanned the vehicle, trying to figure out the source of the gas fumes. I caught Stench watching me in the rearview mirror.

"No paint tonight?" I asked. I tried to sound eager. Like I was looking forward to whatever was coming.

"Don't need it," Stench answered. His smile turned my spine to ice.

"What is our mission tonight?" Joe asked. "I'm sorry we were late—we didn't get to hear it."

Stench's smile just grew wider in reply.

"Mr. Stench gives us information on a need-to-know basis," Petal said into my ear. "He doesn't really like questions."

A leader who expected his followers to obey without asking questions. I flashed for a moment on those faces I'd seen on Mount Rushmore. Our country was founded on debate.

Did Stench know that? If he did, he obviously didn't care.

The muscles in my back and shoulders, and even my jaw, tightened as the van rolled into town. I felt Petal tense beside me. What was going to happen? *Where* was it going to happen?

We rode down the short main street, then hung a left. I took in the rows of houses. Imagining the people sleeping inside.

Was one of them Stench's target? Was he planning to use the gas to burn down one of these houses?

No. Another couple of turns and we were on a much more commercial strip. Fast-food places. A strip mall with a mini-mart. A sporting goods store. Parking lot.

Stench made a left and parked across the street from the parking lot. "Everybody out," he ordered.

I noticed he had a paper bag in his hand when he climbed out of the van. Wet splotches had appeared in the paper.

I made a point to position myself behind Stench, downwind. The gas fumes were coming from the bag.

Stench led the way across the street. A high aluminum fence circled the car lot. Stench nodded to Mondo.

Mondo pulled a pair of bolt cutters out of the back of his pants. With one snap, the lock fell off the gate. Mondo opened it for us with a bow.

Rows of bright-colored pennants flapped over our heads. A giant neon sign that read SPORT UTILITY SALE glowed in the showroom window.

They weren't kidding. The lot was filled with SUVs, SSRs, Hummers. A jeep that was probably seven feet wide. Even a monster truck that was probably more to attract people to the lot than anything else.

Solar Man let out a tortured groan behind me.

Petal shook her head. "Commercials make you think driving these things are about going off-road. Getting back to nature. But they destroy the environment."

"And no matter how often we say it, they won't hear," Stench said. "No matter how many articles we write, they won't see."

He shook his head. "Global warming, smog emissions, dependence on foreign oil . . ."

Einstein Wannabe shook his fists in the air. "No fossil fuel! No fossil fuel!"

Stench put his finger to his lips. Einstein Wannabe instantly went silent.

"We need to do more than speak and write," Stench continued. "We need to save humanity from itself. And the first thing we have to do is get their attention."

Stench pulled a damp cloth out of the paper bag. I got a strong whiff of gas. He unwrapped the cloth. I saw a coil of rope.

I knew instantly what it was for.

The rope was a fuse.

Stick one end in the gas tank. Light the other. The flame would follow the gas-soaked rope all the way to the gallons of gas. Then . . .

"Which of these gas-guzzling demons should be our victim?" Stench asked. "I say that one." He pointed to a big red SUV.

Mondo, Solar Man, and Wannabe Einstein let out a cheer. Stench started toward the vehicle.

I glanced at Joe. I could tell by his face we were in agreement. No way were we letting this happen.

"Stench!" I shouted.

He half turned, not looking pleased at the interruption.

"You think it's wrong to eat anything with a face. You want to live in peace with the entire planet," I called.

"That's right," Stench answered.

"Doesn't that include human beings?" I demanded.

"We have faces," Joe added. "We live on the Earth."

Stench jerked his thumb toward the SUV. "That is *not* a human being."

"Some human makes his living selling it," I answered. "Some human will lose thousands and thousands of dollars."

"To learn a *lesson,*" Stench said. "Haven't you been listening? I do care about humanity. I'm trying to save lives."

"We're all going to die if people don't start listening to Mr. Stench!" Einstein Wannabe agreed.

"People have to see the light!" Solar Man chimed in. Stench turned back around and strode toward the SUV.

Joe nodded at me.

And we both launched ourselves at him.

I hit Stench behind the knees with one shoulder.

We both went down hard. Stench on the asphalt, me on top of Stench.

He managed to flip over on his back. He used both feet to kick me in the chest.

I flew off him, but shoved myself to my feet a second later.

Joe had managed to get one arm wrapped around Stench's throat. He was clawing at Joe's face, but Joe wasn't letting go.

I figured it was time to go for the gut. Stench's stomach was vulnerable to attack. I backed up to get a little speed going . . . and found myself dangling in the air, thanks to Mondo.

His arm was like a vise. I tried to execute a roll, but I only moved about an inch.

Mondo strode over to Joe. He snatched him up and stuck him under his other arm.

"Take them to the van," Stench ordered. "Solar Man, I give you the honor of lighting the fuse."

I felt like a sack of groceries. It was humiliating. Mondo wasn't even breathing hard when he dumped Joe and me back into the van.

He positioned himself in front of the open door.

Less than five seconds later, the others came racing back across the street. They hurled themselves inside.

We all stared out the window as the SUV exploded.

# 15.

## NOWHERE TO HIDE

"I'm very disappointed in you two," Stench told Frank and me as he drove away. "I thought I could trust you."

I stared at the back of his head. How much did I want to get my arm wrapped around his neck again? Pretty much more than anything. But Mondo was sitting right next to him. As usual.

Want to take a guess at what was second on my list of wants?

If you guessed coming up with a foolproof escape plan, give yourself a big gold star. Because now that Frank and I had "disappointed" Stench, I thought some very *unheavenly* things were going to happen to us when we got back to Heaven.

So, about that foolproof escape plan. We needed one, fast. From a van zooming through the desert at about seventy miles an hour.

Hmmm.

My brain was one big blank. I looked at Frank. There didn't seem to be a lightbulb over his head either.

The ride back to the compound felt like it took minutes instead of the usual half an hour. *Think,* I ordered myself as we passed the NOW ENTERING HEAVEN sign. *Think.*

Hardly any time left.

I looked over at Frank again. He deliberately moved his gaze to the van's sliding door.

And I got it.

Between Frank and me, I was closer to the door. I pretended to tie my shoe to get a little closer.

The van slowed down as we reached the rows of tents. I made my move. I yanked open the door and hurled myself out.

Pain in my knee. In my shoulder. Sand up my nose. Down my throat.

"Get them!" Stench yelled.

A hand grabbed my arm. Pulled me to my feet.

I peered into the darkness.

Frank. It was Frank.

We tore down the closest row of tents. No point in ducking into one of them. Almost every tent held a Stench follower.

And it wouldn't take the others long to search the dining hall or the lab or the tents that held other supplies. We definitely couldn't go back to the copter tent.

Racing out into the desert probably wasn't the smartest move either. It was a death trap with no food or water.

I stumbled, went down on one knee—the same one I'd landed on when I jumped out of the van. I found myself staring at a wooden shovel.

I took a moment to look around. We were in the garden.

"Frank! The compost heap!" I whispered. I dashed over to the large heap of vegetable peelings and started to dig with the shovel. Soon we heard other voices:

"They couldn't have gotten far!"

"Check all the unoccupied tents!"

"They're going to pay!"

The voices were getting closer. I dug faster. When I had a hole just big enough for Frank and me, we slid in.

FYI: slimy vegetables down the shirt—don't try it.

"There's no place to hide!" a guy called. I thought it was Dave.

"I assume they started back to town. Perhaps they found their bikes, although they would have made noise." That voice was definitely Stench's. "I'm sure they'll want to tell the police who blew up the SUV."

"Bikes. Good idea," Frank whispered.

He'd found our bikes. Shoot.

"We have to go after them. We can't let them get to the authorities," Stench demanded.

I heard the sound of footsteps moving away. "They're leaving," I said. A piece of old cabbage slid toward my mouth.

"Now what?" Frank asked. "We can't stay in here forever."

I spit the cabbage away from my mouth. "I think it's kinda homey," I answered. I thought for a moment. "We can't try to find our bikes right now. We only know one road out of here, and we could run right into Stench and the van."

"Too bad the helicopter doesn't have a stick," Frank said. "From the air, it would be no problem to find our way out of the desert."

I thought for another moment. "You know what we should do?"

"What?"

"Stench and Mondo are both away from the compound," I answered. "It's the perfect time to search Stench's house."

# 16.

# SURPRISE!

Joe and I made a quiet trip to our tent for my lock picks. I was glad I'd decided to pack them. (I wasn't sorry about the clean underwear, either. I was pretty sure my current pair was filled with rotten rutabagas.)

Afterward we crept through the dark compound to Stench's house. Joe held a microflashlight for me while I got to work. It's not like there were any streetlights or anything.

The lock was pretty basic. I stepped inside the house and automatically felt for a light switch, even though I knew I wouldn't find—

Wait. My fingers actually felt a little plastic switch! I hit it. The room flooded with light.

"Whoa!" Joe exclaimed. He walked in and shut the door behind us. "This place is—"

"—*not* ecofriendly," I finished for him.

It wasn't just that Stench's house was wired for electricity. The lines must have been run underground. He had a refrigerator. My eyes darted around the large room. And a TV. And a computer— the latest version. High-tech.

Joe headed straight for the fridge. He pulled out a couple of bottles of water and tossed me one. "I don't know about you, but I swallowed a cup of sand. And some slimed-out cabbage."

I unscrewed the water, rinsed my mouth, then walked across the room to spit in the sink.

"Oh, man, Stench is such a fake." Joe had his head back in the fridge. "Unless they've figured out how to make a cow without a face. He has steak in here. Hamburger."

"Let's see if we can find something ATAC will be more interested in," I said. I figured the computer was the place to start.

Joe yanked the biggest desk drawer free and sat down on the floor with it. "Come to Papa," he muttered as he started shifting through the papers.

Stench hadn't bothered with a password. I guess he thought the lock on the door and Mondo were security enough.

I hit the Quicken icon. That program would let me see his banking records. How a guy gets and spends his money can be pretty interesting.

"Oh, sweet," Joe exclaimed. "That SUV Stench made Solar Man blow up? It looks like Stench *owns* it." He waved the pink slip.

"I don't get it," I said. "What was the point? What's the point of all of this? I mean, Stench obviously doesn't believe anything he says."

Joe shrugged. I turned my attention back to the computer and ran my eyes down a list of deposits and withdrawals. I hit PRINT.

"Did you find something?" Joe asked when he heard the printer cranking up.

"Oh, yeah. Stench has gotten several payments from a company called Petrol International," I told him. "Big ones."

"Petrol—as in oil? Oooh. Stench has been a bad boy." Joe raised his eyebrows as he scanned the printout. "A very bad boy. Turns out it wasn't just that SUV he owned. He owns the whole dealership."

"He's destroying the environment left and right," I said. "Hey, I just thought of something. How weird is it that this place didn't get touched when those townies came rampaging through?"

"Pretty strange," Joe agreed. "This building kind of stands out."

"I bet Stench paid them off. For some reason, he wants everyone here whipped into a frenzy."

"Ready for his plan. Whatever it is," Joe said.

I grabbed the sheet of paper from the printer. Which was right next to the landline phone.

*The phone!*

"Joe! Phone!" I burst out. "We can get some help."

"I can't believe I didn't think of looking for a phone first thing." Joe snatched up the receiver.

"Drop the phone, Hardy!"

# 17.

## STENCH'S PLAN

I dropped the phone. If I didn't, I figured Stench would order Mondo to pound me into the ground.

"How do you know our real names?" Frank demanded.

Right. Stench had called me "Hardy." I'd been so shocked to see him and Mondo, it hadn't quite registered.

Stench walked over to the leather sofa on the other side of the room and sat down. "We found your motorcycles in the desert," he answered. "Traced the registrations."

He waved his hand at Mondo. Mondo stalked toward me and Frank. He reached into the kangaroo pocket of his sweatshirt and pulled out some rope.

"We know you're not an environmentalist," I told Stench.

"That rope is very low-tech," Stench shot back as Mondo began to tie my hands together. "It looks like you boys have been busy." Stench nodded toward his desk. "How brilliant am I?"

*The guy's a complete loon,* I thought as Mondo tied my feet together. I wouldn't have been surprised if Stench's eyes started twirling like wind turbines.

"How brilliant is this place?" Stench looked from me to Frank. "Oh. You didn't put it together."

He shook his head, making a disappointed clucking sound with his tongue. "Well, I work for an oil company."

"Petrol International," Frank said. Mondo was tying him up now.

"And what do I do for them? Well, I'll tell you. I gather up wackos." Stench brought his hand up and began counting off on his fingers. "Solar Man: my first little wacko. Samuel Fisk: my Einstein-loving wacko. Petal Northstar: my little idealistic wacko. Janet Simkins: my intellectual wacko."

Stench smiled up at the ceiling. "I'm proudest of bringing Janet here. She might really have come up with something revolutionary."

I felt like puking. "So you get paid to make sure no one develops a good alternate energy source."

"You got part of it," Stench said.

"Oh, you are so sick," Frank burst out. "I get the rest. Your job was to encourage these people to do violent things. You wanted them to look bad."

"You got it. No one wants to listen to people who are throwing paint and blowing stuff up," Stench said. "I like you two. You're smart," he added. He pulled out a cigarette and lit up. "Too bad I'm going to have to kill you."

Gulp.

I mean, I don't know what I thought Stench would do to us. But my brain hadn't gotten to murder.

"And I know exactly when I'm going to do it," Stench told us. "Tomorrow. It's Earth Day—or, at least, close enough. It was a couple of months ago. But because it's my birthday, I've chosen to celebrate Earth Day again with you."

He started tapping his toe. Then he began to sing the "Happy Birthday" song. Except half the time, he turned it into "Happy Earth Day." And he made the last line, "I'll kill the Har-dees."

Catchy.

You know what I needed right now?

Yeah. A foolproof escape plan.

I felt like Frank and I would need to be Houdinis to get out of here. We were both tied up hand and foot—and Mondo wasn't taking his eyes off of us.

"I know exactly how I'm going to do it, too," Stench continued.

I didn't really want to hear the details of my demise. But knowing what Stench had planned would make it easier to avoid whatever it was.

I hoped.

"It's going to be part of my birthday present to myself. For my birthday, I'm going to blow up a nuclear power plant."

He said it like it was nothing. Like for his birthday he was going to buy himself a pair of underpants.

"You're insane!" Frank sounded horrified.

"Oh, no. Nuclear power is *evil.* It could destroy the oil industry," Stench answered. "I've gone over the plans very carefully. The Diablo Power Plant is twelve miles from San Luis Obispo. I'm going to crash the drone into it."

The drone. Right. The helicopter with no stick.

"Great technology," Stench continued. "Very similar to what we used in Afghanistan. I can fly it anywhere from the ground. You two will be able to get an up-close look. Because you'll be inside."

He turned to Mondo. "Isn't that perfect? Even if the plant doesn't blow, these two will die. And when their bodies are found, they'll be accused of terrorism."

A blast of nausea hit me as I imagined the headlines. Imagined Mom and Aunt Trudy reading them.

At least Dad would figure out the truth.

Stench stood up. "I'm so excited. I can't wait to get started. Mondo? Would you?"

For the second time I found myself pinned under Mondo's meaty arm. He carried me outside and walked me around the building. There he dumped me into a large wooden cart that stood there. The second he stalked away I started working on the ropes. Rubbing them on the edge of the cart. The friction heated up my wrists, but I didn't feel the ropes give at all.

I stopped when I saw Mondo carrying Frank toward the cart. He tossed my brother in next to me. Then he pulled us toward the tent with the copter.

Stench trailed behind us, humming his Birthday/Earth Day song.

When we reached the tent, Mondo unlaced the flap and pulled it open wide. I could see the drone inside. The death machine.

Stench pulled a remote out of the pocket of his long white robe. He hit a button, and the drone rolled out of the tent.

"Load it up!" Stench cried. He actually clapped his hands like an excited little kid.

Mondo grabbed Frank and started toward the drone. "Petal, help!" I shouted.

She was the only one I could think of who might help us. *Might.* She liked Frank. Maybe she liked him enough to go against Stench.

"Petal!" I shouted again. "Frank needs you!"

"Like you, Petal is a little tied up right now." Stench laughed so hard that he snorted. "I made a joke!" he cried. "Your little Petal is tied up—in the desert."

Mondo came back for me and tossed me into the drone cockpit next to Frank. "What do you mean? What did you do to her?"

Stench walked up to the side of the copter. "I just did what I had to do. I found out Petal was sneaking information to you. So I had someone tie her up and leave her in the desert."

"She'll die out there!" Frank yelled.

"That's the point," Stench answered. "Everyone can't have as exciting a death as the one I've prepared for you and your brother."

He stepped back and hit a button on the remote. The propeller began to spin.

"So the note we got telling us to check out Stench's house came from Petal," Frank said. His eyebrows were pulled together.

140

"Yeah, she likes you even more than I thought," I said.

"That can't be the reason. You don't go against your beliefs because you like someone," Frank answered.

The propeller spun faster.

"Uh, can we talk about the Petal situation later?" I asked Frank. "I think we're about to have liftoff."

Not that there was anything to do. If we managed to hurl ourselves out of the copter, Mondo would just shove us back in. Maybe when we—

"Drop the remote, Stench!"

I twisted around and saw Petal with her bow and arrow. She had an arrow pointed at Stench's head.

"Get her, Mondo!" Stench ordered.

"Take one step toward me, and your boss gets an arrow through the brain," Petal told Mondo. Her voice was cold and harsh.

But it turned warm when she called out to Frank. "Don't worry. I'm gonna get you out of there, Frank!"

I assumed when she got Frank out, she'd get me out too. I mean, I'm his brother. Right?

"Dear Petal, Petal, Petal," Stench crooned. "I taught you better than that. I taught you to love all living things."

"I can love a scorpion, Stench. I can love a rattler. But I can't love you," Petal shot back.

She let the arrow fly. It hit a tree six inches away from Stench's head. "You know I'm a lot better shot than that. Take it as a warning." She strung another arrow and pointed it at the center of Stench's forehead. "Mondo, untie them."

Mondo came toward me—with a knife in his hand. Within a second all the saliva in my mouth had dried up.

Thankfully, he used the knife to cut my ropes free. Then Frank's.

We burst out of the helicopter.

"Drop the remote, Stench," Petal instructed.

"No."

Petal didn't repeat herself. She pointed the arrow downward—and shot the remote out of Stench's hand.

"Get him!" Frank shouted.

Frank got to Stench first. Tackled him. I jumped on his chest, using my weight to pin him down.

He didn't even struggle. He was staring at something over my shoulder, eyes wide. I couldn't resist taking a quick look.

The drone had risen off the ground!

"Grab it, Mondo!" Stench shouted.

I punched him in the jaw. "You aren't the one giving orders anymore," I told him.

Stench suddenly bucked, knocking me half off him. His elbow landed square on my nose, and for a second, all I could see was red dots in front of my eyes. Everything was pain.

The second my vision cleared, I managed to grab one of Stench's ears and twist. It doesn't sound like much, but it can really hurt. And it gave Frank the chance to shove Stench over and get one of his hands pinned behind his back.

"Joe, duck!"

I obeyed Frank without thinking and pressed myself flat against the ground. My hair ruffled as the drone passed above me.

"I don't know how to work this thing!" Petal exclaimed. She jabbed at the remote. "I'm trying to make it land."

Mondo lunged at her. Petal darted away, still punching the remote's buttons.

The copter jerked up, up.

Mondo made another lunge.

Then the helicopter slammed into the ground.

As it exploded, I was hit with a wave of heat. Stench twisted onto his side. "Mondo!" he cried out.

A human figure staggered out of the fireball.
Mondo. He took three steps, then collapsed.

"Mondo!" Stench wailed again. And I realized
he was crying. Blood and tears streaked his face.

It was over.

# 18.

# ROAD TRIP!

Dave and his dad raced up to us. A few seconds later Einstein Wannabe appeared. His hair was wilder than ever. More people appeared every moment.

Before we could answer their questions, we had to deal with the flaming remains of the drone. We quickly formed a bucket brigade—after tying up Stench.

As the buckets of water passed down the line, I couldn't help wondering what would happen to all these people. Janet could probably get a job anywhere. But what about Solar Man?

Working together, it didn't take long to put the fire out. Then Joe, Petal, and I gave everyone in the compound as much of an explanation as we could.

Not fun.

In the background, Stench kept calling us liars. But with the blackened coptor sitting in the compound, most people believed us.

After all questions were answered, I felt it was time to wrap this case up. "I guess we should go call for—"

"Do you hear that?" Joe interrupted.

I tilted my head down and listened. Was I just having a delayed stress attack? Or was I really hearing a *real* helicopter?

I scanned the sky. Sure enough, a copter was incoming.

Ducking, Frank and I ran toward it after it had landed. Was it one of Stench's oil company bosses? Who else would be showing up in a helicopter?

The answer: our dad.

"What are you doing here?" Joe cried as Dad hopped out of the copter.

"Does that mean you're not happy to see me?" Dad asked.

"Just surprised," I told him. "How'd you find us? We barely found this place ourselves."

"That fireball helped!" Dad answered. "I was in California on a mission. I heard you two were out of cell phone range, and I thought maybe something had gone wrong. I decided to do a flyover."

Joe rolled his eyes. He hates it when Dad gets overprotective.

In this case, though, we sort of did need our butts saved. Sort of. We were just about to call for help. But somehow, calling for backup wasn't the same as being rescued by your dad. A little embarrassing.

"Do you wish I hadn't come?" Dad asked, his voice a little sharp. He'd clearly caught the eye roll.

"No," I answered. "Are you kidding? We've been eating tofu for days. We're dying to get out of here."

Joe smiled. "Yeah. We were just wrapping things up. And we needed a lift."

"And who's this?" Dad asked. He jerked his chin toward Petal. She was doing that hanging-back-but-not-going-away thing.

I waved her over. "Dad, this is Petal Northstar. This is our dad, Fenton Hardy."

"I'm Paula Northum, actually," Petal—or Paula—said.

"I knew your parents didn't name you Petal," Joe jumped in. He turned to Dad. "This girl saved our lives. Twice."

Dad shook Paula's hand. "Then I'm especially glad to meet you."

"I still don't get why you were helping us. You're part of the compound," I said.

"It's because she loooooves you, Frank," Joe butted in.

I hate to say it, but I blushed. Paula did too.

"I was in the compound undercover," Paula said. "I'm kind of an amateur detective myself. I live near here, and I wanted to find out what bigger plans Stench might have."

"And what do your parents think about this?" Dad asked. He pretty much had to. Being a parent himself.

"They're cool about it," Paula answered. "I'm home schooled, so I could be here without messing up my grades or anything. My parents and I have a lot of trust between us. They know I can take care of myself—and I've cracked some pretty intricate cases in these parts before."

She smiled at me. "At some point I started to think you were a detective too. I didn't want to blow my cover—but I wanted to help you out."

"You mean Frank and *me*," Joe muttered. "Hi, I'm Joe. Have we met?"

"Definitely," Paula said, smirking. "You and Frank." She was still looking only at Frank, though. "Anyway, that's why I wrote you the note about Stench's house."

Paula shifted awkwardly from foot to foot. "Well, I guess you'll be leaving soon. Me too. I should go pack up my stuff."

She took a couple of steps away. Then hesitated.

"Frank," Joe whispered. "She told you she loves you. She saved your life two times. Give her your e-mail address, you moron!"

Maybe he was right, I guess. But couldn't we just go home and get to our next case?

I stepped up to Paula. My tongue had done that weird tripling in size thing, but I managed to get out a few sentences. "Uh, you want to keep in touch? That would be cool."

She gave me her e-mail. I gave her mine. You know, I probably will write. It's easier to write to girls than to talk to them—because you don't have to look at them. And they can't see you be all dorky.

"So what was *your* mission?" Joe asked our dad.

"Top secret consulting job for a high-tech security agency. You should see some of the stuff they have," Dad answered. "Motorcycles that would put yours to shame. Everything yours have, but with video cameras built right into the handlebars. Night vision headlights. Tires of a light metal alloy that can't be punctured."

"Stop," Joe begged. "I'm going to be drooling in a second."

"We have to look for our bikes," I said. "We had to ditch them in the desert, and Stench found them. Who knows what he did with them."

"I guess we might have to fly home." Joe sighed. "I'd already picked a stop on the way back. There's this mermaid show that sounded really cool."

"I forgot to mention—the security company did give me a bonus for a job well done," Dad said.

*Say it, Dad. Say it,* I silently pleaded.

"A couple of prototypes for the newest bikes. Gassed up and in the back of the copter," Dad told us.

Joe and I looked at each other. "Road trip!" we yelled.

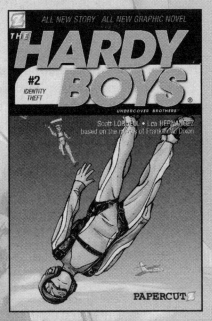

# PENDRAGON

Bobby Pendragon is a seemingly normal fourteen-year-old boy. He has a family, a home, and a possible new girlfriend. But something happens to Bobby that changes his life forever.

## HE IS CHOSEN TO DETERMINE
## THE COURSE OF HUMAN EXISTENCE.

Pulled away from the comfort of his family and suburban home, Bobby is launched into the middle of an immense, interdimensional conflict involving racial tensions, threatened ecosystems, and more. It's a journey of danger and discovery for Bobby, and his success or failure will do nothing less than determine the fate of the world. . . .

### PENDRAGON

by D. J. MacHale

Book One: The Merchant of Death
Book Two: The Lost City of Faar
Book Three: The Never War
Book Four: The Reality Bug
Book Five: Black Water

Coming Soon: Book Six: The Rivers of Zadaa

From Aladdin Paperbacks • Published by Simon & Schuster

## Time to Hit the Beach . . .

"Um, Mom," I said as I toyed with my scrambled eggs, "Joe and I would like to go down to the Jersey Shore for a week. Could we go?"

"By yourselves?" Aunt Trudy broke in.

She was sitting between us, looking from one of us to the other like we were out of our minds.

"I don't know, Frank," Mom said. "You boys just got back from a trip, and now you want to go away again so soon? Fenton, what do you think? Shouldn't they be spending more time at home?"

Dad lowered his newspaper—the one he likes to hide behind whenever there's a family dispute—and looked straight into my eyes.

I tried to signal him that this was important.

He seemed to get it. Turning to Mom, he said, "Well, dear, it is the summertime, after all. I think the boys are old enough to go to the beach on their own."

"Probably get themselves into more mischief," Aunt Trudy grumbled.

"It's true," Mom said, balling her napkin up into a knot. "Fenton, they only just got back—why do they have to leave again? Can't it wait till next week?"

I gave Dad another look. This couldn't wait.

# THE HARDY BOYS
## UNDERCOVER BROTHERS™

**Available from Simon & Schuster**

# THE HARDY BOYS

## UNDERCOVER BROTHERS

**#3**  Boardwalk Bust

**FRANKLIN W. DIXON**

**Aladdin Paperbacks**
New York   London   Toronto   Sydney

This book is a work of fiction. Any references to historical events, real people, or real locales are used fictitiously. Other names, characters, places, and incidents are the product of the author's imagination, and any resemblance to actual events or locales or persons, living or dead, is entirely coincidental.

❧ALADDIN PAPERBACKS
An imprint of Simon & Schuster
Children's Publishing Division
1230 Avenue of the Americas
New York, NY 10020

Copyright © 2005 by Simon & Schuster, Inc.

THE HARDY BOYS MYSTERY STORIES and HARDY BOYS
UNDERCOVER BROTHERS are trademarks of Simon & Schuster, Inc.
ALADDIN PAPERBACKS and colophon are trademarks of
Simon & Schuster, Inc.
Designed by Lisa Vega
The text of this book was set in Aldine 401BT.
Manufactured in the United States of America
First Aladdin Paperbacks edition June 2005
10  9  8  7  6  5  4  3  2
Library of Congress Control Number: 2004116378
ISBN-13: 978-1-4169-0004-7
ISBN-10: 1-4169-0004-7

# TABLE OF CONTENTS

# Boardwalk Bust

# 1.

## In Too Deep

Being buried alive is no fun. No fun at all.

Let me set the scene:

A waterfall of corn was raining down on me. The grains felt like millions of BBs as they bounced off my head.

A mountain of grain was rising like sand dunes all around me. It was at least ten feet deep. It had the consistency of quicksand. I was sunk into it almost up to my knees, and it was trying really hard to suck me down.

Meanwhile, the falling grain was sending up a billowing cloud of dust. I was totally choking on it.

Nice, huh?

It was mostly dark inside this grain bin, except for a distant square of light high above that threw

1

faint shadows here and there. Corn was pouring through the hole—coming through the conveyor belt that a certain bad guy named Bill Pressman had started.

His intention? To kill me and Frank.

Why? That's a long story. But right now we were in trouble.

I could just make out my brother Frank. He was about twenty feet away from me, but it might as well have been twenty miles. He was well out of reach, and buried even deeper than I was.

"Joe!" I heard him yell over the roar. "Where are you?"

"Over h-here!" I shouted back, choking on the dust. "We've got to do something!"

"No, duh. Ya think?"

"Okay, genius," I said. "What's your brilliant plan?"

And, as usual, Frank had one. Over the years, I've come to count on his uncanny ability to pull impossible schemes right out of his ear.

"Joe, you've got to get out of here and shut off the conveyor!"

Uh, hel-lo. Anyone see me stuck in a pile of corn?

"I'm up to my knees in corn, bro," I said. "How am I supposed to do that?"

"Hey, I'm up to my chest! Just figure out a way—you've got to get over to that ladder . . . up there on the wall."

"Are you kidding me? I can hardly move—"

"J-Joe," he gasped, "I feel like I'm gonna be c-crushed if it gets much higher. . . . It's . . . gonna have to be you."

I could tell he wasn't joking now.

Desperately, I tried to wiggle free. I swung my body back and forth. When I had a little play, I shifted my weight to my right leg, which was on the low side of the corn pile, and twisted myself loose.

Then I rolled over, so I was lying with my back against the ever-shifting mountain. That way I could do things like breathe and see.

All right, so it wasn't so hard.

Meanwhile, the corn kept raining down, adding to the pile. The dust made it hard to see anything.

"Okay," I shouted. "Now what?"

"Shine your flashlight on me."

I pulled out my light wand—sort of a combination laser cutter and flashlight—and pointed it at him.

I could make out Frank now. He was holding up a pretty sweet gadget of his own.

"Use this grapple line," he said. "Catch!"

3

He tossed it to me. Luckily, I didn't miss it. It would have been buried under the corn for sure.

By this time I'd gotten Frank's intention. I aimed his gizmo at the ladder and fired.

The strong nylon line shot out and wound itself around one of the rungs of the wooden ladder. The hook at the end of the grapple dug into the wood.

I pressed another button on the handy-dandy contraption, and it reeled itself back in, drawing me forward. I was pulled up the slippery slope, gliding with ease. Before I knew it, I was on the ladder, climbing free of the death trap that still held my brother.

I kept climbing until I got to the door in the wall. The door was locked, of course—from the outside.

These guys thought of everything.

"I'll just use my laser cutter," I said, pocketing the grapple line and pulling out my other gadget.

"No!" Frank screamed. "Joe, grain dust is highly flammable—explosive, even! You'll blow us both to smithereens!"

"Hmmm," I said, stuffing it back in my pocket. "All righty, then. No lasers."

I tried brute strength instead.

Luckily, the lock was old and rusty, and it popped after five or six solid hits from my well-developed shoulder.

"Yes! Hang in there, Frank—I'll just be a second."

I scrambled down the ladder attached to the outside of the grain bin. As soon as I hit the ground, I hustled over to the switch that shuts off the conveyor belt. The machinery ground to a halt.

*There.*

I was surrounded by an eerie silence, broken only by the sound of my own heart pounding.

Luckily, Farmer Pressman seemed to be nowhere in sight. I realized with a sharp pang that he was probably gone for good, escaping justice in spite of all we'd done to catch him.

But there was no time to think about that now—I had to help Frank. I just hoped he was still breathing.

Along the side of the grain bin, I spotted a strange-looking yet familiar device. I recognized it from a newspaper article I'd read the week before. It was one of those new safety devices—what did they call it?

Oh yeah, a grain rescue tube!

But there was a complication. Between me and the rescue tube stood a cow. And not just any cow, but the cow that had kicked me in the eye just about an hour before.

Don't even ask. I was lucky it didn't blind me, and I'd be luckier still if I didn't have a black eye to show for it.

I yelled at the cow to move, but she didn't seem to get it. Cows are not the brightest.

Finally I lost my temper. I ran at the cow and shoved her out of the way.

"Moooo," she complained. But at least she didn't kick me this time.

I hooked the two halves of the rescue tube to the grapple line. Then I climbed to the top of the ladder, pushed the button on Frank's gizmo, and dragged them up after me.

Inside, the grain was no longer pouring off the conveyor belt. But Frank was now buried up to his neck, and I had to be careful coming near him.

One false move and I could have set off an avalanche, burying Frank in corn. Once I had the two halves of the rescue tube in place around him, I hammered down both sides with my fists, so that Frank was surrounded by a sort of plastic cocoon.

"Now start scooping out the grain," I told him.

"Can't," he gasped. "Can't move. Can barely . . . breathe. . . ."

I could see that the remaining grain inside the tube was squashing him pretty good. I realized I was the one who was going to have to get that corn out from around him and give him the space to haul himself out. So I hurried back outside, found

6

a small shovel, took it back inside, and started digging him out.

Finally, after about fifteen minutes, Frank was able to wiggle himself up by the handles and get out. "I'm never eating popcorn again," he told me as we climbed the ladder out of there.

"No cornflakes for me."

"Corn muffins?"

"No way."

"I'm with you, bro."

We planted our feet on solid ground, and boy, did it ever feel good.

"No corn chips either."

"Okay," said Frank. "Glad we've got that straight. Now let's go get our bikes. We've still got a criminal to catch."

# 2.

## Ride Like the Wind

We peeled out of there on our motorcycles, Joe and I, leaving a cloud of dust behind us.

We raced down the farm's driveway—really more like a long dirt road—zipping past the cornfields of Pressman Acres toward the main road.

The corn really was "as high as an elephant's eye," but Farmer Pressman, that no-good crooked slimebucket, was not going to be around to reap the benefits. That is, not if the sheriff had done his job and set up the roadblock like I told him to.

I couldn't really get a good breath till we were back on the asphalt of the main road again, tooling toward home.

About those bikes of ours. Just so you know, these are not just ordinary sport bikes. They've got

600 cc engines, huge twin caliper brakes, digital gauges, titanium-tipped exhaust pipes, twin front ram-air scoops—and that's just for starters. Add in a few nifty little trick gadgets straight out of James Bond, along with a whole lot of style—like the flaming double red Hs painted on the sides—shake well, and you've got yourself one *outstanding* ride!

I looked to my left at Joe and felt a rush of joy go through me. We'd almost been buried alive in that grain bin.

Breathing was good.

When Joe saw the flashers up ahead, he shot me a look—I could see the surprise on his face even under the visor.

I just nodded, trying not to be too much of a wise guy. But it was me, after all, who'd insisted on putting that phone call in to the sheriff—just in case we were walking into a death trap (which it turned out we were).

Joe had called me a wimp for bringing in the police. Now I was tempted to rub it in—but I controlled myself. If you're intelligent, like me, you don't bait people—especially when they're muscle-bound and temperamental, like Joe, and thus likely to knock you flat on your rear.

We slowed down as we passed. Three squad cars were blocking the road, and Pressman's huge

SUV was slung sideways in front of them.

There were skid marks where he'd hit the brakes. Soon there would be burn marks on his wrists, too. Those nylon handcuffs were chafing him as he sat with his back against a tree, trying unsuccessfully to work himself free.

Joe and I didn't stop to chat. We had been working undercover on this case. It wouldn't look good for the local sheriff—or for ATAC—if the newspapers found out that a couple of high school kids were involved.

This wasn't Bayport, after all. It was western New Jersey, and I doubt if they'd ever heard of Frank and Joe Hardy, "amateur teen detectives," around there.

It was just as well if the police took all the credit. ATAC is allergic to publicity. And as card-carrying members of ATAC—American Teens Against Crime—so are we. As we roared by the roadblock, Joe gave the sheriff a little salute. I didn't want to look like a jerk, so I saluted too. The sheriff smiled and waved.

Farmer Pressman saw the exchange, and it must have dawned on him who the guys under the visors were, because his eyes lit up like fireworks.

"Hey, you lousy kids!" he screamed.

The rest of what he said I couldn't hear. Sport

bike engines are really loud, especially when you gun them. I really didn't want to hear what he had to say, though, to tell you the truth. It wasn't going to be anything nice.

We left him to choke on our dust, and to meditate on the fact that crime doesn't pay.

I could tell Joe was laughing by the way his chest was bobbing up and down. It was funny *now*, sure—but I myself wasn't ready to start joking about it. We'd come pretty close to getting smothered.

Very uncool.

Pretty soon Joe stopped laughing. His eye was probably starting to hurt where that cow kicked it. Talk about *embarrassing*.

For the rest of the ride back to Bayport, we just concentrated on the highway and the wind in our faces.

Of course, at that point, we would have settled for a beat-up old Volvo. Anything was better than eating corn dust. It was good to be alive and on the way home.

We pulled into the driveway and parked behind Dad's old Crown Vic—the one he took with him when he retired from the police force.

It's an oldie but goodie, if you know what I mean. It's still got all the super-charged extras police cruisers have (and some others that they don't).

Dad was leaning against the fender with his legs and arms crossed and a sarcastic expression on his face. He'd been waiting for us.

"Well, nice of you two to show up. I was beginning to worry about you. What in the world happened?"

"We were reaping what we sowed," Joe said with a grin, shaking the last stray grains of corn out of his pants.

"Lucky you didn't meet the grim reaper," Dad answered. I could tell he was not amused. He stood up and started walking over to us as we put our kickstands down and our visors up.

"I just got a call from Chief Collig. He says the sheriff over in West Hoagland, New Jersey, reported the capture of a major drug smuggler."

Dad came up right between us and stopped. He crossed his arms again and continued, "This guy was a well-known local farmer, apparently. That factoid rang a bell. I remembered something about you two going off to visit a farm somewhere."

He looked at Joe, then at me. "Do you boys have something you want to tell me?"

Joe and I couldn't help grinning at one another. "Don't worry," I said. "We're untraceable."

"Nice work," Dad said, finally giving us a smile.

"Glad you're okay. Now go inside and get cleaned up. Your mom and Aunt Trudy have been waiting for you, and you look like something the cat dragged in."

Dad really does worry about us. It's not because he doesn't think we can handle ourselves in a tight spot. He knows we can.

It's just that he knows he's responsible for *everything*.

He's the one we took after, the one who taught us everything we know—up to a point. He's the one who inspired us to become amateur detectives years ago, when we were still little kids.

But most importantly, he's the one who founded ATAC and made us its first two agents. So like I say, it's not that he doesn't trust us—it's that he hates putting kids in harm's way. Especially his sons.

"Oh, and also," Dad added, "Trudy said something about sheets."

Sheets?

"Ugh," Joe said, putting a hand to his forehead. "I forgot—it's our day to help with the folding!"

Oh, right. Joe and I exchanged a quick look.

Our clothes were a mess, all ripped. I had scratches all over my arm from fending off Farmer Pressman's Dobermans. And Joe had the beginnings of a really magnificent black eye.

No way did we want to face Mom—and especially not Aunt Trudy—when we looked like we'd just been through a torture chamber.

Dad was staring at Joe's black eye now. He put a hand up to it. Joe flinched at the touch.

"What happened, son?"

Joe hesitated, so I just jumped in. "He got kicked by a cow."

"Shut up," Joe muttered, shooting me a look.

"A cow?"

"I . . . thought it would be a hoot to milk it," Joe said with a sigh. "You know, we were just hanging around in the barn, waiting for this scuzzball to show up . . ."

"Well, you'd better get in there and wash up before your mother and aunt see you like that," Dad said. "That way, you won't have to explain any of this."

We started for the kitchen door.

"And Joe—you might want to do something about that eye. You don't want to go telling people you got in a fight with a cow and lost."

"Dad's right," I said. "You might want to put some makeup on it."

Joe scowled at me. "Do I look like I would wear makeup?"

"Suit yourself," I said with a shrug.

14

We went into the house through the kitchen door. There are back stairs from there that lead up to our bedrooms—and, more importantly, the bathrooms.

We tiptoed our way along and were almost around the corner to the stairs when we heard Aunt Trudy's voice booming out from the living room. "Frank! Joe! I hear you clomping around in there!"

She came into the kitchen with Playback on her shoulder.

Playback is our pet parrot, and he loves to perch on Aunt Trudy's shoulder and nibble on her earlobe. It's probably because she lets him get away with it.

Aunt Trudy doesn't have any kids of her own, and she sure doesn't spoil us, either—but I'm telling you, as far as she's concerned, that parrot can do no wrong.

The funny thing is, when we first brought Playback home she hated him. She was totally grossed out by the way he pooped all over everything.

But one thing about our Aunt Trudy—she's a tough old bird. Tougher than Playback, anyway. Before too long, she had him toilet trained! No lie. That bird would not poop anywhere but in his cage, and from that time on, he was Aunt Trudy's baby.

"Got a good lie?" Joe whispered to me.

"I'll make one up."

"Oh, my goodness!" our mom gasped when she came into the kitchen and saw us.

"Holy mackerel!" Aunt Trudy nearly dropped the folded sheet she was holding.

Playback whistled long and low. "Aaawrk! Bad boys! Bad boys!"

"Joe! Your eye!" Mom said. "What in the world happened to you two? And no crazy made-up stories this time."

"Well," I began, "we kind of got caught in this grain bin . . . doing some research on farm safety devices . . ."

"Yeah!" Joe chimed in. "It's an over-the-summer school assignment!"

"Grain bin?" Aunt Trudy repeated. "Summer *assignment*? Ha! A likely story. They were probably at it again, Laura—chasing after another gang of crooks!"

"Now, Gertrude," our mom said, putting a calming hand out. "Don't condemn the boys before you check the evidence."

She went over to Joe and gently picked off a few grains of corn from his collar. "See? Corn. They're obviously telling the truth this time."

"Hmph," Aunt Trudy said. "Don't tell me. Evidence or no evidence, I know these two, and they've been up to no good."

"Crime-fighting isn't exactly being 'up to no good,' Aunt Trudy," Joe said.

Aunt Trudy raised one eyebrow, and Joe stopped right there.

"You'd better get yourselves cleaned up," she said. "These sheets will be all wrinkled by the time they get folded."

"Hop to it!" Playback squawked. "Hop to it!"

We ran up the stairs and got washed and changed as fast as we could, then came back down and started folding the sheets.

This has been a regular drill around our house since Joe and I were five years old. Every Saturday, Mom and Trudy wash the sheets, and Joe and I fold them. At this point we could do it in our sleep.

Still, Aunt Trudy never stops telling us how to do it just right. She's a laundry fanatic, coaching us like we're medical students doing our first brain surgery. Everything has to be done *exactly* her way.

"Pull on it—no, not like that . . . that's better. Left front corner over right rear, now right front over left rear . . . and make sure the corners match up!"

Et cetera.

After a half dozen or so sheets, we were just about done folding when the doorbell rang.

"I'll get it!" Joe said, eager to be the first one out of there.

Too late. I had already beaten him to it, dumping the sheet in his arms and heading for the front door.

"Hey!" I heard him shout behind me.

I opened the door—to find a Girl Scout, of all things.

"Hi!" she said, flashing me a big smile that showed off her very shiny metal braces. She had to be at least thirteen, maybe closer to fifteen. Kind of old for a Girl Scout . . .

"Wanna buy some cookies?"

She held out a box of Thin Mints.

"Um, no thanks," I said. "I think we've still got a few boxes from the last time. Hey, come to think of it, weren't you just here last month selling cookies? I thought it was a once-a-year kind of thing."

"Oh!" she said, her cheeks reddening. "Well, that was, um, another Girl Scout troop. Yeah, that's right. Our troop does it a month later." She laughed nervously.

"Oh, yeah? How come?"

"Um, just to be different?"

She shrugged her shoulders and giggled some more.

This was getting weird.

I had half a mind to say, "No, thanks" again and get it over with. We had enough Girl Scout cookies in the pantry. But this girl was pretty cute—even with her braces. And when cute girls smile at me, it always makes me nervous. I kind of choke up and, well . . . I start acting like a complete moron.

"Hmmm," I said. "How about some vanilla Trefoils?"

"Um, no," she said, shaking her head. "We're out of those. Try these Thin Mints instead."

Again, she thrust the box of cookies at me.

"No, really," I said, pushing them away. "I don't even like chocolate and mint together. It's . . . not my thing."

"Frank?" I heard Aunt Trudy calling. "Are you coming back in here? These sheets aren't going to fold themselves."

"Coming, Aunt Trudy!"

I turned back to the Girl Scout. "Look, I've gotta go," I said. "Sorry. Maybe next time."

"You dummy," she said, freezing me in mid-turn.

"Huh?"

"Just take them, okay?"

"I don't underst—"

Before I could finish, she shoved the dreaded box of Thin Mints into my hand.

*"They're not cookies, doofus,"* she whispered, widening her eyes and staring at me.

"Not . . . cookies?"

"Nuh-uh."

"Ooooh. Okay, then," I said, getting it at last. "Sorry. I'm a little dense sometimes."

*Especially around girls.*

"Bye!" she said, giving me a wave and another big metal smile. "Good luck."

I opened the box, just to take a peek. Sure enough, there were no cookies inside. Instead there was a video game CD, with a label that read: BOARDWALK BUST.

*Good luck?*

Hmm. Maybe Joe and I were going to need it.

Turns out our cute little friend was no Girl Scout—she was from ATAC. And she had just brought us our next case.

# 3.

## Shore Thing

I was in the living room, trying to do, by myself, what is impossible to do without someone else helping you: fold a queen-size fitted bedsheet.

And where was Frank? At the front door, talking to some girl.

I could hear them from the living room—when Playback wasn't screeching, that is. That parrot was busy using his feathers to mess up the sheets we'd already done. His idea of fun.

It's a strange thing about Frank and girls. They make him go all weird. He starts acting like a complete geek, which is not normally him. Well, maybe it is, just a little—but not as much as when girls are around.

Funny thing is, it seems to make the girls like Frank more than ever.

It gets me *crazy* sometimes. Frank can't dance, has no smooth moves, no dimple in his chin, no big muscles. All of which I've got in spades, by the way. But that doesn't seem to matter at all. Girls like Frank's bumbling shy act better.

I just don't get it.

Finally, Frank came back into the living room, and we started folding sheets again.

"What was that all about, dear?" Mom asked him.

"Girl Scouts," Frank said, looking at the floor. "Selling cookies."

"Well, I hope you didn't buy any," Aunt Trudy said. "Why, they were here just last month. I think it's nervy. How many cookies do they expect one household to buy?"

"Aaarrck!" Playback started in. "Get lost! Scram! Fuggedaboudit!"

"I didn't buy any," Frank said.

Then he noticed we were all staring at the box of Thin Mints sticking out of the back pocket of his cargo pants.

"Oh . . . these were a . . . uh . . . a free gift!"

"*Free gift*?" Aunt Trudy said, raising an eyebrow. "Well, now, that's different!" She smiled. "Frank, why don't you put them out on a platter and let's all have some?"

"Cookie! Cookie! Playback wanna cookie!" the parrot screeched, flapping his wings.

The panic in Frank's eyes was plainly visible, but he was looking at me. His back was to Trudy and Mom—and it was a good thing, too.

Obviously, he needed my help. I didn't know why, but I knew enough not to ask.

"Hey, Frank," I said, snapping my fingers. "Don't you and I have to finish that farm project for school? You know, write up the report?"

"For school?" Aunt Trudy said, raising her eyebrow so high it was halfway up her scalp. "It's *July*!"

"It's part of our summer project," I explained. "We have to do a blog. Daily entries. And we're way behind, aren't we, Frank?"

"Uh . . . yeah!"

"Hmmph." Clearly Aunt Trudy didn't buy it.

Lucky for us Mom was there. "Oh, let them go, Trudy," she said. "Can't you see they're tired of folding?"

"It's all that amateur detective nonsense," Trudy grumbled. "I don't know why you put up with it. If they were mine—"

"I know, dear," Mom said in the most soothing

voice you ever heard. "It's just *awful*. You boys are going to cut down on all that amateur sleuthing, aren't you? Promise me."

"Sure, Mom," we both said, crossing our fingers behind our backs. "You bet."

"All right, then, go on," she said. "We'll see you at dinner."

"Liar! Liar! Pants on fire!" Playback squawked as we ran up the back stairs to Frank's room.

That parrot is gonna get it one of these days, I swear. He's just lucky I'm a bird lover.

*"Greetings, and welcome to Ocean Point, your very own paradise on the Jersey Shore!"*

Frank and I sat glued to the computer monitor as the CD came on.

At first it looked like a typical travel advertisement aimed at potential tourists—except that it was computer animated, like any video game.

Our "host" was a voice-over, and the pictures showed a boardwalk crowded with happy beach-goers. There were people eating ice cream cones, cotton candy, and hot dogs. Little kids raced around in their bathing suits playing tag. In the background was the beach, with surfers riding the waves and swimmers bobbing up and down in the water.

Then the whole picture went to static. When it

came back into focus, we were staring at the face of Q.T., the director of ATAC.

"Hello, boys," he said, not smiling. (Q.T. never smiles.) "Unfortunately, there seems to be a bit of trouble in this particular slice of paradise. Trouble in the form of a rash of burglaries."

The monitor showed pictures of broken display cases, shattered plate glass, and bits of gold and silver scattered around everywhere.

"In the past month three jewelry stores in town have been broken into, causing heavy losses to the stores' owners. More serious, though, is the effect a crime wave could have on a beach resort like Ocean Point. The tourist season is just starting. You boys have got to stop these jewel thieves in their tracks before they scare the tourists away."

"Some time on the beach sounds good," I said to Frank, but he wasn't listening. When he's concentrating, nothing breaks through to him.

"In recent years, Ocean Point has become a haven for young people like yourselves," Q.T. went on. "And since the local police seem to be stymied, I thought we'd put you two on the case. You'll find some spending money and one or two other things we thought might come in handy. Good luck—and you know where to reach me if you run into any trouble you can't get out of."

"Yeah," I said, "how come we didn't try that when we were in the grain bin?"

"No cellular service," Frank reminded me, his eyes still glued to the monitor. "Dead zone."

*Dead zone.* Yeah, I'd say that grain bin was a dead zone, all right. We were lucky to have those gadgets on us.

*"As you know, this CD will reformat to an ordinary music CD in five seconds. Your mission, as always, is and must remain top secret."*

Frank and I silently counted to five. Sure enough, the picture went to a neutral background pattern, and music by the Surfaris started blaring out of the speakers. If Mom or Aunt Trudy had happened to open the door and peek in, everything would have looked normal—and that was the idea.

"Hmmm . . . jewel heists, eh?"

I reached into the cookie box and pulled out a nice-sized wad of cash. "Yes!" I said, starting to count it. "There's a good $500 here! You and I are gonna have a par-taaay on the beach!"

Frank gave me a smile and shook his head. "Born to be wild," he said, and shook out the rest of what was in the box.

There was a cheap disposable camera and a night vision telescope that collapsed down to the size of a shot glass.

"Hey, this is pretty cool," Frank said, playing with the scope.

Then he spotted the PDA. "Sweet!" he said, picking it up and turning it on. "Here we go. We've got all the names and addresses of the jewelry stores that have been hit, and some others that haven't been—yet."

He scrolled down and whistled. "Wow! Two hundred thousand dollars worth of stuff stolen from one store alone!"

"I've got a great idea," I said, hefting the wad of cash. "You and I could ride our bikes down there, but . . ."

"Yeesss?"

"Well, I don't know about you, but I'm starting to feel sore all over . . . and we'd be sitting in Sunday traffic for hours and hours. . . ."

"So . . . ?"

"Well, we've got enough money that we could *fly* down there," I suggested.

Oh, yeah—by the way, Joe and I are certified pilots, another one of the cool pluses of being ATAC agents.

"I don't know, Joe. That money has got to last us for who knows how long."

"Dude, how long could it possibly take to round up a gang of jewel thieves?" I said. "And anyway, the sooner we get there . . ."

"Okay." Frank gave in. "I guess you're right. I

*am* sore all over. Flying down will be relaxing."

"Exactly!" I said, slapping him—gently—on the back. "Now you're getting into the beach party spirit!"

"There's just one problem," Frank said, looking up at me.

"Yes?"

"How are we going to explain this to Mom and Aunt Trudy?"

I thought for a minute.

"Easy," I said. "We'll lie through our teeth."

# 4.

## Lies, and the Lying Liars Who Tell Them

When Joe says, "We'll lie through our teeth," he means *I'll* lie through my teeth.

Joe's a terrible liar. I don't know if he's just too honest, or just a bad actor. All I can say is that somehow, whenever we have to fib our way out of—or into—a situation, it's always me who winds up doing the talking.

I've come to accept this. I used to fight it, but eventually I realized it was no use.

If we wanted our parents to let us fly down to the Jersey Shore for a few days of unsupervised "rest and relaxation," I was going to have to come up with a good line of baloney. No way could we risk revealing our true purpose.

There's a very good reason why ATAC is top

secret, see. If bad guys knew about it, they might try to get even with us agents—or even our families. On the other hand, you can't get information out of someone who doesn't know anything. So the fewer people who are in on the secret, the better.

Not that Mom and Aunt Trudy don't get suspicious sometimes.

It goes back to the days when Joe and I were kids, solving cases we weren't supposed to even get involved with. We got pretty well known there for a while, but ever since Dad created ATAC, we've tried to keep our activities quiet.

That means a whole lot of lying to everyone we know, except Dad. I don't like it, and neither does Joe, but it's the price we have to pay if we want to fight crime in a big way.

So the next morning I had my bag of lies all ready to go.

"Um, Mom," I said as I toyed with my scrambled eggs, "Joe and I would like to go down to the Jersey Shore for a week. Could we go?"

"By yourselves?" Aunt Trudy broke in.

She was sitting between us, looking from one of us to the other like we were out of our minds.

"I don't know, Frank," Mom said. "You boys just got back from a trip, and now you want to go away again so soon? Fenton, what do you think?

Shouldn't they be spending more time at home?"

Dad lowered his newspaper—the one he likes to hide behind whenever there's a family dispute—and looked straight into my eyes.

I tried to signal him that this was important.

He seemed to get it. Turning to Mom, he said, "Well, dear, it is the summertime, after all. I think the boys are old enough to go to the beach on their own."

"Probably get themselves into more mischief," Aunt Trudy grumbled.

Aunt Trudy loves us, but she's always afraid we're going to get hurt. And I guess she has reason to be nervous. Joe and I have gotten into more dangerous situations as kids than most people do in their whole lives. "And how are they going to get there?" she continued. "Not on those motorcycles, I hope! Do you know how dangerous those things are? And look at the way they looked last night!"

"It's true," Mom said, balling her napkin up into a knot. "Fenton, they only just got back—why do they have to leave again? Can't it wait till next week?"

I gave Dad another look. This couldn't wait.

He cleared his throat. "Um, actually, I've got the wood for the new backyard fence being delivered next week. I was hoping the boys could help me with that. This week would be better."

"Well," Mom said, turning to me and Joe, "I hope at least you won't take your motorcycles this time. I'd feel better if you gave them a rest for a while."

"We won't, Mom," I promised. "Right, Joe?"

"Nope," he said, giving her a smile and crossing his heart.

"They still have buses that go down there from the city, don't they?" Mom asked.

"Um, actually," I said, "we thought we might fly down."

I'd been saving this information till we got permission to go. Now I sprung it on them, knowing full well how they'd react.

"Are you *serious*?" Aunt Trudy said.

"What? We're licensed pilots," Joe pointed out.

"Yes," Trudy agreed. "But that doesn't make you *good* ones."

"Now, Trudy," Dad said, "I've flown with the boys, and they're both perfectly fine pilots."

"Then why is it that every time they fly, something terrible happens?" Trudy asked.

"Mayday! Mayday!" Playback screeched, flapping his wings. "SOS! We're going down! Mayday! Mayday!"

"Shhh!" Trudy silenced him, giving him a cornflake. "Last time they flew a plane, as I recall, there

32

was engine trouble—or at least that's what the story was."

"It *was* engine trouble, Aunt Trudy," Joe said.

"Really? Well, it just so happens Adam Franklin is an old friend of mine. He swore up and down that he'd looked over that engine six ways from Sunday before you boys took the plane up."

Joe and I exchanged a glance. We knew we were caught in a lie. That plane hadn't had engine trouble—it literally had a monkey wrench thrown into it. And it wasn't Adam Franklin, our trusty airplane maintenance man, who'd thrown it.

"And then there was the time before that. What was it, a mysterious hole in the gas tank?"

"Look, it's probably just a run of bad luck," said good old Mom. "I know my boys, Trudy, and they're certainly not reckless pilots."

"So it's settled then?" I jumped in, before anyone could say anything else about our flying skills.

"Just be careful," our dad said, putting a merciful end to the discussion. "You boys have enough money for your trip?"

I thought of the cash that had come in the cookie box. I also knew that, thanks to ATAC, the flight down to Ocean Point would be covered separately.

"We'll be fine," I said.

"All right, then," Mom said. "When do you mean to go?"

"Right after breakfast," I told her.

Joe had already shoveled his breakfast down his gullet. I now followed suit, and we got out of there. We had a mission to start, and I didn't want to have to tell any more lies—at least not to our family.

As we left the kitchen, I heard Playback serenading us, displaying his usual sense of humor.

"Mayday! Mayday! We're goin' down, boys! SOS!"

"You sure she's fit to fly?" I asked Adam Franklin as we climbed aboard our two-passenger Piper—Joe at the controls, me sitting behind him to navigate. We'd called about an hour ahead so he could get our plane ready.

"Oh, you bet!" Adam said, taking off his Red Sox cap and scratching his bald head. "Last time your Aunt Trudy gave me what for about it!"

"Hey, that's ancient history," I said. "Don't worry about it, Adam. Let's focus on this time."

"No prob," he said, giving us a wave and patting the silver side of the plane. "She's in perfect shape. Weather's good too. You boys have a nice flight. Take my word for it, it'll be a safe one—long as you don't do any loop-de-loops."

Soon we were airborne and headed south.

We picked up the Jersey Shore at Sandy Hook and kept it in sight as we went. We passed over Long Branch, Monmouth University, and the Shark River Inlet.

It was right about when we hit Long Beach Island that the fog bank rolled in from out of nowhere.

Within the space of two minutes, we were flying totally blind, relying only on our dashboard compass for direction. These little one-engine jobs don't have radar, in case you were wondering. You're basically not supposed to fly them in bad weather.

"Where did this stuff come from?" Joe asked, frowning at the fog. "I thought Adam said the weather was going to be fine."

"You know Jersey. If you don't like the weather, wait a minute."

"I know our luck with airplanes," Joe replied. "And so does Aunt Trudy."

"Just keep us headed the right way," I told him. "This can't last long."

Mmm hmm. Famous last words.

The fog lasted for a good ten minutes. And when we finally came out of it, there was another plane coming right at us.

# 5.

## Beach Bound

"Bank left!"

I didn't need Frank screaming in my ear to know what to do. In that moment I was all instinct. I pulled on the throttle and my stomach turned as we banked hard left—so hard that we were upside down for a moment before we came back around.

"Whew!" I said. "That was close!"

"Too close," Frank agreed. I could feel him grabbing my leather jacket for all he was worth. He was holding on so tightly that I couldn't move to maneuver the plane.

"Dude, let go of me," I said. "I've gotta fly this thing."

He let go, but the plane kept bucking. "What's going on?" I asked.

36

Frank looked behind us, then yelled, "There's something caught on our tail!"

Just for a second, I risked letting go of the controls to get a look.

Sure enough, there was a big piece of cloth caught on our tail. It was flapping wildly in the wind, dragging the back of the plane down. If we didn't get it off, and quick, it was going to make us stall out.

*Not good.*

Neither of us needed to say anything. We both knew we had only one option—one of us had to climb out onto the fuselage and pull the cloth free, or we were going to take a fatal dive into the Atlantic Ocean.

"I'll go," I said.

"No! You stay put—just try and keep us steady."

Before I could argue with him, Frank pulled back the cockpit cover and climbed up and out, onto the top of the fuselage.

I couldn't bear to watch, and anyway, I had to keep the plane sure and steady so he didn't fall off. We were a good thousand feet up, and as good a high diver as Frank is, there was no way he could have survived a plunge like that.

I happen to be a crackerjack pilot, but this plane was getting almost impossible to control. (*You* try keeping a small airplane steady with someone climbing on it!) The closer Frank got to the tail, the more he was throwing off the plane's balance, and the harder my job was getting.

I felt a sudden easing of the drag, and a minute later Frank tumbled back into his seat behind me. "Whew!" he said. "That was exciting."

"What in the world was that thing?"

"One of those banners—you know, the ads planes fly back and forth over the beach?"

"You're kidding," I said. "That plane that almost hit us . . ."

Now it was clear what must have happened. We'd avoided hitting the plane, but the banner it was trailing got snagged on our tail. We were just lucky it had snapped off the other plane, or it could have dragged both aircraft down.

"It took a little chunk out of our tail," Frank told me. "How's she flying?"

"Not too bad," I said, "but we'd better take her down before we lose anything else."

"Where are we?"

I looked around and saw the familiar shapes of Atlantic City's many casinos in the distance. "There you go."

"Atlantic City? But that's forty miles from—"

"I know, dude," I said. "We'll just have to get

there some other way. I'm not risking it. We've had enough excitement for one flight."

He didn't argue. I guess we were both a little shell-shocked. First the grain bin and now this— and all in the space of twenty-four hours!

We finally landed at the Atlantic City airport and phoned Adam to let him know what had happened. Adam's in on the ATAC secret, luckily. He said not to worry about it, that he'd take care of it with a few phone calls.

Now the only problem was how we'd get to Ocean Point. We're not old enough to rent a car, and our bikes were back in Bayport. Being stranded in Atlantic City with a bunch of cash may be some people's idea of a good time, but we had a mission to accomplish in Ocean Point, and no way to get there.

"How 'bout a taxi?" Frank suggested. He pointed to a row of cabs parked outside the terminal building.

"No way," I said. "Ocean Point is forty miles from here. Do you know how much that would run us? We'd be blowing a big chunk of our budget before we even got there! And I am primed for some serious spending."

Just then I felt somebody tapping me on the shoulder.

"Excuse me, son," a deep, booming voice said. "Did you say you needed a lift to Ocean Point?"

I turned around and took a good look at this human megaphone. He was a big, brawny guy—I guessed about fifty years old, six feet, maybe 230 pounds, with a bushy head of brown hair that was getting gray around the temples.

This guy looked like he spent most of his time out in the sun. His tanned face brought out the whiteness of his big teeth when he smiled. The smile looked like a professional dental job—a really expensive one.

"Yes, sir," Frank said. "We were headed there in our plane, but we had a little trouble with it."

"Oh yeah? What sort of trouble?"

I told him about our near miss. He shook his head and frowned.

"Mmmm, yeah. Some of those banner pilots are real cowboys," he said. "You boys are real lucky to be alive."

"You can say that again," I said.

"Name's Bump," he said, holding out his hand. "Bump Rankowski."

I shook it, and he nearly crushed my hand in his grip. *Whoa.* This guy was strong. "Joe Hardy," I said. "And this is my brother Frank."

"Good to meet you, Frank," Bump said, crushing Frank's hand in turn.

I flexed my own, just to make sure it wasn't broken.

"So you say you're headed to Ocean Point? Well, that's where I'm headed too—just got clearance from the tower. Would you like a lift? No charge."

To tell you the truth, getting back in a plane just then was the last thing I wanted to do, and I'm sure Frank felt the same. On top of that, we didn't know this guy from a hole in the ground, and who could tell what kind of pilot he was?

On the other hand, if he *wasn't* a terrific pilot, either of us was plenty good enough to help him correct a mistake or get out of a jam.

Besides, what better choice did we have? Opportunity was knocking, and we weren't about to let a lucky break go by.

"Excellent!" Frank said.

"Sweet," I agreed. "You're sure it's not—?"

"No problem," Bump said. "I've got me a four-seater. Unless you've got company, I count three of us. You ready to fly?"

He gave us another dazzling smile and put a powerful arm around each of our shoulders. "Come on—she's parked right outside."

"This is really great of you, Mr. Rankowski," Frank said.

"Please, call me Bump. Nobody calls me by my last name. Not once we've shook hands."

"If you don't mind my asking, "Frank said, "how did you get—"

"The name Bump?" he finished, laughing. "*That's* how—check her out, boys. She's good for a bump or two, all right!"

Removing his arms from around our shoulders, he pointed to a Day-Glo red Cessna parked across the runway. The teeth and eyes of a great white shark were painted on the sides.

"Awesome!" I said, going over to take a closer look. "Oh, man! This thing rocks!"

"Meet Jaws. She's my pride and joy," Bump said, patting the side of the plane. "Go on, hop in."

"Whoa," Frank said, admiring the instrument panel. It was all sporty; all the dials were phosphor white.

We got strapped in while Bump started going through his preflight checklist. "My birth name was Arnold," he said, "but I never liked it. So when people started calling me Bump, I let 'em."

He started the engine. "So, what brings you boys to Ocean Point? Little vacation?"

Frank gave me a look of caution—like I didn't know to watch what I said. I mean, give me a break! "Fourth of July weekend," I said. "Gotta hit the beach, right?"

"You bet!" Bump said. "You look like you could use a break, Joe. Get punched in the eye, did you?"

"Um, sort of."

"Kicked, actually," Frank volunteered.

I kicked him in the ankle to keep him from saying anything else about it. "It's a long story," he said, wisely leaving it at that.

"Well, anyway, you can't find a better beach than Ocean Point. Best spot on the whole Jersey Shore—and I oughta know. After all, I'm the mayor."

"The mayor?" Frank said, sitting bolt upright in his seat. "Wow!"

"Yup, that's me—live and in person."

Bump gunned the engine, and we started taxiing down the runway. The noise was deafening, but Bump had the kind of voice that can cut through anything—a politician's voice. "Lived in Ocean Point all my life. You want to know something about the place, I'm the guy to ask."

Frank and I exchanged a quick look. This was a perfect chance to start our investigation—but we had to be careful. Bump Rankowski seemed like a friendly guy, all right, but as the mayor of a town with a crime wave, he might be sensitive to certain kinds of questions.

We sat back and waited till Bump got us airborne. He did a slow turn, and we headed back north, keeping the shoreline on our left. There was no trace of the fog bank that had nearly killed us.

"Boy, the weather sure changes fast around here," Frank said.

"You got that right," Bump said. "Gotta keep your eyes open when you're flyin' the beach."

"Flying the beach?" I repeated.

"I'm a banner pilot too," Bump said. "I own a six-plane outfit. You see a banner being flown this week, it's probably me or one of my boys." He pointed to a big white button above his head. "See that? That unfurls the banner."

"You own the company?" I asked.

"That's what pays for things like this baby." He patted the ultra-high-tech dashboard with its expensive wood and gold trim.

I thought of the pilot who'd nearly killed us less than an hour ago. "You weren't up flying today, were you?" I asked.

"Naw, not with the fog," he said. "I grounded my entire fleet at four o'clock when we got the forecast. . . . Oh, I get what you're thinkin'! No, it wasn't me, or any of mine. Ha! That's funny!" He laughed hard, slapping his knees.

It wasn't *that* funny.

"Are there other companies that fly the beaches?" Frank asked.

"Oh, yeah. There are three or four outfits that run advertising up and down the shore. Some of 'em will hire any old pilot too—sounds like you boys ran into a real cowboy."

"I don't think he saw us coming, any more than we saw him," Frank said.

Bump shook his head in disgust. "He shouldn't even have been up there. Once fog rolls in, it's way too dangerous—well, I guess I don't have to tell you that!" He laughed again. "Listen, I'll try to find out who it was. Can't let him get away with shenanigans like that."

I hated to see somebody get fired, especially since there was no way it was intentional. "Aw, that's okay," I said. "I think we'd rather just let it go. . . ."

"Now, you just leave it to me," Bump said, turning back to look at us. "It's my job to keep my town safe, and that's what I'm gonna do." He nodded slowly. "I know people, and I can get things done. You just watch me."

There was something about the way he said it

that gave me a chill. Underneath his friendly politician act, I could see that Bump Rankowski wasn't somebody you'd want to cross.

The sun was setting, and lights were coming on all along the shore. "There's Ocean Point now!" Bump said, pointing to a cluster of lights in the distance. "Beautiful, isn't she?"

We nodded in agreement, staring down at the town as we approached. I could see a boardwalk with lots of stores, restaurants, and attractions. There was even a small pier with rides and arcades—sort of a miniature version of Seaside Heights or Asbury Park.

"Looks like a good time," I said, giving Bump a wink.

"Oh, you boys are gonna flip for it," he assured us. "No place like it."

Frank cleared his throat, and I knew what was coming. "Um, didn't I read something somewhere about some robberies happening there recently? What was it, jewelry stores?"

I could see Bump's face freeze into a mask. His smile was still in place, white as ever, but his eyes had changed somehow. Behind them, the wheels were working.

"Oh, that," he said, forcing a laugh. "Just a once-in-a-blue-moon kind of thing. You know, people come into town from all over. Once in a while, there's bound to be a bad apple."

"Right," Frank agreed, but I could tell he was starting to get suspicious.

---

<u>SUSPECT PROFILE</u>

<u>Name:</u> Arnold "Bump" Rankowski

<u>Hometown:</u> Ocean Point, New Jersey

<u>Physical description:</u> Age 48, 6', 230 lbs., ruddy complexion, deep suntan, graying hair, always smiling, big teeth.

<u>Occupation:</u> Mayor of Ocean Point

<u>Background:</u> Wealthy entrepreneur/politician who was born in Ocean Point and wound up as its mayor. Never married. No children.

<u>Suspicious behavior:</u> The sense that he's got a secret.

<u>Suspected of:</u> Is he hiding what he knows about the jewel thefts?

<u>Possible motives:</u> Saving his town's reputation, maybe?

---

"Has the thief been caught yet?" Frank asked.

"Not yet," Bump said, staring straight ahead as he pointed us toward the landing strip. "But we've got the best police department on the whole shore, and they're on the case. Don't you boys worry. Ocean Point is as safe a spot as you'll ever find."

He brought us in for a perfect landing, and we taxied to a stop outside the small terminal building. "Come on," he said. "I'll drive you to your hotel. Where are you staying?"

"Well, we hadn't figured that out yet," I said. "Any suggestions?"

"Are you kidding?" he said. "I've got a million of them."

He drove us to the Surfside Inn, just half a block from the boardwalk. "Here you go," he said, pulling over. "Best spot in town if you're on a budget—and most kids your age are."

"Thanks, Mr. Rankowski," Frank said. "I mean, Bump."

"Don't be strangers, now. If you need anything, you can find me at City Hall, over on Main Street."

"Well," Frank said, as Bump pulled away in his big black Lincoln. "That was interesting."

"Weird," I said. "What did you think of our new friend?"

"He's definitely a politician," Frank said. "You've

48

got to take everything he says with a grain of salt."

"Did you see how he froze up when you mentioned the robberies?"

"Definitely."

"I guess he's not happy that the news is getting around."

"Would you be, if you were the mayor?"

"Good point," I said. "Well, I don't know about you, but I'm beat. Let's check in, get some supper, and hit the sack."

"What, no partying?" Frank said, giving me an elbow in the ribs.

"Shut up," I said.

# 6.

## Ocean Point

I woke up the next morning when the sun rose over the horizon and shone right smack into my face. It glinted over the ocean, magnifying the light till it was blinding. There was no way to keep on sleeping.

"Oh, man," I said to Joe, who was holding his pillow over his head to keep the light away. "You forgot to close the curtains!"

"*I* forgot?" He threw his pillow at me. I threw mine at him.

"Close the curtains," he said.

"Me? Why me? You're closer to the window."

"Because, dude," Joe groaned. "I hurt all over."

"*You* hurt? Hey, I'm the one who almost got crushed in that grain bin!"

"Big deal," Joe said. "I'm the one who got kicked by a cow!"

"I'm the one who went out on the wing of the plane!"

"Okay, okay," Joe said, hoisting himself up and going to close the curtains. Half a minute later he was back in bed and passed out.

Despite my victory, I couldn't get back to sleep, so I took a hot shower instead. It took some of the soreness out of my muscles. Then I went downstairs to check out the scene.

It was a gorgeous summer morning. The hotel was only half a block from the boardwalk. In between was a miniature golf course, already packed with kids and their parents.

It was a little early for swimming, but by ten o'clock, lots of people would be on the beach and in the water. It was going to be a hot one.

I had some pancakes at the restaurant up the block, then went back up to the room to wake Joe. Time was a-wasting. We had to get started if we wanted to nail our serial jewel thief.

Joe was already up, out of the shower, and in his bathing suit. "Time to check out the scenery!" he said. "I'm feeling ir-res-istible today. Hey, how does my eye look?"

"Better," I lied. "It barely shows. Still, you'd better

come up with a good story to explain how you got it."

"Whatever I do come up with, you'd better back me up."

"Don't worry about it."

"Come on, let's hit the beach."

"Joe, don't you think we'd better do some investigating first? I mean, we're here on a case, remember?"

Joe gave me a look. "All work and no play makes Frank a dull boy."

"How 'bout we go to the jewelry stores that got hit, and see what we can find out?" I suggested.

"Later," Joe said, admiring himself in his new bathing suit. "Gotta take a swim first."

"Joe . . ."

"Maybe do a little surfing . . . we could rent boards. . . ."

"Joe . . ."

"Hey, there's information to be dug up on the beach, too, right? Right?"

I sighed, shook my head, and went to get my suit on.

There's no arguing with Joe sometimes. Like when the surf looked this good.

Hang on, I've got to step in.

In his heart Frank *knew* I was right. There was no better way to get the lay of the land than to go out and do what everyone else was doing.

In Ocean Point that meant swimming. It meant surfing. It meant beach volleyball, cruising the boardwalk, hitting the arcades and amusement park rides, finding cool junk and funky T-shirts in the gift shops and stores. It meant checking out the sidewalk artists and performers who were everywhere in this honky-tonk beach town.

And ah, yes, taking in the bikini parade. *Awesome.*

It meant eating at pizza joints and soft ice cream stands, hot dogs and pretzels and cotton candy . . .

Suddenly I realized I hadn't eaten breakfast. "Frank," I said. "Let's stop and get something to eat."

"No thanks," he said. "I already ate."

"Huh? When was that?"

"While you were sleeping."

Frank can be so annoying sometimes.

"You didn't bring me anything back?"

"I didn't know what you'd want."

*Yeah, right.* "Okay, well, I've gotta eat something. *Now.*"

"Whatever," he said.

We went outside and headed for the boardwalk. Right away I spotted a sign that read: SALTWATER TAFFY—HOMEMADE!

Sounded good to me. I always like to sample the native cuisine. We started heading over.

Over at the amusement park on the nearby pier, we saw some kids screaming on the Ferris wheel. There was a tattoo parlor called Rat-a-Tattoo, and a sign that read: FREAK SHOW—TICKETS $10!

As we entered the saltwater taffy place, we saw this guy behind the counter who—I swear— looked like he was *made* out of saltwater taffy. He was fat, and flabby, and bald, and slightly green. He was reading the morning paper.

"Hi, I'd like some taffy," I told him.

He lowered his paper and slid off his stool. "What flavor you want?" he asked. He had an accent—Russian, it sounded like.

"I don't know . . . the pink," I said.

"Strawberry . . . good choice. How much you want?"

"I don't know," I said. "Enough for breakfast."

He didn't bat an eyelash.

With a big, scary-looking knife, he sliced off a

piece of the sticky stuff, slipped it into a plastic bag, and handed it to me. "Six-fifty," he said.

While I was fishing out my wallet, Frank asked him, "Is there really salt water in saltwater taffy?"

The guy smiled. His teeth were all rotted out and black, naturally.

"Nah!" he said. "Good question, though. Most people assume it's made out of salt water. Americans, they aren't very curious. You're a smart boychick."

"Smart what?" Frank said.

"Boychick. Russian for boy. So *you* want some taffy too?"

"No, thanks," Frank said. "My brother's the one with the sweet tooth."

"Smart kid," the man said, chuckling. "Thinks about his teeth, they shouldn't get cavities."

He turned to me. "You should be more like your brother. Maybe then you won't get black eye."

"How do they make taffy?" Frank asked him, before I could tell the guy where to get off.

"*They? I* make it! Right here in the store."

He pointed to a big machine in the back of the shop that was churning a load of gooey green taffy in spirals, over and over and over again. "That's how we do it. Gotta spin for four hours to get the right softness. You buy it in supermarket, it's not the same thing."

"I bet it isn't," Frank said, looking at the man's newspaper. "So, what's all this about robberies in town? Any idea who's behind it?" Frank asked, pointing at the front page.

Now I saw why he'd been wasting his time on this slob. Frank never stops thinking.

"If you ask me, everybody here has racket. This is just the same thing, only big-time. Everybody is con artist."

I bit my lip. What were Frank and I, if not con artists? Making people believe we were just here for a little fun in the sun, while all the time we were really tracking down a brazen thief?

While they were talking, I was trying to break off a piece of taffy to start chewing on. It didn't want to stop stretching, though, and pretty soon I was fighting with it, backing up toward the window.

Suddenly something grabbed me by the hair.

"Aaargh!"

"NO!" the taffy man shouted. "Don't go there! You'll get stuck!"

"Thanks for the warning," I said, holding onto the hair that was now stuck to one of the big wads of fresh taffy hanging in the shop window. "A little late, but much appreciated. Could you please help me get free of this?"

Frank came right over, but the guy just stood

there shaking his head. "You not gonna get it off like that," he said.

He came toward us with his big knife. Before I could stop him, he cut me loose from the hanging taffy. Now there was just a small piece of it stuck to my hair.

"Don't pull on it, or your hair's gonna come right out," he told me.

"Well, how am I supposed to get this off of me?"

"Joe, don't panic," Frank told me.

"What do you mean, don't panic?"

"Salt water," the guy said.

"What?"

"With salt water, will come right off. You'll go in the ocean, bim-boom, it comes right off you hair."

"Whew. What a relief," I said, backing out the door. "Well, bye. Nice talking to you. Come on, Frank—I've gotta get this off right *now.*"

We crossed the boardwalk and went down the wooden stairs to the beach. There we were, surrounded by kite flyers, Frisbee flippers, volleyball players, and boogie boarders. Everywhere we looked, there were blankets spread out, with cute girls busy getting tans.

"Hi!" one of them said as we passed.

For a fatal moment, I forgot what was attached to my hair.

"Hi yourself," I said, putting on my smoothest move. "What's up? Looking for some company?"

She giggled, and now both she and her friend were checking us out. I sat down next to the one who'd said hi.

I could tell Frank wanted to get on with our job here, but he saw that I was determined not to be rude to our fine new friends, so he sat down too.

Within ten seconds the two girls were surrounding Frank—as far from me on the blanket as it was possible to be. "What is that thing in his *hair*?" I heard one of them whisper in Frank's ear.

"And what happened to his eye?" the other one asked, looking at me.

"Um, it's a long story," I said, standing up before they could see how red my face was getting. "Frank will tell you all about it. I've gotta go cool off in the water. . . ."

I ran for the ocean as fast as I could.

*What a doofus!* How could I have forgotten how geeky I looked with that taffy sticking up from my hair?

Later, I promised myself, I'd go back to that store and get my money back.

The water was cold when I dove into it, but after ten seconds of screaming, I started to get used to it. Then I got busy scrubbing the stupid taffy off.

Lucky for that guy, he wasn't kidding. The taffy came right out.

Too bad I still had that black eye. Frank was right—I should have gotten some makeup for it.

I came out of the water, feeling embarrassed but ready to get on with my life. I saw that the two girls both had their arms around Frank and were laughing their heads off. Frank looked like the cat that ate the canary.

I was about to go over there and remind him that we were supposed to be fighting crime when I noticed something I'd never seen before. It was a huge drawing in the sand, probably created with rakes. Very cool.

I looked at it more closely and saw that it was really an advertisement. THE SHORE THING: FINE JEWELRY, it read.

There was a guy with a metal detector walking across the beach, slowly waving it back and forth. He was about to step right on the embossed ad— on the Y in Jewelry, to be exact.

"Hey!" I called out to him. "Watch where you're walking!"

He stopped and looked up at me with a face that would freeze a furnace.

This was perhaps the ugliest dude I'd ever seen. And his expression was even uglier. He kept staring at me as he marched forward, stomping right through the artwork.

I made a mental note to tell Frank about him. A mental note that I immediately proceeded to forget.

"Come on, lover boy," I told Frank when I reached the little threesome. "We've got work to do."

"Sorry," Frank said to the girls as he rose. "Joe's right. We do have to go."

"Aw, what's your hurry?" the taller of the two girls said.

"Wait a second," said the other. Whipping out a pen from her beach bag, she wrote her phone number on Frank's palm. "See you soon?"

"S-sure," Frank said.

I pulled him away before he could say anything to embarrass himself.

We were about to hit the boardwalk, looking for the first of the jewelry stores on our list, when we heard someone screaming behind us. We turned around to find a whole group of people shouting.

"That little girl out there!" I heard someone say, pointing toward the ocean. "She's drowning!"

There were lifeguards on this beach, but I didn't see any of them running to help. In fact, the lifeguard chair nearest to us was empty. But it wouldn't have mattered if there were six lifeguards swimming toward the drowning girl. Frank and I were already racing toward the water.

I could see her now—a little girl of about eight, drifting way out over her head, flailing her arms and screaming for help.

Just as Frank and I were about to dive in, we heard a loud voice behind us.

"EVERYBODY OUT OF THE WATER!"

It was the lifeguard. He was standing on the ladder that led up to his chair, holding on with one hand. In the other he was holding a megaphone.

"Out of the water!" he repeated. "Sharks! Sharks!"

Suddenly, like a human wave, all the people in the water—most of whom had been swimming toward the drowning girl—were turning back and heading for shore.

But not me and Frank. Sharks or no sharks, somebody had to save that little girl's life.

# 7.

## All in a Day's Work

Joe and I are both on the Bayport High swim team. He does short sprints and relays. I hold the school record in the 4 x 400 medley. But it doesn't matter how fast you swim—sharks can swim faster.

The best thing to do was not to think about the danger. We just had to focus on saving that little girl. Every few strokes I'd stop and try to get a bead on where she was. But by the time we were within thirty yards or so, all I saw was the fin, sticking up out of the water.

"You dive down and get her!" I heard Joe shout from somewhere to my right. "I'll fend off the shark!"

I wanted to argue with him, to take on the more dangerous job myself, but there was no time. The little girl's lungs would be full of water by now, and she'd sink like a stone if I couldn't grab her first.

I dove underwater, keeping my eye out for a sinking girl or a swimming shark.

There she was, sure enough. There were still bubbles rising from her mouth and nose, which meant she still had enough air to keep her suspended in the water. But that wouldn't last long.

I strained every muscle in my body to get to her before it was too late.

*There!*

Throwing her over my shoulder, I held her tight and made for the surface. My own lungs felt like they were going to burst, but I just kept kicking, hoping I'd get some air before I passed out and sent both of us to a watery grave.

I broke the surface just as I was starting to see stars. The world went white for a split second, and then I could hear myself gasping.

Not a peep from the girl, though.

I looked around for Joe, and saw him swimming toward me, holding something by a rope.

A surfboard!

"Some shark," he said as he got near us. "It was turned over, with the fin sticking up."

He brought the board over, and I hoisted the

little girl onto it. Then Joe and I got on opposite sides of the board and swam for shore.

I only hoped it wasn't too late to save our little surfboarder.

No sooner had we got to the beach than a crowd gathered around us. I flipped the girl over onto her stomach and pushed down on her abdominal area. Water gushed out of her mouth. I pushed again, and she started coughing her lungs out.

She was going to make it!

"Make way!" I heard the lifeguard's angry voice barking through the megaphone as he pushed his way through the crowd.

Then he grabbed me by the shoulder. "Back off!" he ordered. "I'll take care of this."

I'm not a hothead by any stretch of the imagination, but nobody—*nobody*—manhandles me and gets away with it. Especially not a lifeguard this dumb. If that girl hadn't still been lying there, needing help, I would have laid into that guy right then and there.

Or maybe not. This guy was a specimen, even for a Jersey Shore lifeguard. From the looks of him, he might well have been a contestant in body-building contests.

He was wearing a thick gold chain around his neck and another around his left wrist—but you could tell that with one flex of his muscles he could have snapped those chains easily.

"Leave my brother alone," Joe said. Next thing I knew, he had pulled the guy away from me and spun him around.

"Hey!" the lifeguard said. "Get your hands off me, punk!" He reared back and let go a left hook that caught Joe smack in the eye—the one that wasn't already blackened.

Now, Joe is a black belt in aikido, and a pretty fair hand at tae kwon do, too—but I know he wasn't thinking straight right then. See, the whole point of the martial arts is to fight with your mind. Not your emotions.

And Joe gets really emotional sometimes. Especially when he's been sucker-punched in the eye. He can get really *angry*.

And who could blame him for being caught off guard? I mean, here we'd just saved this little girl's life. We thought high fives and pats on the back were in order—not the hard time this rockhead lifeguard was giving us.

I could see that Joe was furious. He shook off the pain and squared his body toward his attacker. "Come on," he said. "Let's see you try that again, now that I'm ready for you."

The lifeguard was happy to oblige.

But this time Joe was too quick for him. He ducked out of the way, and at the same time grabbed the guy's arm and helped it along in the direction it was already going.

Then Joe gave a slight yank. The poor slob flipped in midair and came down hard on the sand. The fallen lifeguard muttered something filthy and cracked his knuckles, getting ready for another attack.

"Leave him alone!" one of our blond friends yelled. She stepped right between them. "Those two guys are heroes, you jerk. You should be thanking them!"

"Yeah!" our other friend said. Several others in the tight circle surrounding us agreed.

"Lay off!"

"Put a sock in it!"

"Hey!" the lifeguard yelled, brushing the sand off himself. "Everybody back off! I'm in charge here, and what I say goes!"

"Actually, what *I* say goes."

Everyone turned to see where the booming voice had come from. There stood Bump Rankowski—*Mayor* Bump Rankowski.

"Oh, hi, Mr. Mayor," the lifeguard said, suddenly looking a whole lot smaller and weaker.

"What's going on here?" Bump demanded.

"Um, these two guys disobeyed my orders to clear the water."

"And why'd you order the water cleared?"

"Shark spotting, sir," the lifeguard explained.

"There was no shark, Bump," Joe interrupted. "It was just this surfboard's fin, sticking out of the water. And this little girl was drowning."

The little girl was sitting up by now, with her head tucked between her knees. She coughed every few seconds, but it was easy to see she was going to be all right.

Her mother had found us all by then and was kneeling down, brushing the damp hair out of her daughter's face.

"My baby," she kept saying. "My baby . . . I just went back to our room for a minute. But I could have lost you!"

Well, yeah. Who leaves their little girl on the beach alone for as long as she did?

"What's your name, son?" Bump asked the lifeguard.

"Um, Chuck. Chuck Fatone, sir."

"Chuck Fatone, hmm? I'm gonna remember your name, son," Bump said, shaking a finger at him. "I'd better not hear it again, unless it's to say you saved somebody's life. Understand?"

Fatone gave Joe and me a murderous look

# SUSPECT PROFILE

**Name:** Charles "Chuck" Fatone, aka "Chuckie"

**Hometown:** Trenton, New Jersey

**Physical description:** Age 22, 6'3'',
220 lbs. of solid muscle, movie-star suntan, blond,
buzz-cut hair, perpetual angry expression
on his face.

**Occupation:** Lifeguard

**Background:** Grew up tough, got tougher. Likes
bodybuilding, being a lifeguard, impressing girls
in bikinis. Doesn't like anybody getting in his way.
Never married. Never will be. Children? No way.

**Suspicious behavior:** Not acting faster to save
drowning child. Picking a fight with Joe. Just
being a generally nasty guy.

**Suspected of:** Jewel theft, maybe? Bad things
(like burglaries) are generally done by bad guys
(like Chuckie).

**Possible motives:** Greed. Rats love cheese, and
there's no cheese like expensive bling-bling if
you're a rat like Chuckie.

before turning back to the mayor. "Yessir," he said, his mouth twisted into a bitter sneer.

"I hope so," Bump said. Then he turned to the assembled crowd. "All right, everybody. Excitement's over. There was no shark attack. You can rest assured, everything's under control."

Bump's cheerful tone seemed to calm the crowd, and they started to disperse. I could see why he was a successful politician. Everyone just naturally seemed to follow his orders.

"All is well, everyone. Continue having fun on our beautiful beaches. Don't go home without visiting our many fine shops—and make sure you spend lots and lots of money!" At this, he laughed with the crowd. "Oh, and don't forget to use sunscreen!"

With these words the tension was broken. Calm was restored. It was just another wonderful, sunny, hot day at the beach.

"Come on with me, you two," Bump said, throwing an arm around each of our shoulders. "I've got something I want to tell you."

He guided us to a shady spot underneath the boardwalk. Then I felt his grip on my shoulder tighten.

"Listen here," he said. His voice suddenly had a steely note in it. "Trouble seems to follow you boys—first the airplane thing, now this."

"But—"

"Trouble is *not* good for business," he continued. "Not good at all. People don't vacation in places if they're scared a shark will bite them. Got that?"

"But we weren't the ones who—," Joe tried to tell him.

Bump wasn't listening, though. "When the tourists don't come, business gets bad. Really bad."

"But we didn't—"

"And when business gets bad, mayors don't get reelected. *Comprende?*"

What could we say?

"Yes, sir."

"Yes, sir."

"Yes, *Bump,*" he reminded us, his best politician's smile flashing back to life. "Call me Bump."

He took out a handkerchief, mopped his brow, and turned back to join the crowd on the beach, waving and smiling at everyone.

"Enjoy, everyone! Enjoy Ocean Point—Pearl of the Jersey Shore!"

# 8.

## Scene of the Crime

Well, *that* was interesting. It was a whole other side of Mayor Bump that we hadn't seen before. There was something else to the guy, underneath his salesman personality. Something gritty and distrusting. It made me wonder what else he knew about the robberies going on in his town—and what he might have reason to hide.

I remembered his words: *"When business gets bad, mayors don't get reelected."*

"Hey, Frank, " I said, "I'll bet if we tell Bump we're here investigating the robberies, he'd have a lot more information to give us."

"Yeah, but we're not going to do that, Joe," he said. "If ATAC wanted him to know, they would have told him we were coming."

Frank was right. We were here undercover, and we'd have to stay that way as long as possible—even if it meant we didn't get access to key information.

And, as our dad says, "There's always another way to get the dirt."

We walked over to a big map bolted to the railing of the boardwalk. Frank fished in his bag and pulled out his PDA. "Let's see," he said, scrolling down with his pointer. "Okay, here are the stores that were robbed. Let's see which is the nearest."

The Shore Thing was the obvious choice—it was just a block off the boardwalk, a little ways south. The other two places were farther down, so we'd be going the right way.

"How's your eye?" Frank asked me.

"Which one?"

There was no way around it—I was now going to have *two* black eyes.

"Guess I should call you raccoon-man," Frank said, snickering.

"Smile a little more when you say that," I said, and headed for a gift shop I'd spotted up ahead. "I'm gonna buy me some shades. Pronto."

I already had a pair for flying, but I'd wanted a pair to just kick around with on the beach, and now seemed the perfect time to go shopping. Within minutes I found a cool pair. Metal. Shiny. Plastic.

"How do I look?" I asked Frank.

In response, he turned and walked away. Who can blame him for being jealous of my looks?

The Shore Thing was not what I'd expected in a jewelry store by the boardwalk. From the fancy awning to the insanely expensive stuff in the display windows, this place reeked of class.

I should have known. Only a place like this could afford to pay for that advertisement engraved in the sand.

"Hey, Frank," I said, catching up to him before he went inside, "how are we gonna handle this?"

"What do you mean?"

"What are we gonna say?"

He smiled. "Leave it to me. Just follow my lead, and let me do the talking."

*Okay. Why not?* I followed him inside and waited to see Frank's latest game begin.

A bell tinkled somewhere, and this woman came out from the back of the store. Her heels were high, her dress looked like a million bucks—and so did she.

"Can I help you boys?" she asked, giving us the once-over. I could tell by the look in her eyes that she didn't hold out high hopes for us as customers.

"I was looking for a ring for my girlfriend," Frank said.

One of her eyebrows arched. "Aren't you a little young to be thinking about marriage?"

"Oh, no, it's nothing like that," Frank said quickly. "Just a ring—with her birthstone."

"Okay," the woman said, going over to the display cases and opening one up. "What's her birthday?"

"April 1," Frank blurted.

*April Fool's Day!* Man, he is a smooth liar! He should have been an actor.

What am I saying? He was acting in that store!

"Ah," the woman said with a smile. "She's going to cost you. Diamonds are the birthstone for April."

"D-diamonds?" Frank repeated, sounding like our parrot, Playback. I knew what he was thinking: "Why didn't I pick a different month?"

Guys know nothing about birthstones.

"How about a nice cubic zirconium?" the lady in the dress suggested.

"You mean a fake?" Frank said.

74

"Well, yes, but a very good one. She'll never know." She gave Frank a wink.

And stupid Frank, instead of saying "Okay," said: "I wouldn't lie to my girlfriend."

The woman laughed, and I could see that Frank had won her over. "Nice boy," she said, patting him on the cheek. "She's a lucky girl."

Frank went beet red. "So, could we see the diamonds?"

She laughed again and went to get a tray of diamond rings to show Frank. "Your friend's a big spender," she told me.

"My brother," I said.

"Don't you ever take those sunglasses off?" she asked me.

"Never," I said.

Okay, it was lame, but what else could I say? I wasn't going to take off my shades and show her my raccoon eyes!

"Ma'am," Frank said, "I heard this store got broken into pretty recently. Is that true?"

She froze. She turned. She gave Frank a long, hard look, decided he wasn't a criminal about to rob her, then brought the tray of diamonds over to him. "True," she said.

I could see that she was still shaken up by what

75

had happened—or by the fact that Frank was asking about it.

"Were you here when the store was broken into?" Frank asked.

"No, it was overnight."

"Huh," Frank said. "Did the police catch the guys?"

"Are you kidding?" she said. "Do they ever catch anybody? They're way too busy giving parking tickets to my customers."

"So was there a big mess?" Frank asked. "Did they break all the windows and stuff?"

"No, not at all," she answered, pushing the tray of diamond rings toward Frank. "Funny, huh? Now, this one's not too expensive. . . ."

Frank examined the ring she was holding up. From where I was standing, about ten feet away, I couldn't even see the stone. It had to be tiny.

"How much is it?"

"Fifteen."

"Fifteen dollars? I'll take it!"

"Fifteen hundred dollars," the woman corrected him.

"Oh," Frank said. "Never mind."

She smiled out of one side of her mouth as she put the ring back. "Maybe something . . . smaller."

"So, about the break-in," Frank said—but he was pushing too hard now.

The woman looked right at him, then at me, and then back at Frank. "You didn't come in here to buy diamonds," she said, her voice suddenly low and hoarse.

"Uh, no, ma'am," Frank said.

"What do you want from me?" She grabbed the tray of diamonds and started backing away toward the display cases. "Why are you asking me all these questions?"

"We're trying to track down the jewel thieves," Frank blurted out. "We're detectives, ma'am."

I couldn't believe it! We were supposed to be undercover here, and he was blabbing about it to a total stranger!

"Private detectives?" the woman asked.

Wisely, Frank let her believe it. She knew too much about us already, if you asked me.

"Yes. We look young for our age. Believe me, we're on your side," Frank told the lady.

She seemed willing to listen—maybe because Frank had made such a nice first impression on her.

"I've already told the police everything," she said. "Why can't you ask them?"

"Ma'am," Frank said, "whatever you told them,

it obviously wasn't enough for them to catch the crooks. There've been two more robberies since, and still no arrests."

"If you know all that, what do you want from me?"

"Why don't you just tell us what happened—from scratch. There might be a little detail in there that the police missed. It could be the key piece of the puzzle—you never know."

She curled over the counter and put her head in her hands. "It had to be an inside job," she said in a low voice. "The security alarm never went off. There were no signs of break-in."

"Who do you think could have done it?" I asked her. "You must have some ideas."

She sighed. "I've thought about it ever since that night. I thought it might be this guy who owns Long John's Silver over on Atlantic Avenue, but then I found out he'd been robbed too—the day before I was."

"Is there anybody else who might know how to beat your security system?" I asked.

"Not that I can think of . . ." Her eyes suddenly clouded over. "Wait a minute." She paused. "No, that's a terrible thought. . . ."

"What?" Frank prodded her.

"I did fire one of my younger employees a few weeks ago, a man in charge of maintenance and cleaning . . . because he kept coming in late. But—"

"It's something," Frank said. "Maybe he was angry and decided to get back at you by robbing the place."

"But why would he rob the other two stores, then?" she asked.

"She's got you there, Frank," I said.

"Well, what's his name, anyway?" Frank said. "We can at least go talk to him."

"I'll give it to you," she said, "but please—don't harass him in any way. He's probably innocent, and I wouldn't want him to be angry at me. . . ."

Something about the way she said this made me think the woman was deathly afraid of her former employee.

"His name is Ricardo Myers."

"Where can we find him?" I asked.

"Well, somebody told me he got a job tattooing up the beach . . . on the pier, I think. You could ask around there."

"Thanks," said Frank, getting up. "We will." He shook her hand. "You've been very helpful . . ."

"Mary," the woman told him. "Mary Fleming.

Here's my card. Please call me if you find anything out."

"You got it," Frank said, and then we were out of there, the little bell tinkling behind us.

I could feel Mary's eyes following us as we headed back toward the boardwalk and the pier.

"What do you think?" I asked Frank.

"About what?"

"About her. Mary Fleming."

"Smart lady."

"Good-looking, too."

"Huh? What's with you today, Joe?"

"Nothing. I just wonder if you let her good looks blind you, that's all."

"Blind me to *what*?"

"Maybe she gave us a good lead," I said. "And *maybe* this guy Ricardo is our man. But it's also possible she's sending us on a wild goose chase. That's all I'm saying."

"Joe, she got robbed," Frank said. "She's a victim, not a suspect."

"She knows we're here investigating," I reminded him.

"So?"

"So, she's now officially dangerous."

"You are *so* weird," Frank said, laughing and shaking his head.

"Hey, Frank. You know what? It's even possible she robbed her own jewelry store."

<u>SUSPECT PROFILE</u>

<u>Name:</u> Mary Fleming

<u>Hometown:</u> New York, NY

<u>Physical description:</u> Age 37, 5'7", 125 lbs., frosted blonde hair, elegant looks, expensive clothes and shoes.

<u>Occupation:</u> Businesswoman

<u>Background:</u> Grew up on Park Avenue, moved to the shore after her divorce. No children. Owns her own business and a house on the beach in nearby Avalon, as well as an apartment in the city where she stays in the winter. Devoted to her business and to making it grow. Drives a hard bargain.

<u>Suspicious behavior:</u> Knows her own security system. A calculating mind and very expensive taste.

<u>Suspected of:</u> Robbing two jewelry stores, plus her own (just to give herself an alibi).

<u>Possible motives:</u> Need or greed—insurance payments can come in very handy.

"What? Why would she do that?"

"I don't know—but there could be a reason. All I know is, there's something about Mary Fleming that I don't like."

# 9.

## X Marks the Spot

Joe is totally nuts, okay?

I don't know, I must have been looking good that week, but for some reason I'd been getting a lot of attention from girls—and women.

And Joe, who now had two—not one, but two—black eyes, was getting more and more jealous by the minute.

I mean, take that poor woman, Mary Fleming. He kept insisting she was some kind of dangerous criminal.

In the past he'd often been right about these hunches of his. But I think this time his black eyes had him seeing things that weren't there.

We got over to the pier in about five minutes.

Most of it was enclosed, and from outside I didn't see any tattoo parlor signs.

"Let's have a look inside," I said.

We did, and we were immediately hit by a wave of noise—dings and rings and blowing horns, and hundreds of human voices, shouting, screaming, laughing. There was the smells of popcorn, salt-water taffy, cotton candy, sunscreen, and people—the good, the bad, and the ugly.

"Hey, Frank, check it out!" Joe said, nudging me and pointing to a sign that read: SOLLY'S SIDESHOW FREAKS. "I've gotta see the sword-swallower—and the bearded lady, too!"

"Later, Joe," I said. "First we talk to Ricardo, okay?"

But Joe was already buying our tickets. He's just too fast for me.

So we went inside, and there were all the freaks and geeks: a guy maybe five feet tall who must have weighed about 800 pounds; a lady with a long beard that looked real and hung down to her belly button; a guy eating fire and swallowing swords; a lady with (if you believed her—and I did) over 500 piercings.

Then I noticed the tattooed man. "I bet he can tell us where to find Ricardo Myers."

I wandered over to the guy. He was busy making muscleman poses so people could snap his picture. His face was covered with tattooed spider webs, and he was in shorts, so everyone could see that his whole body was totally covered with tattoos.

"Wanna take a picture?" he asked me when I reached the front of the little crowd that surrounded him.

"No, thanks," I said. "But can I ask you something?"

"Sure, pal. Go ahead, shoot."

"Doesn't it . . . hurt to get those?"

He laughed. "No pain, no gain."

"Well, what if you wanted to get them removed?"

"Why would I wanna do that?"

I didn't want to upset him, so I just shrugged. "No reason, I guess."

Especially if you *like* being a sideshow attraction.

"Actually, I was thinking of getting a tattoo," I lied. "But I want it done by somebody really good."

"Excellent idea," he said. "Nothing worse than bad art you have to wear."

"I heard about this guy, Ricardo Myers? He's supposed to be good. You know him?"

Tattoo Man smiled and pointed to his face. "He did my spidey-web."

"Cool!" I said. "Know where I can find him?"

"Sure—all the way out on the pier. Place called Rat-a-Tattoo."

Oh yeah—we'd seen that place.

"Thanks!" I said. "Um, keep up the good work!"

I flashed him a thumbs-up and got out of there before I said anything else that would get me into trouble.

"Come on, Joe," I said, dragging him away from the bearded lady. "Let's go find Ricardo."

Rat-a-Tattoo had a psychedelic-style sign above its entrance and a crowd of tattooed and pierced kids hanging out in front.

"Excuse us," I said as we made our way past them. "Coming through."

They stared at us like we were from the moon. A few of them smiled and laughed, thinking we were here to get our first tattoo or piercing.

Inside, we looked around. There were sample drawings hanging from all the walls. You could pick any of these for your tattoo, or bring your own drawing. In the center of the store were cases of rings and pins to stick through whatever hole you had the guys behind the counter poke in you.

There was a curtained doorway, behind which the actual "procedures" were being done, judging by the howls of pain that were coming from back there.

Now, to find Ricardo Myers.

## JOE

Joe here. Frank can be a pretty cool guy, but sometimes he turns into something else.

How should I put it? A geek? A nerd? A totally hopeless loser?

Here we were, in this tattoo palace, surrounded by girls in halter tops that showed off their belly button rings.

And Frank? He was standing there like a frozen yogurt on a stick. This girl was standing right in front of him. She had a tattoo of a shark on her stomach, and she was rolling her belly at him so the shark seemed to swim.

Man, I wished I could take off those shades of mine and introduce myself. Why, that week of all weeks, did I have to get stuck with two black eyes?

I couldn't take any more of this.

I went over to a guy who was, according to the plastic tag on his shirt, the store manager. "That guy over there?" I whispered in his ear. "That's my brother. He wants a nose ring, but he's too shy to ask about it."

"Cool," said the guy, and went over to talk to Frank. I couldn't hear what he said, but Frank looked at him like he was from Mars. Meanwhile, the girl with the shark tattoo moved on, giving up on Frank.

*Victory!*

"Hey, Frank, come on!" I said, playing like I was him and he was me. "We've got work to do!"

Frank came over. "This place is giving me the creeps," he said. "Let's find Ricardo."

"He's gotta be back there," I said, indicating the curtain.

Over it was a sign reading: EMPLOYEES ONLY. We waited for the manager to turn his back, then sneaked behind it.

Back here, there were little cubicles on either side of a long, brightly lit room. In each cubicle someone was getting pierced or tattooed.

Five of the workers were female. That left three possibilities, and two of them looked like they were at least fifty years old. Mary had said Ricardo was young.

We tried the other guy, who was dressed in shorts and sandals but no shirt. He had a ponytail that hid the tattoo in the middle of his back, but I could see that it was some kind of snake wound around its prey.

This guy was obviously not someone to be messed with.

"Ricardo Myers?" Frank said.

Snake Man looked right at him.

"Who wants to know?"

He left off what he was doing and said to his customer, "I'll be right back." Coming over to us, he said, "Who are you?"

"I'm Frank Hardy, and this is my brother, Joe."

"Yeah? So who sent you?"

"Actually," Frank said, "we're looking into the break-in at The Shore Thing. We wanted to ask you a few questions."

"What are you, cops?"

I could see that Ricardo was getting angry, but the steam wasn't quite coming out of his ears yet.

"Not cops, really," Frank said. "We're sort of checking it out on our own. Turns out some people are saying you might be involved."

"Oh, yeah? Like who?"

"Um, I'm not at liberty to say," Frank told him.

"That Fleming lady," Ricardo said bitterly. "I hate that woman—she's a snob, man. She thinks if you're tough, you must be a criminal."

## SUSPECT PROFILE

**Name:** Ricardo Myers

**Hometown:** Newark, New Jersey

**Physical description:** Age 23, 5'7", 160 lbs., hair in ponytail, several tattoos.

**Occupation:** Tattoo artist, may have mystery occupation on the side.

**Background:** Grew up in the 'hood, spends summers at the shore. Considered a tattoo artist. Hurting for money, throws away whatever he has by betting it at Atlantic City. Hates rich people and snobs.

**Suspicious behavior:** His hatred of Mary Fleming and his dread of cops.

**Suspected of:** Jewel theft.

**Possible motives:** Revenge on his ex-boss. Need to pay his debts (gamblers often owe lots of money to loan sharks).

"So . . . I guess it's good she fired you, then?" I said.

"Hey! Nobody fires me!" he snapped, grabbing me by the arm. He was so angry, and so strong, that I thought he was going to snap it right off. "Get it?"

"I get it, I get it!" I said. I would have said anything right then, just to make him stop.

Then, just as suddenly as he'd grabbed me, he relaxed his grip and let out a little laugh. "Yeah, man. I like it better here. I make my own hours. Plus I can express myself, y'know? Get into my art."

"How's the pay?" Frank asked.

Good question.

"Stinks." Ricardo's smile vanished.

"How do you get by, then?" Frank asked.

Ricardo's face got ugly in a hurry. "Bug off, okay? It's none of your business how I get by. Mind your own business!"

He gave Frank a shove that sent him into the wall, hard.

Man, talk about mood swings! This guy needed medication, or some serious help.

Frank stayed cool. He just worked out the kinks in his neck and said, "What I really want to ask you, Ricardo, is—"

Just then, the manager lifted the curtain and saw us. "Hey! No customers back here!" he said.

"Oh, sorry," Frank told him. "We're just going."

"Now!"

"Okay, okay," I said, getting between them to give Frank a little more time.

"Here's the question, Ricardo," I heard him say behind me. "Who do you think did it?"

"That's easy. If you're askin' me, I say Mary did it herself."

"Mary?"

"Yeah, man. I bet she ripped off those other two places, then knocked over her own store, just to make herself look innocent."

"Out! Now!" the manager yelled.

"We're going, we're going!" I told him as he shoved us along. "Take it easy, dude. No harm, no foul, okay?"

I heard Ricardo shouting after us. "Hey! If I'd ripped off two million bucks' worth of bling, you think I'd be sitting here doing ankle tattoos for twenty a pop?"

*Good point.*

With a brief good-bye, we walked out of the shop and headed back down the pier.

"So, what do you think?" I asked Frank.

"Ricardo agrees with you about Mary Fleming. So maybe you're right, Joe. I'll tell you one thing, though—it's hard to think when you're hungry. Let's get some lunch."

"I'm down with that. It's one o'clock already."

We emerged onto the boardwalk and headed for the nearest hot dog stand. We put in our orders and were waiting for our Jersey-style Texas Wieners when we heard screams. Loud screams, coming from the beach.

# 10.

## Buried Treasure

At first we thought it might be somebody drowning, or maybe even a shark attack—a real one this time. But the people who were screaming weren't even near the water. They were in the dry sand, gathered around in a big circle about five deep.

It took us a while to push our way through, and the noise was deafening. Maybe there was a rock star in there, I thought. Poor guy—it sounded like they were tearing him to pieces.

Then we got to the middle of the circle and saw what was really going on.

There was this guy with a metal detector—a truly ugly guy, with hairy moles on his face, really bad teeth, and a scraggly beard.

But that's not what had everybody so crazed.

They were screaming about what he was holding up in his hand: *a huge diamond ring!*

People wanted to get close and see it—the find of a lifetime. They wanted to touch it; to fantasize that they were the ones who'd found it. Metal Detector Man let them get close, but he wouldn't let anyone lay a hand on it.

The crowd was growing, pushing in on us. The rumor must have been racing its way down the beach. Joe was shoved into me, and I banged into the guy on my left. And what do you know, it was Chuck Fatone, the lifeguard! Good thing he wasn't paying attention to us.

"Where'd you find it?" someone asked the lucky man.

"You think I tell you where I find it?" he said in what seemed like an even thicker Russian accent than the taffy man's, and he started laughing his head off.

"I wonder why he told anyone in the first place," I said to Joe. "You'd think he'd have kept it to himself."

"Maybe someone saw him pick it up," Joe said.

"Yeah, I'll bet that's what happened."

"Hey, Frank, I ran into that guy this morning," Joe said. "I meant to tell you about him. He was messing up a really nice sand advertisement."

"A what?"

"An ad drawn in the sand."

"What are you, kidding?"

"Nope—somebody paid to have this ad done in the sand, and that dude messed it up on purpose."

"Hmmm . . ." I said. "That gives me an idea."

I went up to the guy and said, "Excuse me, sir, but I'm from the National Ad Agency, and—"

"What you want?" the guy said in his thick accent.

"This morning you defaced an advertisement of ours. You're going to have to pay for the damage."

"I not pay nothing!"

But before he knew what was happening, I'd snatched the ring from his hand and tossed it to Joe.

"Get a quick look at it!" I yelled as the guy flew at me. "Memorize it, Joe!"

"You not from advertising agency!" the angry Russian yelled, taking a swing at me. I got out of the way just in time. "You crook! Give me back diamond ring!"

"Here you go, buddy," Joe said, tossing the ring back to him. "Nice diamond—congratulations."

The guy snatched the ring out of the air and went to pick up his metal detector. Then he turned back to me. "If I see you again . . ." he said, and pretended to slit his throat with his finger.

I got the message loud and clear. And hopefully, if Joe had gotten a good look at the ring, I wouldn't need to bother him again.

"Well?" I asked him as we backed away from the crowd.

"About two karats, I'd guess. Brand new. And it had an inscription on the inside in cursive: 'Melissa & Fred 4 ever.' With the number 4."

"Good job, Joe."

"So you think it's one of the stolen items?"

"I don't know, but it shouldn't be too hard to find out. Come on."

"Where we going?"

"Back to The Shore Thing."

"Why not check the other two places first?"

"That was an expensive ring," I said. "And The Shore Thing seems to specialize in pricey stuff."

 **JOE**

Joe here. Mary Fleming didn't seem happy to see us. Not until we told her about the ring on the beach. After that, she was all action. She checked in her inventory book, and then in her ledger of current orders.

"Yes, here it is—it was scheduled to be picked up today. 'Melissa & Fred 4 ever.'"

"Whoever stole it must have dropped it," Joe said.

A reasonable guess, I had to agree. At that moment it occurred to me that the ring was found on the beach, right near the pier where Ricardo Myers worked.

Hmmm . . .

"Thanks, Ms. Fleming," I said. "We'll try to get the ring back for you."

"Thank *you,* boys!" she said, waving good-bye. "Thank you very much!"

She seemed happy about it, which I took as a good sign. If she'd stolen her own stuff, it wasn't likely she'd have dropped it on the beach, and it was even less likely that she'd be happy it was found.

Ricardo Myers had tried as hard as he could to point the finger at her. I wondered what more was going on there. What did he really have against her—and how far had he gone to get even?

We went back to the spot on the beach where the crowd had been. There was no sign of our ugly Russian friend with the metal detector.

The crowd had broken up, but all along that part of the beach, people were on their knees, screaming and yelling.

And digging.

Not far from us, a large, dark-haired girl was gouging away with a beach shovel she must have stolen from some poor little kid.

"Hey!" I called to her. "What's going on?"

She looked up at me, her eyes wide and wild.

"You'd better start digging!" she said.

"Digging for what?"

She grinned from ear to ear. "So far they've found three diamond rings and a silver bracelet in the sand!"

*JOE*

# 11.
# Gold Rush

If you've never seen a whole crowd of people go crazy, let me tell you—it is an incredible sight.

People on the beach were running in every direction. As soon as they found what they thought was a "lucky spot," they dropped to their knees and started digging.

Word must have been spreading, too, because more and more people kept coming down from the boardwalk to the beach. Some of them already had shovels or magnifying glasses. Everyone was screaming and shouting.

Can we say "madhouse"?

It was the California gold rush all over again!

"Hey, Joe," Frank said, nudging me with his elbow. "Check it out."

He nodded toward a big knot of people. I had to crane my neck to see what was going on.

Looked like everyone was crowding around some guy who was selling *metal detectors*! This guy had a little stand set up, and he was selling detectors as fast as he could take people's money.

"That guy is some kind of businessman," I said.

"Joe," Frank said, "doesn't it strike you as a little odd?"

"Odd?"

"Somebody finds a ring, and fifteen minutes later, this guy's got enough metal detectors to make a killing selling them? You think that's a coincidence?"

"I guess it is kind of strange."

"Come on," Frank said. "Let's go find out how he got so lucky."

It took a little while to get to the front of the line. Nobody likes people who cut. But our instant tycoon wasn't going anywhere—not while his supply of metal detectors held out.

From the looks of it, he must have brought a whole truckload of them. "How did he get them here so fast?" I wondered out loud.

"Maybe he knew there would be a jewelry hunt."

"Huh?"

"If he stole the stuff himself, he could have

planted it here, knowing somebody was bound to find it. Then all he had to do was be ready with his merchandise."

"Yeah, but Frank, he didn't even *have* to do that. He could have just taken off with the stolen jewelry. Why even bother?"

Frank, as usual, was ready with an answer: "Because it's hard to find a buyer for stolen jewelry. Remember, that first ring was engraved. And the store owners must have put out a list with descriptions of the stolen merchandise. Jewelry is unique. It can be tracked. Even pawnshops would be given the list by the police, and they'd be watching for stolen goods."

My reasoning still led me to think it would be easier and more profitable to just steal the jewels and run.

We were edging closer, and now we could hear our man shouting at a customer.

"I don't give bargain!" he was saying. "You want bargain, go someplace else! Here, is one price fits all. You buy, or no buy, what I care?"

Hmmm . . . our man had a thick Russian accent, just like the guy who found the first ring. There seemed to be quite a community of Russians here in Ocean Point—the saltwater taffy man, these other two . . .

I wondered if maybe they were all in this together.

"Frank, it could be the Russian Mafia!"

I felt like I'd stumbled onto the solution. With one stroke of pure genius, I'd cracked the case!

"Easy, there, Joe. Just because three people have the same accent, it doesn't make them all criminals."

My bubble instantly burst, and I came back down to Earth. "I guess you're right. But you've got to admit, it's a possibility."

"One of *several*. We'll add it to our list, okay?"

"You want buy?" the Russian guy asked us. We'd reached the front of the line.

"What we want," I said, "is to know how you knew to show up here just in time to cash in on this treasure frenzy."

The guy scowled at me. He had a big, bushy mustache that drooped down on either side of his mouth, and his gray hair was long and wild. He obviously hadn't combed it in a *very* long time.

"You shut face, okay?" he said to me. "Why it's your business what I do? Is free country!"

"You've got to admit," Frank said, "it *is* pretty suspicious looking, your getting here so fast."

"What you are, junior police officers?" the man asked, sticking his chin out at Frank, then at me. "I come to this country to make decent living and be free. Not to live in police state, okay? Now, get lost. In this country, I have right to sell what I want."

"Nobody's arguing with that, sir," Frank said, trying to calm the guy down.

"Is free enterprise!"

"Yes, sure . . . um, what's your name, sir?"

"None of your business."

"No, of course not. I just wanted to call you by your name, that's all. My name's Frank Hardy, and this is my brother, Joe."

The guy made a face, but decided to back down a little. "Vladimir Krupkin," he said, and gave us a little nod. "Now get lost, okay? I busy now. You want talk, come back later."

"Just one question, Vladimir," Frank said, "and then we'll leave you alone, okay?"

Vladimir looked at the crowd behind us. "Make quick," he said.

"You were right about us," Frank admitted. "We *are* kind of junior police officers. And the thing is, we know that some of the jewelry people are finding was stolen from local jewelry stores."

Vladimir crossed his arms on his chest. "Really?" He didn't look one bit surprised. "So you think I steal jewelry, then bury in sand, then come here to sell metal detectors?"

## SUSPECT PROFILE

**Name:** Vladimir Krupkin

**Hometown:** Moscow, Russia

**Physical description:** Age 45, 5'10", 220 lbs., graying, uncombed hair, pot belly.

**Occupation:** Opportunist. Something different every time you look.

**Background:** Grew up in Russia, came to America to escape Communism. When Communism fell, he didn't go back because he'd gotten several good rackets going.

**Suspicious behavior:** Showing up on the beach with a ready-made business to exploit an opportunity he couldn't have known was coming unless he was in on the thefts.

**Suspected of:** Conspiracy involving jewel theft.

**Possible motives:** Money.

Then he let out a laugh so loud you could hear it in Atlantic City. "You think Vladimir is such a stupid? Why I steal jewelry and then throw away? Is crazy! Ha!"

He had a point—it didn't make any sense. But

then, nothing about this case was making much sense. Yet.

We could still hear him laughing as we climbed the stairs to the boardwalk.

"I can't think when I'm hungry," I said to Frank.

"That's right—we never got our Texas wieners!"

We ate our lunch, topped off by some of the best soft ice cream cones we'd ever had, and tried to get our heads straight about this case.

"Mmmm," I said, licking off the chocolate drips before they fell on my shorts. "Nothing like ice cream for clearing the mind."

"Mmmm," said Frank, nodding in agreement.

"So—something's rotten in Ocean Point."

"Definitely."

"But what? And who's behind it?"

"That *is* the question."

"So what's the answer? Got any ideas?" I asked. *Stupid question.* Frank *always* has ideas.

"Let me ask you this, Joe: Who would benefit if a bunch of people found jewelry lying around the beach?"

"Um, the people who found the stuff?"

Frank rolled his eyes. "Besides them."

"Okay, um . . ." I stared at my dripping ice cream cone. Then it hit me. "Ice cream vendors!"

"Right. And?"

"Hot dog stand owners, and tattoo parlors, and hotel owners, and parking lot owners, and restaurants, and clubs . . ."

"Exactly. And so on. If thousands of people want to come to a place, prices go up, and all the local businesses profit."

"And your point is . . . ?"

Frank smiled. "It's the one motive that explains everything that's happened so far."

"Yeah, sure. The only problem is there are hundreds of merchants in Ocean Point, and they'd probably all benefit—"

"—except the jewelry stores, maybe. But they'd get their insurance money," Frank finished.

"Right. How are we going to figure out which one of them is behind the scheme?"

Frank nodded. "Or which *ones*? It could be a bunch of them working together in a conspiracy."

"So how do we narrow it down?"

All this time we'd been working on our cones, and Frank had now finished his. He bought a bottled water and used some of it to wash his sticky hands. Then he handed it to me, because I was more of a mess than he was.

"I don't think," he said, "that a little popcorn stand or souvenir store owner would throw away millions of dollars of jewelry just to increase tourism. Only a very wealthy person could afford to throw away gold and diamonds. Anyone else would try to turn it into straight cash."

"Okay. That still leaves us with a lot of people as suspects—and most of them we haven't even met yet."

Frank didn't answer. Instead, he turned around and started talking to the ice cream vendor, an older guy who looked like he'd been around here forever.

"Excuse me, sir."

"Yeah?"

"Do you own this place?"

"Me?" The guy laughed—a big, hearty belly laugh. "I don't own the shirt on my back, kid."

"Well, who does own it?"

"Same guy who owns half the shops and restaurants on the boardwalk—Carl Jardine."

"Carl Jardine? Is he the richest man in town?"

"Oh, by far," the guy told Frank. "He's a multigazillionaire. You'd think he'd spread it around a little—give his workers health benefits or something—but no. He just uses his money to buy up more stuff."

The guy was on a roll now. Frank just let him go on, nodding once in a while to show he understood and sympathized.

It's amazing how being a good listener makes people open up to you and talk their heads off.

"You think he works hard, like everybody else? No way!" the man said, his voice starting to get a little loud. "No, he spends all his time on the beach, building sand castles and stuff."

Frank chuckled.

"You think I'm kidding?" the man added. "That's him right down there! You don't believe me, go see for yourself!"

# 12.

## The Richest Man in Ocean Point

We walked over to the railing near the beach and scanned the area, expecting to see a man building a sand castle.

What we saw was the Taj Mahal.

I kid you not—this sculpture was so big that the man building it looked like a midget next to it. He could barely reach the top of the Taj's tower to finish it off. In fact, he was standing on a big cooler to do it.

We thanked the ice cream man for his time and headed over to meet the richest man in town.

The closer we got to it, the more incredible Jardine's sand sculpture was. The thing was the size of a small house, but it was the details that were really amazing.

I'd seen pictures of the Taj Mahal—a tomb built by an emperor for his lady love. A lot of people say it's the most beautiful building ever built.

Jardine had done it proud, down to the lakes and gardens that surround the building. The lakes even had water in them! He must have lined them with something so the water wouldn't drain out.

Fascinating. I wondered about the mind of this man. It was obviously brilliant and talented, but was it also the mind of a criminal?

"Mr. Jardine?" I said.

"Yes?"

"I'm Frank Hardy, and this is my brother, Joe. We're Junior Chamber of Commerce members in our home town, Bayport, and we're doing a piece for the September edition of our high school paper. . . ."

"Oh, you want to interview me, huh?" he said, squinting up at us.

He had to be seventy years old, but Carl Jardine was still in good shape. He wore a beach hat, bathing suit, and flip-flops, and his skin was tanned and leathery. This guy had spent a lot of time in the sun. But he had a pretty good build for an older guy.

"All right, why not?" he said. "That's pretty good, tracking me down on the beach like this. I like initiative. Key to success!"

# SUSPECT PROFILE

Name: Carl Jardine

Hometown: Asbury Park, New Jersey

Physical description: Age 72, 6'2", 200 lbs., gray hair, leathery skin, well-preserved older man.

Occupation: Retired. Or is he . . . ?

Background: Grew up in Asbury Park, moved to Ocean Point as a young man. Bought first taffy stand at twenty-three. Now owns dozens of properties and businesses. No one knows what he does with all his money, except to buy more businesses. Could his empire have a shaky foundation? One that needs shoring up with illegal schemes?

Suspicious behavior: Mostly circumstantial. He fits the profile, spends lots of time on the beach, and wouldn't blink at throwing away tens of thousands of dollars worth of jewelry just to bring in more customers to his many, many businesses.

Suspected of: Seeding the sand with stolen jewelry. Lying about it.

Possible motives: Money, money, and more money. Some folks can never have enough.

He kept working as he spoke. I don't know what he thought he was doing; his Taj Mahal looked pretty perfect as it was.

"This is incredible!" Joe said, meaning the sculpture.

"Did it all myself," Jardine said. "I do everything myself. Only way to get something done right!"

"I understand you're the richest man in Ocean Point?" I said, trying to steer the conversation around to our case.

"I wouldn't know about that. I don't go counting other people's money."

"You don't need to count it if you're throwing it away—or burying it in the sand." Joe muttered the last part under his breath. But it wasn't quiet enough for my taste.

But if Jardine had heard him, he didn't let on. "I've done pretty well, though. Got quite a few businesses going, but they mostly run themselves at this point. I collect the checks and put them in the bank. I'm seventy-two years old—I've got more important things to do than work in an office."

He scraped a bit of extra sand off one of the Taj's walls.

"How did you get started in business?" I asked him.

"My first venture was a little saltwater taffy store on the boardwalk," he said. "I've still got that place. Rented it out to a Russian fella." He fell silent, and started inspecting his work for any stray grains of sand.

"So, you were saying . . . ?" I prompted him.

"Well, saltwater taffy was big in those days. We didn't have fast-food places on our boardwalk back then, or ice cream shops. I was one of the first attractions. I had a couple dozen taffy places all up and down the shore. Now I've got lots of other businesses as well."

"Would you say you have any enemies in town?" I asked.

"Enemies? Well, I guess you don't buy up half a town without running into some opposition. To win those kinds of battles you have to be strong."

He laughed. "Put that in your article! Tell them I'm retired now, doing what I love. I've done over fifty of the world's great buildings in sand, and I've got lots more to go before I sleep. And tell your readers I'm a man at peace with myself. I wish everyone the best, and I just want to be left alone."

I could appreciate that, but we had a job to do. There was no way we could leave him alone—not when he fit our suspect profile better than anyone else we'd come across.

We'd gotten as far as we could with the teen reporter jive. It was time to level.

"I'll be honest with you, sir," I said. "We're actually looking into the jewelry store robberies that happened here recently."

"You're . . . not really interviewing me for an article?" He seemed disappointed.

"Not for our school paper, no," I admitted. "You see, sir, we figure that whoever's been scattering the stolen jewelry on the beach for people to find, they must not have much need for the cash that jewelry could bring."

"Ah," he said. "Someone like me, eh?"

"I'm afraid so."

"You think I robbed those stores and buried thousands of dollars in jewelry to create a tourist boom, out of which people like me would make millions. Is that right?"

"More or less," I said.

"Let me tell you something, young fellows," he said, stopping work for the first time since we'd arrived. "I understand your theory. I can see that you've given it some thought. But you've got the wrong culprit. I have so much money that I have no need to make more. I already have more than I could spend in a lifetime. I'm a happy man. So if you'll please leave me alone, I'd like to get back to work."

Oh, well. At least he thought it was a good theory.

"Sir, one more thing," I said. "You've been around here a long time, and you know a lot of people. Who do *you* think is behind it?"

Jardine knitted his bushy eyebrows. "I think," he said, "that your theory is fundamentally sound. But you need to adjust your sights lower—to a level of wealth lower than my own, but not at the bottom of the ladder, if you know what I mean. Go find a list of the members of the Chamber of Commerce or something. That ought to get you started."

"How many people do you think are on that list?" Joe asked.

"Dozens, I should imagine."

"Frank, how are we ever going to interview them all? We've only got a few days to figure this out before we have to go home."

"You might as well forget it, then," Jardine said, turning back to his work. "You'll never find the ones behind it. To catch them, you'd have to monitor this beach day and night!"

I pulled Frank aside for a moment. "We could do that, right?" I said. "It would save us our hotel bill if we camped out on the beach."

"Forget it," Jardine said. He must have overheard me. "There's no camping allowed in Ocean Point. The boardwalk lights go off at 3 A.M., and it's dark as pitch out here after that, especially when there's a new moon, like tonight. How would you even see anyone in the dark?"

He turned back to his Taj Mahal, and Joe and I looked at one another excitedly.

Carl Jardine was right—it would be dark as pitch. But what he didn't know was that, courtesy of ATAC, we had a night vision telescope!

The richest man in Ocean Point had given us our next plan of action: an all-night stakeout on the beach.

# 13.
## Stakeout!

We went back to our hotel and tried to get a couple hours of sleep before dinner. We were going to be up all night, after all, and we didn't want to fall asleep on the job.

When we woke up, it was around 6 P.M., and we were both hungry. We got dressed, packed all our overnight essentials in a backpack, and headed downstairs to get some dinner.

We were waiting for our food to come and going over the case when I spotted the two blondes from the beach. They were in jeans and tank tops now, but they were still unmistakable.

I just hoped they didn't see us. I'd left my shades in the room, figuring I wouldn't need them overnight on the beach. But I hadn't figured on this. The last thing I wanted was them seeing me with *two* black eyes.

"Yoo-hoo! Frank!"

Ugh. Too late.

They came right over to our table and sat down with us. The girl next to Frank nudged up really close to him—so close that he moved in toward the wall of the booth a little, edging away from her out of sheer embarrassment.

The girl on my side of the table didn't move in on me at all. Instead, she leaned over the table toward Frank.

The one across the table gave me a look. "Eeeuw!" she squealed. "Look at your eyes!"

Her friend next to me took a close look. "Omigosh, you look like a—"

"I know, a raccoon," I said.

"Right!"

"That lifeguard socked you pretty good," the girl across the table said.

"Hey, I didn't know it was coming," I said, defending myself.

It would have been nice of Frank to say something right about then, but he was so shy in the presence of these two girls that he never opened his mouth.

"You should have decked him," the girl next to me said.

"Yeah," the other agreed. "You really wimped out."

I was about to argue with her, but just then our food arrived.

"So, Frank, what are you doing tonight?" the girl next to him asked.

"Um, Joe?" Frank looked at me pleadingly. Obviously, he didn't know what to say.

"We're, uh . . . spending the evening with our parents," I said.

Talk about wimping out. But it worked.

"Your parents? Ick. Sounds totally boring. We're going clubbing."

"Really?" I said. "Have a nice time."

"Oh, we will," said the girl across from me. "I don't know about you, though."

Finally, they got up and left, and we were able to eat our meal in peace. "Do me a favor, Frank," I said, "next time we're on a case, try to stay away from romantic entanglements."

"Romantic entanglements?"

"Whatever, just steer clear, okay?"

I guess I was being a little hard on him. After all, it was me who introduced us to the girls, not him. Still. How frustrating was this?

"Come on," Frank said as we pushed away our dessert plates. "Let's go nail us a criminal."

• • • •

By eight o'clock the beach was deserted, except for one or two couples strolling hand in hand as the sun went down.

Frank and I both agreed that no one would be planting jewelry on the beach in broad daylight. We also agreed that the most likely time would be after 3 A.M., when the boardwalk lights would go off, plunging the beach into almost total darkness.

We had a long time to wait. We probably didn't need to be out here yet, but we didn't want to miss anything if it happened earlier than we thought. We took up positions under the boardwalk, and Frank fished out the night vision scope from the backpack.

"Okay," he said as he snapped it open and scanned the empty beach. "Bring it on."

"Well?" I asked. "What do you see?"

"Just a few drunks . . . some couples making out . . . there's a guy fishing . . . uh, a bunch of seagulls . . . a homeless guy . . ."

"All right, all right, never mind. Just tell me when you see something interesting."

Frank smiled at me. "You'll get your turn, little brother. Just be patient."

I *hate* when he calls me "little brother." He's only eleven months older than me, you know. And I look older and more mature.

Anyway, hours went by. I was sorry I hadn't brought my MP3 player to pass the time. Ten o'clock, eleven, midnight, one . . . and still two hours to go before prime time! This was truly going to rank among the most boring nights of my life—especially if our criminal didn't show up.

At three o'clock all the lights went out. Suddenly, I couldn't see my hand in front of my face. It took all of about ten minutes before I could make out Frank, still staring through the scope at the beach.

"Am I going to get a turn, or are you just going to hog that thing?" I asked.

"Here," he said, giving it to me. "If you're going to keep on nagging me about it . . ."

"We're supposed to share," I reminded him. "They only gave us one of these."

That got him. He sat down and lapsed into silence. The only sound now was that of the waves crashing in.

The spot we'd chosen for our stakeout looked out on the stretch of beach where the first ring had been found. Most of the jewelry had been dug up within view of our position. The town pier was on our left, maybe fifty yards away.

I was looking that way, peering through the scope, when I thought I saw something move.

Maybe it was just a homeless guy, prowling for crabs to eat or a place to sleep.

*Or maybe not.*

I nudged Frank. "Under the pier," I whispered. "Something moving."

"Let's go check it out," he said.

Still staring through the scope, I emerged from our hiding place and headed toward the pier with Frank on my right, holding on to my arm because he couldn't see where he was going.

Suddenly he let out a grunt, and I felt him let go of my arm.

"What the—?"

Then I felt something hard come down on the back of my head. As I crumpled to the sand, all I could see were stars.

# 14.

## Neck-Deep in Trouble

Joe was down—I could see that much.

I was down too, but not out. I struggled to my feet and swung.

Within seconds, my right fist plowed into something soft.

"Ooof!"

A massive shape in front of me doubled over, and I kicked hard at it.

Then I was jumped from behind—by not one, but two guys. The second got his hands around my throat.

I tried to wrestle the second guy off me, but he wouldn't budge.

Meanwhile, the guy I'd brought down before was slowly recovering. He got to me before I could get free of his friend, and socked me so hard in the stomach that I thought I was going to lose my dinner.

I sank to the ground and felt a series of hard kicks delivered to my kidneys. I tried to protect my face and to make the rest of me as small a target as possible. It hurt—but I could sense my attackers getting tired. And it wasn't anything I couldn't handle.

"Tie them up!" the other man said.

Rope was wound around my hands, and the guy was busy tying them behind my back when I heard a loud "Oof!" and he let go.

"Get away from my brother, screwball!"

Joe was back in the fight!

My hands were now tied too tightly for me to help. The two other assailants quickly ganged up on Joe. I heard a loud *crack,* and then Joe yelling, "Ow! My eye!"

He has the worst luck sometimes.

Another minute or two and Joe was lying beside me on the ground, getting his hands tied in the same style as mine.

"Should I bash their heads in?" one of them asked the other.

"Nah," one of his companions answered. "No marks, remember? Now go over behind that piling and get the shovel."

I tried to place their voices, but they weren't familiar. As for their faces, there was no way to make them out in the pitch darkness. Not without our night scope, and who knew where that had fallen?

"Shovel?" the first guy repeated. He didn't sound too bright. "We gonna bury something?"

"Yeah, lamebrain. We're gonna bury these two—alive."

I could see now where things were heading, and it wasn't anyplace good. From the sound of the waves hitting, we were right near the waterline. And it was low tide. If they buried us here—and they were already digging the hole—all traces of digging would be wiped out by the rising tide before the sun came up. No one would ever find us until the day—years from now, maybe—when a hurricane or nor'easter rearranged the beach and made the dead rise.

Once the hole was deep enough, we were both thrown in alive, and they started to shovel the sand back in. When they were done, only our heads were above the sand.

Whoever was doing this wanted us to suffer before we died. Hmmm . . . we must have been annoying somebody pretty badly. To me it meant that our investigation was coming close. Too close for a bad guy's comfort.

And mine, too, actually. The water didn't look too great from this vantage point.

"Who are you?" I asked the men who'd accosted us. "Why are you doing this?"

I didn't think I'd get an answer, but it was worth a try—especially since at least one of them didn't seem too bright.

"None of your business," the answer came back from the darkness.

"Who hired you?"

"What makes you think somebody hired us?" the voice said. "Maybe we're just doing this for fun."

"Fun? You think this is fun?" Joe raged.

"Sure! I can just picture you two as the tide comes up. You'll drown real slow . . . if the dogs and vultures don't get you first! Hahahaha!"

"Hahahaha!" came the echoing laugh of one of his companions. They sounded like hyenas.

"Wait," I said calmly. "Whatever you're being paid, we can double it."

"Oh, I doubt it. I doubt it very much. We're going to make a killing on this one! Hahahaha!"

"Hahahaha!"

"Come on, guys—let's leave these two alone. They've got a lot of thinking to do . . . about how curiosity killed the cat! Hahahaha!"

"Hahahaha!"

The laughter was driving me nuts.

Within seconds they were gone, taking their shovel—our only hope of escape—with them.

For a few moments there was dead silence. Then Joe spoke up. "My nose itches."

There was no sense in telling him to scratch it. This sand was hard packed. We weren't going to just slip out like we would from dry sand.

And did I mention we were tied, hands and feet?

Not good.

"How's the rest of you?" I asked.

"I got punched in the eye again."

"Oh, no."

"Same one the cow kicked."

"Ouch."

"Oh, well. At least now I won't have to worry about how it looks."

There was another long silence. Then:

"Does this remind you of anything?" Joe asked.

"Yeah. Farmer Pressman's grain bin."

"Ding-ding-ding! Yes, that's right, for one hundred dollars!"

"Only now we're buried much deeper," I added helpfully.

"And we have no gizmos to help us."

"And our hands aren't free, let alone our legs."

"So, we're history, right?"

"Wrong!" I said. "Don't give up, Joe. I'll think of something."

I think he believed me. Joe has a lot of faith in my mental powers. But right at that moment, I myself didn't have much faith in them. In fact, I didn't have a clue.

# 15.

## Miracles from on High

We were buried up to our necks, about six feet from the waterline, and the waves kept breaking closer and closer to our heads. I was having flashbacks to our grain bin rendezvous. I hadn't really wanted a repeat performance so soon.

"I just want to say, Frank, that it's been awesome having you for a brother."

I don't know what made me say that. Of *course* we were going to get out of this. Frank was going to think of something at the last minute, and it would all be okay.

But Frank didn't look too happy. He was busy spitting out the salt water he'd just swallowed. High tide was fast approaching.

And so was something else.

"Frank, look!"

The way we were buried, I could see the light easier than Frank could. But we could both hear the sound of the engine. It was coming straight for us.

"What is it?" I asked.

He squinted his eyes to protect them from the glare of the light. "Can't see what kind of vehicle it is . . . but it must be one of those machines that rake up the garbage at night."

Frank and I both screamed as loudly as we could, hoping to get the attention of the driver. The light seemed to turn our way and get brighter. The machine kept coming, and the engine was now drowning out both the surf and our screams.

"We're saved!" Frank kept shouting like an idiot. "We're saved!"

I wasn't so sure. It was pitch dark out here, and in spite of the headlights, the driver might not see our heads poking out of the sand. He might just mistake our heads for plastic garbage bags or something, and rake them up into the jaws of his machine.

Our cries for help became screams of terror as the "grim reaper" descended on us. There was no way the driver could possibly hear us over the roar of the vehicle's engine.

Then, at the last second, there was a shriek of

brakes. The metal monster came to a stop about three feet from our heads.

As if that weren't enough, a big wave chose that very moment to crash over us. When it retreated, we were left gasping and coughing.

Help came in the form of a beautiful dark angel's face, bending over mine. "Whoa!" the angel said. "What the . . . What are you two doing here?"

*Good question.*

"It's a long story," Frank said. "But we haven't got much time. Could you please just dig us out first?"

"Um, yeah, sure," the angel said. "You're lucky I've got a shovel in there."

She went over to her tractor and came back with one. She started digging Frank out while I had to chill, holding my breath whenever the waves came crashing over me.

Pretty soon Frank was able to use his arms to haul himself out. Then the two of them came over to dig me up.

Her name was Naomi, she told us—Naomi Thompson. She was wearing sweats, and her hair was done in cornrows. She was the one who embossed the advertisements in the sand, using her tractor and its nifty rear attachment to make those amazing drawings.

"You're lucky I spotted you," she said. "I just happened to be circling back around, or I wouldn't have had my lights pointed so close to the water."

"Well, thanks for saving us," Frank said.

"No problem. Are you gonna tell me how you wound up like that?"

"Sure," I said. "How about we tell you all about it over lunch tomorrow?"

She gave me a look. "I've heard that line before. How 'bout you tell me first, and *then* we decide about lunch?"

So we told her everything we knew. She's been out on the beach every night; if anybody'd been out there, scattering jewelry in the sand for tourists to find, Naomi might have seen him—or her.

But no. Apparently, it had been pretty quiet. "I've seen a lot of weird stuff poking out of the sand since I started working here," she said. "That's why I bring the shovel with me. But I've never seen anything as weird as two guys' heads."

We borrowed her shovel and filled the two holes back up. That way, in case anyone came by the next day to check on us, they wouldn't know we'd escaped.

"Well now," I said to Naomi when we were done. "What about our lunch date?"

"Um, Joe," Frank said quickly. "Let me remind you about something."

"Huh?"

"Whoever tried to kill us—at this point, they think we're dead."

"Yeah? So?"

"If we want them to keep thinking that, we can't go around in broad daylight, taking girls out to lunch in restaurants."

"Sorry, Naomi," I said, realizing he was right.

"That's okay. Maybe after your eyes heal up."

*Ouch. Forgot about those.*

She got back into the driver's seat. "Gotta get back to work."

"Where can we find you?" I asked.

"Me? I'm out here every night, from 3 A.M. to 5 A.M. Princess of Darkness, that's me."

She revved up the engine and put the tractor in gear. Soon she was just a spot of light retreating up the beach.

"So," I said. "We're ghosts, huh? Cool."

"Yeah," Frank said with a smile. "You know, for a ghost, I feel pretty alive."

"Me too. Thanks to Naomi."

Frank looked up at the stars. "Yeah, good thing she came by, or we'd probably be sunk." He paused for a moment. "Great night, huh?"

I looked up at the sky. And suddenly, something hit me.

Hard.

Smack in the forehead.

"What the—?"

# 16.

## A Bump on the Head

I heard something smack Joe on the head, and an instant later, his cry of pain.

"Ow!"

I turned around, ready to drop-kick whoever was attacking us.

But there was no one there at all!

Something had knocked Joe in the head. There was no doubt about that. He was on his knees, holding his forehead.

"Are you all right?" I asked him.

"Dang, that hurts!"

"Are you bleeding?"

He checked. "I don't think so—but I'm gonna have a lump the size of a—"

He broke off and reached down for something that was lying in the sand. "Hey, Frank—check this out. This must be what hit me!"

He held it up, and I took it from him. It was a heavy gold bracelet—the kind that locks together and looks like you could attach a heavy chain to it.

But where had it come from?

We were down by the water—too far from the boardwalk or the pier for someone to have thrown it. And there was no one near us on the beach, at least as far as we could see in this darkness just before dawn. Besides, to make such an impact, that bracelet had to have come from a really far distance. . . .

Then we heard it—the drone of an engine high above us. I looked up, and there it was: the red blinking lights of an airplane.

Suddenly, all the pieces of the jigsaw puzzle began to come together in my mind.

So *that* was how the pieces of jewelry were finding their way onto the beach!

"Joe," I said, "who do we know around here that has a plane?"

"Bump," he said, feeling the one on his forehead. "Bump Rankowski."

"Exactly. He's got a whole fleet of planes, he

said. He employs pilots to fly them up and down the beach during the day. But what if he paid those pilots *extra,* in *cash,* to do a little night work—say at 3 or 4 A.M., digging a couple of holes on the beach?"

"Could be," Joe agreed. "And he's got motive, too, Frank—more tourists on the beach means more advertising business, right?"

"Not to mention the real motive—that, as the mayor, he'd benefit from a big rise in tourism. It would make him *very* popular with the local business owners—except, of course, the ones he's been robbing!"

"We've gotta nail this guy," Joe said, gritting his teeth and rubbing the swelling bump on his noggin.

Was this about catching a criminal, or about nailing the guy who kept beating Joe up? I couldn't tell, but I figured I'd hit the ball into his court for a change.

"So how are you planning to nail Bump?" I asked.

"Huh?"

"You're so eager to get him in cuffs, how are you going to do it? You've got to have proof, remember?"

Joe frowned, and rubbed his forehead. "Isn't this proof enough?"

"Nope."

"Yeah. I guess not."

I suddenly found myself yawning. It dawned on me that we'd been up all night. It had been a long day, to say the least.

"Why don't we sleep on it, Joe?"

"Sleep?"

"Yeah, sleep—remember it? I, for one, happen to think better when I'm not dog tired. Besides, Bump—if he's our guy—thinks we're dead, right? If we want him to keep thinking that, we'd better get out of sight before sunrise."

"We're going to have to show our faces eventually," Joe said.

"Yeah," I agreed. "But not until we've got a plan."

 **JOE**

Joe here. So we snuck back to our hotel room without anyone seeing us. It wasn't hard—at 5 A.M. there aren't many people out and about. Bump would probably still be out at the airport.

I got a bag of ice from the machine in the hallway and put it on my face, which was hurting all over.

Frank was out cold and snoring, but I was so tired that I managed to fall asleep anyway.

He had set the alarm for 10 A.M. Five hours isn't much, but I felt a whole lot better when I woke up, I can tell you that.

Frank went down the hall and got us some breakfast from the vending machines. Donuts and tarts, mmm mmm. Now *that's* my kinda breakfast!

We sat out on beds, eating and trying to come up with a plan of action.

"We've got to be sure it's him first," Frank said, munching on a frosted donut.

"You're not sure? *I'm* sure!"

"I'm pretty sure. But I don't want us to take down somebody and then find out that they're innocent. That would compromise ATAC."

"All right. So what should we do next?" I asked.

"Well, I think we should do an Internet search— see if it tells us anything."

"Okay. Only we didn't bring a laptop. What do you want to do? Go to Bump's office and ask him if we can borrow his computer?"

I was being sarcastic, obviously. But Frank gets oblivious sometimes, especially when he's hatching a plan.

"I was thinking more of the local library," he said.

"What if somebody spots us there?"

"We'll have to take that chance."

"Let's say it is him, Frank—then what?"

"Hmmm . . ."

Frank massaged his eyes with his palms for a minute, then came up with an idea. "He goes up in his plane at night, right? What if we stow away and go with him?"

A big smile spread over my face at the thought. *Beautiful.* We catch him in the act—a couple of ghosts come back to life!

"Okay then," Frank said, obviously noting my approval. "Compromise: We'll do both: Internet search and stow away."

"Deal."

We finished eating and headed over to the library. It was just across the street from city hall, so we had to be careful. There was no sign of Bump Rankowski, thank goodness, but those two guys who jumped us on the beach might have been around somewhere.

We didn't know what they looked like, but they must have known our faces.

Of course they wouldn't be looking for us, because they thought we were dead.

First time death was in our favor.

Inside, we went right over to a bank of computers, well-hidden from general view behind a row of bookshelves. Frank sat down and did a search for Bump Rankowski.

A bunch of stuff came up—about his businesses, his first mayoral campaign, his winning a flying contest. . . .

"He's running for reelection in the fall," Frank pointed out.

"So?"

"So, if he wants to get reelected—and he sure seems to like the job—he might be tempted to start a tourist 'gold rush,' right?"

"Totally. I'm convinced, Frank. It's him. Let's get out of here and take care of business."

"Wait a second. Cool your jets, Joe. There's no proof in here—not enough to go on."

"But Frank—"

"We've got to have more than this," he insisted.

Then it hit me.

"Hey, remember he said Bump wasn't always his name?"

"Right! Now what was it . . . ? Adam? Something with an A . . ."

I suddenly remembered. "Arnold!"

"That's it!"

Frank keyed in Arnold Rankowski, and a moment later we hit the jackpot. There was an article from the *Sea Bright Gazette,* dated 1984, all about the arrest of one Arnold Rankowski on charges of petty thievery—from a jewelry store!

"Paydirt!" Frank said, and printed out the article.

There were more, too—our boy Arnold had three more minor offenses to his name.

No wonder he'd changed it!

"So here's our case," Frank said, gathering all the printouts together. "Three felony arrests along with two misdemeanors. Suspended sentence for the first felony, community service for the second, three months in Rahway State Prison for the third. Nothing since 1985."

"How did he ever become mayor?" I said. "Wouldn't somebody have dragged out his past during the campaign and used it against him?"

Frank did some more searching.

"Hang on," he finally said. "November 7, 1992. Front page of the *Ocean Point Gazette*: 'Rankowski Wins in Squeaker.'" He scrolled down and continued reading: "'Arnold "Bump" Rankowski was elected mayor yesterday with 52 percent of the votes counted. Steve Lyons conceded defeat at 10 P.M. Most observers agreed that Rankowski's heroic efforts last week in spotting and putting out a potentially devastating fire at the amusement pier helped erase the negative effects of his somewhat shady past.'"

"I'll bet he set that fire himself," I said.

"I wouldn't put it past him," Frank agreed. "Bump seems to have a way of manipulating events to suit himself."

"I'll bet he robbed those three jewelry stores, Frank," I said. "He figured he'd drop the loot on the beach, create a gold rush, and get reelected by a landslide!"

"And Joe, think about this—as mayor, he could have waltzed into police headquarters at any time and pulled the codes for the jewelry stores' alarm systems off the police computer!"

"Huh?"

"Stores with alarm systems hooked in to police and fire headquarters have to provide them with the codes to disable the system."

"Ah, I get it," I said.

"I think we're getting a pretty clear picture of Bump Rankowski," Frank said as he got up.

"That slimeball. Let's not forget, he tried to have

us killed when he realized we were close to cracking the case!"

We had our man, all right. All we had to do now was catch him red-handed.

Tonight was the night—and I could hardly wait.

# 17.

## Up in the Air

We called a cab to come get us at our hotel and bring us to the Ocean Point Airport. I took the precaution of calling one from Atlantic City. Sure, it was expensive, but there was no way we could be sure the local cab owners weren't FOB: Friends of Bump.

The airport closed at 11 P.M. I was fairly sure Bump wouldn't be doing his treasure dumping before then. Trudging through the terminal building with a big sack of jewelry would be pretty hard for anyone to miss.

Besides, it had been nearly 4 A.M. when Joe got smacked on the head by that bracelet. My bet was that Bump didn't show up till well after 2 A.M.

Joe and I waited in the darkness across the road from the terminal until everyone had left for the night, and most of the lights had been turned off. Then we ran across the road and hopped the chain-link fence that separated the terminal from the runway.

It was easy to find Bump's plane—those shark teeth and eyes stood out even in the semidarkness. You could even make out that the plane was bright red. It almost glowed in the moonlight.

We had to do this all in a hurry. At any moment a car passing by on the road might shine its headlights right at us—or an airport employee we hadn't accounted for might decide to check the planes out.

Anything could happen.

So we jogged over to Bump's pride and joy. The canopy was locked—no problem, though. I fished out my pocketknife and jimmied it. Sure, the destroyed lock might make Bump suspicious when he saw it, but if our plan worked, he'd be behind bars before he had a chance to notice.

We quietly raised the canopy and climbed inside. Only after we'd shut it behind us did we feel we could relax.

At least for now.

"Got the camera?" Joe asked.

I patted the pocket of my windbreaker. The cheap disposable camera ATAC had given us was there, ready and primed for action.

"Got the night scope? You found it after we got dug out, right?"

I took it out and gave it to Joe, and he started scanning the airport on the other side of the clear plastic canopy.

"What's the use of doing that?" I asked him. "We'll see the headlights when Bump parks his car."

"And what if someone drops him off down the road, and he walks the rest of the way and ends up taking us by surprise?"

I didn't think it was too likely, but I agreed that Joe had a point.

Still, as the hours wore on and there was no sign of Bump Rankowski, it started to get boring—and tiring.

We were still sleep-deprived, and we had to keep nudging one another to stay awake, especially once it got past 2 A.M.

When 4 A.M. came and went, Joe began to get really antsy. "He's not coming. It's not him. We've got this all wrong, Frank."

"What?"

"It's somebody else—one of our other suspects. That lifeguard, Chucky Whatzizname. Or the tattoo guy, Ricardo. Or one of the Russian guys."

"Joe . . ."

"I don't want to waste our time waiting for a guy who's not coming."

"Okay, wait a minute," I said. "First, I'll remind you that you're the one who was so convinced it was Bump, from the minute you got hit with that bracelet. Second, someone's dropping jewelry out of a plane. Bump has a plane—in fact, he owns a fleet of them. He's got motive, opportunity, and means."

"All right, but now I think I was wrong. He's still not here, right? What time is it?"

"Five minutes later than the last time you asked."

"Come on, wise guy. What time?"

"Four ten."

"And still no Bump. I rest my case."

Wouldn't you know it, just then a pair of headlights came into view down the road, swinging right toward the airport.

When the car pulled into the lot and stopped, it was time to hunker down and get ready. We settled ourselves behind the rear seats of the plane, completely hidden from view.

The canopy opened, and Bump's sizeable figure appeared in silhouette. I could hear him breathing hard as he settled himself into the pilot's seat and closed the canopy over his head. "That's funny," he mumbled. "Coulda sworn I locked it. . . . Oh, well."

Joe and I looked at each other. We were trying hard not to make a sound. We couldn't see Bump, but we could hear him going through his checklist, humming a happy little tune as he went.

*That scum,* I thought. *He thinks he's killed a couple of kids, and that makes him want to burst into song!*

I knew Joe felt like jumping him then and there, so I put my hand on his arm, reminding him that we had to wait until we had the evidence we needed.

Bump got the engine going and nosed the Cessna onto the runway. Soon we were airborne—but not without a struggle. With me and Joe on board, the plane was about 300 pounds heavier than Bump realized, and he had to give it a bit more lift than he thought.

"What the—?" I heard him grunt. "What's wrong with this thing?"

After a minute, he'd figured out how to get us

up to a safe altitude. He circled around, no doubt heading for the beach.

Two minutes later we heard the pilot's side canopy window open. Then there was the jingling of the sack of jewels he was carrying with him.

"Now!" Joe mouthed.

I sprang up, camera in hand, and fired off three pictures before Bump knew what hit him.

"What the—? HEY!"

He dropped the bag and tried to hide his face. The plane yawed and pitched crazily, and Bump had to grab the controls—which kept him from going after us.

"Who's that?" he shouted. "Who's that back there?"

But we weren't back there any more. Leapfrogging the seats, we were now right behind him.

"You!" he gasped.

"Sorry we're not dead," Joe said.

With that, he grabbed Bump's left arm, twisting it behind his back. Bump's right hand came off the controls, and I grabbed it—but only until his foot lashed out and caught me in the head.

I let go, reeling backward, and the plane did a full, sickening rollover. Joe almost wound up going out the open window.

And Bump had time to recover his wits.

He backed into Joe, trying to force him out the window, while flailing at me with his feet.

The plane was still rolling over, and it was all I could do to steady myself. Finally I twisted around and sat on Bump's outstretched legs.

My back was toward him, but now I could grab the throttle and try to steady the plane. I mean, there was no point in catching Bump if we all wound up dead in a plane crash, was there?

Maybe we should have thought this through a little better.

But then, this was the fun part.

Joe was dangling out the window, but Bump was too busy choking me to push him the rest of the way out.

I elbowed Bump in the ribs until he let go, then swung back around, dodging a punch on the way.

Joe had managed to fall back into the plane, and Bump was climbing over the seats, headed for the rear. I kept hold of the throttle while Joe faced him down.

"It's two against one, Mayor," Joe said, balling his fists and slowly closing in for the finish. "I think you should give up."

Bump reached down behind the backseat—right

where we'd been crouching down in the dark—
and drew out a big, fat pistol.

"Maybe this evens things up," he said, pointing
it right at Joe's face.

# 18.

## Defying Gravity

It was a little too dark, and I was a little too distracted, to tell exactly what kind of pistol was staring me down. Believe me when I tell you, though, that it was plenty big enough to blow my head off.

Especially from three feet away, which is where Bump was standing.

Frank was busy with the controls, but if he didn't do something fast, it wouldn't matter if we crashed or not.

But what was he supposed to do? If he made a move, it was the big bang, and *good-bye, Joe Hardy*!

"So," Frank said to Bump, "you're going to shoot us?"

"Only if I have to," Bump answered, wiping the blood off his mouth. "I'd rather not mess up my plane. I'd much prefer it if you boys would jump. You know, I thought you two had washed away with the tide."

"We got lucky," I said.

Bump laughed. "Right. Well, I guess your luck has just run out." He cocked the gun. "Now, are you gonna make me shoot you? Or are you gonna cooperate?"

We didn't answer. I was pinned down and couldn't risk moving, and Frank was steering the plane.

"Out that window will do," Bump said, pointing to it with one hand while the other held the gun right at me.

"You first," he said to Frank.

I saw Frank's eyes shift, and I knew what he was thinking. A quick jerk on the throttle, and maybe it would throw Bump off balance enough for us to overpower him.

But there was no guarantee of success. And if he messed up, I was dead.

"And no funny business," Bump said quickly, "or your brother gets a big fat bullet in the head."

Obviously, he'd read Frank's mind, same as I had.

"Slowly, now," Bump told him. "Not one false move. Hands off the controls."

Frank did as he was told. He gave me a long look, then climbed out the window. Headfirst.

Nice acting, bro. Nice.

I could see him clinging to the wing. The plane, dragged by his weight, started to bank to the left.

"Now you," Bump said to me. "Turn around and start moving."

I followed Frank out the window, and I didn't try jumping Bump. I didn't know how we were going to get out of this alive. All I knew was, I trusted my brother and his convoluted brain. I had faith that Frank, as always, had a plan.

"So long, boys!" Bump yelled before closing the window behind us. He grabbed the controls, but he was still fighting our weight, which was now dragging the plane to one side.

"Quick!" Frank yelled to me. "We've got to get to the center. Climb on top of the fuselage."

I followed his instructions. It was hard to hold on—the plane had to be going eighty miles an hour, and we were at least a thousand feet up.

The wind was so powerful it pushed me back along the top of the plane. I slid until I hit the tail—which was right between my legs.

*OW!!*

I winced in pain. Could it be worse?

At least I wasn't going to fall off from this position. I guess.

Now I saw Frank, sliding back toward me. His right foot hit me square in the head. Right into my black eyes.

*OW!!*

Yeah. It could be worse.

At least now we were both firmly attached to the plane, with good footholds and handholds.

Just in time, too, because Bump had realized we were there and was trying his best to shake us off.

He was doing rollovers.

We held on with sheer muscle power, fighting gravity, until Bump had to right the plane or risk crashing.

In fact, now that Frank and I were firmly attached to the tail section, the whole plane was dragging—so much so that it might tip upward and stall out at any moment.

Frank looked back at me.

"What do we do now?" I asked him.

"Look behind you!" he yelled.

I did—and there, trailing behind us, was a big,

long banner. EAT AT RON'S LOBSTER SHACK, it said.

"How did that get there?" I shouted.

"One of us must have hit the release button by accident! Joe—it's our way out of this!"

"What?"

"Climb out on the banner!"

"Are you crazy?"

"We'll make it into a parachute!"

"A parachute?"

"Aunt Trudy, Joe! Remember? Bottom left corner, top right corner . . ."

Now I saw what he was getting at.

It was a long shot, all right. But it just might work.

I waited for a moment when Bump wasn't trying to shake us off. Then I eased myself around the tail, grabbed onto the banner, and swung myself off the plane. Gradually, little by little, hand over hand, I let myself out toward the far end, while Frank followed behind me.

I watched as he took out his pocketknife and flipped it open. "Ready?" he called to me.

I nodded.

"Grab your two corners!" he shouted. "And hold on!"

He cut the cord holding the banner to the plane, and with a sudden snap, we were floating free.

*Plummeting* free is more like it, really.

I spread my hands wide, trying to keep the banner as open as possible.

The tug on my arms was tremendous. Good thing I'd worked out before we left.

Across from me, Frank was grimacing as he held his corners. The veins in his neck looked like they were going to pop out.

The ocean was getting closer by the second. I could see it in the dawn's early light. We were right over the shore and drifting toward the beach. If we hit the sand at this speed, we were goners.

I looked up for a second, and I saw Bump's plane spinning downward, out of control. The shock when we'd cut our weight loose must have made him stall out!

As we got closer to a deadly crash-landing, I stared at the beach below us. I was more terrified than I'd ever been in my life.

Was this it? Were we really going to die like this?

My whole life flashed before my eyes in a second. Dad, Mom, Aunt Trudy, all my friends . . . and most of all, Frank, who was going through the same thing, I'm sure.

*BOOM!!*

I heard the explosion—Bump and his plane

hitting the water at 100 miles an hour. *Well, he got what he deserved,* I thought.

Small satisfaction, though. In about five seconds, we'd be as dead as he was.

I closed my eyes and braced for impact. . . .
*KATHUNK!!!*

*Am I dead?*

My mouth was full of sand. So were my eyes. They stung.

I hurt all over.

But . . . if everything hurt, I couldn't be dead, right?

"Joe, are you okay?" It was Frank's voice.

He was alive too!

I spat a wad of sand out of my mouth. I still seemed to have all my teeth. This was good.

I tried to open my eyes. It took a while to get the sand out of them and actually see anything.

Finally, I saw Frank standing over me, covered with sand—but very much alive.

I stood up—slowly, carefully—and stared at the mound of soft sand that had saved both me and Frank from certain death. . . .

It was the Taj Mahal. Carl Jardine's amazing sand sculpture!

Funny.

Perfect.

His masterpiece was totaled, all right—but *we* were still whole. Which proves one thing: It's lucky to be smart, but it's even smarter to be lucky.

FRANK

# 19.

## There's No Place Like Home

We paid a big chunk of money to get driven back to Bayport by limo. Both Joe and I were way too sore to drive, and neither of us wanted to hop in a plane again anytime soon.

We'd spent the whole day being checked over at the Ocean Point Community Hospital (lots of bruises, but amazingly, no broken bones—thanks to Aunt Trudy and her Code of Perfect Sheet-Folding).

The police didn't believe our story at first, but when they found some of the stolen loot in the desk drawer of Bump's office at city hall, they decided to let us go.

We could have hung around for a real vacation, but Ocean Point was the last place we wanted to be right then. Both of us felt like Dorothy at the end of *The Wizard of Oz*: "There's no place like home."

We rolled up in front of our house and slowly, painfully, got out of the limo.

Mom and Aunt Trudy were out front, weeding the flower garden. Playback was perched on Trudy's shoulder, as usual.

"What the—?" Mom gasped when she caught sight of us.

I knew we were in for it.

"What have you boys been up to *this* time?" Aunt Trudy asked. "Look at them, Laura—they're black and blue all over. You boys have been getting into fights again, haven't you? Don't deny it!"

"Now, Trudy," said good old Mom, "I'm sure if the boys were fighting, it's only because they were provoked."

"Oh, *right*," said Trudy. "'They're good boys, your honor!' *Hmph*!"

"Now, Trudy," Mom said, "let's not jump to conclusions. I'm sure Frank and Joe can explain everything. Let's go inside and have some lemonade, and they can tell us all about their adventures on the Shore."

Lemonade? Yes, please.

Between the driveway and the kitchen, I was sure I could come up with something to tell them.

Something that wasn't the truth, but that would sound enough like it to satisfy them.

"Liar, liar, pants on fire!" Playback squawked, staring straight at me.

I put a hand on Joe's arm before he could go for the parrot.

"By the way," Aunt Trudy said as we crossed the living room, "those sheets you folded last Saturday? All wrong. I had to do them over again—corners weren't lined up at all! When are you boys *ever* going to learn?"

"Now, Trudy," Mom said, "the boys are all bruised and banged up. Let's not pester them about the sheets. After all, perfectly folded sheets aren't a matter of life and death."

Ah, but how wrong she was!

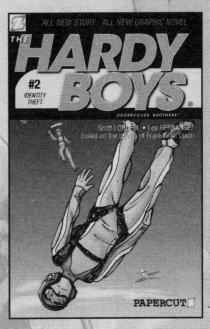

# PENDRAGON

Bobby Pendragon is a seemingly normal fourteen-year-old boy. He has a family, a home, and a possible new girlfriend. But something happens to Bobby that changes his life forever.

## HE IS CHOSEN TO DETERMINE THE COURSE OF HUMAN EXISTENCE.

Pulled away from the comfort of his family and suburban home, Bobby is launched into the middle of an immense, interdimensional conflict involving racial tensions, threatened ecosystems, and more. It's a journey of danger and discovery for Bobby, and his success or failure will do nothing less than determine the fate of the world. . . .

### PENDRAGON

by D. J. MacHale

Book One: The Merchant of Death
Book Two: The Lost City of Faar
Book Three: The Never War
Book Four: The Reality Bug
Book Five: Black Water

Coming Soon: Book Six: The Rivers of Zadaa

From Aladdin Paperbacks • Published by Simon & Schuster

## *Around and around and around it goes . . .*

A baseball cap came flying through the air. The carousel was going faster and faster. I saw a woman's pocketbook get pulled off her arm by the centrifugal force created by the wild ride. Popcorn flew through the air, yanked out of the tubs the kids on the merry-go-round were holding.

The carousel spun even faster. The tinkly music started to sound warped as the ride whooshed by.

"Look out!" Joe yelled as a camcorder came flying toward me. I ducked just in time.

"Somebody stop that thing!" a nearby father shouted. His face was white with fear.

# THE HARDY BOYS

## UNDERCOVER BROTHERS™

**Available from Simon & Schuster**

# THE HARDY BOYS

## BOYS

UNDERCOVER BROTHERS™

**#4**  **Thrill Ride**

**FRANKLIN W. DIXON**

**Aladdin Paperbacks**
**New York  London  Toronto  Sydney**

This book is a work of fiction. Any references to historical events, real people, or real locales are used fictitiously. Other names, characters, places, and incidents are the product of the author's imagination, and any resemblance to actual events or locales or persons, living or dead, is entirely coincidental.

❧ ALADDIN PAPERBACKS
An imprint of Simon & Schuster
Children's Publishing Division
1230 Avenue of the Americas
New York, NY 10020

Copyright © 2005 by Simon & Schuster, Inc.

All rights reserved, including the right of
reproduction in whole or in part in any form.
THE HARDY BOYS MYSTERY STORIES and HARDY BOYS
UNDERCOVER BROTHERS are trademarks of Simon & Schuster, Inc.
ALADDIN PAPERBACKS and colophon are trademarks of
Simon & Schuster, Inc.
Designed by Lisa Vega
The text of this book was set in Aldine 401BT.
Manufactured in the United States of America
First Aladdin Paperbacks edition June 2005
10  9  8  7  6  5  4  3  2

Library of Congress Control Number: 2004117445
ISBN-13: 978-1-4169-0005-4
ISBN-10: 1-4169-0005-5

# TABLE OF CONTENTS

*JOE*

# 1.

# RUMBLE!

"He's always come through for us and he will now!" Riff yelled.

A burst of music rang through the air.

Onstage, one of the big musical numbers in the summer stock production of *West Side Story* was just about to begin. Backstage, my brother Frank had just been stabbed in the stomach.

"Frank!" I cried, trying to keep my voice down.

With all the actors either onstage or in one of the dressing rooms upstairs—and the stage manager nowhere to be found—it was just Frank and me against DJ and Big T, two of the nastiest lowlifes I'd ever met.

Frank and I had been sent to investigate a drag-racing ring. We'd never expected it to lead us to a

1

theater with a play in mid-performance! DJ and Big T were two of the main criminals in the racing ring. They stole from anyone and anything to finance their expensive automotive habit.

DJ stood over Frank, who slumped on the floor holding his stomach. His mouth was open in a silent O of pain and disbelief.

Like most brothers, Frank and I have our differences. He's got no sense of humor; I've got a great one. He spends way too much time looking things up on the Internet library reference sites; I spend way too much time playing games on my Xbox. And most recently, that mysterious attraction he holds for girls made it impossible for me to get noticed by Angela Mendes.

But I really didn't want him to get stabbed. Not even a little. I could barely believe my eyes. I mean, we've escaped a million life-threatening situations on our missions for American Teens Against Crime, or ATAC for short. How could Frank get stabbed by some degenerate at the Croton-on-Hudson Theater? These losers were trying to steal the box office money the summer stock company was raising for the When Wishes Come True Foundation.

Guys like that shouldn't be able to stab my brother.

DJ—a small, wiry creep with long greasy hair

and an even greasier smile—glanced at me over Frank's crumpled body. DJ had the chipped teeth of a fighter. He grabbed the metal lockbox the money was in and headed for the exit.

But the only way out was onto the stage.

DJ yanked aside the curtain—only to find twenty or thirty fake gang members dancing across the stage.

I shook my head, trying to clear it. Right after Frank took the knife, everything seemed to slow down to molasses pace, like someone hit the SLOW button on a remote.

I had to get to Frank. But I'd been in the middle of a fight. I turned to face Big T, a beefy guy with cropped hair and the typical tough-guy tattoo around his bicep.

I'd meant to turn back to Big T. Instead, I turned back to his fist.

Coming right at me.

And someone had hit the PLAY button again, because his fist was coming in *fast*.

I've taken a lot of punches on my ATAC missions, and I know that big guys usually throw these roundhouse punches. All the way around their bodies, leading with their shoulder. No matter how fast they move, there is always time to step toward them and get inside the arc of their fist.

So that's what I did.

As fast as possible, I moved close to Big T to get my head out of the way. Then I bent my knees and sidestepped out of range.

I had to get to Frank, who was still lying on the floor. And making a weird gesture with his hand.

What was he doing?

He pointed up and then at the wall. Then he did it again.

Maybe he was just in so much pain that he was having spasms.

DJ decided not to run out on stage. I guess disrupting the show in front of a packed audience would call too much attention to him and Big T. He whirled away from the curtain and took off for the ladder leading to the catwalk that ran across the top of the stage. I started after him.

But I couldn't move. Big T had grabbed the back of my jacket.

No problem. I wriggled out of it and took a few steps toward Frank.

He kept making those weird gestures. And his eyes were unmistakably saying, "Pay attention, bonehead."

Then I got it. He was signaling me.

See, as I mentioned before, I had a thing for Angela, the actress who was playing Maria in *West Side Story*. She was totally gorgeous, and she was only in town for the summer. So I had come to more rehearsals than I could count. I knew all the words to all the songs, all the steps to all the dances, and all the props and sets that moved on and off the stage. And so did Frank. Because the only way I could get Angela to come over and talk to me was to bring Frank with me. He's like a force of nature—girls love him. The problem is, he's so shy with them that he turns into a big dork when they're around. But for some reason they all like him. Including Angela.

Frank and I were there the day the summer stock director—in a fit of his self-proclaimed genius—got his carpentry team to rig up a special effect for the play. At just the right time in "When You're a Jet," the gang leader Riff kicks a trash can for emphasis. The can is supposed to fly off the stage—and I mean *fly*.

To get this effect, the can was connected by a nylon fishing wire threaded through a pulley system to a heavy sandbag. When the stage manager got the right cue, he'd make the sandbag drop to the floor backstage, pulling the trash can up and through the air.

I glanced up. The sandbag dangled ten feet above and just a few feet to the right of Big T's gigantic melon of a head.

I looked back at Frank. He was still lying on the ground, but he was close to the rope that needed to be untied to trigger the bag. So I turned on Big T with my fiercest look.

He laughed at me.

All I had to do was get him to step under the bag. I knew I couldn't get close to him. He was too big and too dangerous. And I knew he wasn't afraid of me, so he wouldn't run. But I also knew that Big T was not too bright—we're talking ten-, maybe twenty-watt bulb here. All I had to do was let him think he was going to win.

So I let him come to me. I sidestepped so he had to move under the bag.

The entire time I listened for the cue from the stage. No sense in ruining the show just because we were having a fight. The actor playing Riff was supposed to say, "I'm only gonna challenge him," and then kick the can. That was the cue for the sandbag to drop.

Frank was gesturing frantically for me to get Big T under the bag. But Angela would be so upset if the show got ruined by a special effect going off at the wrong time.

I needed to wait for just a few more lines, so I circled again. Big T continued to follow me, step-ping after me as if connected by a leash.

There!

Frank scrambled up to his feet. Big T stopped, surprised that Frank was moving so fast. Come to think of it, so was I. But I had no more time to wonder about it because . . .

"I'm only gonna challenge him," Riff sneered. He kicked the can.

Frank released the rope.

Wham!

The sandbag came down on cue—right on Big T's head. No one on stage or in the audience was any the wiser. And certainly Big T wouldn't be either. He was out cold on the floor.

I ran over to Frank.

"Are you okay?" I whispered, reaching to steady him. But he didn't need my help.

"I'm fine, Joe." He handed me the gleaming knife. "It's one of the stage knives. Retractable blades."

I pressed the point of the knife against the upturned palm of my hand. Sure enough, it slid back into the handle like it was supposed to.

"I pulled it on that loser and let him think he took it from me." Frank shook his hand in the air, sending tiny droplets of blood flying. "I cut myself on his stupid ring, though."

"It's a good thing Big T isn't the sharpest knife

in the drawer." I stabbed Frank in the shoulder with the fake blade. He didn't think my joke was funny. He never thinks my jokes are funny. Of course, I didn't think his pretending to be stabbed in the stomach was funny either.

Frank pointed at DJ, who was climbing down from the catwalk on the other side of the stage right now. With the metal cash box in one hand, the ladder was slow going, but he was still getting away. With all the money.

"We have to go after him." Frank started toward the ladder.

But I knew it was hopeless. We didn't have time to get all the way across the length of the stage. It would take too long to maneuver through all the props and sets stored backstage.

Luckily, I had a Plan B.

"Hey, Frank, can I have this dance?" I pointed at the stage.

"What?"

The Jets were just going into another of the director's bright ideas. The gang members start on our side of the stage and do this weird step-step-raise-your-knee-snap-with-your-arms-by-your-sides thing a few times across the stage. They looked like idiots every time they did it. But it got them across the stage pretty fast. We grabbed a couple of extra period hats and ran to the back of the line.

Suddenly we were out in the bright lights with the actors. Being onstage wasn't what I expected. You can barely see the audience at all. Just the first few rows and then darkness. It was a little like being alone, with just the other performers.

Except that off to the side of the first row, peering in from one of the exit doors, was Angela! Oh, man. Was she there to watch the scenes she wasn't in?

Well, not anymore. Now she was watching Frank. And so was I.

He stepped. Then stepped again. Then raised his knee—and saw Angela looking right at him.

*Uh-oh,* I thought.

My pumpkinhead of a brother stopped. Right there in the middle of the stage. He stood frozen, blushing from head to toe. I rolled my eyes. Frank can do anything except deal with cute girls.

I sped over to his side and poked him in the ribs.

Frank jumped back into action. We skipped the snap and just ran with our arms by our sides. We stayed behind the rest of the guys and caught up by the time we started stepping again.

Once we hit the other side, we ducked offstage, with no one the wiser. Well, except Angela, that is, and probably some of the guys onstage. But the show must go on, right?

We ran back into the darkness just as DJ was getting to the bottom of the ladder. It took a few seconds for our eyes to adjust after the bright lights of the stage. When they did, I saw DJ trying to get *his* eyes to adjust—to the fact that Frank was up and around instead of lying there with a knife in his stomach.

DJ ran toward the back exit, with Frank and me in hot pursuit. "We can't let him get out the door," I cried in a stage whisper.

If DJ got through that door, he'd be able to get to his hot rod. Our awesome, state-of-the-art motorcycles could catch his car, no problem. Only our bikes were in the front parking lot, all the way around the building.

If he got out the door, we'd lose him. And the money for the When Wishes Come True kids.

And we couldn't yell out for help, because then the show would come to a screeching halt and people might want their money back.

Besides, Frank and I always catch the bad guy. We've never been on a mission we couldn't handle.

Then I remembered. The stage manager had told me they stored tall scenery pieces under the stage. They lowered them down through a long trapdoor in the stage—three feet wide by fifteen feet long.

The crank to open the trapdoor was on this side of the stage.

"Make sure he doesn't get past that yellow painted area," I told Frank. He'd been so busy stammering and trying to avoid Angela whenever we were here that he'd never heard about the trapdoor. "And you stay out of it."

Frank nodded.

I ran to the side wall, where the crank was hidden behind the spiral staircase that led up to the dressing rooms. I'd have to do this quickly and just like the stage manager had showed me. There was some trick to get the crank going.

Too bad I couldn't remember what it was.

DJ ran into the yellow area, approaching the door. He glanced over his shoulder.

Frank threw the knife at him.

DJ dodged sideways—and stayed in the yellow area.

"DJ," Frank said—loud enough to hear, but quiet enough not to disturb the play. "How dumb are you? It's a fake knife."

The taunt stopped DJ just long enough for my brain to kick into gear. I remembered the trick. I wedged myself on the other side of the crank, with my back to the wall next to it, and put my left leg onto the handle. I pushed with all my strength.

The trapdoor opened.

And DJ disappeared as the floor vanished from underneath him.

Well, almost. At the last second he grabbed onto the edge of the floor.

He held on, dangling. And it was a long drop. Frank leaned over. "Here. Take my hand."

DJ looked at Frank's hand, then at the money box he'd have to drop if he did. His indecision cost him. His hand slipped and down he fell.

I knew he'd be okay, but it was going to leave a mark.

I walked up next to Frank. "Greed is a heavy burden," I joked.

Frank just looked at me and shook his head.

# 2.

## SPECIAL DELIVERY

"And just where have you two been all day?" Aunt Trudy greeted us as we walked through the front door.

I shot a look at Joe. His clothes were still covered in dirt from the fight backstage. I quickly stuck my scraped-up hand in the pocket of my jeans. "We were at the theater," I said.

"The *theater*?" Mom sounded skeptical.

"Yeah. There was a summer stock production of *West Side Story*."

Now even Dad looked skeptical. We'd never told him we'd been hanging out at the summer stock theater lately. Joe had been too embarrassed about the theater part of it. I'd been too embarrassed about Angela having a crush on me. "The

13

girl who stars in it is incredibly hot," Joe put in.

Mom and Aunt Trudy exchanged a smile, and Mom shook her head.

"Nice save," I murmured to Joe. I'm such an idiot around girls that I avoid them as much as I can. But Joe is always flirting with someone—and he'd spent half the summer flirting with Angela. Aunt Trudy and Mom would totally believe that he went to a play just to score points with a girl.

Dad was still studying the grime on Joe's shirt. He frowned. Dad's the only one who knows that we work for American Teens Against Crime—ATAC. Even though he cofounded the organization, he still worries about us when we're on missions. Obviously he could tell we'd been in a fight.

"How was it?" he asked. Mom probably thought he was asking about the play. But I knew he really wanted to know about our mission.

"It was great," I told him. "Not a single hitch."

"Sounds like your girl is a good actor in addition to her incredible hotness," Mom teased Joe.

"You should have put on a clean shirt if you wanted to impress her," Aunt Trudy added. "You look like you've been rolling in a pigsty. I expect you to wash up before dinner—and that is in exactly ten minutes."

"Pigs! Pigs! Pigs!" my pet parrot, Playback,

14

squawked from his perch on the back of Dad's chair.

Mom squinted at Joe's filthy shirt. He shot me a panicked look. Our mom's no fool—she works as a research librarian. It's not easy to keep her from finding out about our missions. And if she got a closer look at Joe's shirt, we'd be busted for sure!

The doorbell rang.

"Saved by the bell," Joe said. He rushed over and pulled open the front door.

"Pizza delivery!" The teenage guy on the porch wore an idiotic red-and-white uniform with a big red scarf tied around his neck. He held up two pizza boxes. "Two cheese pies," he announced with an Indian accent.

"All right!" Joe cried. "Nice going, Aunt Trudy."

Aunt Trudy frowned so hard I thought her face might crack. "I didn't order pizza. I made a big chef's salad."

"Oh." Joe turned away from the door, bummed.

"Sorry," I said to the pizza guy. "Looks like there was a mistake."

He shrugged. "Well, you can have the pies anyway. If I brought them back, they would just get cold."

"Really?" I asked. "Cool."

"Cool?" Aunt Trudy repeated. "You think a meal

filled with enough cholesterol, saturated fat, and sodium to choke a horse is *cool*?"

"Saturated fat!" squawked Playback. "Cool!"

"Actually, if these are plain cheese pies, they're not so bad," Mom put in. "The extremely high levels of saturated fat and sodium are usually found in pizza that contains meat—you know, a sausage or pepperoni pie. A plain cheese is fine." She winked at me. "As long as you don't eat it every day."

"Well, I think we should leave the pizza to the boys," Dad said, standing up. "Us old folks can dig into that salad." He ushered Mom and Aunt Trudy toward the kitchen.

That was weird. Dad loves pizza. Why would he want to let Joe and me have it all?

I turned back to the guy at the door. He was watching our parents leave the room. As soon as the kitchen door swung closed behind them, his whole expression changed. With one hand, he pulled the dumb red scarf off his neck.

"You're not really a delivery guy, are you?" I asked.

"Nope. I'm from ATAC," he replied. "My name is Vijay Patel."

"What are you talking about?" I said, playing dumb. ATAC is a secret organization. This kid could be trying to get us to spill information about our work—and we had no way of knowing who he really worked for.

"Oh. Sorry." Vijay bent down and put the pizza boxes on the doormat. He stuck out his hand to shake.

I grabbed on and did two hard up-and-down shakes followed by a wrist-grab, then a fist-touch, and finally one last up-and-down shake. "Okay, Vijay, you know the handshake," I said. "So you must really work for ATAC."

"Yes. I'm still a trainee. In fact, you two are the first real ATAC agents I've met." Vijay looked embarrassed. "I almost forgot that I had to identify myself with the secret handshake."

"No problem," Joe said. "We just have to be careful. Sometimes people set traps for us."

"I know," Vijay told us. "I've read about a lot of your cases in the ATAC files. You're two of our top agents!"

"Thanks," Joe said with a big grin. "It's nice to have a fan. How long have you been with the organization?"

"For a year," Vijay said. "I used to solve crimes in my neighborhood in Calcutta when I was little. I've always wanted to be a crime fighter."

"How long have you been in the United States?" I asked.

"My family moved here from India when I was twelve," Vijay said.

I heard the sound of plates clanking in the kitchen. We had to finish up with Vijay before Mom decided to come back out. "I guess our father recognized you as a fellow ATAC-er," I said. "Are you here on official business?"

"Yes." Vijay bent and opened the top pizza box. Inside was a video game disk. The title on the game read, THRILL RIDE.

Vijay handed me the disk, while Joe groaned in disappointment. "That's not real pizza?" he complained.

"No, but this is." Vijay picked up the second pizza box and gave it to Joe. "The folks at ATAC knew you'd be hungry after your last mission!"

"They're a class operation," Joe said happily. He's easy to please.

"There's one more thing," Vijay added. He pulled a tiny metal square from the pocket of his uniform. "We just used these in my last training session. I thought you guys might like one—it could come in handy."

"What is it?" I asked, taking the little silver box. "Some kind of cell phone?"

"No, it's a pocket strobe," Vijay explained. "Push

this button on the side, and the box will emit a flash of powerful light. But only for a second."

"So it's like a camera flash?" Joe asked.

"If it's a strobe light, it's much more powerful than a camera flash," I said.

"Yeah, it's really bright," Vijay agreed. "But you never know when you need some light."

"Cool. Thanks, Vijay," I said.

He tucked the now-empty pizza box under his arm and gave us both the secret handshake again. "I can't wait to tell the other trainees I met Frank and Joe Hardy," he said. "You guys are legends."

"Legends," Joe repeated as I closed the door behind Vijay. "I like the sound of that."

"Don't get so full of yourself that you forget we have a new mission," I told him. "Let's go pop this disk in the system."

Upstairs in my room, Joe dug into the pizza while I stuck "Thrill Ride" into my gaming system.

A video of a roller coaster came onto the TV screen. People screamed as they turned upside down on a wicked coaster loop. Another rockin' coaster followed; then another.

"I like this mission already," Joe mumbled through a mouthful of pizza.

"Amusement park rides are built to thrill," a

deep voice said over the coaster montage. "Gravity-defying turns and deadly dangerous drops. But it's all fun and games. Isn't it?"

The image zoomed in on the screaming face of a young guy, swooping straight into his mouth, open in a yell of terror, and ending in blackness.

"Uh-oh," I murmured. I had a feeling this mission *wasn't* going to be fun and games.

The blackness turned gray, then lightened to a black-and-white still photo of an old amusement park on a paved lot. Judging from the grainy photo and the strange clothes the people wore, this picture had been taken at least seventy or eighty years ago.

"Uncle Bernie's Fun Park," the deep voice announced. "Amusing and delighting the people of Holyoke, Massachusetts, since 1924."

The picture faded out and was replaced by a photo of a middle-aged woman smiling sweetly at the camera.

"Maggie Soto," the voice said. "Age forty-five, a schoolteacher and a mother of two. She was killed last week at Uncle Bernie's Fun Park."

I heard Joe gasp. I put down the slice I'd been eating. Pizza didn't seem so good all of a sudden. What had happened to this woman?

As if he could read my mind, the announcer

explained, "Maggie was riding on the Doom Rider roller coaster when the ride malfunctioned."

Maggie's smiling face vanished and was replaced by a picture of the coaster. It looked just like any other medium-sized roller coaster. No loops, but a lot of big drops and a few tunnels.

"In the second tunnel, a large piece of interior scenery broke off the ceiling," the announcer said. "The collapse happened immediately above Maggie's car. It injured her spine, and she died a few hours later."

"Aren't roller coasters inspected for safety like every day?" Joe asked.

"Uncle Bernie's Fun Park is maintaining that Maggie's death was an accident," the announcer said. "Their safety inspections are up-to-date, safety inspectors found nothing wrong with the coaster tracks or the cart she was riding in, and the local police have determined that no one had a motive to harm Maggie Soto."

"So what's our mission?" I asked. Sometimes the mission disks are so detailed that it almost seems like they're interactive.

Sure enough, the announcer answered as if he'd heard me.

"Your mission is to check out the amusement park," he said. "We here at ATAC are not convinced that this incident was an accident. We suspect that there may have been foul play, and you boys have to find out for sure."

I shot a look at Joe. "Before something else happens," I said.

"Before someone else gets hurt," the announcer finished. "This mission, like every mission, is top secret. In five seconds this disk will be reformatted into a regular CD."

Five seconds later, an old Aerosmith song blasted out of the TV speakers. But I was still thinking about Maggie Soto. What had really happened on that ride?

# 3.

# DOOM RIDER

"You boys be careful," Dad said early the next morning.

I was tempted to roll my eyes, but I held back. Dad says that every time we leave for a mission. You'd think he was a regular father, the way he worries. Not Fenton Hardy, ex-cop and cofounder of the coolest crime-fighting organization ever. Dad was the one who recruited Frank and me to the ATAC team, but I guess that doesn't stop him from worrying about us.

"I'm still allowed to be concerned for your safety," Dad said. "Okay, Joe?"

"Yeah," I agreed. Obviously he knew what I was thinking even if I didn't roll my eyes. That's

23

because he's such a great investigator—he can read people's body language.

Frank was still putting on his motorcycle helmet, but I was geared up and ready to go. I couldn't wait to get on the road. Sitting on my tricked-out cycle in the driveway was no fun at all.

"We'll be careful," Frank assured our father. "Are you going to tell Mom where we're going?"

"I'll say you went to an amusement park," Dad said. "I just won't say why."

"Sounds good. See you later." I revved up my bike, and Frank and I took off. In the sideview, I could see Dad standing in front of the house, watching us go.

The truth is, I feel better knowing he's got our backs. But I would never tell him that.

It took us almost four hours to get to Holyoke, Massachusetts. But four hours on the bike feels like no time. I could ride that thing all day!

We pulled into the parking lot of Uncle Bernie's Fun Park. The photo on the mission disk had been really old, but the amusement park still looked exactly the same. The lot was paved with old white concrete, grass grew up between the cracks, and the boards that made up the welcome sign looked like they were ready to collapse into sawdust.

"They haven't updated this place much," Frank commented.

"Not since the Dark Ages," I agreed. In fact, the only thing about the park that looked new—well, post-1970, anyway—was the roller coaster. It rose above the park, all gleaming metal and black paint. The way it loomed over the rinky-dink rides from the 1920s made the coaster look like some kind of monster.

"Let's go," Frank said.

I hopped off my bike and headed for the ticket booth. It was an old-fashioned wooden one that looked like a phone booth. "This is the best mission ever," I said. "Can you believe we've been *assigned* to go on amusement park rides?" Even if Uncle Bernie's was an old park, it would still be cool to go on the bumper cars and the slide.

"Don't get too excited," Frank warned. "Remember, that poor lady died here last week. And she may have been murdered."

That's my brother, always a downer. "I know," I said. "And I intend to find out what really happened." I couldn't get Maggie Soto's face out of my mind. If she'd been a victim of foul play, I wouldn't rest until her killer was behind bars.

"Let's check out the place first, get a feel for who

works here," Frank suggested. He paid for two admissions to the park and led the way inside.

The first attraction we came to was a flume ride. The cars were cool because they looked like real logs that had been carved into little canoes. But the water was only a foot deep and there were no big drops. I like a flume ride that dumps you fifty feet and creates a humongous splash. Still, the flume was packed with people, and the line had to be a half-hour wait. It was pretty hot out—I guess people like to get into whatever water they can find.

"Look at the girl running the ride," I said to Frank. She was about our age, with long dark hair pulled into two braids. That might have looked dorky on some girls, but she was gorgeous. On her the braids looked flirty and a little punk.

"She doesn't seem very suspicious," Frank said. "She just looks bored."

The girl yawned as she pushed the button to start the next log flume on its way down the fake river.

"I didn't think she was suspicious. Just hot," I informed my brother. He's so dense when it comes to girls.

"I think we should talk to that guy," Frank said. He nodded toward a gangly looking man dressed in a blue-and-white striped suit. The dude was seriously tall. He must've been at least eight feet. He towered over the crowd as he walked forward. And there was something weird about his gait. There could only be one explanation: He was walking on stilts.

As the crowd cleared in front of him, I could see that I was right—the bottom half of his wide striped pants fluttered in the breeze as he walked. The stilts underneath were connected to his super-big shoes.

"Hey!" Frank called up to the guy. "You're pretty good at that. How long have you been stilt-walking?"

The guy peered down at us as if he was surprised that anyone was talking to him. I guess he didn't get much conversation way up there.

"Too long," he said. "I've been working at Uncle Bernie's for twelve summers now. This is my last one."

"How come?" I asked.

The guy pulled off his straw hat and mopped his brow. "Twelve years, no raise," he said. "I'm sick of it. Next summer I'm gonna find some other place to work. I could make more money with a traveling carnival." He slapped the hat back on his head and stomped off through the crowded park.

"O-kay," I said. "He's not too happy here. You think that makes him a suspect?"

Frank shrugged. "We don't even know if there was a crime yet. I don't think we can start calling people suspects."

"Check out the haunted house," I said. "I love haunted houses."

"That one looks pretty lame," Frank replied. "The back door is even open."

Sure enough, one of the employee-access doors to the house stood open. The outside of the door was painted to look like a column that was part of the mansion, complete with a spiderweb stretched over the top. But with the door open, the whole illusion was ruined. We could see right into the darkness inside and hear the screams of the people within.

As I watched, an elderly man in a faded blue jumpsuit came out of the haunted house. He was pushing a bucket with a mop sticking out of it. He let the door slam behind him without even caring about the noise it made.

"I'd like to talk to him," I said, following the old guy.

We caught up to him in a tin maintenance shed behind the kiddie swing ride. "Excuse me," I called.

The old guy turned around. "Whaddya want?" he growled.

"Uh . . . are you the janitor here?" I asked.

"Not anymore," he said. "Now I'm called the maintenance coordinator." He rolled his eyes.

"Why?" Frank asked.

"Because I asked old Bernie for a raise," the man said. "So he gave me a new job title instead."

"A new job title but no money?" I said. "That doesn't seem fair."

"Tell me about it. Bernie expected me to be thrilled. Seemed to think a new title would raise my self-esteem." He broke into a dry laugh that sounded more like a cough. "I don't care about self-esteem. I just wanted to make more than minimum wage."

"How long have you been working for Uncle Bernie?" Frank asked.

The man squinted at him suspiciously. "Why are you kids so curious?" he asked.

"We were thinking of applying for jobs here," I said, thinking fast. "We figured we'd ask what kind of employer Uncle Bernie was."

"He's the worst employer in Massachusetts," the man said. "Stingy and mean. Why, when that lady died on the coaster last week, all Bernie cared about was the bad publicity. He didn't even call her family to say he was sorry."

"Wow," Frank said. "Were you here when it happened?"

"Of course," the maintenance man said. "I'm always here. You think old Bernie gives us any time off?"

"Did you see the accident?" I asked. "Do you know how it happened?"

"Nah. I was clear across the park, cleaning up a milkshake that spilled on the teacup ride." The man turned to go inside the shed. "My advice to you boys is to get a job somewhere else. Anywhere else." He shut the door behind him.

"One thing's clear. Uncle Bernie isn't very popular," Frank said.

"But that still doesn't help us figure out what happened to Maggie Soto," I said.

"Let's head over to the roller coaster," Frank suggested. "We need to look at the scene of the crime . . . or the accident."

"Right." I glanced up. It wasn't hard to spot the coaster—the thing was the biggest ride in the park. You could see it from everywhere. I led the way toward it, past the game booths and around the carousel.

"Hang on," Frank said. "I need a drink after that long drive up here." He got in line at an old-fashioned concession cart on wheels. A pretty Asian girl manned the cart while a big, muscular bald guy stood nearby. He was obviously the one who pushed the cart from place to place. One entire arm was covered in tattoos, while the other just had one, a picture of a cat with the name LULU underneath.

"Hi. Two Cokes, please," Frank told the girl when it was his turn.

"Sure." She reached into the portable ice chest to get them.

"Hot out today, huh?" I said, flirting. "I hope you get a break soon."

The muscular guy snorted. "Yeah, right," he said. "We don't even know what a break is."

"Come on, Jonesy, it's not that bad," the girl replied. "We get time off for lunch."

"Ten minutes. Barely enough time to down a burger," Jonesy muttered.

Frank frowned. "You get only one ten-minute break a day? That's illegal."

Jonesy shrugged. "Tell it to old Bernie. He only cares about the law when they're here to investigate."

The girl made a face. "It's true. When the cops were here last week, all of a sudden we got an hour for lunch and ten-minute breaks twice a day. Once their investigation was over, it was back to no breaks at all."

"How long were the cops here?" Frank asked.

"Two days," the girl said. "They had the whole roller coaster roped off."

"It must've been a shock to have a death here," I said. "You guys must've been really upset."

"Just upset that it wasn't old Bernie who got killed on the coaster," Jonesy said. He smiled, revealing sharp gold teeth where his canines should be.

The girl shook her head. "Don't mind Jonesy," she told me. "He's always cranky."

"What about you?" I asked. "Do you like working here?"

"Not really." She gave me a big smile. "But I like it when there are cute customers to talk to."

I opened my mouth to flirt back . . . and that's when I realized that she was now gazing at Frank. *Smiling* at Frank. She'd forgotten I was even there.

What *is* it with him and girls?

"Can we get some service, please?" snapped a woman behind us. She had three little kids pulling on her arms.

"Sorry," I said, stepping aside. Frank grabbed the Cokes and followed me.

"What do you think about that big guy?" he said. "Sounded like he really wants to do Bernie in."

"You think maybe he tampered with the roller coaster?" I asked.

"Maybe," Frank said. "We'd better make sure the

## SUSPECT PROFILE

**Name:** Samuel "Jonesy" Jones

**Hometown:** Albuquerque, New Mexico

**Physical description:** Age 29, 6'2", 250 lbs. Bald. Tattoo of his childhood pet, Lulu, on left arm.

**Occupation:** Concession worker at Uncle Bernie's Fun Park

**Background:** Child of divorce. Grew up in a run-down section of town.

**Suspicious behavior:** Heard to say that he wished Uncle Bernie harm.

**Suspected of:** Tampering with the roller coaster.

**Possible motives:** Revenge against Uncle Bernie's unfair treatment of his workers.

roller coaster was tampered with before we jump to conclusions."

We downed the sodas on the way to the coaster. I was surprised there wasn't a line wrapped all the way around the ride—usually roller coasters are the most popular rides at amusement parks.

"I bet people are staying away because they're freaked out by the accident last week," I said.

"Nope." Frank pointed to the front entrance of the coaster. "The ride's just closed."

I stared at the big black-metal gateway to the coaster. A neon sign read "Doom Rider." The words blinked on and off in an electric blue color. But a chain over the entrance made it clear that no one was allowed on.

"No way," I groaned. "If the cops are done investigating, why is it closed?"

Frank went closer to the chain. There was a small sign attached to it. "'Closed for repair work,'" he read aloud. "Looks like we can't get in this way."

"Then we'll have to find another way in," I said.

Frank nodded. We walked casually along the fence that surrounded the Doom Rider, looking for a back way in. But the fence went all the way around the coaster without a single break.

"What do we do now?" I asked.

"There has to be some kind of employee access," Frank replied. "And there should also be an emergency exit."

I glanced around. The coaster was all the way at the end of the amusement park—you had to walk past all the other rides and games to get to the Doom Rider. Since it was closed, there weren't many people around today. Just the lonely roller coaster and a few tin sheds.

"That's it!" I cried.

"What is?" Frank asked.

I gestured to the tin sheds. One of them had a KEEP OUT sign on the door.

"I'm guessing that's the emergency exit from the Doom Rider," I said. "This old pavement isn't strong enough to support the weight of the coaster. There has to be newer concrete underneath. And probably a control room or something."

"Good thinking," Frank said.

We went over to the door. I kept a lookout while Frank picked the lock on the doorknob. We always bring our lock picks with us on missions.

"We're in," he told me. We slipped through the door.

Just as I'd expected, the door led into a stairway that plunged under the ground. We hurried down and found ourselves in a storage room built of concrete underneath the old paved-over land. On one side was a mess of electronics. That had to be the control system for the coaster.

"It's like a garage," Frank said. "There are coaster parts all over the place."

"Yeah, but we're here to check out the ride, not the parts," I said. "Look!"

In the center of the room, a ladder led up to a trapdoor in the ceiling. That had to be where the storage room connected to the actual roller coaster.

We climbed up and made our way through to the coaster. Without the cars going, the whole thing just looked like a series of ladders and train tracks that criss-crossed every so often. "What are we looking for?" I asked Frank. "The cops already investigated the Doom Rider."

"Then we're looking for anything they missed," Frank said.

"Well, it wasn't the cars that malfunctioned," I said. "And it wasn't the tracks. It was one of the tunnels."

Frank glanced around. "I see one tunnel on the other side of the coaster," he said.

"And there's another one right over there." I pointed to a fake mountain made of some kind of plaster. The coaster tracks shot through it about fifteen yards from where we stood. "Let's check out that one first."

We made our way along the tracks until we reached the tunnel. It was at least ten feet off the ground, so we had to climb the tracks like a ladder to get inside. The tunnel wasn't very long—only about twenty feet or so. The fake mountain arched up and over the coaster, but the ceiling was low. I

36

love when roller coasters plunge into a tunnel—the ride designers make it look as if you're going to crash right into something. My guess was that whoever designed the Doom Rider wanted this tunnel to give that impression too.

"Perfect," Frank said. "We picked the right tunnel on the first try." He inched along to a spot in the middle of the tunnel. "Here's where it collapsed."

I followed him to the place where the roof had fallen onto the tracks. There was plaster dust everywhere, so I pulled my T-shirt up over my mouth to help me breathe. A gigantic chunk of the hard plastic ceiling of the tunnel had fallen away from the metal bars that made up the frame. The blue sky peeked through, sun glinting off the tracks.

I let out a whistle. "This is serious damage."

"No wonder Maggie got killed when all this stuff fell on her," Frank said. "Her head would've been only a foot below the ceiling."

"There's no way she could've avoided being hit." I didn't like to think about that nice woman in such a scary situation.

"The police and the safety inspectors checked the roller coaster car, the safety restraints, and the tracks," Frank said.

"Yeah, but did they check the cave-in itself?" I asked. "From what it said on our mission disk, they only checked the coaster, not the cave-in. What would make something like this happen?" I stood up on the tracks and stuck my head through the hole in the roof. The edges of the plastic were sharp and twisted where the material had broken away, but none of the bars of the frame were broken. "It wasn't structural damage," I told Frank. "The steel bars are intact."

"So something made the hard plastic and the plaster decorations break," Frank said.

"And I think I know what caused it." From where I stood, I could see a small piece of thick red cardboard stuck on one of the sharp plastic shards. I stuck my arm carefully through the broken roof and snagged it. Then I jumped back down into the tunnel.

"What is it?" Frank asked.

"I think it's a piece of a spent shell," I told him. "From an M-80 firework."

"Could an M-80 have done this much damage?" Frank wondered.

I thought about it. "An illegal M-80 could. They can contain as much as two grams of flash powder. That's why they're illegal—they're dangerous."

"People still sell them, though," Frank said in

disgust. "But don't you have to light an M-80 to make it go off? How could someone do that while speeding along on a roller coaster?" He frowned.

"You can set up a slow-burning fuse," I replied. "Somebody could have planted the M-80 on the top of the scenery and lit a really long fuse. It just happened to burn out when Maggie's car was passing underneath."

Frank looked grim. "There's our answer. Maggie Soto's death was no accident. Somebody brought this roof right down on her head. On purpose."

I opened my mouth to answer him. But before I could say a word, a strong arm slipped around my neck. Someone was attacking from behind!

# 4.

# AN EXPLOSIVE DISCOVERY

"What's going on here?" The man with his arm around Joe's neck didn't look happy. "Who are you kids?"

"My name is Frank Hardy," I said quickly. "And that's my brother, Joe." Our ATAC training had taught us that the best way to deal with a violent situation is to keep calm.

"What are you doing in here? Can't you read?"

"We saw the 'Keep Out' sign," I admitted. "Are you a security guard?"

"No!" the guy bellowed. "I own this place. And I want to know why you boys are sneaking around in my roller coaster when it's clearly closed." He squeezed Joe's neck harder. "Did you punks have something to do with the accident last week? Did you come back to get rid of evidence?"

"No!" I cried.

"So you're Uncle Bernie," Joe choked out. "We were hoping we'd get to meet you."

Uncle Bernie seemed surprised to hear that—especially from someone he had in a choke hold. He relaxed his grip on Joe's throat but kept holding his arm. "How do you know who I am?" he asked.

"We came here to offer you our help," I said, thinking fast. "My brother and I are sort of amateur detectives. We've solved a lot of cases back in Bayport, where we live."

"What's that got to do with me?" Uncle Bernie growled.

"We read about the tragedy here last week," Joe said. "It was in all the papers."

"And we saw that the police ruled out foul play," I said. *Even though they were wrong,* I added silently.

"But they still didn't have an explanation for why the cave-in happened, did they?" Joe asked. "We thought we could help you figure it out."

Joe shot me a look, and I knew we were both thinking the same thing. After everything we'd heard today about Uncle Bernie, it didn't seem likely that he'd want our help. In fact, it was more likely that he'd been the one to explode the M-80 on his own ride. Maybe he wanted to get the park closed down so he could collect on the insurance money. Maybe he'd had a motive to kill Maggie Soto that the police didn't know about. I wasn't sure. But the one thing I knew for certain was that I didn't trust him.

"You two think you're smarter than the cops?" Uncle Bernie snorted.

"No," Joe said. "But we did find something that they missed." He held up the piece of red cardboard.

"What's that?" Uncle Bernie asked.

"We think it's part of an exploded M-80," I explained. "Probably an illegal one that had enough power to blow that hole in the ceiling."

Uncle Bernie glanced up at the twisted plastic and the sky above it. He sighed and let go of Joe's arm.

"I knew there was no safety violation," he mumbled. "But why would someone want to explode my roller coaster on purpose? I could get shut down for something like this."

He almost sounded sincere. Sincerely upset.

"This place means a lot to you, huh?" I asked.

"It's my whole life," Uncle Bernie answered. "I inherited the park from my dad, Bernard Jr. And he inherited it from *his* dad, the first Bernard. My grandfather founded the place. And we Bernies have been running it ever since."

"So you've never worked anywhere else?" Joe asked.

"Sure I did," Uncle Bernie said. "But when my father died, I came right back here to take over for him. It's what we do in this family. This amusement park is our legacy." His face puffed up with pride. "One day my son will inherit it, and he'll be the fourth Uncle Bernie in charge here."

"Your son's name is Bernard too?" I couldn't help thinking that would be confusing at a family reunion.

"Yep." Tears welled up in Uncle Bernie's eyes as he mentioned his kid. Hard to believe this gruff and nasty guy had it in him. "Little Bernie. He's twelve."

Uncle Bernie suddenly turned and punched the wall of the tunnel. More plaster came falling down around us. Joe coughed.

"Little Bernie was sitting right behind that lady," Uncle Bernie said. "Right there when this thing collapsed on her. I was afraid he'd be traumatized by what he saw."

I nodded sympathetically.

"But you say somebody exploded an M-80 on the roof?" Uncle Bernie shook his head. "That means someone wanted the collapse to happen. And maybe they weren't after that lady. Little Bernie was right there too. He could've been killed!"

"Maybe he was the real target all along," Joe said. He turned to me.

"I think we should talk to Little Bernie," I said.

Uncle Bernie nodded. "You boys go right ahead. He's probably hard at work somewhere in the park."

"Do you know where?" Joe asked.

"Not really. He rotates, does a little of everything." Uncle Bernie beamed as he talked about his son. "Tell him I said it's okay, otherwise he won't want to leave his post. He lives for this park—he'll be a terrific Uncle Bernie one day."

Uncle Bernie said good-bye and headed off for his office to make some phone calls.

"It's a little weird that he doesn't know where his own son is," I said. "Didn't he say the kid is only twelve?"

"He probably figures his son is safe in the amusement park," Joe replied. He squinted at something over my shoulder. "But I'm not so sure. Check that out."

I turned to see what Joe was looking at. The Ferris wheel was slowly jerking its way around in the start, stop, start, stop motion that meant it was still loading riders on.

"What?" I asked. "It's just a Ferris wheel." I hate those things. They're totally boring. But Joe loves Ferris wheels. "Something looks strange to me," Joe said. "See that woman?"

I put my hand up to shade my eyes from the

45

bright sunlight. Joe was pointing to a woman about halfway up one side of the Ferris wheel. She sat in a cart with her son, who looked to be about four or five years old. "What about her?" I asked.

"She's struggling." Joe studied the Ferris wheel for another second. Then he took off at a run.

"Whoa," I muttered. I sprinted after him. I knew that if my brother was running toward something, he was going to need backup.

"Look out!" Joe yelled, pushing his way through the line of people waiting for the ride.

"Hey! No cutting!" a guy about our age yelled.

Joe ignored him and shoved his way to the front. I followed.

"Shut down the ride," Joe told the girl at the foot of the wheel. She was about to close the door on a cart that had just been loaded with passengers.

"I-I don't control it," she said, surprised.

"Who does?" I asked.

"Tommy," she said. She gestured toward a guy sitting on a little metal chair about ten feet away. He was reading the newspaper, one hand resting on the lever that started and stopped the wheel.

I shot Joe a look. "I've got it," I said. I ran over to Tommy and pulled the newspaper down. "I need you to shut off the wheel," I told him. "Can you do that?"

He glanced up, confused. "Sure. But why?"

I didn't really know the answer to that. But one look over my shoulder showed me that Joe was pointing up at the woman and her son. "That lady is in some kind of trouble," I told Tommy.

He pulled a pair of binoculars from under his chair and trained them up at the wheel. Then he jumped to his feet. "The safety bar is open!" he cried.

I grabbed the binoculars and looked. Sure enough, the black bar that was supposed to be locked into place across the passengers' laps was hanging open in midair. The woman clung to her son, her eyes wide with terror as the little boy wailed. His mouth was open and tears ran down his cheeks. But from way down here, I couldn't even hear him.

"Call security," I ordered Tommy. "We've got to get them down."

"We can't move the wheel," he said. He pulled a metal locking device over the control lever. "They're already halfway up. In order to get their cart to the bottom, they'd have to go up over the top. There's more wind up there. And the motion of the wheel might swing the cart so much that they'd fall out."

"Can't you put the wheel in reverse?" I asked. That way, the woman and her son would be getting

47

closer to the ground the entire time. If they fell, they might not be hurt as badly.

Tommy shook his head. "It doesn't go in reverse."

I jogged back over to Joe and the girl. "There's no way to lower them down," I told him.

"Then we'll have to go up there and get them," he said. "The little kid is so scared, he's squirming all over the place. I don't think she can hold him for much longer."

"But how will we get him down?" I asked. "We can't climb with the little boy in our arms."

"We need rope," Joe said.

I turned to Tommy. He was on his walkie-talkie, summoning security. But I didn't think we had time to wait for them to arrive.

"There's a hose in the emergency fire panel," the girl said. "Could you use that?"

I checked out the panel. It was a short metal cabinet bolted to the edge of the platform where we stood. Through the glass door, I could see a fire extinguisher and a flattened fire hose all wound up. Somewhere below the cabinet there must be a pipe to send water through the hose in case of a fire on the Ferris wheel.

"That will have to do," I said. "Let's just hope it's long enough."

Joe pulled his T-shirt down over his elbow and

smashed the glass front of the cabinet to get to the hose inside. As he unrolled it from its spool, I turned to the girl.

"Good idea," I told her.

She blushed and smiled up at me.

I turned away fast. I hate when girls look at me like that. It turns my brain to mush—and I needed my brain right now. I had a Ferris wheel to climb.

The hose reached its full length. It was still attached to the spool.

"We need it to be loose," Joe said.

I grabbed the hose, wrapped the end around the metal spool, and pulled it taut. Luckily the metal was sharp on the edges. With a sudden yank, I was able to snap the hose free.

"Let's go," Joe said. He slung the hose over his shoulder and ran to the edge of the platform.

"What's the plan?" I asked, following him.

"I think we both need to get up there," Joe called over his shoulder. He jumped up and grabbed one of the bars of the Ferris wheel, then pulled his legs up over it.

"One of us to hold the cart steady, the other to tie the rope around the boy?" I guessed.

"That's right." Joe climbed to the outside ring of the Ferris wheel. All the carts were attached to this ring by giant metal bolts. The ring itself was built

49

like a huge curved ladder, with steel slats running horizontally between the verticals. Joe began to climb it quickly.

I kept up with him. It was easy to climb at the beginning, just like playing on the monkey bars back in elementary school. But when the wheel started to curve, we had to hang from the slats, holding our weight with our arms and legs wrapped around the bars. It was much slower going that way.

"We need to get on the outside of the wheel," I told Joe. "So we can just crawl up the bars."

"Catch the hose," he replied. He let go of the bar with one hand and tossed the hose down to me. I managed to grab it as it fell through the air. I slipped it over my arm and took hold of the bar again.

Meanwhile Joe had pulled himself through two of the horizontal slats. He worked his way to the outside of the wheel, then reached down for the hose.

As soon as the weight of it was off my shoulder, I pulled myself up through the bars too. We hurried up the curve of the wheel on the outside.

The cart with the woman and her kid was almost at the top of the curve. As we got closer, I could see her frightened face. The little boy was still screaming and crying, squirming around in fear.

His mother held him with one arm and clung to the back of the cart with the other. I could see that she was getting tired.

"Please help," she called as soon as she spotted us. "I can't hold on for much longer!"

We put on a burst of speed and reached her cart. Joe tried to grab the safety bar to pull it back in, but it was swinging out from the cart. "It's too far away," he grunted.

"It won't close anyway," the woman said. "The lock is busted."

"Frank," Joe called. "I'll hold the cart steady. You get the rope around this boy."

I nodded, inching my way toward the cart as Joe tied one end of the hose around the rim of the metal Ferris wheel. He wrapped a loop or two around his own arm to help him stay balanced. Then he sat on the edge of the wheel and reached out for the cart. He grabbed the back of it with both hands and hung on.

I raced up to the cart. Standing on one of the metal slats, I leaned over the top of the cart and pulled the loose end of the hose toward me. I had to get the kid tied up fast. Joe wouldn't be able to hold us all still for long. I knew my brother and I could hold on if we needed to, and I figured the woman could, too.

But the little boy was so terrified that his eyes were squeezed shut and he thrashed around in fear. If he started to fall, he wouldn't be strong enough to grab onto something and hold himself up.

"It's okay, buddy," I told him. "We're gonna get you down." I slipped the free end of the rope around his waist and pulled it snugly around him. Then I wrapped it again so that another loop went between his legs. I tied it tightly around him so that the whole combination would work as a sort of seat for him to sit in.

The kid was so surprised to see me up there that he had stopped screaming for a second. His teary eyes met mine.

I grinned at him. "Don't worry," I said. "My brother and I are gonna lower you down the side now."

The kid's face paled. *Uh-oh,* I thought. *Is he going to start crying again?*

"We do this all the time," I told him, trying to make the whole thing sound like an adventure. "It'll be fun. It's just like mountain climbing."

The kid's chin trembled.

"Now you have to be brave while I lift you out over the side," I said. "You can be brave, can't you?"

The little boy blinked at me. Then he nodded.

"Okay. You be brave, don't worry, and you'll be down on the ground in no time." I reached in. He wrapped his arms around my neck and I lifted him out of his mother's embrace. She looked scared, but she reached out and grabbed onto the back of my shirt.

"In case you start to wobble," she explained. "I can try to hold you until you get your balance back."

I nodded. "Thanks." I hoped I wouldn't need the help. But it wasn't easy standing on the rim of the wheel like this. The wind whipped against my face.

"Is the rope tied tight?" I asked Joe.

"Yup," he said.

"Then here we go." I slowly turned toward the outside. I eased myself down into a sort of sitting position, with my back against the cart. Joe held the cart still, and the woman hung onto my shirt until I was braced against the wooden cart.

"Now you have to let go of me," I told the kid. "I'm going to swing you outside of the wheel."

He closed his eyes and let go.

I eased the hose down through my hands, slowly lowering the little boy down along the side of the Ferris wheel. I moved only an inch at a time—any more than that and he would've dropped too fast and gotten scared.

I looked up at Joe. He still had the hose looped around his arm.

I was out of rope. The little boy dangled ten feet above the ground. "I need some slack," I called to Joe.

He untangled his arm from the two loops of hose. I lowered the little boy down another foot.

His mother bit her lip. "What do we do now?"

I had no idea.

But down on the ground I spotted three security guards rushing around. "Help is here," I told the woman. "Security will know what to do."

I had a good view from up here. I saw one of the guards run over to a maintenance shed and pull out a ladder. He dragged it over to the Ferris wheel and they set it up under the little boy.

A guard climbed up and quickly untied the kid, handing him down to one of the others. Then he gave me a thumbs-up.

I relaxed my muscles. So did Joe. The kid was small, but it had still been a strain to hold him on the rope this whole time.

"Thank you," the woman breathed. "Thank you so much."

"We're going to climb back down," I told her.

"Will you be able to hold on if they move the Ferris wheel? The only way to get your cart to the bottom is to turn the ride on and send you up and over the top."

She nodded. "I'll be fine. It's just when I had to hold Devon that I couldn't hold on to the cart. Now it's no problem—I have both hands free."

"We'll see you at the bottom, then," Joe told her. He untied the hose, pulled it up, and slung it back over his shoulder.

We climbed back down the rim of the Ferris wheel.

At the bottom the little boy—Devon—ran up and gave me a high five.

Tommy turned the Ferris wheel on and moved it slowly around until Devon's mom reached the platform. The security guards helped her out, and Devon rushed into her arms.

Tommy went to check out the broken safety bar while one of the guards let the other riders off, and another guard put a RIDE CLOSED sign on the fence surrounding the Ferris wheel.

"That's two rides with mysterious problems," Joe murmured. "Do you think this was an incident of sabotage?"

"I don't know," I said. "I'm just glad we were here to help before anything too bad happened."

"We have to get to the bottom of this," Joe said.

"You're right. We need to get back to the investigation." I led the way toward the exit from the Ferris wheel. "Let's go talk to Uncle Bernie's son."

# 5.

# THE REAL TARGET?

"Hey, can you help me?" I called to the cute girl at the concession cart. "I'm looking for Little Bernie Flaherty."

"Little Bernie?" Jonesy growled from his post at the end of the cart. He was busy pushing it past the fifty-foot-tall slide. "What do you want with him?"

"We just want to talk to him," Frank replied. "We're doing a paper on family businesses, and we hear he's going to inherit this place."

Jonesy laughed, but he didn't seem amused. "He'll inherit a broken-down dump. One more accident like that Ferris wheel thing—or the roller coaster last week—and they'll shut this death trap down."

57

"It's summer," the cute girl pointed out. "Why are you doing a paper?"

"Um . . . for extra credit," Frank said.

"Oh." She didn't seem so interested in talking to us now that Frank had made us seem like total nerds. What did I tell you? He's clueless around girls. "Little Bernie is in the ticket booth," she said.

Jonesy pushed the cart away from us, and I watched her disappear after him.

Frank headed over to the ticket booth. We'd already bought our admission tickets, but we waited on line anyway. No sense in getting everyone else in the line upset. When we got to the front, I had to stop and take another look.

No way was the guy in the ticket booth Little Bernie. Uncle Bernie had said his son was twelve years old. But this dude was gigantic! He had to weigh at least three hundred pounds and he was so tall that his head almost brushed the ceiling of the booth.

"She sent us to the wrong guy," I whispered to Frank as we approached.

"I don't think so," Frank murmured. He grinned at the ticket seller. "Are you Bernard Flaherty the Fourth?"

The guy grunted. "Who wants to know?"

"I'm Joe Hardy and this is my brother, Frank," I

said. "Uncle Bernie said we could talk to his son about the accident last week."

"Is that you?" Frank asked.

"Yeah. I'm Little Bernie."

I had to look down at my feet to keep from laughing. Little Bernie was the biggest person we'd seen all day!

"How old are you?" Frank asked.

"I'm almost thirteen," Little Bernie said. He rolled his eyes. "Don't tell me, I know—I'm big for my age."

"You sure are," I said. "When I was twelve I was totally puny."

"So my dad told you to hang out with me?" Little Bernie asked. "Cool!"

He grabbed the shade that was hung above him and pulled it down over the window. On the outside, the word CLOSED was written in fading paint. Little Bernie stepped out the side door of the ticket booth.

"Let's go," he said cheerfully.

I glanced back at the people waiting in line. "What about your customers?" I asked.

Little Bernie shrugged. "They'll wait."

"That doesn't seem fair," Frank said.

"Oh, all right," Little Bernie grumbled. "I'll send someone over to cover for me." He stuck his head back inside the booth and picked up a phone.

While he called for backup, I pulled Frank aside. "I can't believe he's only a kid," I said.

"Some people grow faster than others," Frank pointed out. "But it seems like he's inherited his lack of charm from his father."

"Yeah," I said. "I wonder what else runs in the family."

Little Bernie came back out and let the door slam closed behind him. "Someone will be here soon," he said. "You guys want some cotton candy?"

"Sure." I followed Little Bernie back into the amusement park. I felt bad for the line of people waiting to buy tickets, but what else could we do about it?

"Aren't you too young to be working here?" Frank asked.

"Yeah. That's why I don't get paid," Little Bernie said. "I don't really work at the park . . . officially."

"But you were selling tickets," I pointed out.

"Duh," he said. "My dad makes me work in different jobs all over the stupid park. He says I'll learn the ropes that way."

"You mean you'll learn the amusement park business?" Frank said. "So you'll know how to run the place someday?"

## SUSPECT PROFILE

<u>Name:</u> Bernard Flaherty IV

<u>Hometown:</u> Holyoke, Massachusetts

<u>Physical description:</u> Age 12, 6', 304 lbs. Frizzy red hair, pale skin.

<u>Occupation:</u> Seventh grade student; works at Uncle Bernie's Fun Park.

<u>Background:</u> Child of divorce. Mom left.

<u>Suspicious behavior:</u> Doesn't care about his family's amusement park.

<u>Suspected of:</u> Sabotaging the Doom Rider roller coaster.

<u>Possible motives:</u> Resents his father.

"Yeah." Little Bernie stopped at another one of the wooden concession carts. This wasn't the one with Jonesy and the cute girl. A gruff older woman manned this cart.

"Three cotton candies," Little Bernie told her.

She handed them over with a sour look on her face.

Frank reached for his wallet.

"No way," Little Bernie told him. "You're with me. And mine are free because I practically own

61

this dump." He sneered at the woman. "Now get back to work," he said in a fake stern voice. Then he laughed at his own "joke." The sour-faced woman turned away, annoyed.

Little Bernie might not *look* twelve years old, but he sure acted like it.

"Thanks for the cotton candy," Frank said. "It must be cool to get all this stuff for free."

"I guess." Little Bernie grabbed a handful of cotton candy and shoved it in his mouth. "I get to go on all the rides, too. As many times as I want."

"That's awesome," I said truthfully.

"I know," Little Bernie replied.

"So you spend lots of time here?" Frank asked. "Even during the school year?"

"Every day after school," Little Bernie said. "We have to close the park for three months in the winter because it gets too cold. But otherwise me and my dad are always here. It's like we live here."

I stuck some cotton candy in my mouth and waited until it melted away. I couldn't tell if Little Bernie was bragging or complaining about his life at the park.

"Where's your mom?" I asked.

"She left," he said. "She used to work here too, but she got sick of it. She wanted my dad to let someone else run it."

"And he wouldn't?" Frank asked.

"Are you kidding?" Little Bernie scoffed. "This place is the only thing my dad cares about. That's why they got divorced. She said he loved the park more than her."

"Do you live with your dad?" I thought I knew the answer to that one already. Uncle Bernie didn't seem like the kind of guy who'd let his son grow up away from the family amusement park.

"Yeah. I see my mom on weekends." Little Bernie downed the rest of his cotton candy. "Dad wants to make sure I know how to run the fun park. He didn't want Mom moving me to some other state or anything."

Now I *knew* he was complaining.

"That must be tough," I said.

Little Bernie blushed. "No way," he replied. "I have the perfect life. Most of the kids at school only get to go to an amusement park like once a year. If they're lucky! But I get to be here all the time!"

"I bet you know every nook and cranny of the park," Frank said admiringly.

"Definitely," Little Bernie bragged. "I know some stuff even my dad doesn't know."

"Like what?" I couldn't help but ask.

Little Bernie lowered his voice as if he were

telling us some big secret. "Well, most of the rides have, like, basements below them."

I thought about the "basement" we'd found underneath the Doom Rider. I nodded.

"The basements are connected by all these little tunnels!" Little Bernie added excitedly. "They used to be for maintenance, I guess, but no one has used them in years. You can get all over the park without ever going above ground."

Frank raised his eyebrows. I knew what he was thinking: Tunnels like that could be very useful if you were trying to sabotage the amusement park rides without getting caught. Still, I doubted that Uncle Bernie was really in the dark about those tunnels. Little Bernie might think his dad didn't know about them, but I had gotten the sense that Uncle Bernie knew the park like the back of his hand.

Little Bernie seemed to be waiting for an answer. "Wow," I said. "That's really cool. Can you show us?"

He shook his head. "Are you crazy? I would get in huge trouble if I took you guys backstage. Customers are only supposed to see the face of the park, that's what Dad says. They're never supposed to see how things really work or it spoils the illusion."

"Okay," I said. I didn't bother to tell him we'd

already been "backstage" today. "So listen . . . did you see anybody climbing on the roller coaster last week?"

Little Bernie blinked in surprise. He'd obviously forgotten that Frank and I were here to talk about the accident.

"Uh . . . no," he said. "Why would someone climb on it?"

"We think somebody set off a firecracker and it caused the roof to collapse," Frank explained.

Little Bernie looked doubtful. "Must've been a pretty big firecracker," he said.

"Yeah, it was. More like a weapon," I told him. "Lots of people think firecrackers are toys, but they can do serious damage. And this one was probably more powerful than what's legally allowed."

"Wow." Little Bernie's eyes were wide. "It *was* loud. I thought the noise was just from the ceiling falling down. But I guess it could've been an explosion."

"Your dad told us you were right behind the woman who got hit," Frank said.

Little Bernie nodded.

"I . . . I don't want to scare you," Frank began.

Little Bernie puffed his chest out. "Nothing scares me."

Frank shot me a questioning look. I nodded.

Little Bernie was just a kid, but if he was in danger, he had the right to know.

"Well, we were thinking maybe somebody was trying to harm you instead," Frank told him.

Little Bernie gulped. "M-me?"

"Can you think of anyone who might want to hurt you?" I asked.

"Sure," he said. "Lots of people."

"Like who?"

"Well, there's that Richardson guy."

Frank pulled out the little notebook he carries everywhere. "Who's Richardson?"

"He's this loser who wants to buy out my dad," Little Bernie said. "He keeps trying to get Dad to sell him the park."

That didn't sound like something Uncle Bernie would want to happen. But I didn't see what it had to do with Little Bernie. "Why would Richardson want to hurt *you*?" I asked.

Little Bernie shrugged. "I don't know. Maybe he's just trying to scare my dad into selling. Or he wants it to look like the rides are dangerous or something."

"If the park was forced to close, Uncle Bernie probably would be more willing to sell it," Frank said. "Who else might want to hurt you, Bernie?"

Little Bernie scratched his mass of red hair.

"Uh . . . this kid from school really hates me. I had to kick him out of the amusement park a couple of weeks ago."

"How come?" I asked.

"He was getting rowdy, causing all kinds of trouble." Little Bernie tried to look tough as he said that, but it didn't really work.

"What's his name?" Frank asked.

"Chris Oberlander. He's a punk, that's what my dad says. I caught him spray painting on the walls of the boys' room."

"What was he painting?" Frank asked.

Little Bernie blushed. "Uh . . . pictures of me. My head on a pig's body. But that's not all. He also threw a match into a trash can."

"Sounds like trouble," I agreed. "Anyone else?"

"Yeah, there's Big Jim. He runs the snack bar. He might try to get me."

"Why would he be after you?" I asked.

"'Cause he's a know-it-all. He's been working at the snack bar for thirty years, so he thinks he's a total expert on the fun park."

"He probably is," Frank said.

"So what?" Little Bernie replied. "I'm still the one who's gonna own it. So he doesn't like me. He tries to charge me for hot dogs and everything. Can you believe that?"

I shrugged. I could believe it.

"What about people who would like to see the park get closed down?" Frank asked. "Maybe whoever set off the explosion wasn't trying to hurt you at all. Maybe they just wanted to make Uncle Bernie's Fun Park seem unsafe. This Richardson guy is a suspect like that. Can you think of anyone else?"

Little Bernie frowned. "My mom, I guess," he said slowly. "Her name's Karen. She'd probably get half the money if the park got sold. But she wouldn't do anything like that. Especially not with me on the roller coaster."

"Probably not," I agreed. But I noticed that Frank wrote down her name anyway.

"Okay. Thanks for your help, Bernie," Frank said.

"Are you guys gonna take off now?" Little Bernie asked.

"Yeah, we have to check out all the people you just told us about," I told him. But before I could even take a step, an ear-piercing scream rang out.

# 6.

## NOT-SO-MERRY-GO-ROUND

Another scream rang out, and the sounds of people shouting filled the air. Two men raced past us.

"They're heading for the carousel!" Joe cried. He took off running, and I followed. I heard Little Bernie huffing along behind us.

When we reached the carousel, I had to push my way through a crowd of people just to see what was happening. I couldn't believe it—the thing was spinning out of control! Where was the carousel operator?

"Is it supposed to go that fast?" I asked Little Bernie.

He shook his head. "No way. But it's been running fine since 1935. I don't know what's wrong with it to make it go so fast now."

"We have to stop it," Joe said. "People might get hurt."

On the carousel, I saw the worried faces of mothers whizzing by. The kids on their painted horses were crying. One little boy puked over the side of the ride.

"Bernie, do you know where the controls are?" I asked.

Little Bernie was watching the out-of-control ride, shocked. "Uh . . . yeah. But they're inside. I mean, they're in the middle of the carousel. There's no way to get to them while it's turning."

Just then, the carousel operator came running back, looking panicked. "What's going on?" he shouted, then turned to Bernie. "I had to go so bad I couldn't wait—just left for a second. How could this happen?"

I looked at Joe just as he rolled his eyes. What kind of guy would leave a ride full of kids running? This place had problems—big problems. A baseball cap came flying through the air. The carousel was going faster and faster. I saw a woman's pocketbook get pulled off her arm by the centrifugal force created by the wild ride. Popcorn flew through the air, yanked out of the tubs the kids on the merry-go-round were holding.

The carousel spun even faster. The tinkly music

started to sound warped as the ride whooshed by.

"Look out!" Joe yelled as a camcorder came flying toward me. I ducked just in time.

"Somebody stop that thing!" a nearby father shouted. His face was white with fear.

A loud scream caught my attention. I saw a girl—maybe ten years old—hanging on to one of the poles at the edge of the merry-go-round. One foot was off the ride, and the wind was pulling her harder every second. She couldn't hold on much longer.

On the next go-round, she was going to fall for sure.

I glanced around the area. People were everywhere, screaming, crying—all watching the carousel. Even the park workers had abandoned their booths and carts.

Finally I spotted what I was looking for. A game booth had a bunch of stuffed animal prizes hanging from the top of it.

I sprinted over to the booth, leaped up, and grabbed the largest animal I could find—an enormous stuffed bear.

The girl was still screaming.

A glance over my shoulder showed me that she was already falling off the ride.

"Joe!" I yelled. "Think fast!" I hurled the bear at him.

Joe jumped into the air, grabbed the bear, and threw it to the ground just as the girl went flying off the carousel. She winged through the air, screaming the whole way.

Then she landed on the bear.

I drew a huge sigh of relief. Joe shot me a thumbs-up.

The girl's mother ran over to pick her up. As they hugged, the girl was still crying. But she hadn't been hurt at all.

Still, we couldn't relax. The ride was still spinning way too fast, and before we knew it other people would fall off too.

"There's a horse coming loose!" someone yelled.

Sure enough, one of the poles holding the painted horses had been jarred loose from the top of the carousel. It was going to come off any second.

"Hit the dirt!" Joe bellowed.

Everyone around us dropped to the ground, covering their heads. I heard a sickening creaking sound, then the horse—still on its pole—sped through the air over my head.

The pole speared one of the wooden concession carts, knocking it onto its side.

"Cool!" Little Bernie cried.

"We're just lucky no one was on that horse," I told him.

This was getting serious.

"Let's go," I told Joe as I ran past him. I took a leap and landed on the carousel, lying on my side. The force of impact and the speed of the ride made me roll along the floor, banging into the poles of the horses. From here, the velocity of the thing seemed even greater. The faces of the people watching were just a blur as they whirled past.

I spotted Joe getting ready to jump. I stood up and pulled my way along by the poles. When he jumped on, I was there to grab him so he didn't get thrown right off again.

"We have to get to the middle," I shouted. But the wind whipped the words right out of my mouth.

"What?" Joe yelled. I couldn't hear him over the crazy music and the noise from the spinning ride. But I could read his lips.

I pointed to the center of the carousel. That's where Little Bernie had said the controls were.

Joe nodded.

We had to get there. But it wasn't easy. The centrifugal force from the ride was pulling everything—and everyone—toward the outside edge of the platform. But we were trying to get to the *inside* edge. All the force of the wind and the ride were working against us.

I grabbed onto the nearest pole. I wrapped my arm around it and hung on with all my might. Then I held out my other hand to Joe.

He grabbed my wrist and I grabbed his.

Using me to stabilize him, Joe let go of the cart he was hanging on to. Immediately, I felt him wobble backward. The ride was trying to force him to the edge. I held on tight to the pole and to my brother, straining the muscles in my arms.

Little by little, Joe made his way forward against the centrifugal force. When he reached the pole behind me, he grabbed on. I let my muscles relax for a second while Joe wrapped his arm around that pole. Then he reached out for me.

We did the whole thing again, this time with me pulling myself along using Joe to stabilize me. With his help I got to the pole on the very inside edge of the platform. I grabbed on, then pulled Joe along until he was beside me.

We eased our way down the pole until we were sitting on the floor. The force of the ride was even stronger here. I fought against it, reaching toward the edge of the platform. I grabbed it as hard as I could and held on while I lay down on my stomach. My legs stretched back along the floor. I held on to the inner edge of the platform for dear life.

Next to me Joe did the same thing.

From that position I could see the machinery of the carousel. Well, I could see where it was, anyway. We were spinning around so fast that the machine looked like a blur of black and gray. It was impossible to tell what was wrong with it.

Sparks shot off the mechanism as we spun even faster.

"It smells like something's burning," Joe yelled above the noise of the ride.

"We have to stop this thing before it blows," I yelled back.

I squinted at the machine. There was a wire—a thick orange wire like the one Dad uses as an extension cord when he puts up the Christmas lights outside the house. As we whirled around the center, I kept my eyes on that orange line. After about five spins around, I was sure: The wire led away from the carousel machinery.

"There's an extension cord," I shouted to Joe.

"I see it," he replied. "It leads underneath the ride. It must go out to the park somewhere."

"You think that's normal?"

"Who knows?" Joe yelled.

I sure didn't know anything about how amusement park rides worked. But it seemed strange that someone would need to plug in the carousel. My best guess was that the orange cord was somehow responsible for the ride going out of control.

"I'm gonna pull the plug," I yelled. "You have to keep me steady."

"Right!" Joe managed to undo his belt while holding on to the platform with one hand. As he pulled it out of the loops, the belt was torn from his grip by the force of the ride. It slithered toward the edge of the platform.

I slammed my sneaker down on it, pinning the belt to the ground. Never lifting my foot, I bent my leg and drew the belt toward me.

Finally Joe was able to grab the belt. He yanked it up to the pole and looped it around. Somehow he managed to get it buckled around the pole and his leg. He made it as tight as he could, then shot me a look. "In case I have to let go of the pole to hold on to you," he explained. "As long as I'm tied on, we won't fall."

"If you say so." I wasn't sure his plan would work. But the first thing we learned in our ATAC training was that you always need to take safety precautions.

Still holding on to the pole with one hand, Joe reached out and grabbed the back of my belt. He held me steady as I let go of the platform and leaned out toward the machine in the middle.

The centrifugal force was trying to yank me backward and sideways all at once. Joe held on, but I knew he couldn't do it for long. The force was too strong.

The orange cord whizzed by in front of me. I grabbed . . . and missed.

In no time we were back around. I grabbed for it again. My hand grazed the cord. I saw the orange line move a foot or so. Then the ride pulled me away from it again.

"Frank, come on!" Joe yelled.

I knew he couldn't hold on to me much longer.

The orange cord came by again. I stuck out both my hands and lunged toward it.

Success! The cord jumped off the ground and came spinning around with me. It felt hot in my hands.

But the ride kept spinning. The cord wrapped once around the machinery, then tightened.

"Uh-oh," I said.

"Let go!" Joe yelled.

I released the cord just as it snapped taut. The ride kept spinning, but the cord stayed where it was. If I'd still been holding on, it would have pulled me to a stop so fast I'd have gotten whiplash.

I tumbled backward past Joe. I was rolling toward the edge of the platform. I grabbed the first thing I saw—the hoof of a painted wooden horse—and held on.

Back in the machinery, the cord was still wrapped around as the machine spun. Sparks flew out from the friction between the cord and the metal.

Then the cord snapped.

There was a small explosion somewhere behind me, and the carousel began to slow down.

Slowly the music returned to normal.

Slowly the force pulling us toward the edge lessened.

Slowly the people watching stopped screaming.

But the ride didn't stop. It was back to normal merry-go-round speed, but it just kept going.

"Let us off of this thing," a mother holding a toddler begged.

Joe unbuckled his belt from the pole, hopped up from the platform, and jumped down into the middle of the ride. He grabbed a giant lever and pulled it.

"The ride is still on," he called to me. "I turned it off!"

I laughed. After all that, the carousel's simple on-and-off switch still worked.

The ride slowed to a halt, and the crowd rushed

forward to help people off. Joe climbed back up onto the platform and slapped me on the back.

"I know I always say carousels are boring," he told me. "But that was the best ride ever!"

# 7.

## INNOCENT BYSTANDER

"You guys are so cool!" Little Bernie cried, rushing up to us. "What went wrong with the ride?"

"I'm still not sure," I admitted.

"I heard an explosion from somewhere behind me after the cord snapped," Frank said. "Somewhere away from the carousel itself."

"Let's go see," I said. I made my way through the crowd of hugging people and crying children. Then I circled the merry-go-round until I found what I was looking for—the orange cord. It came out from underneath the carousel just as I had suspected. I followed it across the walkway and to a locked utility closet. The cord ran under the door and disappeared inside. "Can you open this door?" I asked Little Bernie.

"No problem. I have a passkey," he boasted. He pulled a key from a chain around his neck and unlocked the closet. "No way," he breathed.

Inside, attached to the orange cord, was a power generator.

"Someone hooked a generator to the carousel to make it spin faster," Frank said. "But who—"

A siren ripped through the air.

We spun around to see an ambulance come screeching into the crowd of people. Two EMTs leaped out of the back and rushed over to a guy lying on his back near the harpooned concession cart.

"Oh, no," Frank said. "Did he get thrown from the carousel?"

By the time we got through the crowd of gawkers and reached the ambulance, the EMTs were already pulling a sheet over the man's body.

"What happened?" I asked.

"We're not sure," the EMT replied. "Looks like a heart attack."

"Was he on that carousel?" Frank asked.

I peered down at the poor man. Then I kneeled and took a closer look. "This wasn't caused by the carousel," I said. "He's got a bee crushed in his hand."

The EMT knelt next to me. "Where?"

I pointed it out. The EMT turned the guy's hand over, revealing a tiny swollen hole. "The bee stung him, he crushed it, and then he died," the EMT said. "Looks like the bee might be related to his death."

"He must've been allergic to bees," I guessed. "He went into anaphylactic shock, and nobody noticed in all the hysteria about the out-of-control carousel."

"Then his death was still caused by the sabotage to the carousel," Frank said grimly. "At least indirectly. If people hadn't been distracted by the ride, someone might have noticed that this man needed help."

"It's true. If we'd gotten here sooner, we could've given him a shot of adrenaline and saved his life," the EMT said.

"You don't know that," Little Bernie put in. "It's not fair to blame the carousel."

"It's yet another example of unsafe rides at this amusement park!" a loud voice broke into our conversation. "This is the second accident in two weeks!"

It was a tall man in a dark suit and tie. His face was bright red and sweaty. *That's what he gets for wearing a suit on a hot summer day,* I thought.

"You!" the man shouted, pointing at Little

Bernie. "You should be ashamed of your father, allowing this run-down old park to stay open."

"Who let you in?" Little Bernie demanded. "Security!"

"I paid for a ticket like anybody else," the man said. He raised his voice, trying to get the attention of the other people gathered around the carousel. "This place should be shut down! How many people have to die here before the state takes action? Somebody should sue them!"

"Who is this guy?" I asked Little Bernie.

"John Richardson," he told me. "Security!"

So this was the businessman Little Bernie had told us about earlier. The one who had a motive to hurt him.

"What's going on here?" Uncle Bernie came huffing and puffing over to where we stood.

"You've had another accident on one of the rides, Flaherty," John Richardson said loudly.

"No one was injured on the carousel," I told Uncle Bernie. "But—"

"Richardson, I thought I told you to stay away from this park," Uncle Bernie interrupted. He didn't seem to want to hear about the carousel disaster.

"If I were you, I would seriously reconsider the offer my company made you," Richardson said more quietly. "My offer of a million dollars is the best one you're going to get for this place."

"Yeah, so you can turn it into a strip mall or a condo park or some other ugly piece of suburban sprawl," Uncle Bernie spat.

"I want to turn it into a parking garage, actually," Mr. Richardson said.

Uncle Bernie looked ready to explode. "A *garage*? Are you crazy? This park has been in my family since 1924! It's my whole life, and my father's and his father's. It will be my son's one day. And you think I'm gonna let you turn it into a *garage*?"

"Look, Flaherty," Mr. Richardson said. His face was getting red again. "It's only a matter of time before you get shut down for all these safety violations—"

"There haven't been any violations," Uncle Bernie interrupted. He glanced nervously at the people standing nearby. Most of them were watching this conversation with interest. "These incidents were accidents, plain and simple."

"—and once the park is closed, our offer to buy it will be a lot less money," Mr. Richardson continued. "You'll be begging us to take it off your hands."

"Do you think we really can sue him?" a woman asked Mr. Richardson. "My daughter's hands got all scraped up from holding on to the merry-go-round when it was out of control."

"Yeah, and one of the carousel horses banged up my knee," a nearby kid added.

Uncle Bernie's eyes bulged. I could see that he was about to panic.

"Hey, Dad," Little Bernie said, tugging on his sleeve.

But Uncle Bernie ignored him. He shook off his son's hand and climbed up onto the carousel. "Attention, everyone!" he yelled.

"This ought to be good," Frank murmured. "How's he gonna make all these people forget about wanting to sue him?"

"I apologize for the unfortunate malfunction on our carousel," Uncle Bernie announced. "We here at Uncle Bernie's Fun Park take your safety very seriously. And that means the carousel will be closed until we can find out exactly what happened."

"You mean exactly who hooked it up to some extra juice," I said.

"In the meantime, to show how sorry we are, I'd like to offer everyone in the park a hot dog on the house."

The murmuring of the crowd grew more cheerful.

"In fact, I'll throw in a free ice cream cone for each kid, too," Uncle Bernie added.

Immediately a cheer went up from all the kids in the crowd. People streamed toward the snack bar, smiles on their faces.

"Wow," Frank said. "Looks like all it takes is a free hot dog and people will forgive anything."

"Not me," I replied. "I still want to get to the bottom of these so-called accidents. Although I wouldn't mind a free hot dog first."

I glanced over at Little Bernie. He was smirking at John Richardson, and Mr. Richardson didn't look too happy about it.

"Don't go gloating yet, kid," Richardson said. "This place will be mine, one way or another." He stalked off.

Little Bernie grinned at me. "That guy's such a loser," he said. "You dudes want a hot dog? I can take you to the front of the line."

"Sure," I replied. We followed him over to the snack bar. Normally I'd feel bad about cutting in line, but everybody there seemed happy to let us go first. Several of them slapped Frank and me on the back as we walked by. Even if they weren't planning to sue Uncle Bernie, they still considered us heroes for getting the carousel to stop.

The guy who served us our hot dogs didn't look too cheerful, though. He sneered at Little Bernie, and he sneered at us.

I didn't care. That dog hit the spot!

"What do you think about John Richardson?" Frank asked as we left the snack bar with our food. "He looks like a suspect to me."

## SUSPECT PROFILE

**Name:** John Richardson

**Hometown:** Boston, Massachusetts

**Physical description:** Age 48, 5'10", 166 lbs. Thinning brown hair, face flushes easily.

**Occupation:** Land developer

**Background:** Unclear right now.

**Suspicious behavior:** Was present when carousel went out of control. Has made veiled threats to Uncle Bernie and Little Bernie.

**Suspected of:** Sabotaging the Doom Rider roller coaster and the carousel.

**Possible motives:** Wants Uncle Bernie to sell him the amusement park so he can tear it down.

"Yep," I agreed. "It's obvious that Uncle Bernie isn't willing to sell to him. But if he got the amusement park closed down, Uncle Bernie would probably change his mind."

"You think so?" Little Bernie asked.

"Sure," Frank said. "If the park is really closed for good, your dad would have no reason to keep the land. He'd have to sell it and start over somewhere else."

Little Bernie stopped walking.

"What's up?" I asked.

He took another step, then staggered backward a little. "I . . . I don't feel so good," he said.

"Are you sick?" I asked. "What's wrong?"

"It's the . . . the . . ." Little Bernie's eyes rolled back in his head. Then he collapsed on the ground.

# 8.

# ROTTEN MEAT

Little Bernie lay crumpled on the blacktop, unconscious.

Immediately I knelt by his side. I was grateful for my emergency medical training. "Bernie, can you hear me?" I asked. I lightly grabbed his shoulder and repeated the question.

"No answer," Joe said. "Check his airway."

"Help me roll him." Little Bernie was too heavy for me to move quickly. Joe bent and helped me push him over until he lay flat on his back.

I tilted Little Bernie's head back and gently lifted his chin. I eased his mouth open a little. There was still no response.

"Is he breathing?" Joe asked.

I bent over Little Bernie's face and put my cheek

89

next to his nose and mouth. I watched his chest for signs of breathing. In a second I felt air coming from his mouth. His chest rose and fell. "Yeah, he's breathing." I put two fingers to Little Bernie's neck and felt for a pulse. "His pulse is strong," I told Joe.

"Okay, let's get him into the recovery position," Joe said.

I pulled Little Bernie toward me while Joe pushed from behind to help move him. As he rolled, I lifted his arm over his head and Joe crossed one of Little Bernie's ankles over the other. Soon enough we had him lying on his side. His knee had bent because of the crossed ankles, so he lay propped up by his knee and arm.

Joe and I stood up. At this point in the emergency medical treatment, we were supposed to go get help. But somehow I didn't think Little Bernie needed an ambulance. He was breathing fine, his pulse was normal, and his skin looked the same as ever. He hadn't grown pale, or flushed, or turned green or blue like he would have if there was something really wrong.

"Doesn't seem like he choked," Joe said. "He can breathe."

I nodded. "And if he'd gotten a bite of bad meat, his color would have changed. Or his pulse would be racing . . . or *something*."

Little Bernie's eyelids fluttered, then opened. "What happened?" he asked.

"I don't know," I told him. "What do you remember?"

Little Bernie slowly sat up. "I was eating a hot dog."

"Yeah. Then what?" I asked.

"Something tasted funny . . . and that's all I remember." He frowned. "Do you think it was poisoned? You said someone might be trying to hurt me, right?"

I glanced around. Practically everyone in the park was eating a hot dog right now, and nobody else was keeling over. So it wasn't likely that the hot dogs were bad, or poisoned. On the other hand, the guy who'd given us the dogs had been scowling at Little Bernie.

"It's possible that your hot dog did this to you," I said.

Joe nodded. "You were in the roller coaster when that accident happened, and you're the only one who got sick from the hot dog. It seems like the perp could be trying to target you."

"Well, if the hot dog was tampered with, that means somebody in the snack bar knows about it," I said. "And you told us the guy who runs the snack bar doesn't like you."

Little Bernie nodded. "Big Jim. He hates me."

"Joe and I will go have a talk with him," I said.

"Okay." Little Bernie got to his feet. "I better get back to work before my father notices me slacking off."

"Don't you want to swing by the nurse's office?" Joe asked. "To make sure you're okay?"

"Uh . . . nah," Little Bernie said. "I feel fine now."

"All right." I didn't see Uncle Bernie anywhere, so he didn't seem likely to notice Little Bernie. But I was done hanging out with this kid, anyway. We needed to do some hard-core investigating. "Go to the nurse if you start feeling sick again. See you later."

Little Bernie took off with a wave, and Joe and I headed for the snack bar.

The crowd of people looking for free hot dogs had finally died down, and we found the scowling guy wiping the countertop.

"Are you Big Jim?" I asked.

His scowl grew deeper. "Nobody calls me that except old Bernie. My name is James Buchanan."

It didn't seem like a good time to mention that Little Bernie also called him Big Jim.

"Sorry, Mr. Buchanan," I said.

"Do I look big to you?" he interrupted. "Old

Bernie thinks it's funny to kick people when they're down."

I wasn't sure what to say. Big Jim was only about five foot four, pretty short for a guy. He seemed to have some kind of issue about his height, so I decided to ignore his comment.

"You don't seem to like Uncle Bernie very much," I said.

Big Jim glared at me. "Like him? I hate him!"

"How about his son?" Joe put in. "Do you hate him, too?"

"Why shouldn't I?" Big Jim snapped. "That little brat acts like I work for *him*. I don't care who his father is, he should show some respect to his elders!"

"Did you know Little Bernie got sick just now?" I asked. "He ate one of your hot dogs, and then he just collapsed."

Big Jim leaned across the counter, still scowling. "And?" he said.

"And he said he got a funny taste in his mouth just before he passed out," I said.

"I see." Big Jim leaned closer to me. He might be a short guy, but he was still pretty intimidating. "So you think I slipped the brat a bad hot dog. Who are you kids?"

"We're looking into the accidents here in the

park," Joe replied. "We're sort of amateur detectives."

"Then go harass someone else!" Big Jim roared. "You punks listen to me: I've been making hot dogs for thirty years! My dogs are all beef and there's nothing wrong with them. It's bad business to go around poisoning your customers— especially when one of them is the owner's son. I'm no fool. I can't stand the idea of working for that Little Bernie one day, but I didn't poison him. Now get out!"

I shot Joe a look.

"Let's go," he said.

We took off.

Outside, Uncle Bernie's Fun Park was anything but fun. Every ride had a long line snaked around it, the air was thick with humidity, it had to be at least ninety-five degrees, most of the kids were whiny, and the parents looked miserable.

"I think we need a break from this place," Joe said.

"We haven't made any progress on the case," I pointed out. "We have a bunch of suspects, but no evidence."

"I know. That's why we have to clear our minds," Joe said. "Spend an hour or two not thinking about Uncle Bernie. Then we'll have a better perspective on things."

## SUSPECT PROFILE

**Name**: James "Big Jim" Buchanan

**Hometown**: Riggs, Massachusetts

**Physical description**: Age 61, 5'4", 150 lbs. Wiry frame, long hair in a ponytail, constant scowl on his face.

**Occupation**: Manages the snack bar at Uncle Bernie's Fun Park.

**Background**: Has been making hot dogs for thirty years.

**Suspicious behavior**: May have poisoned Little Bernie's hot dog.

**Suspected of**: Sabotaging the Doom Rider roller coaster and the carousel. Poisoning Little Bernie.

**Possible motives**: Hates Uncle Bernie. Resents the fact that Little Bernie will inherit the amusement park.

I rolled my eyes. Joe is so obvious sometimes. "All right, what do you really want to do?" I asked.

"There's a water park half a mile away," he said with a huge grin. "We passed it on the way up, and it's scorching out. Doesn't a water slide sound sweet right now?"

I had to admit, it did.

Still, with water parks came girls. Girls in bathing suits. Girls Joe would want to flirt with. "I don't know," I said. "Maybe we should stay here and keep looking around."

A little kid wandered past us, wobbly from the teacup ride. He turned toward me—and puked all over the ground.

"Okay," I said. "Water park it is."

# 9.

# DOWN THE WORMHOLE

Splash World. I could hardly believe Frank had agreed to come here. Water parks are the coolest things on the planet!

"This place has a surfing pool!" I said, studying the map of the park.

Frank was busy looking around. "It's a lot newer than Uncle Bernie's."

"Yeah," I said. "This information map says the place opened only two years ago."

"It must get a lot more business than Uncle Bernie's does," Frank said thoughtfully. "I wonder if the owners of Splash World are planning to expand. They'd need Uncle Bernie's land to do that."

Unreal. I was trying to forget about our mission

for an hour or two, but Frank brought it right along with us. "You're not supposed to think about Uncle Bernie right now," I said. "Or about Richardson, or Big Jim, or anybody else. We're here to have fun."

"Okay." Frank squinted at the map. "Let's go on the Roundabout River."

"You're such a baby," I scoffed. "That's for little kids. All you do is sit in a stupid tube and float around the park."

Frank rolled his eyes. "What do you want to do?"

"There's a four-story-tall water slide," I said. "And two covered slides. Those are the coolest."

"Excuse me," said a voice next to me. "Do you mind if we look at the map with you?"

I looked down to see two gorgeous girls around our age. One of them had long curly dark hair and big brown doe eyes. The other one was taller, with strawberry blond hair and long legs. They both wore bikinis.

And they were both looking at Frank.

"Sure. You can squeeze in here with *us*," I said pointedly, but it was no use. It was happening again: That mysterious magnetic power Frank seems to have over girls was drawing these two right over to him. It's just *not* fair.

"Thanks," the dark-haired girl said. They both stepped in front of us, and we all looked at the map for a few seconds.

"I think we should go on the Roundabout River," the tall one said. "What do you think, Lisa?"

Lisa—the brunette one—nodded. "That sounds like a good way to start. We can see the whole park from the river and then pick our next ride." She gazed up at Frank. "Do you guys want to come with us?"

"Sure," I said quickly. "We were planning to start with the Roundabout River too."

"We were not," Frank put in. "You said it was boring and that it was for little kids."

Lisa and her friend shot me dirty looks. I shot Frank a dirty look. Was he really so clueless? Did he seriously not get that I was trying to find an excuse to hang out with two cute girls?

"You don't have to come on it, then," Lisa told me. "Renee and I will go with your friend."

"He's my brother, actually," I said, putting on my best flirtatious smile. "And I was just teasing him about the ride."

"You were not," Frank argued. "You wanted to go on the covered water slides."

The tall girl—Renee—raised her eyebrows. "Those things are terrifying. You couldn't pay me to go on one of those. Let's go to the river, Lisa."

They walked off toward the Roundabout River, and I glared at Frank.

"What?" he said.

See? He's completely clueless.

"Nothing. Let's go to the covered slides," I grumbled. If we couldn't hang out with the cute girls, we might as well have fun.

The line for the Wormhole was kind of long, but I figured it was worth the wait to go on the biggest, twistiest covered slide in the park. The Wormhole was a supersteep one-person water slide with a black metal roof covering the whole thing. I couldn't even see where the slide ended, but I figured it shot you out over a deep pool somewhere else in the park. Most covered slides spit you out about ten feet above the water. So after a terrifying ride down a pitch-black slide, you get to have a little free fall to thrill you at the end.

"I love water parks," I said.

"I know," Frank replied. "You love them so much you don't even care that we've been on line for a half hour already."

"We're almost there," I said. "We're on the stairs now." Everybody knows once you're on the stairs up to the high platform of the slide, you're in the home stretch.

Even so, we waited for another fifteen minutes.

"You're gonna thank me for this," I promised Frank. "The information map said that the Wormhole slide changes direction three times while you're in the tube."

"So?"

"*So,* it's amazing," I said. "You're completely enclosed in the metal slide, you've got water running down your back, you can't see where you're going . . . you're totally at the mercy of the Wormhole."

"As long as it's wet, I'll be happy," Frank said. "It's way too hot out."

Finally we got to the top. From here I could see out over almost the whole park, with its wave pool and whitewater rafting creeks and the Roundabout River encircling all the other rides. The Wormhole was just a big black tube, a circular opening maybe three feet wide with only blackness inside.

I watched the kids in front of me as they disappeared into the tube one by one. The park worker at the ride instructed them to grab onto the top of the tube, stick their feet into it, and let go. As soon as they did, the force of the water rushing down the tube pulled them inside. They vanished into the blackness almost immediately.

The park worker waited for a minute or so and

then let the next person on. I knew you couldn't have two people in the tube at once, so the whole ride probably only lasted for a minute. But so what? It would be worth it.

I was next in line. I was so pumped. "Can I go in headfirst?" I asked the worker.

He just laughed. "No. Trust me, it'll be scary enough feet first."

"I hope so." I glanced at Frank. "See you on the other side!" Then I grabbed onto the top of the tube, stuck my feet into the Wormhole, and let go.

The water was freezing! It pulled me along so fast that before I knew it, the light from the entrance was gone and I was in total darkness, whipping along superfast. I could barely even tell where the top of the tube was—I didn't have time to think about anything.

Suddenly my feet hit a wall and my whole body jerked to the right.

I gasped in surprise. But before I could even catch my breath, my feet hit another wall. I jerked left.

And kept speeding downhill. There was one more turn to go . . . but when would it happen?

Just when I thought I couldn't fall any farther, my feet hit the wall again. I slid right around the turn.

My feet hit another wall. And stopped.

The sudden stop brought the weight of my whole body down onto my ankles. My knees buckled, and I started to fall. But the tube was so narrow that my knees hit one wall and my back hit the other. I stayed there, crouched, for a couple of seconds, just trying to catch my breath.

What was going on?

*Keep calm,* I told myself. That was the first rule of dealing with a crisis—every member of ATAC had it drummed into their heads. *Take stock of your surroundings, then figure it out from there.*

I was standing on a blockage in the tube. There were only supposed to be three turns, and I'd gone through all three. So this must be the bottom of the tube. But it was blocked.

I pushed down with my toes, then slid my feet around, trying to figure out what was blocking the tube. It was something smooth and flat that felt a little bit like the rubber they use to make trampolines.

*Okay, that's not helpful,* I thought. I tried to figure out some other details.

I wasn't standing straight up, as far as I could tell in the dark. The whole tunnel seemed to be at an angle so that I leaned more to the left than the right.

The tunnel was narrow—only one arm span across.

It was pitch black.

And water was pouring down on my head.

*Uh-oh,* I thought. Water ran down the length of the whole tunnel. And if the bottom was blocked, that meant the water couldn't escape. It would start to build up into a pool at the bottom.

I lifted one foot. Sure enough, the water had formed a puddle on top of the blockage. It was up above my ankle already, and rising fast.

I had to get rid of the blockage—fast—before the water backed up even further.

I stomped down as hard as I could. It didn't move. I braced my arms against the wall of the tunnel and stomped down with both feet at once. It still didn't budge. I tried a few more times. Nothing.

A sound came from the tunnel above me. Sort of a whooping yell.

My blood ran cold.

*Frank!*

The worker at the top had waited for a minute, then let Frank into the tube. Any second now, he was going to land on top of me!

*It's okay,* I thought. *Maybe the impact will knock this blockage loose.*

I flattened myself against the side of the tunnel and braced for the hit.

Frank's feet walloped me in the shoulder, and he crumpled on top of me, pushing me back down to my knees. The water sloshed up into my mouth.

"Hey!" Frank yelled.

I pushed at him. "Get off of me!"

He pushed against the side of the tunnel and scooted up enough for me to stand again. "What's going on?" he called down.

"The bottom of the tube is blocked," I said. "I can't push it loose. Even the weight of two of us didn't knock it free."

"That's bad," Frank said. "There's water coming down."

"I know."

"The water will fill the tube and we'll drown," Frank said.

"I know," I repeated. "We have to find a way out. Fast, before someone else comes down."

"They put up a chain behind me so the workers could change shifts," Frank said. "No one else will be down for at least a few minutes."

"Good. Then no one else is in danger," I said. "But we're still in deep trouble."

"If we can't go down, then we have to go back up," Frank called.

"How can we climb all the way back up?" I asked. "This thing is really steep. And what about all those turns?"

"I can reach the first turn from here," Frank said. "I'm gonna pull myself up over it."

The darkness was so total that I couldn't see him at all. But I felt the weight that had been pressing down on me ease as he pulled himself up.

The water had reached my waist now. I had to start climbing. But how? Every time I tried to push off the wall, my foot slipped against the smooth metal. The water made everything slick.

"I need a little help!" I called.

My brother's hand smacked me in the face.

"Sorry!" he said. "Grab on."

I grabbed onto his wrist. I figured he must be lying on his stomach above the turn. He pulled me up out of the water. I felt the tube change directions. Up here we could crawl forward, but the water rushing down made it difficult. In front of me, Frank lost his balance and was swept back down the tube.

"Look out!" he yelled.

I swiveled around and pushed my feet against the wall opposite me. This way I could block his path and keep him from falling back down to the bottom of the tube.

*Oof!* He slammed into me.

"I think I get to go first from now on," I complained. "That's twice I've had to break your fall."

"Joe, the water's up over the turn already," Frank said. "It's rising fast."

"Let's get going." I led the way, crawling along the tube until I reached the next turn. "These two turns were really close together," I called back to Frank. "Maybe we can put our feet on the first turn and then pull ourselves up on the next one."

"Yeah," Frank's voice reached me through the darkness. "But then the tube goes straight up for at least thirty feet. How are we gonna climb that?"

I pulled myself up onto the next turn. Extending my arms over my head, I felt the final turn of the tunnel. I dragged myself up until I could look straight up the rest of the tunnel. Up above—*way* up above—I spotted a tiny circle of light. "I can see the top!" I yelled.

"How can we get there?" Frank yelled back.

I took a deep breath and tried to assess the situation calmly, the way Dad always did. We had a narrow space, and an almost vertical climb. What should we do?

It hit me like a bolt of lightning.

"It's a chimney!" I called.

"What?"

"Like in rock climbing, when there's a crack in the rockface big enough to climb in. We can use our hands and feet to brace ourselves against the wall and inch our way up."

"Got it!" Frank called. "But we have to go fast. The water is rising."

I pulled myself the rest of the way up into the tunnel and stuck my foot against the wall, about knee-high. I leaned across and pushed both hands against the same wall. Then I bent my knee and lifted my other foot. I pressed that foot against the wall under my butt. I was suspended in the tunnel, holding myself up between my arms and legs. Pushing hard against both walls, I straightened my back leg and lifted my body as far as I could. Now that my bottom leg was straight, I bent the other one and stuck it against the wall in front of me at knee-height. I took a split second to rest, then did the whole thing again.

Slowly I inched up the tube. I heard Frank doing the same thing below me.

My arms and legs were aching with the effort, and my lungs were working overtime. But I kept my eyes on the little circle of light above. I tried to ignore the water pouring down on top of me. It made the tunnel slippery, so I had to push hard against the walls to avoid sliding down.

Finally I reached the top. The sunlight dazzled my eyes for a few seconds, so I stayed put in the tunnel to let my sight adjust.

"Hurry up, Joe!" Frank called from below. "The water's up to my legs."

With a final exertion, I pushed my back hard against the wall and moved one of my arms up to grab the top of the tunnel. I held on tight and pulled myself up and over the top. Then I collapsed on the platform and tried to catch my breath.

"Dude!" cried the park worker standing two feet away. I heard gasps from the people at the front of the line.

"My brother's in there," I said.

The worker rushed over to the tube and pulled Frank out. He dropped down next to me on the metal platform. "My biceps are aching," he muttered.

"Where did you dudes come from?" the worker demanded. "You're not supposed to climb back up the slide."

"The bottom is blocked," Frank said. "Don't let anyone else go in. We almost drowned."

The worker stared at us in shock for a moment, then looked back into the tunnel. When he saw the water almost to the top, he yanked the walkie-talkie from his belt and got help.

The people standing in line were evacuated from the platform and the stairway, and someone at the bottom of the slide removed the blockage. By that time Frank and I had recovered enough to talk to the Splash World security guard who'd come to take our statement.

"What was over the bottom of the slide?" I asked.

The guard was a middle-aged woman with a long blond braid down her back. She looked embarrassed. "Someone put the cover on," she admitted. "When the ride is closed, we put rubber covers on the top and bottom of the tunnel. To keep the raccoons out and make sure the slide doesn't get all mucked up with falling leaves and stuff."

"You mean somebody purposely closed off the end of the slide while people were going down it?" Frank asked. "We could've been killed. You're just lucky it was us and not some ten-year-old kids."

"I know." The guard frowned. "The story I'm getting is that the worker at the bottom thought the Wormhole was already closed for the shift change. He didn't think anyone else was coming down, so he put the cover on."

"Do they usually cover the slide during a shift change?" I asked.

"No," she replied. "But it was this guy's first day on the job. He says he got confused. Needless to say, he's been fired."

Frank and I exchanged a look. Had this worker really just made a mistake? Or was he trying to hurt us on purpose?

"Is the worker still here?" Frank asked.

The guard shook her head. "We had him escorted off the premises. Splash World takes safety violations very seriously—"

"Thanks, but we've heard this speech today already," I interrupted her. "Can you tell us the guy's name?"

"Marc Krakowski," she said.

Frank wrote the name in his notebook, and we made our way down the long staircase.

"It's too bad we can't talk to the worker who did this," Frank said. "I'd like to know if he's connected to Uncle Bernie's Fun Park in any way."

"We'll have to go back to Uncle Bernie's to find out," I said. "But first I could use a nice, boring ride on the Roundabout River."

We snagged some inner tubes and plopped ourselves in the slowly moving water. "Now this is the way to relax after some chimney-climbing," I joked. "What a workout!"

"We've got a problem," Frank said. "We have no

idea who's been sabotaging the rides at Uncle Bernie's—and maybe here, too. There's no way we'll be able to solve this thing and get back home today."

"Let's call Dad and tell him we're gonna crash up here," I suggested. "We passed at least five motels on the way to Uncle Bernie's."

After we got off the ride and changed back into regular clothes, we headed back out to our bikes.

It was quieter in the parking lot. I pulled out my cell phone and dialed home.

Luckily, Dad answered the phone. If it had been Mom or Aunt Trudy, I would have had to lie. And I hated lying to them.

"Hey, Dad," I said.

"Joe. Are you boys all right?" Dad sounded worried.

"We're fine." I glanced at Frank and he shook his head. I knew what he meant: Don't tell Dad about our near-death experience in the Wormhole. The last thing we wanted was to freak out our father. Besides, we *were* fine. We'd gotten out of the scrape like we always do.

"No problems," I said into the phone.

"Where are you?" Dad asked.

"Still up in Massachusetts," I said. "We're at an amusement park."

"I see." Dad doesn't say much, but then he doesn't have to. I could tell by his tone of voice that he knew we weren't here for fun. He never asks for details about our ATAC missions. But he always knows when we're on ATAC business.

"The thing is, we kind of lost track of time," I said. "We won't be able to make it all the way home tonight."

"Hmph," Dad said. "You're sure everything's okay?"

"Yeah," I said. "We just need a little more time. We thought we'd stay in a motel up here."

"All right," Dad replied. "I'll tell your mother she can expect you home tomorrow."

"Thanks, Dad," I said.

"Be careful, Joe," he told me. "Call if you need anything."

"We will. Bye."

I hung up and turned to Frank. "Well?" Frank asked.

"He's not happy," I sighed. "But he knows how it is on ATAC business. We'll get some sleep tonight. And then tomorrow we'll finish the mission and be home by dinnertime."

# 10.

# WORKING OUT

"Are you gonna eat those pancakes?" Joe asked me the next morning at breakfast.

I was busy staring out the window of the diner, thinking about the situation at Uncle Bernie's Fun Park. Joe reached across the table, ready to grab my last two pancakes with his fork.

I pulled my plate away.

"There are two suspects left who we haven't actually met and questioned yet," I said.

"You're doing work over breakfast?" Joe groaned. "Okay, so we have Big Jim, and John Richardson, and both Bernies. Who else? What about that big guy, Jonesy? He really hates Uncle Bernie."

"Maybe," I said. "But I was talking about Uncle

114

Bernie's ex-wife, Karen," I said. "Remember, Little Bernie said she'd get half the money if the park was sold."

Joe shook his head. "I don't think so. She wouldn't put her own son in danger. Little Bernie almost got hit by the Doom Rider cave-in, and somebody may have tried to poison him yesterday. It's hard to believe his mom could be involved in any of that."

I agreed with him. Even Little Bernie had said his mother wouldn't do anything like sabotage the rides. "Okay, so we cross her off the suspect list for now. That leaves one person. The kid from Little Bernie's school."

"The one who got rowdy at the park until Little Bernie threw him out," Joe said. "What was his name?"

I checked my notebook. "Chris Oberlander."

Joe glanced around the diner. "Pay phone," he said, pointing. "I bet there's a local phone book."

We headed over to the phone and grabbed the book from the counter underneath. Joe flipped through to the O section. "There are two Oberlanders in Holyoke," he reported.

"Give me the first number," I said, picking up the phone.

I got an answering machine.

But when I called the second number, a woman picked up. Maybe it was Chris Oberlander's mother.

"Hi," I said, trying to sound younger. "Is Chris there?"

"No, he's not," she said. "He went to the gym. Is this Ryan?"

"Um, no. This is his friend Frank," I told her. "Chris goes to Gold's Gym, right?"

"Planet Fitness," she corrected me. "Should I tell Chris you called, Frank?"

"No, that's okay. I'll probably see him at the gym. Thanks!"

I hung up and gave Joe a thumbs-up. "Planet Fitness, here we come." We paid at the counter and hurried out to our bikes. It took twenty minutes to find Planet Fitness. We could have used the hypersensitive GPS on our bikes to find the gym, but it's much more fun to ride around on the motorcycles and just look for places. When I'm on my bike, I never want to get off it.

But soon enough we spotted the gym. It was a medium-sized building with floor-to-ceiling windows in the front. Inside I saw the usual assortment of exercise machines, free weights, and cardio equipment.

"I wonder if Chris Oberlander is a musclehead,"

Joe said. "That could be bad if he really has it in for Little Bernie."

On the front door was a flyer advertising free introductory sessions at the gym. I pointed it out to Joe on the way in.

"Hi! Welcome to Planet Fitness!" the girl at the front desk chirped. "How can I help you guys?"

"We're interested in the free introductory session," I told her. "We're thinking of joining."

"Great!" she said. "Just fill out these forms and you can use the facilities for the next hour."

"Thanks." I took the forms and we filled in our names and put fake addresses in Holyoke. The whole time I kept looking around the gym. Which of these bodybuilders was Chris Oberlander? None of them looked young enough to be in school with Little Bernie.

"Maybe Chris is a high schooler who knows Little Bernie," I suggested to Joe.

"Could be. At least there are two of us if we have to fight a bodybuilder," he joked.

We handed our forms to the girl at the desk. "Hey, can you tell us if Chris Oberlander is around?" Joe asked her.

"Sure," she said. "He's over there in Free Weights."

I looked where she was pointing. There were three huge guys lifting weights on the blue mats in the corner. "Which one?" I asked. "We're new in town and Chris is a friend of our father's. We're supposed to meet him here."

The girl smiled. "He's the one in the green shirt."

"Thanks." We headed over toward the big guys and the free weights. None of them wore a green shirt.

But the skinny little geek hidden behind them did.

Joe stopped short. "That little kid?" he asked.

I checked the guy out. He didn't look like he could lift a telephone off a receiver, much less a barbell. He was struggling to do a bicep curl with what had to be a two-pound weight.

"He's no killer," Joe said. "Let's just go question him."

"No, we should watch him first," I replied. "Just because he's a twerp doesn't make him harmless. None of the things that happened at Uncle Bernie's Fun Park required strength to pull off."

"True. So let's work out." Joe headed over to one of the treadmills, and I got on a stationary bike. From there we could keep an eye on Chris without him noticing us.

The kid was scrawny, but he was determined. His puny biceps bulged as he lifted his little weight over and over again. His eyes never left the image of his arms in the mirror. His face wore an expression of grim determination.

I was impressed. He was a skinny little kid, but he was trying really hard.

He worked out for another fifteen minutes, sweat pouring down his face. Then, exhausted, he dropped the dumbbell back down onto the rack and went to get a drink from the water fountain.

"I think he's done," I told Joe. "Let's go."

As we slowed down and got off our machines, Chris pulled a gym bag out of one of the lockers near the door. He took off his sweaty T-shirt, pulled a dry one out of the bag, put it on, and stuffed his wet shirt into a pocket on the bag. He then left the building. Joe and I followed.

Outside, Chris headed toward the bike rack. "Excuse me, Chris?" I called.

He jumped, glanced over his shoulder . . . and took off!

Joe shot me a surprised look, then ran after him. We followed him around the corner and halfway down the side street. He wasn't hard to catch—his legs were pretty short, after all.

But just as I reached out to grab him, Chris ducked under my hand and cut right. He sprinted into someone's yard.

I ran after him.

He jumped over a chain-link fence and circled back around toward the gym. "He's going for his bike," I called to my brother.

Joe nodded and ran back toward the gym while I followed Chris through an alleyway and up to Planet Fitness from behind. When he got back to the parking lot, Joe was there waiting for him.

Chris turned—and stopped short when he saw me behind him. He was cornered.

"Don't hurt me!" he wailed.

"I'm not going to hurt you," I told him. "We just want to ask you some questions."

"Do you always run when somebody calls your name?" Joe asked.

"You would too if people were always beating you up," Chris snapped. "Who are you guys?"

"My name is Frank and this is my brother, Joe," I said. "We were hoping we could talk to you about Little Bernie Flaherty."

"Little Bernie sent you?" Chris dropped his gym bag with a thud. He stuck his hands up in front of him, curled into fists. "What, now he's getting other people to come after me? He can't do it himself?"

"Chill," Joe said. "We're not gonna fight you. Put your hands down."

Chris kept his fists up and glared at us. "If you're

friends with Little Bernie, that means you're jerks. Because nobody decent would hang out with that idiot."

"We don't hang out with him," I explained. "We're just trying to figure out who might want to hurt him."

"That's easy," Chris said. "*I* want to hurt him!"

"You do?" Joe asked skeptically. "Why?"

"Because he's been picking on me since kindergarten," Chris said. "He's a big bully. I'm sick of it. Why do you think I'm working out?"

He bent down and unzipped his gym bag.

"Look," he said. He pulled out a huge bottle of vitamin supplements that read BUILD MUSCLE in huge type across the front. "I'm taking these, and I have this creatine powder that's supposed to help me bulk up. . . ." He pawed through a jumble of protein powders and other bodybuilding supplements. "One of these days I'm gonna be big enough to get back at Bernie."

I thought about Little Bernie. He was the biggest twelve-year-old I'd ever seen. Somehow I didn't think Chris Oberlander would ever be that big.

"How else are you trying to get back at him?" I asked.

Chris stopped looking through his bag. "Huh?" he said.

"We heard Little Bernie threw you out of the amusement park for making a scene a little while back," Joe said. "Have you tried to get revenge for that?"

"*He's* the one who made a scene," Chris grumbled. "I didn't do anything."

"But you're still mad at him, right?" I said. "Mad enough to try to kill him?"

Chris stared at me, confused. "Huh?" he said again.

"Someone has been tampering with the rides at Uncle Bernie's. Yesterday Little Bernie got a hot dog that may have been poisoned." I watched Chris's face for any sign of guilt. But he just looked surprised.

"He was poisoned? Did he die?" Chris asked hopefully.

"No!" Joe snapped. "Were you trying to kill him?"

"No way," Chris said. "I didn't know anything about it. I'm not even allowed back into the park—how could I have done any of that stuff?" He zipped his gym bag and stood up. "But if someone is trying to kill him, I hope it works."

Joe looked at me and shrugged. We obviously weren't going to get anything more out of this kid. I had a feeling that he was telling the truth, but you never know.

"Listen, stop taking those bodybuilding supplements," I told Chris. "You're never going to beat Little Bernie physically. The only way to deal with a bully is to stand up to him. Once you show him you're not afraid, he'll leave you alone."

"Easy for you to say," Chris muttered.

"Seriously, those supplements are bad for you,"

Joe said. "They don't really help, and some of them have dangerous side effects. You'll be much better off if you just eat right and keep working out. One of these days you'll have a growth spurt."

I grinned. He sounded just like Mom!

"And take some karate classes," Joe added. "If you know martial arts, it doesn't matter how big you are."

Okay, *that* didn't sound like Mom.

Chris headed off to the bicycle rack, and we went over to our motorcycles. Someone had stuffed a flyer into the seat of mine. I pulled it out.

"What next? Should we go find Little Bernie's mother?" Joe asked, straddling his bike.

"No," I said slowly. "We should go to the amusement park."

"How come?" Joe asked.

I showed him the piece of paper. It was no flyer. It was a note.

And it read, THE EVIDENCE YOU'RE LOOKING FOR IS IN THE HAUNTED HOUSE—A FRIEND.

# 11.
# HALL OF HORROR

"It could be a trap," I said into the microphone in my bike helmet. Frank and I can talk to each other through our wireless mikes when we ride, and the noise-canceling helmets make it as simple and quiet as having a normal conversation. Well, a normal conversation while flying down the road with the wind in our faces and 130 horsepower between our legs. "Sometimes when you get a note from 'A Friend,' it's really from an enemy."

"I know," Frank's voice came through the speaker in my helmet. "But we have no choice. All we know so far is that everybody hates Uncle Bernie and Little Bernie, and lots of people would like to close the park down. But there's no smoking gun to lead us to one suspect."

"Then we'd better hope our smoking gun is in the haunted house," I said. "I love haunted houses, anyway."

I turned my bike into the parking lot of Uncle Bernie's Fun Park.

It was still pretty early—not even noon. The park wasn't crowded yet. The only line I saw was the line at the carousel. It was mostly teenagers. I guess everyone wanted to try out the wild merry-go-round after yesterday. I just hoped there wouldn't be a repeat of that unpleasant incident.

We made our way to the haunted house. The neon HALL OF HORROR sign was on, but there was no line. There wasn't even a park worker in sight.

"Do you think it's open?" Frank asked.

"It looks pretty deserted," I said. "But maybe our 'friend' wants it that way."

"Okay, let's go in." Frank led the way.

It was dark inside, like all haunted houses. But somehow after our adventure in the pitch-black Wormhole the day before, this darkness didn't seem so scary.

Spooky organ music drifted in through hidden speakers, and every so often a scream pierced the air. Usually in a haunted house, you hear other people screaming. But these were the canned screams that were part of the prerecorded soundtrack. As far as

I could tell, we were alone in the Hall of Horror.

Something grabbed my arm.

I jumped and spun around.

There was nothing there.

"Cool," I said, relaxing a little. Have I mentioned that I love haunted houses?

"Check it out," Frank said. In the dim light, I could see him pointing to the right. I looked over there and saw a dinner table all set up with fancy china dishes. In the middle was a man lying on a platter. His mouth was open, and an apple was stuck in it like he was the pig at a pig roast.

I chuckled. "That's gross," I said appreciatively.

"We're here to look for evidence, not to enjoy the haunted house," Frank reminded me.

"Oh. Right." I studied the fake dinner set for any sign of the evidence our "friend" had mentioned. But the table and chairs looked just like normal props. The man was obviously made of plastic.

Maybe the apple in his mouth was a reference to Little Bernie's poisoned hot dog? I shook my head. I was really grasping here to find whatever hint our "friend" had left for us.

I left the pathway and stepped over onto the dinner set to check it out.

"We're not supposed to go over there," Frank pointed out.

"No one else is here," I said. "And we're investigating, remember?"

"Just hurry up," he replied.

I got up close to the table and peered down at the apple. It was made of wax, like the fake fruits our Great Aunt May keeps in a bowl on her living room coffee table.

"Nothing here," I said, returning to the pathway.

We kept going.

I passed a portrait of a pretty girl hanging on the wall. It was lit by a small spotlight coming from the bottom.

I checked it out, because the girl was pretty.

But when I got up next to it, her face turned into the wrinkled face of an old hag. Then the flesh dropped off the face and it became a skeleton.

"Cool," I said.

I stopped to look at the picture more closely.

It changed back to the young girl, waited for about ten seconds, and then went through the girl-hag-skeleton process again.

I turned away. The effect was fun one time. But when you saw the whole thing happen again, it kind of lost its interest.

In front of me, a figure lunged from the darkness and grabbed Frank.

He let out a yell.

I ran to catch up, but by the time I got there the figure was gone.

"Who was that?" I asked. "Our friend?"

"No, it was a Frankenstein," Frank said. "Or maybe a werewolf. I couldn't tell."

I grinned. Haunted houses usually had a few park workers in them who would dress up as monsters so they could jump out and scare you. I'd always thought that would be a cool job to have.

I heard a hissing sound, and suddenly the room was filled with smoke.

Was this the trap?

I took a shallow breath. It was only fog from a fog machine. I had a hard time seeing Frank through the haze. And if there were any clues in this room, I couldn't see those, either.

"Joe, in here!" Frank called.

His voice was coming from the left. I moved that way. Soon enough, I spotted him to my right. I stopped, confused.

"Frank?"

"Over here." His voice was still coming from the left, but I could see him standing on the right, gesturing to me with his hand.

I walked toward him—and smacked into a wall.

Not a wall. A mirror.

"All right!" I cried happily. "A hall of mirrors!"

"I still haven't seen anything unusual," Frank said from behind me. When I turned around, he was gone.

He appeared again to the left. "What kind of evidence do you think we're looking for?"

I moved left, and hit another mirror. Where was Frank?

When I turned around, I saw a room filled with . . . me. Reflections of myself looked back at me from every direction. "Who knows?" I answered Frank. "I figure we'll recognize it when we see it."

Suddenly a tall man appeared in the mirrors, standing right behind me.

I spun around, freaked out. No one was there.

"Hello?" I called. "Is someone else here?"

A deep, maniacal laugh echoed through the room. But all I could see was myself, everywhere.

"Frank?" I said. "Are you still in here?"

No answer.

"Frank?"

Someone grabbed my arm. I jumped and let out a yell.

It was Frank.

"There's nothing here," he said. "Let's keep going."

The next hallway was pitch black. It had slimy

things hanging from the ceiling and something that felt like cobwebs stretched across the center. I sighed. "These haunted houses are all the same," I complained. "I was hoping for something scarier."

"I was hoping for some evidence," Frank said.

A woman dressed like a vampire appeared and screamed in my face.

I didn't even gasp. I was getting bored.

"Maybe we should try to go backstage, or whatever they call it in haunted houses," I suggested to Frank. "Our friend didn't say the evidence would be part of the attraction. Maybe there's something hidden through that back door we saw yesterday."

"It's worth a try," Frank said, pushing his way past a suit of armor that had suddenly started moving. "Let's get through the rest of this thing, get outside, and circle around the back."

"Okay." A zombie jumped out in front of me.

I waited for it to leave.

It waved its arms and let out a growl.

"Aaahhh," I yelled halfheartedly. Maybe it would move on now.

"Joe, come on," Frank said from the other side of the zombie.

"Uh, excuse me," I told the zombie. I stepped around it.

As I joined Frank on the other side, the zombie roared again.

Then it grabbed my head with one hand.

It grabbed Frank's head with the other hand.

And it smashed our heads together—hard.

# 12.

# ZOMBIE!

My head was killing me. There was a woodpecker sitting on my shoulder and pecking me over and over with its beak. It hurt like crazy, but I couldn't lift my arm to shoo the bird away.

"Frank."

Seriously, I had a splitting headache. I glanced over and saw that it wasn't a woodpecker after all. It was Playback, my parrot. "Zombie!" he squawked. He kept pecking me in the head.

"Frank."

I recognized my brother's voice, but I didn't answer him. My head hurt too much. And Playback wouldn't stop pecking me.

"Frank, wake up."

*I'm dreaming,* I thought. *Playback isn't pecking me.*

133

"Frank!"

"I am awake," I muttered. "Leave me alone. My head hurts."

I tried to remember if I had any aspirin nearby. My bedroom is only a few feet from the bathroom, and there would probably be aspirin in the medicine chest. But my head hurt too much. I didn't want to move.

"Frank, open your eyes," Joe commanded. "*Now.*"

I opened my eyes. I waited for the sunlight to hit me and make my headache worse, but instead all I saw was darkness. I blinked.

My eyes adjusted to the dim light.

This wasn't my bedroom. And I wasn't in bed.

I was sitting up. In a hard chair. And my hands were tied behind me.

"What's going on?" I cried. "Where are we?"

"I think we're in a dungeon," Joe's voice said.

Wait a minute. Where was he? I could hear him, but I couldn't see him. I turned my head to look around—and the headache got worse. "My head is killing me," I said.

"Mine too," Joe answered. "That zombie smashed our heads together. Who would expect it to hurt so much?"

"It knocked us out," I guessed. "He must've hit us pretty hard."

"No kidding," Joe's voice said.

"Where are you?" I asked. "I can't see you."

"I'm behind you," he told me. "We're back to back, I think."

"Can you move?"

"Nope," Joe said. "My hands are tied behind the chair. And my legs are tied to the chair legs."

I took a deep breath and forced myself to ignore the pain in my head. I couldn't afford to be out of it right now. I tried to move my legs. No good. They were tied to my chair. I tried to move my arms, and felt the ropes bite into my wrists. Now that I was paying attention, I could hear Joe moving around behind me.

I looked around the dim room. The only light came from a fake window up near the ceiling. The "window" had bars over it, and behind it was a tiny patch of what was supposed to be the sky—a pale, yellowish light that didn't actually illuminate anything.

The rest of the tiny room was painted gray, with walls that were supposed to look like blocks of stone. Rusted old manacles hung from the walls on all sides. One set of them had a skeleton hanging by its wrists. A pile of bones and a skull lay in one corner, and an animatronic rat sat and twitched its whiskers at us.

"So I guess our friend wasn't a friend," I said finally.

"Guess not," Joe said. "We knew it might be a trap."

"We should've been more careful," I said. "We didn't take that zombie seriously enough."

"We have to figure out how to get out of here," Joe said. "I really need to get to some aspirin."

"This looks like part of the haunted house," I said. "If we can get out of this room, we should be able to find our way outside."

"Yeah, but first we have to get free of these ropes," Joe pointed out.

The deep, evil laugh we'd heard earlier reverberated through the room. Was it part of the haunted house outside?

"I hope you're enjoying the Hall of Horror," the deep voice cackled. "You're going to die here!"

"Is he talking to us, or to the whole haunted house?" Joe murmured.

"I'm talking to *you*, Frank and Joe Hardy," the voice answered as if it heard him. "You're going to die!"

"Who are you?" I yelled, even though it hurt my head.

"I'm a zombie!" The voice laughed maniacally again. I didn't see what was so funny.

"Why are you doing this? Let us go," Joe called.

"I've had enough of your meddling," the voice boomed. "You have no right to snoop around here and make trouble."

"*You're* the one making trouble," I replied. "We're just trying to help."

"You've helped yourselves into an early grave!" the voice cried. "I'll teach you a lesson about sticking your nose into other people's business. You're going to become a permanent part of this haunted house!"

"What do you mean?" I asked.

"You're going to stay where you are, tied up, with no food and no water . . . until you die." The voice laughed again, echoing off the walls. It really hurt my head.

"Don't bother calling for help," the voice added. "People will only think it's part of the Hall of Horror experience."

A door creaked as if it were opening. It was hard to tell what was real in this place, and what was just part of the scary attraction. "Hey!" I called. "Don't leave!"

"I hope you enjoy your deaths," the voice replied. "You only get to die once."

And then the door slammed.

"Hello?" I yelled. "Are you there?"

"We're not done talking to you!" Frank called.

No answer.

The zombie was gone. Or at least he wanted us to think so.

"Do you think he's really gone?" Joe whispered.

"I don't know," I whispered back. "It's impossible to tell. Did you recognize his voice?"

"No," Joe said. "I think he was using a voice distorter. It could have been Uncle Bernie, or Big Jim, or anyone."

"Well, I think we can cross Chris Oberlander off the list," I said. "He couldn't pull off something like this. This is an inside job. Whoever is doing this obviously knows his way around the haunted house."

From somewhere outside the room, a scream split the air. It was followed by some of the creepy organ music.

"I can't believe it," I muttered. "This ride is actually open for business with us stuck inside it."

"Well, we have to get unstuck," Joe said. "How do we untie ourselves?"

I hesitated. For all we knew, the zombie was still listening in on our conversation. But we didn't have much of a choice. We had to try to escape.

I forced myself to think, even though it made my head hurt.

"We're back to back, right?" I whispered.

"Yeah."

"So if we get closer together, we should be able to reach each other's hands, right?"

"Right," Joe said. "And then we can untie each other's ropes!"

"We've done this a million times," I said. "No problem."

"Unless the zombie's still here," Joe murmured. "We better move fast."

I couldn't move my feet very well, but I managed to push my toes along the ground enough to shove the chair back an inch or so. It made a loud scraping sound against the floor.

"Quiet!" Joe hissed.

"I don't have many options," I replied. I shoved the chair back another inch. Behind me I heard Joe doing the same.

After five more shoves, I felt my arms bang into Joe's chair. We maneuvered ourselves sideways until our hands were right next to each other.

Now that I had something to concentrate on, my head didn't hurt as much. I focused on the ropes around Joe's wrists. It didn't take me long to figure out that the zombie had used a basic square knot. Once I knew that, I had the ropes undone in a few seconds.

Joe quickly untied his legs. Then he came over to my chair and untied my hands. I took care of the ropes on my legs.

We were free!

# 13.

## In the Dungeon

"Let's get out of here," I said. I stood up and started rubbing my wrists where the ropes had been.

"Not so fast," Frank said. "Sit back down."

"Why?" Didn't his head hurt as much as mine did? I had zero interest in spending any more time in this dungeon.

"We still don't know who that zombie is," Frank pointed out. "Our mission isn't over until we catch him."

I sat back down. "How are we gonna catch him by staying in here?"

Frank tossed some rope at me. "Tie it around your wrists—loosely," he said.

I was beginning to understand his plan. "We pretend we're still tied up?" I asked.

"Yeah. That zombie guy has to come back and check on us, right?"

"I don't know," I said as I formed the rope into two loops, like handcuffs. "He said he was just going to leave us here to die."

"Yeah, but he can't really do that," Frank said. "At least he has to come back to make sure we haven't escaped. And when he comes back, we'll jump him."

I stuck my hands through the rope and put my arms behind the chair. It wasn't comfortable, but it was better now that the ropes weren't cutting off my circulation. Still, I wasn't convinced that Frank's plan would work.

"Last time he didn't come into the room," I said. "If he still doesn't come in, how can we jump him?"

Frank thought about it.

"Maybe if we pretend we're asleep or unconscious again, he'll come in," Frank said.

"Why would we be unconscious?"

"From the blow to our heads," Frank suggested. "Or we could just be exhausted with hunger."

"I guess so," I mumbled. "I *am* exhausted with hunger. How long do you think we've been in here?"

"It's hard to tell," Frank said. "It's so dark in here that it feels like the middle of the night, even though it's probably still daylight outside. Wait." He twisted his wrists out of the rope and pressed the backlight button on his watch. "It's about five." Within a few seconds he was back in the rope.

"I hope he comes back soon," I said.

But he didn't. We must've waited at least an hour, pretending we were tied up, listening to the sounds of people screaming and laughing in the halls of the haunted house. Nobody came near the dungeon, though. The zombie must've closed it off somehow.

Finally the screams of people outside stopped. The creepy organ music went away. Everything grew silent.

"It seems like the ride is closed," Frank whispered.

"Could be," I whispered back.

Suddenly we heard footsteps in the hallway outside.

"Play dead," Frank whispered.

I closed my eyes and let my head fall forward onto my chest as if I were deeply asleep, or just passed out.

I heard the jingle of keys, and then a door was opened. I kept my eyes closed as someone entered the dungeon. The footsteps were heavy, and I could hear him breathing.

"Now!" Frank yelled.

I jumped up and shook the fake bonds off my wrists. Frank did the same.

The zombie jumped in surprise, but he didn't back off. Instead he pulled a knife from inside his costume and held it out toward us.

I froze. I hadn't been expecting a weapon. And I figured Frank would be surprised too. We'd been planning to rush the guy, but right now that didn't seem like such a good idea.

The room was so dark that I could barely make out the steel glinting in his hand. With the three of us in there, the place was too small to maneuver. If we tried to run or to fight him, chances were good that one of us would get stabbed.

The zombie laughed. He was going for that same deep, maniacal laugh as before. But he didn't have the voice distorter now—probably he had to use the haunted house PA system to do that.

"You didn't expect me to come armed, did you?" he asked.

He was still disguising his voice, but it wasn't as deep as it had been through the distorter. It sounded familiar . . . but was it Uncle Bernie's voice? Big Jim's? I couldn't tell.

"I decided starvation was too good for you," the zombie went on. "It would take too long, and then I'd have to keep the dungeon closed off." He gave another deep laugh and lunged at me with the knife.

I jumped backward. The knife flashed through the air a few inches from my throat.

"And the dungeon is everybody's favorite part of the Hall of Horror," he continued. "Don't you like it?"

"No," Frank said.

The zombie laughed again. "Too bad. It's the last place you'll ever see."

This time he brandished the knife at Frank. Frank twisted away and jumped over next to me. "We can't keep doing this," I whispered. "The room's too small. He'll hit one of us soon."

"I have a plan," Frank murmured.

But before he could say anything else, the zombie lunged at us with the knife. I couldn't see much in the darkness, so I just spun away from Frank and tried to get behind the dark figure of the zombie.

He'd come through a door—where was it?

I glanced frantically around the room, searching for the way out. But all I saw were the fake stone walls. The door must be hidden in one of the walls.

The zombie gave a roar and lunged forward again. At least the darkness was working against him, too.

"Joe," Frank called.

"Over here," I replied.

"Remember Vijay!" he said.

*Huh?* My guess was that Frank was trying to let me in on his plan, but I didn't understand what he meant. *Remember Vijay?*

I forced myself to keep calm and think it through, even though the zombie was still two feet away holding a knife on us.

Vijay. Vijay Patel, the guy who'd delivered pizza—and our last mission—to the house? What did I know about Vijay?

He was an ATAC trainee.

He was originally from India.

He thought Frank and I were heroes.

He'd given us a pocket strobe light.

*That's it!* I thought. *Frank must have the pocket strobe with him.*

Leave it to my brother to be totally prepared at all times. That's why he's such an excellent ATAC agent.

"I remember," I called.

"Now!" Frank yelled.

I closed my eyes. Even through my eyelids I could see the flash of bright blue light as Frank hit the button on the strobe.

The zombie let out a yelp of surprise. He'd been

blinded by the light in the dark room. I listened to where the yell came from so I'd know where he was in the darkness.

"Now!" Frank yelled again.

This time I didn't close my eyes. I was ready for the flash of light. When it came, I had a brief view of the guy in the huge zombie costume as he stumbled backward. The knife in his hand glinted in the blue light.

I kicked it out of his hand.

The knife clattered across the floor.

Frank hit the strobe again. In the light we saw the zombie running toward the wall. I tackled him to the ground. A second later I felt Frank jump on top of him as well.

"Tie his hands," Frank cried, shoving some of the rope toward me.

We wrestled the guy's hands behind his back and tied them together. It wasn't easy in the darkness.

As soon as we had him tied, I decided it was time to let a little light in.

"He was going for the wall over here," I told Frank. "The door must be hidden here somewhere."

Frank flashed the strobe again, and in the split second of bright light I spotted the outline of a door cut into the "stone" wall.

I felt for it in the darkness and managed to find the edge. Feeling downward, I found a tiny latch. I threw the latch and yanked the door open.

Outside, the halls of the haunted house were lit with work lights—the kind they only turn on when the ride is closed.

Compared with the dim light of the dungeon, it seemed like the brightest sunlight I'd ever seen.

"Okay, let's see who this zombie is," Frank muttered.

I helped him push the guy over onto his back, and then I sat on his chest to make sure he stayed down.

Frank pulled off the zombie mask.

I watched anxiously. Was it Big Jim? Uncle Bernie?

"Get off of me," the zombie whined.

I stared in disbelief.

It was Little Bernie.

# 14.

## MISSION ACCOMPLISHED

"I should've known when I saw how tall the zombie was," Joe said, shaking his head.

I shrugged. "I figured that was just the costume."

"You guys are in big trouble," Little Bernie whined.

"Get up," I told him. "*You're* the one in trouble." We dragged him to his feet and led him through the haunted house. He cried the whole way. He was such a big guy it was easy to forget that he was still just a kid.

Joe found a door labeled EMERGENCY EXIT and pushed it open.

I was shocked to see sunlight come streaming in. When we stepped outside, the park was as crowded and bustling as ever.

"I thought the park was closed for the night," I said.

"It's only two-thirty," Joe said, checking the big clock over the concert bandstand. "Little Bernie must've just closed the haunted house so he could deal with us."

"What's going on here?" Uncle Bernie demanded. He came storming up to us, three security guards behind him. When he spotted Little Bernie, he gasped. "Son? What are you doing in that costume?"

"He was trying to kill us," I said.

Uncle Bernie's eyebrows shot up. "What? That's impossible." He looked his son up and down. Little Bernie kept crying. "He was probably just working in the haunted house, and he tried to scare you. That's the job of the zombie." Uncle Bernie didn't sound too certain.

"The haunted house was closed, remember?" one of the security guards put in. "That's why we were coming here to check it out."

Uncle Bernie's face fell. "It shouldn't have been closed in the middle of the day," he said. "Why was it, son?"

Little Bernie just sobbed even harder, snot and tears rolling down his face.

"Your son is the one who set off the M-80 on the

roller coaster," I told Uncle Bernie. "He also hooked up a generator to the carousel to make it go too fast. For all we know, he broke the safety bar on the Ferris wheel, too."

"And yesterday he pretended to be poisoned by a hot dog in order to throw us off the trail," Joe put in. "He wanted us to think Big Jim had done it, but we didn't fall for it." He frowned at Little Bernie. "We know you're the one who's been sabotaging the park all along."

"That's impossible," Uncle Bernie said. But he looked scared. "Tell me the truth, Bernie."

"Why did they have to come here?" Little Bernie blubbered. "They ruined everything!"

"Did you have something to do with what happened at the water park yesterday, Bernie?" I asked. "Were you trying to get rid of us then?"

"I know a kid who works there," he sobbed. "I bet him fifty dollars he wouldn't put the cover on the tube. I didn't do it!"

"No, you just paid someone else to do it," Joe said grimly.

"What are you talking about?" Uncle Bernie asked.

"A kid named Marc Krakowski tried to kill us at Splash World yesterday," I explained. "Just like

Little Bernie tried to kill us in the Hall of Horror five minutes ago. And just like he killed Maggie Soto on the Doom Rider last week."

"I didn't mean to!" Little Bernie cried. "I just wanted a little bit of the roof to collapse so people on the roller coaster would be scared. I didn't think a stupid firecracker would make such a big explosion. It was an accident!"

One of the security guards pulled out his walkie-talkie and radioed for the police.

Uncle Bernie had gone pale. "But why, son?" he gasped. "Why would you do such horrible things?"

"I hate this stupid park!" Little Bernie cried. "It's the only thing you care about! You don't care about Mom, or me, or anything. Just the dumb amusement park!"

"That's not true," Uncle Bernie protested.

"Yes, it is," Little Bernie sobbed. "I thought if people got scared to come here, you'd have to close the place down. Then we could have a normal life and you would pay some attention to me."

Uncle Bernie looked as if someone had punched him in the gut. "I only care about the park because I want it to be yours someday," he said. "I never dreamed that you felt this way."

"You never bothered to ask me," Little Bernie spat.

A siren rang through the air, and a cop car came driving slowly through the crowd that had gathered outside the haunted house.

Two police officers got out of the car and walked over to take Little Bernie into custody.

He was still crying as they put him in the backseat of their cruiser.

Uncle Bernie turned to us, still horrified. "I . . . I had no idea," he said again.

"I know," I told him. "I'm sorry about your son."

He blinked at me. "I'm sorry he tried to kill you," he said. "I don't know what to do."

"Your son could use a father right now," Joe said. "Frank and I are fine. We can take care of ourselves."

Uncle Bernie nodded slowly. He turned to watch as the cops closed the door on his son. "Wait," he called suddenly. "Wait for me."

He hurried over and got into the backseat next to Little Bernie.

"Maybe now Little Bernie will get the attention he was looking for," Joe said. He turned to me and smiled. "Another successful mission. We got the perp."

"Yeah," I said. "I never expected it to be a kid."

"Want to hit the log flume before we leave?" Joe asked.

I thought about it. But right now, Uncle Bernie's Fun Park was anything but fun. "Nah," I said. "Let's just go home."

"I have a better idea," Joe said. "Let's go back and find Vijay. We have to tell him how his pocket strobe—and some ATAC training—saved us from a zombie!"